The
Deviant
Apparition

The Deviant Apparition

SK Webb

Winchester, UK
Washington, USA

First published by Roundfire Books, 2012
Roundfire Books is an imprint of John Hunt Publishing Ltd., Laurel House, Station Approach,
Alresford, Hants, SO24 9JH, UK
office1@o-books.net
www.o-books.com

For distributor details and how to order please visit the 'Ordering' section on our website.

Text copyright: SK Webb 2011

ISBN: 978 1 84694 949 4

A CIP catalogue record for this book is available from the British Library.

Design: Stuart Davies

Printed in the UK by CPI Antony Rowe
Printed in the USA by Offset Paperback Mfrs, Inc

We operate a distinctive and ethical publishing philosophy in all
areas of our business, from our global network of authors to
production and worldwide distribution.

CONTENTS

Acknowledgements

Lynne McTaggart, for providing much inspiration through books, writings and presentations, particularly the talk she gave at the Oxford Union in 2005.

Resurgence magazine, for being such a bastion of wisdom and sanity.

June M. Spong, for Dorking history.

Thanks also to author Neale Donald Walsch, whose works have helped inspire and shape this story; in particular *Conversations with God - Book 3*, (published by Hodder and Stoughton UK, 1999) from which the wedding vows were derived (used on pages 291-293).

Dedicated to Kris

PROLOGUE

Sometimes things suddenly go backwards or turn inside-out; sometimes what we thought we knew is rendered untrue; sometimes the unexpected becomes the expected, and sometimes time itself seems to be a Grand Master of elaborate games. Light becomes dark. And dark becomes something we must walk through on our own, unguided and without a map. Our boundaries, preconceptions and accepted knowledge are thrown out the window. We think we know time and space and this thing we call existence. Think again.

TV NEWS

CAPTAIN: "Altitude stabilised; all systems good."

CO-PILOT: "Mountains are clear today. No clouds. No cross-winds. No winds at all, really. This is gonna be a cruise."

CAPTAIN: "Yep, textbook stuff; anyway, Benedicto, this route is usually easy – I could do it blindfolded."

CO-PILOT: "Ha! Don't let the passengers hear you say that!"

CAPTAIN: "Yeah! Ha!"

CO-PILOT: "Ha ha!"

CAPTAIN: "Sweet cruisin'."

CO-PILOT: "Yeah."

CAPTAIN: "Er, hey, hang on a minute, Ben, what's that?"

CO-PILOT: "What's what?"

CAPTAIN: "*That!*"

CO-PILOT: "What?"

CAPTAIN: "What's going on? Can't you see that?"

CO-PILOT: "Er…yes, I can! But I dunno what I'm seeing!"

CAPTAIN: "What the? Eh? This is not possible! This…this *can't be happening!* The whole of the mountain range is shimmering…looks like it's *melting!*"

CO-PILOT: "It's…it's not the same anymore! It's not normal! It looks *flatter! And swampy!*"

CAPTAIN: "Yeah, I can see patches of water! It's unbelievable! I just don't know how…"

CO-PILOT: "Well, what's going on? And what are those shapes moving around? Big animals?"

CAPTAIN: "No, they can't be animals! They're too big to be animals! But we're too high up to see what they are!"

CO-PILOT: "Shall we drop down a bit?

CAPTAIN: "Errrrr, no, shouldn't do that…oh, yeah, let's."

A conversation with Mexican air traffic control takes place.

CO-PILOT: "Well? What are they? What do you think it all is?"

CAPTAIN: "Now, what the—?"

CO-PILOT: "Ohhhh! Oh, Lord, oh, Lord! What the fu—?"

CAPTAIN: "It's not just me – is it? You are seeing it too?"

CO-PILOT: "Yes!"

CAPTAIN: "You sure?"

CO-PILOT: "*YES!*"

CAPTAIN: "But what is all this? *How are we seeing this? This is wrong! THIS IS SO VERY WRONG!*"

CO-PILOT: "We've just gotta fly past it! Gotta keep going! We're still on route. Ground speed still the same. The instruments seem okay…"

CAPTAIN: "NO, IT'S NOT OKAY! Oh, Lord!…Benedicto, do you see *that?*"

CO-PILOT: "Uhhhhh…"

CAPTAIN: "*And it's still changing! It's becoming—*"

CO-PILOT: "(Gasp) Holy Mary, Mother of God, pray for us sinners, now and at the hour of our—"

Then came a loud, crashing sound, ending both the flight recording and the lives of all those on board flight 105 bound for Mexico City.

"This is Lyndsey Smith reporting from the scene of yesterday's plane crash here in Mexico. El Volar Airlines flight 105 came down here in the Sierra Madre mountains in north-western Mexico in what can be described as perfectly clear and sunny weather, plummeting from some thirty thousand feet, and crashing into a remote wooded hillside. Authorities now confirm that all two hundred and fifty-six people on board the Mexican jet are presumed dead. The search for the wreckage is well underway, and with the early retrieval through its emergency locator beacon of the box containing the flight recording – commonly referred to as the 'black box' – an investigation can now begin. The wreckage is thought to be scattered across the mountainside over quite a large distance. It has been confirmed by airline officials that communication between air traffic control and the two Mexican pilots had been normal and routine up until just a few minutes before the crash – there seemed to be no hint of any trouble until the last moments. A few minutes ago a statement was released to the media revealing that some rather strange conversation took place between the captain and co-pilot in the final moments before the crash. According to an airline spokesperson their final words as translated from Spanish point to them not believing their eyes about the landscape they were flying over.

"What they saw and what really happened, we do not as yet know. We expect more in this series of press releases to come our way soon, but until then there will be much investigation needed to unravel just what caused this tragic – and so very baffling – crash. What to make of the alleged sightings by the two pilots is something yet to be answered, but until then this remains one of the strangest plane crashes ever. I hope to have an update for you in the ten o'clock news. This is Lyndsey Smith in Durango, Mexico. Back to you in the Channel 4 studio, Tom."

FIREWORKS

Sky rockets shrieked as they soared into the sky, bursting into bloom. Colours exploded, and children gasped and cheered. A succession of reds, greens, silvers and blues came and went, noisily and triumphantly. The icy November wind was ignored by all, despite its insistence that people look away from the heavens and down to their cold hands and fluttering coats. The best firework was left for last: a giant kaleidoscope; a cannonball of light. It was so big and appeared so solid that it looked as though you could step inside it, and for a split second the quickest, most sparked imaginations on the village green had a fantastic moment: to imagine walking into it and seeing and feeling those colours at close proximity; walking on crimson stars, putting your hand through silver orbs and tasting green swirls. If only it would last longer! As the fizzes and bangs and colours faded a mere wisp of smoke lingered.

The crowd of locals remained entranced for what seemed to James Harvey to be rather a long time. Drawn into the celebrations he had let himself be a boy again, and it felt good. He stood still, trying not to think about anything except the brilliant sights he had just seen.

Dreamily looking around, his gaze rested on the nearby village church, which stood on high ground as if in quiet judgement of the frivolity below. He noticed how its silhouette looked dramatic against the silver-grey of the full moon sky. It had a long, slate-bonneted spire that reminded him of a witch's hat. A hilarious irony, he thought. In its blackness and witchiness the church looked closed and off-limits for the night. Around it, wonky-angled headstones jutted out of the ground like decaying old teeth. Some of the bigger, brighter rockets, as they exploded, had illuminated the stained glass windows, revealing their characters and catching them – for a split second only – in some saintly act or holy pose. But no one looked or seemed to notice the church tonight – except for James, who made a point of looking at it at every chance. Its solidity, its craftsmanship and its sheer power impressed upon his mind. And the fact that people had been worshipping there for so many years. Not that he went to church at all – barring the occasional birth, marriage or death – orthodox religion had no place in his bookish and very run-of-the-mill life.

"This is the best fireworks we've had at Spook Hill since the millennium one, don't you agree?" It was old George Hodges, dressed in dungarees with braces and a tatty grey felt hat. He had shuffled up to James's side without James knowing, quite a feat for a man of George's girth and height.

"Hi, George! How are you?"

"I'm well, thank y'lad. Best fireworks in a long time, don't you think?"

"Uh, yeah, I think so. Pretty spectacular, all right. Loved that last one, it was a blinder, eh?"

"It certainly was."

"You keeping well, George? I haven't seen you walking past the house much lately." George liked to walk a lot, and was a distinctive character in the area. He certainly had the longest beard and the wildest looks, looking like, James thought with amusement, a Victorian or Edwardian farm labourer. And not a particularly tidy one either. Hodges, Ploughman of Surrey: James could almost see him out baling hay in the July sunshine or sitting on a sack of seeds chewing on a straw; a character straight out of a Constable painting.

George eyed James and shuffled even closer. Bending to his ear, he said quietly, "Lad, I've been all right. *I've* been all right...but—"

"What?"

The colossal figure looked worried. "There's been some funny goings on up in my street."

"Oh," James replied, uncertain where the conversation was going. "Not that dodgy guy with the campervan again?"

"No, not him. I dunno, lad. Maybe it's me eyes. Prob'ly is. I'm just seeing some strange things. Now, don't go telling anyone this, y'hear. I'd appreciate that."

"Of course I won't. Tell me what you've been seeing." This is going to be one for the opticians, James thought. Oh well, let him get it off his chest.

George's long, grey whiskers were starting to brush James's face and his breath smelled of peppermints.

"I was in me garden the other day, just pottering, y'know. It was about eleven in the morning, normal day, a bit cold but nothing else. No one around. Lovely and quiet, y'know. Anyway, as I was fixing one of me wooden fences I saw something. Just in front of me, well over the fence actually – I can see over it, I'm that tall. There was something where the neighbour's house should have been. Oh, that sounds... Oh God, I shouldn't have said anything! I shouldn't be saying any of this!" He went to walk away, but James grabbed his shoulder.

"No, George, don't go. Tell me. I promise I won't think anything."

He edged back and the whiskers began tickling James again.

"It was some sort of...well, *vision*. The neighbour's house suddenly...well it *wasn't there anymore*. There was an open area and then woodland, going for as far as I could see. *The houses were gone! They were gone!* There were silver birch trees, oaks and whatever, and birds everywhere – I remember lots of crows and magpies. There was an elderly lady and gent out on a walk. Had a dog with 'em, a big one, not on a lead either, and a basket of berries they'd just picked. Couldn't tell ye what sort – red ones, I think. There was also a horse tethered to a tree and a man sitting on the grass nearby. He was closer than the others were – to me, I mean. He looked like he was having a rest, y'know. Sitting on the grass with a pipe – smoking a bleedin' pipe! How many of those do y'see these days! I think it's lovely, smoking a pipe – I've got one, in fact, as you probably know. Anyway, as I looked and watched the man, it started to go well, watery, I should say. It started to go, but very slowly. The man with the horse looked up and saw me at this time. He seemed to go wide-eyed. He stared at me. I stared at him. As we stared at each other the view went – it slowly dissolved away to normal again. Then the houses came back and it was completely normal, as if nothing had happened. Make of that what y'will! There, I've said it! I suppose now y'll think I'm mad. Completely bonkers."

"George, I don't know what to say. I really don't. I'm gobsmacked! That's so…weird. But, er, can I ask you one thing? Please don't take offence."

"What's that, lad?"

"Had you had – how can I say it? – anything at all to, er, to drink? I know it was only morning, so please don't take this the wrong way."

George huffed right in his face. "That's a bit offensive, don't y'think? I really thought more of you, you with yer books and yer brains. In fact you can bog off, you little prat, if that's how y'er gonna think!" He began to walk away.

"George! George! I'm sorry!"

He turned and said over his shoulder, "*No!* I *hadn't* had anything to drink! Not a friggin' drop! I never do have anything till evening either, for your information. And I'm not on any medication that might make me see things. And I hadn't been smoking anything, not even me pipe! Hmmff! I'm off. I'm sure I shall see you sometime." He hobbled off back into the crowd and was gone.

James closed his eyes for a moment, sighed deeply then looked up into the black sky. "*Damn!*"

He walked home, chatting convivially with neighbours as he went. He spent the remainder of the evening at his computer. For over a year he had been researching not only his own family tree, but also dabbling into the past of the village and surrounding places. Motivated by curiosity, he enjoyed being able to peer into the past. Not a lot had happened in the area, admittedly, but he felt it was nice just to know how things had been and not lose sight of where you've come from, collectively speaking. The fascination with history had been a lifelong passion, showing no signs of lessening with age; quite the opposite in fact. He had majored in history for his arts degree, although the years at university were a long time in the past, almost becoming distant history themselves. Why, he often wondered, today's politicians – so sure with their advisors and their righteousness – didn't read history to help them with knowing what to do – or, more to the point, what *not* to do – he couldn't fathom. So many events and patterns repeated themselves it made for easy advice, he thought. History had taught him that many human actions and reactions were the same, no matter what the century and who the leader. The wheel kept turning relentlessly, quickly forgetting its previous rotation.

Feeling very ordinary himself, the lives of other ordinary people fascinated James, and he would often lapse into a deep contemplation of the subject. His collection of family photos was like gold to him, some having been given by family members long since passed. He realised that even though there might now be little or even, more likely, nothing of them left in this world now – often not even a headstone – the photos were solid evidence that all these people had once lived. He could see and feel the fragility and the staggering shortness of it all. A broach or medal in a box; a piece of lace; an autograph book with yellowing pages. This could be all that was left. Snapshot images, memories and stories passed down. Life on Earth was little more than a prolonged snapshot and these things were the articles of life; of terrifyingly short life. But James wished for more. Much more. He was not aware, however, that one should be very careful about what one wishes for, as occasionally wishes are granted, but not always in ways one might have chosen.

If I have been extinguished, yet there rise
A thousand beacons from the spark I bore.[1]

THE WOMAN AT THE GRAVE

A movement caught his eye. Hunched over a grave was a young woman. Her hands were tracing the chiselled letters of the inscription. She looked lost in thought and oblivious to her surroundings. Deeply grieving, he thought. Better give her a wide berth. Her face stayed low. The wind whipped at her coat and he could hear the flapping of the fabric.

James continued his examination of the gravestones, careful not to go near the woman. From selected stones he jotted down names, dates and other details on a sheet of paper. He was all but finished with researching his family and the local area, determined not to dig too deep or become too much of an expert, but had this final bit of work to do.

The wind stepped up, blowing his piece of paper to the ground. He lunged, but as he went to grab it it blew further, slapping on to a headstone, as if clinging on for dear life.

"Shit!" James muttered, running over to the stone. Just as he was reaching down to the paper, another gust came and stole it out of his grasp, carrying it over and flopping it down beside the kneeling woman.

"I'm sorry." James tried to smile politely.

She glanced at the paper then up at him. Her eyes were red. She did not smile. She passed the paper to him.

"Thanks. The wind took it from me. It's getting up now, isn't it?"

She said nothing. As he looked at her, he felt a wave of something – a feeling that he was not familiar with. Something was not right. The woman, pale and unforthcoming, was dressed in a grey overcoat and wide-brimmed hat. She had long, dark hair tied up in a bun under the hat. It was the hat.

She began to look puzzled. James kept looking at her, aware that he probably seemed very rude, but he was unable to take his eyes off her, especially now that she was giving him such a look.

"Are you from around here?" he asked, thinking that she would recoil from what sounded like a corny chat-up line.

She cleared her throat. "I live in Roseberry Lane, just beyond that row of houses." As she turned, pointing towards the houses on the other side of the village green, she suddenly froze. Her arm came down slowly, and she dropped the handkerchief she had been clutching. It tumbled a few times before becoming lodged in a clump of grass between the graves. James looked at her then down at the handkerchief. It was white with lace on the corners and what looked to be an embroidered bouquet of flowers. He stooped to pick it up.

"It's all right, sir! I'll fetch!" She scuttled across, grabbed it and stuffed it into her coat pocket.

As she moved, James realised more about what it was that so unnerved him. She was dressed in clothing more normal for someone living many years ago; her hat, her handbag, the cut of her coat, the long dress he could glimpse. Even her demeanour seemed old-fashioned. He remembered he had heard about there being one or two fundamentalist religious groups in the area, but he knew nothing about them including old-looking hats in their ultra-conservative get-up. He went to walk away, conscious of the time he had spent staring at her. As he turned to leave, he noticed her expression. She was standing looking across the village green, down the hill towards a small row of houses. Her face was ashen and she had her hand across her mouth. She turned to him, whereupon he saw that her eyes were wide, with what looked to him to be terror. She screamed.

"Whoooaaa, what's wrong? Are you all right?"

She was shaking and becoming even whiter. He wanted to place a consoling hand on her shoulder, but did not feel he could risk it.

She looked at him, searching his face as if looking for answers. She then looked back at the houses and the surrounding area.

"Arghhh! What's happened, sir? What's happened? Can you see it? Can you? The houses have changed! *And there are more!* And what is all that noise?" She jumped and clutched James's sleeve. "Oh Lord, have mercy, what is *that thing?*" A black car sped up the narrow lane past the churchyard.

"Steady on! What exactly's wrong? Are you...not well?" Suddenly he knew all about her: she was a mental patient with a penchant for dressing up in strange clothing. Anti-modern, or something. You do get all sorts wandering the streets, even around here, in this conservative Surrey neighbourhood.

"Sir, something has happened and I need some answers...are you able to give me them?" She looked at him with such need that he felt his stomach twinge. He was hoping to go home and do his own thing now, not play social worker or nursemaid to some poor mentally ill person who, for all he knew, could be likely to steal his wallet or even stab him in the back.

He led her gently down the path and across the road to the green. He gestured for her to sit down with him on the park bench, facing a small pond. She hitched her skirts and coat and sat, taking some time to adjust everything. She moved closer to him, still shaking and gasping every few seconds as she surveyed the scene.

James tried to look her in the eye, but she kept looking around. "Tell me your name," he asked in a deliberately calm voice.

"Stepney. Miss Stepney."

"Miss Stepney? Do you have a first name then, Miss Stepney?"

Irritation flashed across her face. "Mary."

"Mary Stepney," he repeated, making sure he could remember for when he was later interviewed by the police or the hospital. "And Mary, you say you live in Roseberry Lane? Is that in the estate?"

She turned to him and scowled. "What isn't in the estate, you strange creature?! The Hood-Andrews own practically this whole area! Even the Prouts are only leasing."

"Uh?," was all James could muster. Better not upset her, he decided; she was most certainly not all there.

"Do you work?" Innocuous enough, he thought.

"Yes," she replied, more happily. "Well, I did. I was employed as a school teacher with a school not far from the High Street in Dorking, but I've left to pursue personal interests."

"Oh, really? What personal interests, if you don't mind me being nosey?"

"I like to write, but father says there's no money in it for a woman. He wants me back at the school. But, although I found it rewarding and a very important job, I just felt I was denying myself so much by being there."

"What subjects did you teach?"

"Mainly reading, writing and arithmetic. And I was coming along with my Geography."

"What sort of things do you write?"

She smiled and looked down at her hands. "I just write short stories. I've been very lucky – I had one published in *The Times*."

James relaxed somewhat. "That's excellent. You should do more. Your father sounds very old-fashioned, I hope you don't mind me saying. Tell him it's the twenty-first century now! Get with it!"

At that she jumped away from him and let go of his arm. "What! Sir, I was wondering about you, then I stopped wondering, and now I am wondering once again. Please tell me that you just have a very poor sense of humour! Twenty-first century, indeed!" She laughed, but it was not a happy laugh.

James gulped. "I'm sorry, Mary. I was just meaning that your father has no right to try to stop you being a writer just because of your sex. I do stand by my words – he is unbelievably living in the past!"

She came closer again, but did not take his arm this time.

"Sir."

"Call me James. Oh, I'm sorry, I should have said, I'm James Harvey."

"All right then – Mr Harvey, what century does *your* father live in?"

"The same one as yours, don't you think? Bit of a strange thing to say." He felt his hackles rise again.

"Well, Mr Harvey – *James* – can you please tell me why the houses are all looking so different today? And, for that matter, why your clothing is a little, er, unusual?" She stuck her chin in the air and looked him sternly in the eye.

"Why did that car make you jump so much? You not used to old bangers?"

"That car? Old bangers?" She repeated the words, but seemed unable to answer.

"Are you really all right?" he asked. "You don't seem...completely, er, completely well."

"Thank you, sir. And you do not look altogether unlike something my cat would cough up after she's been out ratting!"

"Uh! To hell with this! If you're just going to insult me, I'm going home! Goodbye, Mary! Very nice meeting you!"

As he leaned forward to get up off the bench a siren shattered the tranquillity. It was an ambulance from the nearby station. Mary turned in horror.

"Oh, Lord! Such noise! Mr Harvey, where am I?"

He looked seriously at her. "You just said you live up the road. You know where you are. Look, don't bother playing games with me. Has whatever happened been all too much for you? I know you're in mourning for someone who died – is that why you were visiting the grave? Someone you know...I mean, knew."

"Really! You are not afraid to speak your mind, I can tell that! Yes, as I said, I live nearby. But I'm trying to tell you that things are all different today. It all looks the same...but also very different, if you'll be kind enough to try to understand. What was that thing making all that noise just now?"

"You mean the ambulance?"

"Ambulance?"

"Yes."

"Oh. Is it like the things I was reading about in *The Times* a short while ago? There was an article about bringing in motor cars to carry passengers between Piccadilly Circus and Putney. Did you see it, or do you not take *The Times*? They will be able to carry up to eight people at once. Amazing! I shall use it next time I am up in London."

James felt queasy. This was too weird for him.

"No, I didn't see the article. I don't buy a paper; I go online instead to get my news. Tell me about the grave at the church."

She frowned and looked at him icily for a long moment. "That grave is the grave of my dear departed sister, Sarah, God bless her soul. She died of pneumonia last March. Only six years of age, poor wench."

"I'm sorry."

"Now there's just the eight of us left – and father and mother. I'm the eldest."

"Gosh, big family!" James replied. "Mine's only small – me and my sister. And Mum and Dad."

"Where do you live? Do you all reside together? Please don't think I'm being too forward, will you."

James noticed a sparkle of interest he hadn't seen in her eyes until then. "I live alone, up in Turnpike Lane. My parents are in Eastbourne – retired from the civil service in London. And I have a sister. She is the normal one, a daughter as perfect as they could've wished for. Grew up, went to university, won academic prizes one after the other, got married to a perfect man – he isn't really, but they think he is. And she had a couple of lovely children. Oh, don't get me wrong, they're very nice people, kind, decent, respectable...there's nothing at all wrong with them…except that they just go along with everything in the world, you know, without questioning or doing a lot of thinking. I call them sleepwalkers; not to their faces, of course."

"Oh." Mary looked dumbfounded.

"I've always been a bit different – stood out a bit I guess, with my more, I dunno, critical and less accepting approach to life. I probably seem a bit duller and more introverted than her. But I like to think I'm a bit smarter, but, whatever, she remains my parents' favourite. It sucks. But I accept it. Have to. It actually doesn't bother me as much now as it used to, but I'm just telling you."

"Oh, I don't quite know what to say. The odd one out, eh? Where does she live, if you don't mind?"

"They moved out to New Zealand a few years ago."

"Goodness, New Zealand!" she said in a surprised voice.

"Yes. Do you think that's a good thing? Do you think they're lucky?"

"I cannot say, really." She chuckled, continuing, "Yes, lucky if you wish to be living in a mud hut, or as good as, with some very suspicious characters for next-door neighbours. And I hear the gold is all gone now – scarcely enough left to do a tooth. Not like it was, anyway. Mind you, I hear there is a lot of good land there still, and a living to be made without the pressures and shackles of this country."

"Huh? WHAT? You say bonkers things!" James started. "I think you like to pretend. I think it's to get a reaction. Not in acting, are you?"

"No! Thank you, you rude thing! But New Zealand is one place I do know something about! My uncle Richard and his family went out to the colony a score or more years ago. They had a horridly long journey – it took them over three months to get there. Just over a hundred days, Liverpool to Auckland. That is too long for my liking."

"Blimey! What was it, a sailing ship?" He laughed.

"Of course."

James rolled his eyes.

"Oh, and I know Turnpike Lane," she began, sounding more confident again. "Do you know Samuel Hodges, the big man at number ten?"

"*Samuel* Hodges?" James repeated. "No, I don't think so. Not by name anyway. I only know *George* Hodges – you must know him, the giant with the braces and the untamed beard? Always wearing that daft old grey hat."

Mary laughed. James noticed how clear and blue her eyes were, and the way they brilliantly lit up when she smiled. He also noticed how her cheeks broke into dimples. He had always had a thing for dimples. Pity she's permanently out to lunch, he thought.

"No," she replied, "I do not know any giant man George Hodges, nor do I care to, either, by the sound of him! You do make me laugh, James. Although I do worry you might be mad. You're not a hatter by any chance, are you?" She laughed again. There was a faint pink glow now in her cheeks.

"Ha, ha. No. I'm a lowly public servant – I work for the local council, attending meetings and moving lots of pieces of paper around. No, I shouldn't say that, there's a lot more to it than that, and it is all very important and satisfying stuff, dealing with sometimes highly critical issues that matter in the real world."

"What other world is there?"

He smiled. "But it's only what I do in between doing interesting and fun things in my life – which, to be honest, I don't do as much as I'd like. I wouldn't mind more excitement in my life, probably like most other people. But my real job is as an amateur historian – in my spare time. And I suppose I like to read a lot."

"Oh," she acknowledged. "The two go well together."

"Yeah, and I kinda like football, but not obsessed or anything."

"Oh yes, very good."

"I've made myself sound really boring, haven't I?"

"No, no, not at all." She looked at his face intently. "But please explain something to me. Although I have noticed your eyes don't seem to betray any wickedness – one could even go so far as to call them kind eyes – you still haven't told me...why are you dressed in those peculiar clothes?"

As she waited for his answer she looked at him, returning her gaze to his eyes, which were a warm cinnamon brown, almost exactly the same colour as his hair, which although not long, had bits dancing in the wind.

He looked down at his fleece jacket, jeans and trainers.

"Is it something council officers must wear?" she asked.

He laughed. "What's wrong with these clothes? They're all right, aren't they? Anyway, what about your hat? Why do you dress up like you're something out of 1900?"

Mary looked aghast. The smile and dimples were quickly banished. She huffed and looked the other way, fumbling to make sure her handkerchief was still in her pocket, close at hand. After some tense silent moments she turned back and said coldly, "Perhaps, sir, that's because *it is only 1901!* Only one year later! Did you not think of that?"

THE REVELATION

The day had started normally enough but had turned out to be without a doubt the strangest and most unsettling one James could remember. After the surreal meeting and conversation with Mary Stepney it occurred to him that this woman should not be left unaccompanied until help arrived – and help was needed in the form of someone to sort out what was fast becoming a messy situation. Frankly, it did his head in. How this oddly-dressed woman could get her years so muddled was not at all easy to answer. After her wild declaration that the year was 1901 James had become mildly sarcastic as a defence. Assuming she was in her right mind, he couldn't bear to play whatever game it was she was playing, and yet he liked her. It was a peculiar feeling.

After a couple of hours spent sitting together the wind had started to irritate them a little too much, and he pestered her to go home. She agreed, but insisted on him escorting her, her arm linked with his as they walked. When they arrived at the house she was visibly shocked. She told James how nothing looked as it should – not the house, not the garden, not the neighbouring houses, not even the lamp-posts. The street signs were new; there was an extension on number 15 which she said they had not had when she'd set off for the church that morning. Some trees were gone, others were new, and a few oaks were the same only much bigger than they'd been that morning. It was all more built-up, she claimed, more busy; and there were objects around which were new and unidentifiable. On the occasions when a car went past them Mary would turn and stare. On noticing that there were people inside these contraptions her comment was that as they are all going so fast there must be a great many people killed in them every day; it was simply inevitable. James had just smiled, adding that perhaps bicycles and horses were a better idea, to which she heartily agreed. Mary visibly appeared to have trouble figuring out cars and the changes in the buildings and streets; she seemed unable – or perhaps unwilling – to challenge her notion that the year was 1901.

As they stood for several minutes outside what was supposed to be her family home on Roseberry Lane, James eventually said, "Mary, if you're sure this isn't your house anymore, why don't you come home with me? I'm only a few streets away."

She slapped his face with such ferocity that he stumbled.

"YOU'RE MAD! WHAT THE HELL DID YOU DO THAT FOR?" he blurted, holding his hand to his cheek.

"Don't let's pretend you're oblivious! I think you jolly well know why! And do not swear at me!" She stuck her nose in the air in front of him, adding, "I don't quite know what you think of me, Mr Harvey, but I assure you I am not that kind of lady! Just you remember that!"

"I'm sorry! Mary! I *wasn't* being like that! Honest! You've got nowhere to go, or so you say."

She looked down at the pavement then up at the front door of the house. She sighed. "No, you're right. I can tell by the shiny new brass of the lock on the door that my key won't fit anymore. And we never had curtains like those or all those flowers in the garden. They've done a grand job of making the place look lovely, I must say."

"Come on, let's go." James gently took her arm. They walked away, but with every few steps she would turn and look back.

When they entered his house, she gasped. She looked around almost frantically. Not speaking for many minutes, Mary inspected every piece of furniture, every picture on the wall, every ornament and every appliance. She ran her fingers across the screen of the television, over the buttons on the stereo and DVD player, she touched the thermostat of the central heating system, turning the dial. She pressed light switches, delighting every time at the outcome. Shaking her head in wonder she busied herself around the whole of the downstairs, fingering, tweaking, tapping and turning. Pausing to rest beside a radiator she jumped as she felt it beginning to heat. She touched the fabric of the brightly coloured cushions on the sofa and even passed her hands across the frosted-glass drink coasters on the coffee table.

Finally, walking over to James in the kitchen, where he was making tea, she said, "James, please don't think me strange or mad, but…"

IT'S TOO DAMNED LATE FOR THAT! he thought loudly to himself. "What?"

"Is it *really* not…um, is it *really* not 1901 anymore?"

He placed a consolatory hand on her shoulder. Play the game, he thought. "Mary, this will be hard for you, so hard I can't even begin to imagine, but I know you've realised things are not as you think they should be. You seem genuinely unfamiliar with so many things. It's weird for me. It's unbelievable. No, the year is not 1901! And it hasn't been for some time!"

"Well then, what is the year? Tell me! Please!"

He eyed her seriously as he pointed to the date on the kitchen calendar. She stared at it, transfixed. She kept looking at it for some time before slowly turning to look out the window. There she stood without speaking, clasping herself tightly around the waist, rocking to and fro on her heels, looking at the plants, trees, flowers and the cat that slept beneath a shrub by the wooden fence.

After a long silence she spoke. Her voice wavered. "It is all so different. But this is the same place. Just not the same time. It's over a hundred years later! *Over a hundred years!* But how could this be?" Her voice trailed away. She buried her face in her hands.

"Mary, I don't know." He kept wondering if he had become part of some elaborate hoax, some cruel game, and that a TV person would jump out in front of him saying, 'Ha ha, you've been had!' It would be so embarrassing. He couldn't help wonder, after all, to him it seemed a much more likely explanation than her preposterous story that she had somehow inadvertently time-travelled from 1901 to the present.

He made the tea, grabbed some nibbles and they went and sat down in the living room. His mother had always said if someone's upset make them a nice cup of tea, but he felt he really could have done with something much stronger.

Mary stayed the night, sleeping in James's spare bedroom. He had had to clear a lot of things out of the way; it had been a long time since anyone had stayed over (without sleeping in his bed). As the evening wore on Mary had become more placid and fragile, probably, James thought, with the realisation of how incomprehensibly vulnerable she was – that's *if* what she said was true.

* * *

The next day was Sunday. Mary woke early. When they met on the upstairs landing she asked him if he was going to church, and whether there was still a service at 11 o'clock. He said he didn't know, but even if there was he had no desire to go. This then began a long and rambling discussion on religion, which continued right through breakfast. James told her about how he used to be a believer, but went on to reject orthodox Christianity, choosing instead a more radical – but no less credible – set of beliefs based on spirituality, rather than religion. This had both confused and engaged her. He was just getting further into the conversation when there was a ring of the door bell. Mary jumped in her seat, spilling her tea.

It was George Hodges. James ushered him inside.

"Lad, I'd just like to say I'm sorry for storming off like I did, y'know, at the fireworks."

"George, it's all right. I understand. Anyway, I'm sorry for what I said. It was very tactless of me and I'm the one who should be apologising."

"Okay. How 'bout a Fisherman's Friend? Original, extra

strong." George held a packet out towards James.

"Er, no, thanks." James smiled as he got a whiff.

"Oh, 'ang on, do I know this young lady?" he asked, nudging James.

Mary stood up as they entered the kitchen.

George grinned, asking her to sit down again and get back to her breakfast.

"George, this is Mary Stepney. Mary, this is George Hodges. He lives up on Duke's Ride."

"How do you do, Mr Hodges? I know Duke's Ride, sir. You're not any relation of the man at number ten this street, Turnpike Lane, are you? Er, what's his name, Mr Samuel Hodges?" As soon as she had said it she looked as if she wanted to slip through a crack in the floorboards and disappear.

"Eh?" George scratched his head. "Samuel? That rings a bell. But no, there's none of me family living in this street. I think you must be mistaken."

"Yes, you are right, I'm terribly sorry, sir. I think I have got my details confused."

"I did have a grandfather named Samuel, but he's been dead for donkey's years."

"I'm sorry, I've got my names mixed up."

"Oh. All right lass, no worries." He scratched his head, then said to her, "Have I seen you somewhere before?"

"Oh, no! I shouldn't think so."

"Oh. I'm sure it's just me then. I'm always gettin' people mixed up meself." He chuckled.

James forcibly moved George into the living room.

"George, I want to say that I am really sorry I didn't believe you the other day. I should have been more open-minded, I know. I've since been, er, thinking it over, and I know there are many things that happen in this world that can never be explained, at least not by an everyday explanation."

"Well, well! Great! I'm pleased to hear that!" Placing his huge hand on James's shoulder George added, "Well I won't interrupt you any longer. I didn't know y'had company. Is she yer girlfriend?"

"No!" James hissed, not wanting Mary to hear. "She's just a friend who needs somewhere to stay for a while."

"Oh, okay." George tapped the side of his nose. "Won't say a word."

"*George!* George, it's true! You don't know the half of it. We're just friends, *believe me!*"

George grinned. "Oh, it's all right, lad – I do. Just getting you back! Bye now. Oh, and do watch out for any strange goings on like I was telling you about, won't you."

OVER THE GATEPOST

The man, tall, portly and slightly dishevelled, stood resting on the gatepost, catching his breath. He had just finished chopping up wood for the fire and had noticed something appealing about the light. The sun, now beginning to set at the end of Turnpike Lane, was casting a straw-coloured wash, turning everything a creamy gold; even the brown brick of the houses glowed. He smiled weakly. The ache of his bones could not be forgotten, even for a minute, and had been made worse by the chopping.

He glanced at his pocket watch then rubbed his beard and looked into the distance. Rain coming, he thought. He could feel the change in the air and could just make out a layer of dark grey in the sky to the north. It'll be cold, he decided. Just as well I've done the wood.

Holding his hand to his lower back, he was turning to go inside when a movement caught his eye. It was his neighbour scurrying quickly towards him.

"Samuel! Samuel!" the man said with emotion. "I need to talk to you!"

He stopped at the other side of the gate. He looked upset and he smelled of booze laced with stale smoke.

"Pooh! You've been up at the inn!"

"Samuel! Just let me tell you what happened to me today!"

"A'right. There's no stopping you anyway, I can tell."

"I was out in the field earlier, minding my own business, when something queer happened. I'd been out on Bertha, and we'd ridden for miles – been up to old Aunt Bessie's up on Box Hill – and we were almost home, just cutting alongside the Prout's property. We stopped for a rest. I was having a pipe and Bertha was tethered. I was sitting on the grass watching an old couple out with their dog, picking wild berries. Anyhow, I couldn't believe my eyes. I was just sitting there when the view in front of me altered from what it should have been to a vision. Not very nice either, but not bad, mind. I saw this fellow standing there looking at me. Only he hadn't been there a moment earlier. Where he came from I don't know. There were houses all around him too. He was in the yard of one of them, peering over a fence. He was quite tall. He had on dungarees and, well, reminded me of you actually, funnily enough. We looked at each other, then it all just went away, just as silently and strangely as it had come. There, now don't think I'm a lunatic! Please! I did see him and he did see me. But what the vision means I don't know."

"Well, I'll be!"

"Samuel Hodges, is that all you can say?"

The big man stroked his beard and thought. He had heard many a ripping yarn in his time, especially when he lived up north, and this was just the latest one to be added to the list. But the neighbour had never before said anything like this; he was usually a quiet, sober man not taken to excesses of anything – but he did smell of drink tonight.

"Eee, I dunno what to say," said Samuel, glancing up at the approaching cloud, "'cept it's gonna rain any minute now and you'll be caught out in it if you're not careful."

"So you obviously don't believe me!"

"It's not for me to believe you or not. I won't disagree with you though. Queer things do happen and always have. Even round 'ere. Only the good Lord above will know what really happened. Lad, you'd best be off home, it's starting to come down. Don't want you catching pneumonia like that poor wee Stepney lass."

"No, that's true. Well I'll be off. Good evening, Sam."

"Good evening.

GETTING ACQUAINTED

After George departed the house James and Mary resumed their breakfasts. The unusual house guest was like a ship riding stormy seas, surging to and fro; one moment placid and accepting, the next moment possessed by what seemed to be intense fear. When she was calm she was happy, in spite of her constant flow of questions (which were mostly rhetorical). James's nervousness was beginning to show, however, with him becoming increasingly anxious about what he might now be involved in. And, although he could blame nobody but himself for getting into this situation, how long was he to be responsible for her? He wanted to believe her, as insane as it all seemed, but was unnerved by the way that when she was calm, she seemed *too* calm, *too* happy and even able to crack jokes. Her usual demeanour was thoughtful and composed, with an educated yet friendly, straight-forward style of communicating. There didn't seem to be enough of the meek, lace-bonneted Victorian woman, at least not enough to fit his stereotype; she should be more terrified, he thought, if her story was really true. So the two of them swung like pendulums, in isolated alternating movements.

"Would you like me to save the tea leaves for you?" Mary asked, as she got up to clear the table.

"What?" James was awoken from his reverie. There was so much going on in his mind that he was finding it hard to stay in the here and now. "What do you mean?"

"Tea leaves," she repeated. "From the tea."

"I, er, don't have tea leaves. There's no tea pot, they're tea bags."

She looked puzzled. "Bags? Pardon me for saying, James, but is this another new invention? Tea *bags?*" She smirked.

"Yes. It's just tea leaves inside thin paper bags. Plonk it in boiling water. Just very practical. Not romantic, I suppose, like tea from a tea pot. Is that what you're used to?"

"Yes."

"Well, many people still use real tea with pots, but not as many as in your day."

"Oh."

James smiled at her. Seeing this, she ducked her head down and fussed with the dishes.

"What fate did you have in mind for the tea leaves, anyway?"

"Oh, for the floor – the mats. The leaves soak in the dirt and then you sweep them up."

"I see," he acknowledged. "They go into my compost heap. Tea bags decompose into the most fabulous soil for the garden. But don't the tea leaves stain whatever they touch?"

"Not really, so long as they're not too damp. If you want to be on the safe side I suppose it helps if the mat is brown, which most of the mats in our house are, or *were*. My parents' house, I mean."

"Oh, right." James smiled politely. *My God*, he said inwardly, *how am I going to cope with this woman? Every little thing! Nothing is familiar!* Or so she says.

* * *

That afternoon, James decided it might be a good idea to take Mary down to the shops that were open to get her some new clothes. She was, after all, wearing all the clothes she now possessed, or that was the story. He would be a gallant gentleman of the most generous kind – or, more likely, he thought, the biggest mug ever born – and buy her a starter wardrobe, enough for a few days' wear plus a couple of special, dressed-up items. And she needed new shoes – she was clomping about in black lace-up boots that while not looking too out of place in the twenty-first century – where just about anything goes – would not go with much, and did always make him think she was wearing fancy dress. Attracting attention to her was the last thing he wanted, and Dorking was only a small town. After an awkward conversation he succeeded in persuading her not to wear her hat, informing her in no uncertain terms that even though he was a male he knew that hats like that were a thing of the distant past. She found that difficult, commenting that she never ventured anywhere without a hat on her head. Before they went out she fussed with her hair, brushing its long, dark strands with a brush James had, complaining that she needed her own dressing table and all her things. And having her house and family back would be nice too, she added. James could not have agreed more.

He was not, however, prepared for Mary's reaction to the local shops. Although she was familiar with the High Street and the smaller streets that radiated off, she sought out those businesses she said she was accustomed to visiting. First of all she wanted to see the shop where her family used to buy much of their food and household supplies. She led James to what was a glitzy, electronic goods shop. They stood together at the doorway looking in, with Mary glued to the spot, her mouth agape. Double whammy, if she really was from 1901, James thought, starkly conscious of the extra shock provided by the sight of all the strange products on offer. Predictably, Mary soon began pointing and asking what things were.

How, James wondered, do I describe digital technology or a TV or even a vacuum cleaner to Mary? And computers! Don't even go there! Even the concept of pedestrian crossings was alien to her.

"I see the White Horse Inn is still there. Looks quite the same too. Although the wooden picture hanging above the street, the one of the white horse, does look more like a black horse now with just a few white spots! A different breed entirely now! But I see that the Red Lion, the Ram Inn and The Three Tuns have all gone. They used to read out the election results from the steps of the Red Lion Hotel. And The Three Tuns had a big sign outside, painted on the building, that said 'luncheons, dinners and teas'."

"I remember my parents talking about The Three Tuns," James said. "It was pulled down in the 1970s to build more shops."

"Outside The Three Tuns you'd often see the rat-catcher. He'd shout 'Death to the rats!'. He was a filthy man, scurrying around on his hands and knees. I didn't like him or the thought of what he did, although I understood that there could sometimes be too many rats and in the wrong places, and that something had to be done. I used to tell people that the rats would get their revenge on him one day! Anyway, as I always said until I was blue in the face, getting a cat is a better way to keep the rats down."

"A rat-catcher, huh?"

"Yes." She resumed looking around.

"How were people supposed to get rid of rats then? They can spread disease, and stuff!"

"Oh, I know. I understand, but I just would have preferred some other method that didn't involve killing them. A lot of people didn't agree with my opinion on the poor, bedraggled rat-catcher and thought I was mad and silly, but no bother, I thought. I've always been quite the black sheep, always thinking differently from other people. An oddity. And now look at me! Here I am today, even odder!"

"Hey, don't worry. We'll sort you out." *One way or another*, he thought.

"I see that Chequers Yard has gone...as has, well, so much. Did you know there used to be a candle factory over there." She pointed at a shop that now sold mobile phones. "It used to have a sign outside that said 'Let there be light'. And there was a big clock. And over by where those people are crossing the road there used to be a travelling dentist who would come to town every market day and take people's teeth out. That was what he usually did, but he didn't get mine, thank goodness. He'd set up shop on the pavement over there," she pointed to outside what was now an Oxfam.

"Oh, I'm happy to see Woodcocks chemist is still there and still looks much the same. That's an odd comfort. Yes. I like seeing a few things looking much the same. The cars on the road though…are something to behold. *So many!* And such noise! And such speed! And so graceless. The old carriages, horses and bicycles at least gave a sort of charm to the streets. Although you know at the time I didn't realise it. At least we weren't as likely to die just crossing the road. This is a frightening scene. They scare me, James."

"It's so busy along the High Street because the town has the A25 running directly through it – a major road."

"Well, whatever. They seem harsh and unforgiving. And, from what you've said, a pit for you to throw your money into. Yet being in the car coming here was an exhilarating experience and we got here so quickly." She paused.

"See Box Hill?" she said, suddenly laughing.

"Yeah," James answered, glancing towards the hills that lay to the north of the town.

"Before I forget, let me tell you a little story about Box Hill."

"Okay."

"Well, years before I was born – many years before, in fact – there was an eccentric old gentleman – a retired major from the army, from memory. He said that when he died he wanted to be buried on Box Hill on his head."

"On his head?"

"Yes. A hundred feet down, what's more."

"Can I just ask *why?*"

"So that on Judgement Day, when all things will supposedly be turned topsy-turvy, he will be the first one upright!"

"Ahhh, well! What can you say! Original!"

"To get to the top of Box Hill back then one had to cross a footbridge over the river on the track of the old Pilgrim's Way.

They did that – carried him all the way – and they buried the man exactly as he had requested – on his head. Very peculiar!"

"Well, I suppose it takes up less space if you look at it from a practical point of view – surface area, you know."

"I dare say. A good idea nowadays, perhaps then. So, he was an odd man and that was a very odd thing, I'm sure completely forgotten by now, apart from the old memorial up there."

"I've seen it."

"He's long gone and long rotted into the earth, he and all the people who knew him."

James shrugged. "Of course. That's how it goes." He looked her straight in the eye and tried to ignore the sudden sharp feelings of unease that were pricking at him.

As Mary watched a group of teenage girls walking by, her face grew serious. "Does this world not know it's possible to be too liberal? Or, should I say, too vulgar?"

He looked at her. "Huh?"

"No bother. I suppose I am the odd man out now, not them."

After a few awkward silent moments she inhaled deeply. "The smells in the air in town are different now. But all this change is naturally to be expected. It feels so strange to me, like a dream from which I must surely be about to awaken. But I'm beginning to realise that I really am here and that I may be here for some time." She broke off and looked into the distance.

"I can only try to understand," James offered. "I know how I felt when I once returned to the house I grew up in and found they'd demolished it to make way for a block of flats. And an ugly block of flats at that. A slum in the making, I thought. The trees I used to play in had been cut down. Everything had been levelled and nothing was real anymore. There were signs – do not do this, do not do that, no ball games, all that sort of stuff. It upset me a bit. I felt sorry for the kids that lived there. A kid's gotta have trees to play in – plenty of natural areas – and gotta be able to play outside on grass with balls and bikes and stuff, and make dens and huts. What sort of childhood is it without those things? And I felt they'd ruined the character of the street forever, those damned developers and town planners."

She looked at him seriously and nodded. "I can see how that would be upsetting. But do you know what the funny thing is? The house that *I* grew up in all those years ago here *is* still standing. Ironic, isn't it?"

"Yes."

Taking Mary into a chain store renowned for classic clothing for men and women at a reasonable price, James, at first happy and optimistic about their prospects, soon noticed the looks the shop assistants were giving her. A surge of protectiveness went through him. He realised the need to closely guard and watch her for the time being, not only because of what people might think of her but also how she might react to her new surroundings. Mary, the wildcard. James now dearly wished this were just a dream: that he would wake up at some time and come to his senses, and all would be well with him once more – back to his nice, safe, normal life. But it was not to be. The time spent in that store would go down in James's memory as one of his worst shopping experiences ever (and he had had a few). He tried to think, in vain, of a word that meant more than just embarrassed ('mortified' wasn't strong enough). After several unsuccessful changes of clothes Mary was becoming frustrated, so James embarked on a plan of just grabbing garments which were her size (which itself had taken some working out) and would be able to be worn with other items. Getting past the corset issue (which he persuaded her she didn't need – the young women in the shop overheard the conversation and had a giggle over that one), James felt sure the assistants would be thinking he was a controlling husband of the worst kind – even saying what the poor woman could wear! What must he be like at home?

He would stand outside the fitting room waiting patiently as she tried on item after item: dresses, skirts, trousers, shirts, jackets. The shop also sold shoes. And she looked at scarves, hats, socks and gloves. As time went by the shop assistants eyed him more judgementally, shooting him looks of suspicion and even disgust. James wished he had taken Mary up to London, at least there was anonymity up there – and, of course, much more choice. Another perhaps wiser part of his psyche told him one step at a time: Mary was in no way ready for twenty-first-century London just yet!

After James paid the expectedly hefty bill they left the shop, both carrying so many bags that it looked as though they might have cleaned out almost everything in the shop.

"James," Mary began uncertainly as they crossed the street, "how am I possibly to thank you for all this?"

He smiled at her. "It's all right."

"I want you to know how deeply touched I am and how appreciative I am. Thank you very very much for all this. I will pay it back one day, mark my words." She looked across at him, caught his eye and smiled.

He wasn't quite sure what to say. How could he possibly have left her in his house dressed as she was, like a prisoner unable to go out and interact with the world? A secret woman! What would the neighbours say if they had seen her in her old garb hanging out the washing or sitting in the garden when he was supposed to live alone? And, more importantly, what would his parents think if they came up from Eastbourne (which was after all only around an hour and a half away) and found a 'Victorian lady' living with him? They would have her carted away to a mental hospital before you had time to say *"Remember Catweazle? You wouldn't have wanted him to be put in a loony bin!"*

"Mary, it's fine," he replied warmly. "I want to help you, and this is something important for you to have. You need to get out of those old clothes as soon as possible. Please don't slap me for saying that!"

They returned to James's car. Mary was in the throes of

getting used to it. On the ride into town she had been fascinated. She had marvelled at the speed at which they moved and was enthralled by the array of knobs, buttons, switches and things to touch. James kept assuring her that, yes, they were safe (he had to hope he would be right on that one) and that he would answer all her questions later that day. In the meantime he tried to briefly sum up for her the internal combustion engine of his four-year-old Peugeot, and he explained the basic principles involved in driving and parking, and something about the many things you have to do to own and run a dirty and expensive, but oh so practical motor car. And the voice behind the voice was still laughing at him and calling him a pathetic fool.

* * *

James went to work while Mary stayed at home, the arrangement being for her to pay her way by doing cleaning and washing and whatever else she could find to do. James had instructed her on the washing machine (which she loved), the vacuum cleaner (ditto) and the iron (ditto). Genuinely labour-saving devices went down well with her. She happily washed, cleaned and tidied, as well as doing bits and pieces in the garden; however, her going outside was an issue with James, as several of the neighbours had views straight into the property at the front and back. There was, however, an area to one side where no one could see, and Mary was fast becoming partial to taking a chair around there just to get some fresh air and enjoy being outside. But the winter was coming on, and the mildest of late autumn days were becoming difficult to endure, as the sun grew fainter.

To occupy herself she started reading voraciously, like a reader starved of books suddenly let loose in a library. The book shelves in James's house held an impressive collection of eclectic titles. She would never be bored again. Subjects such as travel and health intruded upon the sizeable historical realm, while architecture butted up to the likes of Ray Bradbury and Noam Chomsky. Further along the same literary avenue lived Albert Schweitzer and his curious neighbour, E.F. Schumacher. Then it was astronomy, birds and Thomas Edison. Nothing was in order, adding to Mary's delight as she explored the titles. She set her heart on reading all that interested her, careful to move James's half dozen *Match of the Day Annual*s to relegation at the bottom end of one shelf. Heavy and light, non-fiction and fiction, the sprawl of printed words created a jumbled city of stimulating and occasionally inspired words – enough to entertain his house-guest for the foreseeable future.

* * *

"Give me one I'll know," she asked, as they whiled away a rainy afternoon looking at books.

"Okay, here's one I think you'll recognise." James read the opening sentence from a novel, " 'It was the best of times, it was the worst of times, it was the age of wisdom, it was the age of foolishness, it was the epoch of belief, it was the epoch of incredulity, it was the season of Light, it was the season of Darkness, it was the spring of hope, it was the winter of despair, we had everything before us, we had nothing before us, we were all going direct to Heaven, we were all going direct the other way – in short, the period was so far like the present period, that some of its noisiest authorities insisted on its being received, for good or for evil, in the superlative degree of comparison only.' "

"Goodness! That must be the longest sentence ever written! It *is* just one sentence?"

"Yep!" He replied, shutting the book and replacing it on the bookshelf. "Well, what's it from?"

She smiled. "That was Charles Dickens – *A Tale of Two Cities*. A grand book, to my thinking. I've always thought his powers of observation very sharp, and his understanding of the human condition shines through his writing."

"Absolutely. It's one of my favourites."

"You might say," she added shyly, "that it fits well the current time, do you not think? Those terms are still relevant for the present period, do you not agree?"

"Hmmm," he contemplated. "Yeah, I guess so. Sharp observer yourself."

She smiled and looked away. "Have you anything by Louisa May Alcott?"

"Er, no."

"Ooh, I do like her books. And she herself was an inspiration to me. Someone quite ahead of her time, in my opinion."

"I'm afraid I know nothing about her," James replied. "How about this one?" He grabbed another book. "This is the opening line of another famous novel, 'Tell me, Muse, of that man, so ready at need, who wandered far and wide, after he had sacked the sacred citadel of Troy, and many were the men whose towns he saw and whose mind he learnt, yea, and many the woes he suffered in his heart upon the deep, striving to win his own life and the return of his company.' "

"Oh, truly, I think I know this. I think I can work it out. What, with a big journey and muses and Troy…it must be, oh, I know! Would it be Homer? *The Odyssey* or *The Iliad*? I'm not at all well-versed with Homer."

"Correct enough. It was the first sentence from *The Odyssey*."

"James, I think I'm on a journey a bit like him," she began sadly. "A big journey. Frightening and uncertain. And mine goes further, really, with things he never had to face."

He smiled weakly.

"I feel as though God has forgotten me. Do you have any idea how it feels?"

James couldn't speak. Mary's new-found reality was a harsh one, whether it was truly as she said it was or not. His carefully concealed doubt about the whole thing was almost to the point of overwhelming – but not quite. He had never been called stupid, nor was he in the habit of being overly gullible. To fall or be pulled through, or to somehow seep through the invisible fabric of the physical world – the boundaries of space and time, no less – was something frequently the stuff of science-fiction and, increasingly, of science itself. But was it possible? Did it happen? And, if so, how and why? His gut feeling, normally so wisely guiding and trustworthy, was now mute and unable to help. This time the mind was hell-bent on overruling any hint of anything far-fetched and ethereal. Whose reality was it anyway? And whose reality was real? And, of course, definitions of reality were wont to vary. So with a head perplexed and incapable, his heart decided to stay the course, running on its own power, and enjoying the company of this highly intelligent and stimulating woman, wherever she was really from. He remembered a quote he had once read, it went something like, 'The ultimate arrogance is to confine reality to that which we can understand.'

* * *

James's parents, Frank and Edwina, arrived to visit him one day, unannounced, bringing with them James's four-year-old cousin, Charlie. When the doorbell rang, James and Mary had been watching TV, taking in yet another movie: Mary was fast becoming, in James's opinion, far too enamoured with the big screen in the corner of the room. Even the advertisements were lapped up. And yet he could understand why – if he was to accept, at least for now, her account of where she was from – a flashy, flickering array of coloured pixels could change someone's world to a large extent, and the sheer novelty was hard to resist and probably, James thought, easy for her to get hooked on.

To explain Mary's presence, they had cooked up a story to tell people that Mary was an old friend of his from his days at university, and that they had reconnected via a social networking website. She had read English literature, and lived in the West Country, in a place (hopefully) never to have to be revealed. (He thought he would trundle out "a village somewhere near Glastonbury" if anyone ever asked).

Sitting politely with cups of tea and chocolate biscuits it had all gone well until James's mother, convinced of a serious relationship between the pair, asked Mary where her parents lived.

"My parents are, um, er…" she faltered.

"Mmmm?" Edwina prompted, peering over her teacup. Her mind flittered: in Reigate? In Cardiff? In Australia? Not *prison*, surely?!

"They're, um, dead." Mary looked at the floor and felt herself taking quick, shallow breaths.

"Oh dear, I am sorry," Edwina consoled. Placing her cup on the coffee table she reached across and placed her hand on top of Mary's.

"It's all right," Mary blurted, her eyes welling up. She excused herself and went out to the kitchen.

James glared at his mother. She glared back. A few tense moments passed with no one speaking.

"I didn't know," she eventually hissed. "I am sorry. Really, I am. It makes a change – it's usually your father who upsets—"

Mary returned from the kitchen, smiling. She went over to Charlie, who had been sitting thumbing through a book of James's that had colour photographs of an underwater archaeological excavation.

"Charlie, where do you live?"

He looked up from the book. "Hove, actually."

Mary looked confused and thought for a moment. "Oh, is that Hove – Hove, near Brighton? Not Brighton then?"

"Hove!" Charlie repeated emphatically, before adding, "actually."

Mary giggled. "Mmmm, very nice, aren't you a lucky boy living at the seaside? Charlie, would you like to come with me into the kitchen and play a game?"

"Oooh, what game?" he said, scrambling to his feet and running out of the room with her.

"I'm not telling. Not a dicky bird until you're seated and ready," she answered, shutting the door behind them. They sat at the table and Mary gave Charlie a glass of water. She got herself one and sat facing him.

"Charlie, this game is about funny rhymes. It's not really a game, it's really just making up rhymes. I used to like doing this when I was a little girl. I used to play it with my sisters."

"A long time ago?" he asked plaintively, his eyes taking in her unfamiliar face.

"Yes. A long time ago. Here's my first one. Ahem." She assumed a lilting, theatrical voice. "Boys who dig holes make homes for little moles!"

He roared with laughter, jiggling his small arms up and down and clapping a few times.

Spurred on, Mary followed it with, "Girls who like pearls grow roses in their curls!"

More laughter. The boy's attention was gripped.

"And Charlie," she said, encouragingly, "did you know that boys who like cats send presents of rats?"

"That's funny!" Charlie shouted.

"Can you imagine that? Sending a cat a present of a rat? Here's another one." She was dragging them from her memory. "Babies with smiley faces often win dribbling races."

"Hah!" He squirmed in his chair. "'Nother one!"

"Now, do I know any more?"

"Yes, pleeease!"

"What about you? Can you make up any funny rhymes?"

He scowled and stared into his glass of water, saying nothing.

"Oh, so just a one-sided game, this one? All right, I see. Last one then." Resuming a funny voice, "Girls who eat peas do all their work with ease!"

"Hah! I like peas!"

"Always say peas and thank you!"

Silence.

"HAH, HAH!"

"This is definitely the last one. Boys with big dogs can find their way through fogs!"

Charlie laughed more. Mary decided the bonding work had gone well and that she had surpassed herself. She wondered how she had possibly remembered those silly old rhymes she had made up years earlier, but was pleased that she had.

"You remind me of my little brother," Mary said to him, as she looked at his blonde hair, noticing he had the same shaped head and face.

"What's his name?"

"Johnny," she said quietly. "And I have other brothers, but you don't remind me of any of them. Johnny's a lovely lad, polite, helpful, likes to run around. He'll grow up to be a fine and handsome young man, I dare say. I do miss him." She felt a sharp pang in her stomach and her throat tightened. Her eyes tried to water, and she stifled it by looking up at the ceiling while she changed the subject to that of Charlie's parents.

Eventually taking the boy back into the room with the others, she noticed that they were speaking quietly, almost as if in some sort of conspiracy.

Frank was hurriedly finishing off. "And so they're not wanting anyone to know. They don't want to be made fools of, even though this sort of thing's in the news so much at the moment. Not a word, James, you hear?"

"Okay," James replied.

Mary sat down feeling slightly uneasy.

"Now then, my boy, did you have fun out there with Mary?" Frank asked, scruffing Charlie's snowy head.

"Yes," the boy replied politely.

"Good. Did Mary tell you something funny? We could hear you laughing from here! You're a little riot when you get going, aren't you?" More scruffing of the hair.

"I'm terribly sorry, Mr Harvey," said Mary. "I didn't mean to make so much noise. It's just so lovely to have a child in the house ag—" She stopped herself. "I come from a big family, you see, so there's always been the sound and feeling of children around." She knew she had said more than she wanted to, but it had just slipped out.

"Do you have brothers and sisters?" enquired Edwina, feeling she was back on safe ground.

"Er, yes, I have. Three sisters and four brothers."

"Gosh! That's a big family!" Edwina tried to laugh it off without causing offence.

"There was one more, but she, er, passed away from an illness when she was just six." Mary wondered at herself opening up in this way, far too much. She felt queasy.

"Oh, I am so sorry. May I ask what the illness was? I used to be a nurse."

"Pneumonia," Mary replied.

"Oh, how dreadful. It still kills many people, doesn't it. How very sad." Edwina was secretly wishing she hadn't opened her mouth and had left it at just the parents dead. Now a sister as well! And the poor girl is still only young.

"Not Catholic, are you?" asked Frank.

"Dad!" James snapped. "You can't ask things like that!"

"Oh—"

"No, it's all right," Mary interrupted. "I'm not Catholic. Mother and Father just wanted as many children as they could have."

"Heavens!" was all Edwina could add, knowing her son would jump to Mary's aid if any further questioning took place.

Mary's concentration lapsed, as she thought to herself: *They are still alive. They are not dead.* She fought back tears and tried to be interested in Edwina's stories from the Women's Institute.

With the atmosphere in decline, the visit was ended, much to everyone's relief except Charlie, who had made a new friend and was happy – the only one properly smiling, in fact, when it came time to wave goodbye.

THE GRAVE AND THE HOLLY TREES: PART ONE

The sun, although still very low in the sky, reflected dazzlingly off the pond, causing Matilda to shield her eyes. She moved under a nearby willow for some shade, tugging at her younger brother's sleeve.

"C'mon, under the tree," she instructed. "It's too glary."

"But there's a fish at the surface. I want to feed him." He dragged himself away and they sat on the bench beneath the downy willow.

"Didn't bring any bread though. Nothing," she said glumly.

The boy groaned exaggeratedly.

"Shush! Please don't upset me! If it's not bad enough that today's the 11th of November."

"What?"

"Don't say *what*. The 11th of November. You know very well what I mean. It's been one year."

"But—"

"Shush, Johnny!"

The boy hung his small blonde head between his knees and said nothing. A few minutes of silence elapsed, apart from an unconducted symphony of blue tits, chaffinches, goldfinches and assorted others. The quiet corner of Surrey seemed even quieter than usual.

Abruptly, Matilda stood up. "Johnny – look!" She was fixated on some activity up the hill, in the churchyard. Johnny turned, blinking his eyes, trying to peer into the sun.

"Can't see," he exclaimed, "sun's in me eyes."

"*My* eyes! Johnny, remember your lessons!"

"Well, what? I can't see anything," he said grumpily.

"Come on!" she commanded, pulling his arm.

"Oh, where to *now*? You cart me around with ye like I'm

a...*doll!* Well, I'm not!" He jerked his arms out of her grasp.

"It's *you*, not *ye*," she corrected, but this time with less passion and without taking her eyes off the churchyard. "Johnny, we've got to go up to the church – I think it might be Mary! Oh, please!"

He leapt to his feet. "Mary? Why didn't ye say? Let's go!"

The two children ran up the narrow, almost straight path which led to the church, with just the narrow lane to be crossed. As they approached the roadside they could see a figure crouched in the graveyard, but the early morning sun was blinding, making it hard for them to see many details. With a bit of imagination it could have been Mary, and, innocently enough, they were both determined to see what they wanted to see.

They stopped and looked at each other. The person was visiting one of the graves. And it did look somewhat like Mary from their angle, although they could not see her face.

"Tilly," the boy whispered, "is it her?"

"*I don't know,*" Matilda whispered tensely. They clasped each other's hands. Matilda had a strong urge to call to the person, but somehow it was stifled and unable to escape her lips.

The figure had not moved since they started looking. They could just make out the folds and pleats in the dress and it did look like the long coat Mary usually wore when she went out. The woman's head was down, and dark hair could be seen pinned up in a bun beneath her voluminous hat.

The boy and girl, still holding hands, moved a step closer to her, although still cautiously keeping some distance.

A large group of men on horseback came trotting down the lane, instantly obscuring the children's view, shouting loudly to each other over the sound of hooves clattering upon hard ground.

"Oh, horses, go away! Not now!" Matilda cursed.

"If wishes were horses then beggars would ride!"

"Shush! You always like to repeat what father says!"

He frowned. "So?"

By the time the last horseman had passed, the figure in the graveyard was no more to be seen, although retreating footsteps could be heard, seemingly on the path that led around to the other side of the church.

"Johnny, I can't see her!"

"Eh? Where is she, Tilly? She's gone! Tilly, where did she go?"

"We're not even sure it was her. It might not have been. But it is strange that we can't see the lady anymore."

"I must see if it was her!" At that, Johnny broke away and started running in pursuit.

TWENTIETH-CENTURY BLUES

In Flanders fields the poppies blow
Between the crosses, row on row,
That mark our place; and in the sky
The larks, still bravely singing, fly
Scarce heard amid the guns below.

We are the Dead. Short days ago
We lived, felt dawn, saw sunset glow,
Loved and were loved, and now we lie
In Flanders fields.

Take up our quarrel with the foe:
To you from failing hands we throw
The torch; be yours to hold it high.
If ye break faith with us who die
We shall not sleep, though poppies grow
In Flanders fields. [2]

Rounding a corner Mary spotted a crowd gathered on the High Street. Intrigued, she crept nearer. They were standing solemnly facing the town's war memorial – a concrete monument bearing the names of those from the town who died fighting in the First World War, or the 'Great War', as was inscribed. A sea of white crosses and red poppies washed up at the foot of the cenotaph, the red of the poppies standing out aptly like a pool of blood against the colourless concrete. A solitary bugler played and Mary watched, inching closer until she was part of the crowd. Noticing she was the only person present not wearing a poppy on her front she pulled her coat tightly across her chest and folded her arms.

The minister asked for those with wreaths to lay them. As a small procession walked up and then back from the monument, Mary looked at their faces. As more and more wreaths accumulated the pool of blood grew, soaking rapidly into the grey blandness.

She was struck by the notion that a person could, if they wanted to, think that none of what they were there to commemorate had ever happened – that it was just an exercise in believing. The past – and war, in particular – seemed so foreign in this familiar landscape, of happy buzzing about and 'just another day'; so removed from the day-to-day life one lives in this land, and indeed most of the world. What they were talking and singing and praying about was something so ugly that you could not mention it easily or lightly, this suggestion of something that was not there and perhaps had never been there. Cannon to the right of them and cannon to the left of them – what did Tennyson know? And yet it *was* real. She could see it in their faces. Accepting that it was simply human nature to try to avoid the unpleasant, she wondered whether there were any people alive in the world who never think – or even knew – about what went before or what has been fought over and won in years gone by. What freedoms existed? And what triumphs of the soul? As well as heartbreak. She pondered the modern world, and how the richness and wonder of days past seemed lost to so many now who don't find time to read books and learn. She had noticed those who abhor silence and the depth of being it bestows, who deny their own thoughts by jamming their ears with sound at every chance. Where was the true learning and reflection? she asked herself. As conversations and curriculums changed, so did society. What was real anymore was something Mary began to wonder, as she stood feeling quite alone in the midst of all the people.

A hymn rang out, accompanied by a flock of quacking ducks flying overhead. As the crowd started to sing 'God Save The Queen' Mary sighed deeply and felt her eyes mist over. She reached for her handkerchief and dabbed the corners of her eyes. She looked across the medalled chests. Looking into their faces she wondered what they had witnessed and endured that resulted in them being given their awards: what sights, what sounds, what feelings, what horrors. One old man in particular caught her eye. He was in a wheelchair, with a tartan rug covering his thin legs and an impressive array of medals pinned to his frail chest. Standing beside him was a man around thirty years younger, his hand resting steadfastly on the old man's shoulder. Mary saw – or thought she could see – a swarm of emotions present in the old man, behind his eyes; brown eyes narrowed by time, yet holding much. The depth of some of the expressions she saw around her gave her no doubt that terrible, unforgettable events had taken place; the years little comfort to the rawness still felt. Nonetheless, even with her feelings of profound compassion and regret for wars, she knew that her feelings were empty compared with theirs.

Suddenly, she felt almost ill, she felt an imposter; a voyeur to other people's sadness – people who truly had a right to feel sad. What did she know? A sheltered upbringing, with no real struggle for life and with no need for desperate actions. What did she know about seeing your friends blown apart before your eyes, their blood and organs strewn across your face as you ran next to them, heart pounding and tripping over what you thought were rocks, only to find they were heads and legs and helmets. Only they could know – and still remember, if they weren't lucky – how the echo of your friends' voices still rang in your ears from seconds earlier, when they were with you, running next to you or sitting with you in a hideout. How their voices outlived them was something no one else could ever know. Like how their bodies were revealed in an instant – as quick as an incendiary flash – as being completely fragile and unprotectable, the softest things in the world encased in skin, skin that lay all around you, hanging like moss from the trees.

* * *

"James," Mary began seriously, as they sat reading magazines at the dining room table, "do you know the 11th of November will always remain a special date to me – special in a strange way?"

"Huh?" He didn't look up. "You didn't arrive here on the 11th, it was the week before."

"Well, yes, it was; I don't know how that happened, but that was the date when I was last in my time…in my world. The 11th of November. I got up in the morning like any other morning. I liked the pattern of the numbers, eleventh of the eleventh…one, one, one, one. I like little things like that."

"Armistice Day," he stated, still not looking.

"I beg your pardon."

"Armistice Day…er, you know, sometimes called Remembrance Day. Remembrance Sunday." He paused. "Oh, God." He peered over his magazine at her and remembered that he had made a decision to 'play the game' with her, whatever she was really all about. "I'm sorry, I really shouldn't have even mentioned it." He realised the implications and put the magazine down on the table. "Now what've I started?" he mumbled, rubbing his hands up and down his face. "What've I started?"

"What do you mean, James? What is it?"

He looked at her and saw a face searching for answers, reaching out to him. Another feeling of responsibility struck him. He swallowed hard.

"Armistice Day or Remembrance Day is held on the eleventh of November each year. It's the anniversary of the signing of the peace treaty that ended the First World War."

Mary's eyes widened and her mouth fell open. "The gathering I saw at the memorial – was that—?"

"Yes. The First World War happened between 1914 and 1918 and was referred to as the Great War."

"*Great?* How curious. Yes, I saw the inscription."

"The name refers to the scale of events – unprecedented.

Millions of people were killed between 1914 and 1918."

She gasped. *"Millions? Are you sure?"*

"Completely sure. Oh, but that wasn't the end of it. Along came the Second World War, where millions more died. Even bigger and more grotesque, much worse."

Mary's hand flew up to cover her mouth. *"Second* World War? Oh, Lord! How horrible!"

James thought he saw some colour drain out of her cheeks.

"Yep. The Second World War happened between 1939 and 1945 and was really nasty. I don't think you'll believe me if I tell you. More people were killed. There's no completely accurate numbers, but they reckon on at least twenty-three million people in Russia alone, including people who weren't part of the military – there was severe repression, disease, famine, you name it…and between ten and twenty million in China, again that includes civilians. Almost half a million people in this country. The total for the whole war was estimated at at least—"

"Twenty-three million in one country alone!" she cut him off. "Oh my Lord, oh my Lord! Stop, that's too many to even contemplate, even if they weren't all soldiers! What has happened to this world? Why has it gone mad? *Why has it?* It's mad and evil! *Why?* WHY?" She glared at him. *"I HATE THIS PLACE! I HATE IT! I WANT TO GO HOME!"*

James said nothing.

With a terrified expression, she looked around the room as if she wondered if another, perhaps smaller war might be taking place as they spoke and that someone might leap through a window at any moment bearing a rifle and bayonet.

He softened his voice. "I know this must sound really shocking. It must be really freaking you. I'm sorry that you even have to know. Not that, I suppose, you really do need to, only if you're going to stick around."

"Stick around?"

"Do you want to know more?"

"I, er, I don't know. Um. Oh, yes, I do. Tell me, who were the warmongers? Was it Russia again? Or that blasted Japan?"

"Okay, a potted history of the Second World War. I have some books I can show you which will help my meagre explanation. The perpetrator was Germany, and later Japan as well."

Mary huffed.

"Germany was still unhappy after the way the First World War had ended. A maniac rose to power in 1933, feeding off popular discontent and economic problems, things like that. An opportunist. A man named Hitler. He had this vision of a German empire, a master race: one without Jews, gay people – homosexuals in your time, gypsies and those of certain religions. Oh, and also the physically disabled and the mentally unwell. They were no good either, according to him. He had people killed – exterminated. He tried to conquer most of Europe and beyond. Even this country."

"Truly?"

"Yes.

"So, anyone who was different from a prescribed ideal was a target?"

"Yep."

"Once more this world separates people out...and chooses fates for those they feel completely removed from, would you say?"

"Yes, you could say that."

"Separateness."

"Exactly."

"I used to believe in the great human family, that we are all related somehow, and that our similarities are greater than our differences, but when I hear things like this...it makes me so very sad."

"Couldn't agree more. There was a concentrated air, land and sea war in various places at once. There was a war from the air over this country, London, especially, but lots of places were bombed. They really copped it. Even down here there was the odd bomber that crash-landed – they pulled the last one out of Hazelwood Common only a few years ago. And there are still many unexploded bombs around. The air war over London was called the Blitz. It was very intense, and aeroplanes swarmed overhead like angry wasps seeking to sting as hard and as deeply as possible."

"Oh, how terrible! And all the people? Oh, my poor dear country! My family!"

"Mary, I'm sorry. I'm really not enjoying telling you this, something so horrible. But, for both better and worse, it has shaped the world of today, like it or not."

"Tell me, has London been destroyed? Our greatest city! What's become of it?"

"It's all right now. Yes, a lot was destroyed. Many Londoners were killed by bombs dropping from the sky, especially in the East End. But at least the Germans never actually landed here, we prevented that."

"Good! I know now about these flying contraptions, these aeroplanes – remember I've seen some since I've been here."

"That's right." At least, James thought, that was one hurdle already crossed, thanks to living near the Heathrow and Gatwick flight paths. "There were thousands upon thousands of these aeroplanes all organised together under what is called an air force. Like an army, you know, but using planes."

"Yes, I understand."

"The war spread as far as Australia and the Pacific Ocean."

"Truly? That's hard to believe. A European war spreading to the farthest colonies."

"Well, it wasn't just a European war. There was already one raging in the Far East, and things there just hotted up. There were many Australians, New Zealanders, Indians and so forth fighting over here and in the Pacific."

"Supporting the mother country," Mary chipped in. "I can

understand that."

"Perhaps not so for the Indians though – not their mother country."

"You mean to say we don't have India anymore?"

James laughed. "No! We don't *have* India anymore." He eyed her seriously for a long moment. "That ended in 1947. Sorry, those days are long over! Anyway, as I was saying, Japan joined with the other side, against us and our allies. There was a lot of fighting in the Pacific region; a lot of planes and ships went down out there."

"How dreadful! James," she began furtively, "this is a lot to digest. It's too too much. Did you say the war finished in 1945? May I presume that we won this Second World War?"

"Yes, thank God. We eventually ground down the Germans and Japanese and resisted them enough for them to retreat, tail between their legs. They're now *very* different places though, so don't judge the Germany and Japan of now by what they were then."

"Have you ever been to either?"

"Yeah, Germany. I like it very much."

"Whew! Hard to take in! So the twentieth century was to become a most bloody century indeed! Much blood has soaked into the ground and many, many tears must have been shed."

"Yes. More wars and cruelty than ever before. And let me tell you later about the extermination camps and things like that, although, to be honest, part of me doesn't want to subject you to hearing it."

"It's all right, James," she replied appreciatively, "I'm sure I can withstand the details."

"Nationalism has so much to answer for. It often carries with it varying degrees of irrational hatred and prejudice. With pressure to conform."

"Yes, I'll give you that."

"I guess a lot of things come down to education."

"What do you mean?"

"Well, it's so variable. I was put through the system and processed, Western-style, you know. I was taught subjects in what I now think was a very mechanistic way. Reducing things down, d'you know what I mean? And there could've been more creativity and critical thinking...joined-up thinking. I know not all places are the same and that there's much better education to be had if you know where to go, but I can only talk about where I went. In the sciences we were taught that the world around us is pretty much like a machine, consisting of parts. We were taught that you could really only understand something by looking at its physical parts, you know, like dissecting a frog. Or looking at individual cells of an organism. When I left university I thought I knew so much. But I've since discovered that there's a lot of stuff we weren't taught, like to think outwards, not inwards. The things I studied were all in neat little boxes, little snap-shots, where no hint of a wide-angle view really came into it." He drew breath. By now Mary was staring at him, transfixed. He carried on. "Is that something lacking, or is it just me? Maybe I think too much – I've been told that before! And I'm sorry – I've lived on my own too long, I guess. I suppose I should find myself a wife and settle down, but that's another story. I'm sorry Mary, but, hey, get this: I was never taught how to be truly happy. Or what is really important."

"James, you have rendered me speechless. I don't know what to say. I understand! And I agree! You've said so much and there's not a bit of it that I think isn't right. But is it not the place of your parents to instil love and respect and teach you the things you say you missed learning?"

"Well, yes, I suppose so, but you're in school and with friends so much of the time, so many hours each day, that the stuff instilled by your family can become a little, well, sidelined, I guess. I don't like saying that, but the influence of peer pressure and the media on children growing up are not to be underestimated. My parents were great though. But Dad was in London most of the time, for work. Mum was at work a lot too, not quite as much, but wasn't home enough in my opinion. Blimey, I wouldn't want them to hear me saying all this! But I think I've turned out pretty okay, regardless!"

"Indeed! Don't let's forget, there are always those worse off."

"I know."

"James, my grandmother, bless her soul, taught me many things, the main thing being to think for yourself, and not just swallow what you're told without thinking. She influenced me greatly, and with the sorts of books I chose to read I'm afraid there was no hope for me turning out normal. And I thank God that I haven't! She also used to say that love, truth and beauty are all someone needs to know in this life. Abide by those and all else will fall into place. Bless her, she was so wise."

He looked at her. "Yes, you're right. To *be* those things. But only if people realise that they can be applied to everything in every area of their lives."

Mary looked fascinated.

"And," he continued, "sometimes I wonder what it would be like if people learned less *about* things and focused more on how actually to *be* them."

"Most profound! Dear Mr Harvey, you're actually a very deep and passionate person underneath it all. And very enquiring. There's so much more to you than meets the eye. I think you might just be another black sheep. Hmmmm, perhaps we should form some sort of Black Sheep Society and have secret meetings where we plan revolutions and how to reform the world?"

"Are you taking the pi—" He stopped himself.

She gave him the warmest smile he had seen from her so far. Reaching out for his hand, she gave it a squeeze. "I am now *completely certain* that we are tarred by the same brush."

He continued. "Oh, I'm sorry, I just felt like telling you this, I hope you don't mind. I know I've been ranting a little, but it's just that we all keep so much cooped up inside us. It's good to discuss critically."

"Yes, you're right. James, this Hitler creature had obviously never been taught much about love and respect either."

"Hey, he was a total psychopath! And not just him either, his henchmen were just as bad."

"But where did they come from, all these people?"

"They were obviously there all along, waiting in the wings. But something allowed them to come out and do the things they were able to do. Circumstances. And personal ambition, for want of a better word."

"I have seen hatred in many faces, in many people," she began. "It is ugly and it makes the person ugly. I don't just mean their faces. I have always thought hatred to be like a dark veil that hides people from themselves – from their true selves – for I believe everyone is good underneath."

"Do you?" he queried, visibly mulling it over. "I don't know. I guess most people are, but there's a tiny minority that seem just plain bad. So you think even Hitler was good underneath these layers, these dark veils? Veils of hatred, fear and prejudice?"

Mary thought for a moment before answering. "Of course I don't know enough about him to say, and I am certainly not wishing to make any excuses for him, but I think that whatever of him is, or was, his true essence was good, but that through his life he allowed himself, for whatever reasons, to go bad and be influenced by dark forces."

"Blimey! Interesting answer! Mary, do you believe in the Devil?"

Mary revealed a depth of feeling and thought that impressed James, who had expected an orthodox Victorian viewpoint along the lines of church dogma. Instead, he was shown a point of view which was very close to that of his own, where ghouls and demons exist, but only because people let them, by breathing life into them.

Later, they spoke about other historical events that had taken place since 1901. He handed her a magazine which had a list of wars that one country in particular had started: none other had started anywhere near as many; and the same nation had also attempted to overthrow more than 50 foreign governments (sometimes successfully). Mary appeared stunned. Tangled threads of lies and deception were laid out before her allegedly innocent eyes.

She shook her head. "Hmmfff! Dirty washing made to look clean – a lie does not become the truth when wrapped in a national flag."

James thought he could see her changing slowly as she learned more about the strange world she maintained she had fallen into. He began to pity her. He saw what he thought was a purity of heart and did not want to contaminate it with the hard and bad of today's world. Would she go home again? Would she even be able to? He wondered every day. And the nagging negative voice in his mind kept popping up when he least expected it, poking fun at him and calling him a hilariously gullible fool.

THE GRAVE AND THE HOLLY TREES: PART TWO

"But I tell you, mother, we saw her! We do think it was her! Really there, by the grave! But then she ran off, or something. It must've been her, please believe me." Matilda pleaded.

"Matilda Stepney! Don't be so ridiculous! If it had been her she would have come home, or we would at least see her somewhere. Or someone else would see her and would tell us. Well then, tell me what did you do when you reached her, tell me that?"

"Johnny and I ran around the churchyard searching for her—"

"Whoa! You do *not* run around a churchyard! You must show respect! It is not a playground! I thought I had taught you children that much!"

Matilda replied sadly, "Yes. But it was important. And we weren't playing. But we couldn't see where she went."

"Yes, Mother, that's the truth! We couldn't find her!" added Johnny.

"Yes! Oh, please, Mother! We are telling the truth! It could have been her!"

"Well either it was or it wasn't! You're saying it *was* her then you're saying it only *could* have been her! Well, children, which one was it?"

"We think it would have been her!" said Johnny, emphatically.

"YES! YES!" added Matilda.

"Do not shout at me! Both of you!"

The woman ignored the best attempts of her children to get her serious attention. No amount of standing and lingering in front of her, stopping her walking, was going to make her listen to their far-fetched story; their story she suspected to be partly grief expressing itself in some strange way and partly childhood imagination. The grief, she knew, would mellow with the years although never go completely, and the imaginations would be lost soon enough – the world would do its best to make sure of that.

Matilda thrust her fists in the air in desperation. "It's true! She was the lady we saw!"

"No, it wasn't! It was *not* your sister! I won't hear any more of it!" She kept walking.

"Ohhhh!" Matilda whined.

"It *is* true!" Johnny joined in. "She was at Sarah's grave, talking to her."

"Aargh! *Be quiet!* Your sister was – *is* – better behaved than the two of you put together! She seldom in her life put a foot wrong. Wherever she is, I'm sure she will be taking good care of herself. Perhaps she has found herself a young man. I'm certain there is a good reason for her, er…her absence." She drew a sharp breath then flung her head upwards and pursed her lips, while gazing intently at a large clump of bushes straight ahead of them.

"Look, over by the Prout property, there's a lovely hedge of red holly, all in flower. Shall we pick some for the house?"

FRIENDLY ADVICE

"So what exactly are you saying?"

"I'm saying that this woman has invaded my life."

"Listen, James, she's obviously some sort of nutter. Do you want someone like that in your house? Could be dangerous or run off with your identity."

"What?" James laughed. "You think she's gonna go around saying her name is James from now on?"

"Nah, mate, don't be so naïve. She could sell your identity to someone else. If she's in your house she's potentially got access to your personal documents, your birth certificate, your banking and stuff, you know what I mean?"

"Yeah. I suppose you're right."

"Is it all locked up?"

"Some of it. Not all of it. It's too much of a faff to lock things up all the time."

"James! You're too trusting! You're far too *nice!* If I were you I'd start locking things up the minute you get home tonight. And take the keys with you every time you go out."

"Yeah, I suppose you're right on that one. I'll do it. But I just don't know…she seems so nice. I kinda like her."

"Blimey, you are so naïve!"

James shrugged.

"What's she doing tonight while you're here? Going through your drawers? Hacking into your online banking?"

"You're like her – you're dramatic! I don't know what she's doing. Probably watching TV. She loves it. Or reading. She does that a lot too. Nothing too extreme; she's quite a domestic person."

"Does she mind you going out to the pub while she stays at home?"

"No, not really. If I did it every night I think she'd have

something to say. But I don't."

"I know you don't. When did we last do this?"

"Too long ago," James replied, sipping on his beer.

"Too right. But if she is a nutter…mate, get her out of there, for your own sake. If she's got some, I don't know, condition, or something, there must be somewhere that she can go. There must be a place for people like her, people who don't fit in."

"Doesn't fit in – that's such a bloody understatement! I've even had to tell her all about the wars – the first and second world wars. We got onto the subject by chance, but I tell you Bob it wasn't easy having to talk to her about things like that; it's like I'm some sort of schoolteacher. I had to tell her about how modern society works, and how things are in the world now. Like cars, planes, money, the food we eat, central heating, computers, teabags, hell, it's so hard, Bob, you have no idea."

"You're right, I have no idea. And I'm quite happy like that!"

"But what should I do?"

"Is she a looker?"

"Yeah. But Bob! Don't go down that path! It's not like that! Don't bring that into it! Hell, I'd probably have to teach her the facts of life as well! And to hell with that!"

"To hell with that, all right! But you shouldn't have her in your home if you don't want her there. Give her the heave-ho. Tell her she's got to go out and get a job and then get her own place. You should be able to give her her marching orders. It's your house."

"I know, I know. But it's not that simple."

"Does she have family she can go to?"

"No. Well, she says she hasn't – that they're all dead. It's the story she's telling and she never, for a moment, deviates from it. If she's lying about everything then she's a bloody good actor and should be up for an Oscar."

Bob laughed. "You get all kinds in this world. Deranged." He shook his head. "If I were you, you know what I'd do? This is if

I was being nice to her."

"What?"

"I'd do a little research into her family and find out if she's got any relatives kicking around. Even if they're in bloody Australia I'd be shipping her off! Even if I had to buy her the ticket – one way, of course! At least then you would know and you could take the pressure off yourself."

"Yes! And it might solve the mystery about her origin."

"You don't believe that story for a minute...*do you?*"

"I've been playing along with it, just to keep things harmonious, you know. But, Bob, sometimes I believe it. Yes, there, I've said it. You can stop looking so shocked. But then my senses return and I don't believe her again. I go between the two. I actually *want* to believe her."

"Eh?"

"I don't want to think I'm being lied to in such a big way."

"You're going soft on her, aren't you?"

"There's been all these weird things happening around the world, it's all over the news, you know. I think maybe she could be another one of them. Perhaps it is possible. Not likely, but possible."

"You mean the Unexplained Visual Experiences? UVEs?"

"Yeah."

"Hang on, she's not a visual experience!" He laughed.

"But she is unexplained! And she could be part of...all that."

"You're a nice guy, James. Don't let her walk all over you. If she is telling the truth – and personally I don't believe it for a minute – you must be able to find out somehow. There must be a way. DNA-testing or something."

"She'd hate me if I took her somewhere for tests."

"So?"

"Well, I don't want to make her hate me. I do have some consideration for her. And we do have some really interesting conversations. She's stimulating."

Bob smiled. "I'm right. You really have gone soft on her! Hook, line and sinker. This is going to turn into a relationship."

"No, it's not! It is definitely not! It's not appropriate."

"Not appropriate?" Bob roared with laughter. "Since when has a bloke had to see a woman as appropriate to be able to take her to bed and sha—"

"Enough! It's not like that and she probably wouldn't want it anyway."

"How do you know? Sounds to me as if she would. I think she's soft on you, too. Do you know, she was probably watching you for some time before she accosted you in the cemetery."

"She didn't accost me. We just bumped into each other."

Bob grinned. "Oh well, at least you can stop going around saying that your life is dull and boring now, can't you!"

James, draining his glass, added, "Yep, I sure can, and you, Bob, with all the good advice, it's your round again."

THE ACCIDENT: PART ONE

Mary settled well into her new life as James's house guest and live-in maid. She led him to understand that she was, day-by-day, learning more about life in what she described as a strange new time: being forced to rapidly get to grips with what amounted to a very changed world, and a changed world that touched every area of her life, one way or another, and would doubtless, she indicated, even alter her psyche. James wondered whether it would be like a long holiday coming to a natural close? What was she thinking – and, of course, feeling – about her old life, especially her family? With no photographs to look at he surmised she was reliant on her memory alone, and of the skills of its resident portrait painter. He hoped the forms would stay true and the colours never fade.

"Richard Townsend married Frances Earll. Frances's parents were Thomas and Rhoda. Richard and Frances had eleven chil—" He stopped speaking. Mary had just walked into the room and was wearing some of her new clothes that he hadn't seen her in before.

"Mary, you look...you look *great!*"

She smiled. "Thank you, kind sir, but you do make me blush."

"Is everything all right?"

"Yes," she replied. "Only I could hear you talking and thought I ought to investigate that you hadn't gone *completely* mad, that's all. I know having me living here with you is probably enough to do the trick!"

"Don't be silly. No, saying it out loud just helps me understand my family tree and makes me take it in better. So many branches to learn, you know."

"I see. Why do you need to learn it?"

"I don't really. I'm just very interested in it, in the main lines of those who came before me."

"Like me? I came before you."

"Yes."

"Don't let's pretend that I should be here. You know I shouldn't."

"Mary, don't—"

"I have something to say. I've realised something. That I was likely to have known your grandmother and your great grandmother – I think we may even have been friends for a while when we were at school!"

"Yes," he replied sombrely. "I've thought of that too. But, hey, don't say you shouldn't be here."

"But it's true! You know it is! You can't say you were present when Queen Victoria was on the throne. You don't know what it's like to have her as your queen. I followed the events of both Boer Wars as they happened. And I remember reading about the first modern Olympic Games, in Greece back in 1896. And I remember the Whitechapel murders – Jack the Ripper. JAMES, I AM A VICTORIAN WOMAN!"

"Edwardian," James corrected.

"Oh, for goodness sake! You're so pedantic! Edwardian then! By how many months? Although I don't consider myself to be that – of a different era from Victoria."

"Perhaps not yet. Give it time." James said.

"That implies I'll be returning home. Or do you mean I'm staying here?"

"I'm sorry...I don't know. Of course I don't know!"

"And 'give it time'?" Mary laughed sardonically. "Time is something I thought I understood! But certainly not anymore!"

James reached out and stroked her arm. She quickly calmed down, seeming to welcome his touch.

She sighed. "I must be mad or something, as a poem has just come into my mind. It's one of the few I know off by heart. I only remember it because it's so short." She cleared her throat.

"I'm nobody! Who are you?
Are you a nobody too?
Then there's a pair of us – don't tell!
They'd advertise – you know!
How dreary to be somebody!
How public, like a frog.
To tell your name the livelong day, to an admiring bog!" [3]

* * *

One morning, tired of feeling cooped up and longing for a walk and some fresh air, Mary defiantly left the house. Telling herself she would be careful and avoid people wherever possible, she grabbed her coat and headed out the door. As she walked down the front path she glanced at the birds bustling about in the rowan tree, going from one bird feeder to another. She smiled as she noticed her favourite bird, a robin, shyly foraging about on the ground, hunting for dropped seeds from the feeders amid the natural abundance that existed in the modest cottage garden.

It was a sunny, still morning and the dew shone and sparkled on every surface. The only sound Mary could hear was the birds. A large, wooded common and a long-abandoned claypit now restored to native woodland were close by, together presenting a good home for birds, as well as foxes, deer, badgers and pretty much everything else associated with English countryside. Shutting the low wooden gate she turned to walk through the village towards a tiny lake that she knew was nearby.

A curtain of fog began to fall heavily between her and the immediate world around her. Her mind became flooded with thoughts and images from another existence, of another Mary Stepney, and to her the world she was now in seemed a mirage.

As she buttoned her coat all the way to the neck and pulled the collar around close she could hear her mother warning against catching a cold.

"Oh, Mother!" Mary mumbled to herself. Mother was always worrying about us, always making sure we had a good coat with us and proper shoes and were dressed appropriately. *Oh, where is mother?* She looked up at the sky and saw only emptiness.

She gasped. "Dead. Long dead. Like I am supposed to be. I am supposed to be dead. I should have died years ago."

She walked briskly, looking down at the pavement, feeling at one with its greyness.

"I shouldn't be here. This is not my *time*. It is only my *place*."

A car sped past her, as if to jolt her back to reality. It was loud and seemed to come from nowhere. She jumped and felt the vibrations go through the road and through her. Annoyed by how the driver seemed to care so little for his surroundings she muttered quietly, "What about if a child had run out? Fool!" She had already told James how she thought that some of the roads he had driven her along seemed too dangerous for words. And the notion of a criminal minority repeatedly getting behind the wheel after having drunk alcohol or taken drugs made her tell James a few old tales from years ago of drunk men leaping on to horses and galloping off, wobbling and swaying as they went, only to be found later lying on the ground somewhere, undignifiably, amid their own vomit (or worse). Sometimes, she had laughingly told him, they fell off as they were passing a patch of blackberries or stinging nettles. It was great entertainment (although admittedly a little on the cruel side) to watch them scrambling out of the bushes after they came to.

She continued walking, more slowly now, through the hushed streets. There were many cul-de-sacs with interconnecting footpaths. Most gardens were flowerless at this time of year, so Mary smiled when she saw a front garden decorated with generous plantings of winter pansies and crocuses. The colour leapt out of the background dullness and she started to enjoy herself. After being shut away in James's house for so long it was fun to be able to walk around and look at what everyone was doing – these modern people with their strange modern ways – and with not one of them knowing who she was. They had no idea, she mused, that she had lived up in Roseberry Lane over a hundred years ago! They didn't know that she knew exactly how the area looked in those days and could tell you with reasonable accuracy what the differences were! Oh, she thought, if only they knew! They would collapse from shock! The horror of it all!

Several new streets had been built since 1901 on what had previously been pastureland. Mary's mind found it hard to resist playing a game with itself in which the object was to find something – a house, a neighbourhood, a clump of trees – which looked more or less the same as in 1901, at least according to her memory. James's street, Turnpike Lane, was in what was now known as the older part of Hazelwood, even though Mary had memory of watching the houses being built and regarded the street as being still with bricks fresh from the brickworks and mortar still setting.

As she walked on she entered the newest part of the area, where all the houses had been built during the 1980s. These houses and their plots were smaller and somewhat different in design from the older ones, mainly plainer. Something red caught her eye. The holly was newly out in flower and the sight of the dazzling arrays of bright red berries against the dark green crinkly leaves made her smile. She stopped in front of one particularly tall holly hedge and just stared.

"Hello, old fellow. I see you. Say I see you back, won't you? Have you seen me before? Do you remember me? I think you were standing in my time. I'm sure I've seen you before. Yes, it's true, I am one who has lived a long time. This is *not* my imagination! This is *not* my delusional mind! That is *not true!* For I am unique, like a four-leafed clover – not like everyone else you see before you! So many fools. Their fast cars and their plastic food and their unhappiness! They are the delusional ones! For I am most certainly sane! And awake! Please look upon me differently and do not doubt me, dear tree, for I am you and you are me!"

She noticed so many well-tended gardens that it made her wonder about the amount of spare time these modern people must have. Spare time felt to her like a new concept. Or it had been. Now she had so much glorious time on her hands that she felt she was living a life *of* spare time, with total lack of direction. And gardening for beauty, not just food – what a fabulous thought! She remembered how in her younger years she had heard about the royalty and aristocracy liking their pretty gardens as much as they liked their jewels and ornaments. They would have special plants and trees shipped in from all parts of the Empire; the Monkey Puzzle tree was a favourite of many. Memories of Queen Victoria's Diamond Jubilee flooded back to her. She had loved that; such a happy and festive time they had had back in 1897. The whole family had attended one or two local events, and were loyal subjects. Who wasn't? It still saddened her when she remembered the moment she first heard about the queen's death four years later – two months before her own sister. It seemed that nobody could remember, even vaguely, there having ever been a different monarch on the throne (William IV was long ago, and only in childhood memories of the very old). Sixty-three years of Victoria! Oh, what a monumental figure she was! Oh, what an Empire! The feeling of pride!

She carried on along a footpath that led behind some houses and directly to the small lake. The paved path ended and the way became rougher. She enjoyed how the fallen leaves crunched under her feet and the houses were no longer able to be seen. As she walked lost in her thoughts three boys riding bicycles clattered up behind her going so fast, and only seeing her at the last minute, that one of them clipped her arm with his handlebars as he passed.

She stumbled. "Ow!" she yelped.

The offending boy turned and glanced back at her but kept pedalling.

"You! Watch where you're going! Has sorry gone out of the English language?"

She lumped the boys together with the speeding car driver: reckless, frenetic, careless. There was already a lot about this 'new' world that Mary told herself she could not stand. She wanted it to slow down and enjoy itself more: take time to get somewhere; take time to talk with friends and neighbours; just *take time* – you will all be so much happier, she thought.

She finally reached the small, oval-shaped lake. Only about half of it was open water, the remainder was overgrown with reeds and various aquatic plants: a wild, luxuriant area in the middle of manicured Surrey, it existed as a miniature oasis of calm, untidy beauty. She sighed and sat down at the outside of the fence, leaning against one of the wooden railings, resting her chin on folded arms. Although the lake was about the same size as she remembered, she thought the land and the trees around it looked a little different. There were no frogs to be heard now, but Mary put that down to the time of year. Birds twittered and sang above her, and she thought she could hear ducks not far away. She relaxed and let her mind carry her as it sailed freely.

After some time she was thinking of moving on when the tranquillity was shattered by the sound of two piercing cries, both followed by crashing sounds. She then heard a series of loud shrieks. She had no idea what it was. She raced along closer to where she thought it was coming from and came across one of the three boys on the bicycles. He was the smallest of the boys, and looked to be aged about five. He was no longer with his bicycle. Seeing her, he ran towards her, dripping with water. She could see a small bicycle suspended upside down in the bushes beside the safety rails. The boy's face spoke of terror.

"HELP! MY FRIENDS HAVE FALLEN IN THE WATER! I CAN'T SEE THEM! THEY'RE GONNA DROWN! PLEASE

MISSUS, YOU GOTTA GET THEM OUT!"

Mary looked across the water. She saw nothing except two bicycles half-submerged in the thick of the reeds.

The boy was fixated on her. "CAN YOU SEE THEM?"

"NO! I'M STILL LOOKING!"

"I'm Jack! They're my friends!" He started to cry. He slumped to the ground, wailing.

"Wait on, Jack!" said Mary. "I think I can see bubbles...or something. I don't know how to...no matter. Wish me Godspeed."

Very quickly, she shed her coat and shoes and left them on the fence. She glanced at Jack as she clambered over the fence in a somewhat ungainly fashion, but with such determination that it became clear that nothing was going to stand in her way of getting in there. He followed, but remained out of the water.

She hacked her way through the bushes and waded part way out into the lake. Raising her arms out in front of her, and with a spring forward, she hurled herself into the icy water. She moved below the surface for some distance before coming up for air and thrashing about. Her clothes, especially her dress, were hampering her efforts to move and were almost as difficult to negotiate as the reeds. The boy on the shore shouted encouragement.

Mary's head appeared and she took a deep breath before sinking down again. Jack watched, then became alarmed when she did not return to the surface.

THE BIRDS

It was coming in fast from a westerly direction. It was so sudden and so noticeable that the ten-year-old girl was nearly knocked off her bicycle by a rapidly approaching *parked* car. The quick-moving mass she could see was a dark grey, the same grey as a cloud ripe and heavy with water, but the rest of the sky was blue, making the intruding object stand out starkly. She pulled up and stood astride her bike outside the old oak that marked the boundary of their property. Open-mouthed, she watched the huge grey mass as it got nearer. She told herself that it couldn't be a cloud – it just didn't look like a cloud!

The figure of her elderly neighbour appeared at the front door of her house, looking up. The girl saw her and was going to call out but found she couldn't take her eyes off the sky. The grey mass began to lighten in colour as it came nearer. It started to lose some of its density and it now revealed what it was – birds. A colossal flock. The girl felt sure that it was the biggest congregation of *anything* – birds, animals or even people – that she had ever seen. And it reminded her of a photograph in a book of hers of birds in Africa – but the picture was of millions of pink flamingos, and these were, well, she wasn't at all sure, but she knew they weren't flamingos. Perhaps the neighbour would know. The sound of the birds rose from what had up till then been a very low hum – barely audible – to what was becoming a loud and animated flapping and squawking.

That's weird, thought the old lady, as she wiped her glasses with her always-at-hand spectacle cloth, the sound doesn't seem like individual flaps and squawks at all. She marvelled to herself at how it looked and sounded more like one big thing, just with countless feathers all flapping at once and many noisy parts, all crying out at the same time, working together like players in the world's biggest orchestra. Then the most horrific thought crossed her mind, causing her to spring for cover under the porch roof overhang. It was only then that she saw the girl standing on the edge of the road. Her mouth was hanging open. The old lady suppressed the urge to laugh out loud as she thought of what the young girl may well shortly experience, gastronomically-speaking. Would *that* really, she wondered, be thought of as good luck?! Would it really still be thought of as fortunate if you were struck by not just one but goodness knows how many thousand birds doing what Nature has only made, well, natural? She smirked and then worried about her car parked out in the driveway.

The birds were now overhead, although still very high. Perhaps their doings would evaporate before they hit the ground, the old lady speculated, trying to forget about her car and the laborious scrubbing that would no doubt ensue.

The birds began to circle, slowly and fluidly, as if by choreography. The girl looked at the old lady.

"Hello!" The girl beamed a wide but nervous smile, flicking her long brown hair from her eyes.

"Hello, dear!" She wanted to offer her shelter with her under the porch roof, but something prevented her from doing so. Instead she added grandly, "Have you ever seen anything like it?" Oh, of course the child hasn't! she told herself gruffly. She was only born five minutes ago! What's she had time to see or do yet? Silly old woman!

The girl thought for a moment then replied, "No, I've *never* seen anything like this! Ever, in my whole life! Aren't they big and loud? Why so many? Why are they all in one group?"

Oh, heavens! You tell me! the old lady thought. "Sometimes," she began, "animals – and I include birds in that – want to be together. They have special instincts and behaviours that we don't always understand. They like each other's company – their own type. Like attracts like, you know. They live communally and act as one."

The girl looked fascinated. They both turned their heads to look up again. A bizarre pattern was emerging, caused by the way the birds were now flying. A corkscrew-shaped silhouette was forming in the sky, as the thousands of bodies flew, still circling. The old lady wondered if it was her eyes or whether the birds really were flying in tighter circles each time. As it was impossible from that distance to keep your eye on one individual bird and follow its trajectory, she was left unsure. But the rational part of her mind told her that they couldn't be. If, she went on to ponder, the birds were doing what it looked like they were doing and moving in a way like water draining down a plughole it left her more puzzled than she could remember feeling in a long time. Unless the birds were going up even higher as they entered the central core of the formation – which wasn't normal bird behaviour – they must, impossible as it may seem, be disappearing! But how could they be? Where could they be going? She cleaned her glasses again, this time with more vigour.

"It must be my ruddy eyes! These eighty-eight-year-old eyes aren't quite as sharp as they used to be!"

"Uhhhhhhhh...ooooh." The girl's mouth was open again. She forgot about her bicycle and it fell to one side as she jumped away to run over to stand with her neighbour.

"It's all right, dear! They won't hurt you."

"WHAT ARE THEY DOING? WHERE ARE THEY GOING?"

The old lady could only shake her head in disbelief, her eyes still transfixed on the sky. She now knew they had both seen the same thing – *were still* seeing the same thing – as the birds continued with their incomprehensible disappearing act. It was madness; it was impossible. But it was happening.

Soon there were noticeably fewer birds left in the sky. What remained of the grey, speckly cloud seemed almost to pulsate; its moving parts giving it the semblance of being a single entity. As time passed, the slowly swirling spiral grew smaller and smaller until the last birds circled thinly, eventually vanishing from sight.

The two observers strained their eyes to see any trace of the birds. Nothing. How could so many birds just disappear? And where did they go? The old lady shook her head again and muttered something to herself, still staring upwards.

No one had walked along the road in that time, and only a couple of cars had driven past. Its relative isolation and modest scattering of houses began to play on the old lady's mind as she felt a pang of protectiveness towards her neighbours' child. Whatever was going on must not, she silently declared, harm the child. Whatever freak of Nature has just taken place – for that is surely what it was – must not be dangerous to us, to *her*, especially. The girl buried her head in the old lady's dress, clutching tightly at the fabric.

"It's all right, dear, really it is." She tried to sound consoling. "I'll phone your mum and get her to fetch you, shall I?"

The girl hesitated, then peeped out of the dress, answering with a timid "Okay."

The old lady led the girl into the house. The phone call was made and it was not many minutes later that the door bell rang and the girl's mother was ushered inside.

"Has she been misbehaving herself? I'm so sorry!"

"Did you see the birds, mummy?"

Her mother's eyes widened and she searched the two faces for clues. "Birds? What birds? What on earth are you talking about?"

The old lady sighed loudly and shrugged her shoulders, replying, "Something very odd's just gone on. I don't know, really I don't. I kept her safe – she was out on the road on her bike—"

"I saw her bike out there! She'd just left it lying on the road. I moved it over to the edge, I just hope it was enough. The first fast lorry—"

"And no," the elderly woman interrupted, "she's done nothing wrong. There were these birds and she felt a bit scared and so she came over to me. The birds were absolutely fascinating. I still don't understand."

"What? I'm sorry, do you think you could explain?"

"There was a huge flock of birds. They came from the west. A huge cloud of them. Don't know what sort. Could've been starlings. They spiralled up into the sky. And seemed to disappear up! Just like that!" She gestured with her hands.

The woman said nothing.

"Mummy, it was…it was different from normal birds."

"Are you sure? Are you both sure you were looking at birds and not something else? Not planes flying in a special pattern? The RAF or something on manoeuvres?"

"No! Mummy! It was birds!"

"Yes. Hundreds of thousands of them at a guess. But it looked as if they all just vanished into this spiral, into the sky, you know. Straight up. I think I'll phone a few people and see if they saw anything. There'll be something in tomorrow's papers for sure."

"Well, I hope so. I wouldn't mind finding out what this is all about."

The girl's mother scanned her neighbour's living room for any empty gin or sherry bottles or mysterious pill containers but saw none. Perhaps she'd been mixing prescription pills? But how did her daughter get this story in her head – her normally fairly level-headed daughter? She suddenly remembered a programme she'd heard recently on the radio about the resurgence in old-fashioned storytelling; the well-woven tales and yarns that although often dressed as truth were usually captivating and fictitious in pretty equal proportions. Apparently there was a movement to get kids away from the telly and technology and back on to granny's lap. With a sudden impulse she grabbed the child and headed for the door.

"We must be off. Thanks ever so much for keeping an eye on her." She placed her hands affectionately on her daughter's shoulders and guided her out the door.

"Will you stay for some tea? I'm cutting a whisky cake that my sister sent me down from Scotland."

"Uh, that's very kind of you, but no thanks. Not this time. I think I'd best get this one home, bike included. Her father'll be home soon and he certainly won't want to see her bike squashed like a pancake."

"Cheerio then."

She closed the door, slid the security lock across and walked over to the window that faced west. Looking out, she saw the space where the birds had been. It was back to being a clear blue sky, without a single cloud, as though nothing had happened. The great joke played by Time, where all you have of an event is your memory. And there are those, she thought, that would rub out or deny that some memories even existed – 'doublethink', in George Orwell's terminology. She stood there leaning out for so long that her elbows started to ache. The whisky cake was washed down with some of her own home-made elderflower wine, non-alcoholic of course.

THE ACCIDENT: PART TWO

Mary's head eventually popped up above the surface of the water. She was desperately gasping for air and tugging on something. She had found one of the drowning boys amid the reeds and the gloom of the water and was trying to swim with his head on top of her left shoulder. The young boy's face was ashen and his eyes were closed. She dragged his inert body to the surface and slowly hauled herself and the boy out of the watery death trap. Her teeth were chattering and her body was shaking. Jack tried to help them but was of little use. Mary lay the boy down on his back on the ground.

"Is he going to be all right?" Jack asked Mary.

"I d-d-d-don't know," she stammered, quivering. Leaning over the white body, she looked in his eyes and his mouth before listening to his heart.

"His heart is st-st-st-still beating, j-j-just. He isn't breathing though." Panicking, she rocked his torso from side to side and banged on his chest.

"S-s-s-start beating, will you! Beat! BEAT!" She pushed, she hit, she slapped him across the face. "Do something to him!" she ordered Jack. "Make him breathe! He'll die really soon if he doesn't breathe! Try whatever you can think of! Blow down his throat even!"

Mary turned around fretfully, looking back at the lake. "I've got to go back in and get your other friend now!" And with that she dived in again.

She moved unseen beneath the surface. She started coming up for air more often this time although, it seemed, with greater difficulty. It was taking her longer to catch her breath now, her breaths becoming quicker and shallower, and the chattering of her teeth was getting worse. At one stage after surfacing she didn't open her eyes for a long time. Jack did not notice what she was enduring, however, as he blew down his friend's throat and tried copying what he vaguely remembered being shown at school.

Eventually Mary appeared with the second boy, and it was an obvious strain to pull him along with her, keeping his head above the water. Dropping his leaden body on to the edge of the lake, she collapsed down beside him for a moment, panting and shaking. Then she fumblingly set about examining him. Now without much coordination, she accidentally knocked his head backwards with her knee as she moved. She slapped him and pushed his chest several times, before blowing into his mouth. Although desperately wanting to collapse, she increased her efforts. She hadn't looked at the first boy she had rescued, assuming him to be dead. This second body had pond weed adorning it and blood flowing from gashes on the head, arms and legs. The face was deathly white and the flesh cold to the touch. She fell to the ground for a few moments and lay still.

Making herself sit up again, she knelt beside the second body and said a prayer. She had the dim realisation that she hadn't said a prayer out loud since she had said one the day her sister died. It had been a prayer to save a life. But it hadn't worked. She hoped this one might.

"Oh, Lord, please save these young boys! Please bring their lives back to them. P-p-please may it not be too late. Please, oh Father, please! I beg of you! Please show mercy on ones s-s-so young...with their whole lives ahead!" She kept her eyes shut for a few moments and her lips moved as if adding her own private words.

Jack started crying. He ran around in a circle, wailing and waving his arms in panic. After a while he stopped his crying and looked at Mary without saying a word. Mary held out her arms to him and put them around him, pulling him in close. They both closed their eyes. She appreciated the modest warmth his small body was able to provide.

"It's al-al-all right," she soothed. "They'll be all right."

"How do you know?"

"Because whatever happens, they'll be all right."

"Oh." He sounded confused.

"You see, h-h-heaven welcomes the little ones that get sent there. And many do get sent there, unfortunately. I don't know why it's allowed to happen, but it is. I've known m-m-many babies and children go to heaven. But, listen, when they get there they are given love, completely and unconditionally. For heaven is where truth and love dwell – it is the home of t-t-truth and love. Not like this place."

Jack wailed shrilly followed by uncontrollable sobbing. "I DIDN'T KILL THEM! IT WAS AN ACCIDENT! We tried to ride our bikes along the top of the rails!"

The two hung on to each other and their grief seemed the more inseparable the longer they were there. Despite the cold and the wet they knelt together on the soggy earth at the edge of the lake unaware that they were being watched.

Propping himself up by his elbows was the first 'drowned' boy, or rather not so drowned anymore. His face, although still as white as the snowdrops that grew nearby, had life in it once more. The eyes were open and he was looking on with benign interest.

"I'm s-so c-c-c-cold," he murmured weakly before flopping backwards.

Mary and Jack sprang apart and leapt to their feet. They looked at each other incredulously then laughed and hugged one last time before going over to the boy who was by this time trying to cough up the contents of the lake.

"You didn't swallow any frog sp-sp-sp-spawn, I hope," Mary said, trying to lighten the situation.

The boy groaned.

"Would you p-p-please fetch my c-coat from where I left it?" Mary said to Jack.

He ran and brought it to her. Feeling its dryness and life-giving warmth made Mary crave to put it on, but instead she laid it carefully over the retching boy.

"Jack, p-p-please go now to one of the houses nearby and fetch an adult! Or two adults, even b-b-better! We need to get your friend away from here before he catches pneumonia. QUICK!" Then she added quietly under her breath, "And we'll need an undertaker for the other one."

He was off like a shot, climbing the fence and running as fast as he could over the dry leaves of the track in the direction of the houses.

Mary went to look again at the 'dead' boy. There were no obvious signs of life. Stooping over him, she placed her ear on his chest and felt his wrist at the same time. There was a faint heartbeat, but it was erratic and too slow. Mary racked her brain for knowledge on this sort of thing and decided that she ought to still be trying to revive him even though he wasn't breathing. But, unfortunately, no longer in control of her movements, she fell with all her weight upon him, landing heavily on his chest.

Aargh! Well done! That will have finished him off! she thought, as she started to sob. But the heavy weight had caused water to work its way up and squirt out of his mouth, spilling forth like a tiny spring, running down over his eyes and into his ears and blood-soaked hair. Catching sight of this out of the corner of her eye, Mary let out a small gasp. Spurred on, she twisted around into a sort of semi-crouch. With his head still tilted backwards, she held on to his face for support, by chance covering his nose and cheeks, and blew hard into his mouth.

As if struck by a bolt of lightning the boy's body jolted. He coughed and sputtered noisily and began breathing again, although laboured. Mary cried and laughed simultaneously. She then fell over on to her side, wrapped her arms around herself, shaking. Very soon she became semi-conscious.

Hurried footsteps pounded along the track. Help arrived in

the form of two burly men accompanied by a well-dressed middle-aged woman. The men scooped up the larger of the two boys along with Mary in their arms and carried them over the wooden railings and out of the lake enclosure. The woman managed to carry the lighter of the two boys over her shoulder, with Jack taking some of the weight. Jack retrieved Mary's shoes from the fence where she had left them, and the group trudged as quickly as they could along the track to the woman's house. She had already telephoned for an ambulance, and they had only just set foot inside the house when the vehicle pulled up outside.

The lake water this time of year, the paramedics said as they peeled the wet clothing off the three patients, was so cold that you risked getting hypothermia very easily. Mary regained a modicum of consciousness, enough to wish that her parents and family could be there with her. She wanted to cry but did not have the energy. She could faintly hear her mother scolding her; for what, she wasn't sure, as her mind and body shut down and slipped into a lifeless slumber beneath warm, dry layers. The three were bundled into the ambulance, along with the woman and Jack, and driven away.

* * *

The hospital phoned James and told him what had happened. It had taken them a while to work out who to contact for Mary, as she had no identifying papers or cards on her, and the only item of use to them was a piece of paper found in one of her coat pockets which had a Hazelwood address, a few phone numbers (including the 999 emergency number) and even more strangely, they thought, what seemed to be instructions on how to use the various types of telephones. Upon getting the call James raced anxiously to the hospital and sat with her. By that stage most of the tests and checks had been completed and she appeared to be making a good recovery. She was very lucky, the medics told him, to have suffered from only a mild hypothermia, considering how long she had spent in water and wet clothes. Woollen clothing had helped her stay relatively insulated, they said. They wanted her to stay in hospital, under observation, until all systems were completely back to normal.

The next day she was discharged, as were the two boys. James drove Mary to his house and put her to bed. As she lay before him, weak and pale, he surprised himself by reaching down and kissing her tenderly on the cheek. And then as if a flash had come from a giant mirror reflecting himself he realised what was happening: that he had just kissed the woman he had not wanted to have any feelings for. With the realisation came the acknowledgement that she was getting to him in a way that no other woman had. Women from his past had too often turned out to have an attic full of baggage that they had kept hidden from him for so long before it all fell out, landing on them both, with the woman seeming unable (or unwilling) to try and shift it. Other women had been enticing, and even great fun, but had failed to possess enough intelligence and interest to talk about what James saw as important issues in the world; issues of life, death, the universe – everything. How, he wondered, a person could live in this world, walk on this amazing and awesome earth and not want to talk about these things just baffled and irritated him. Lack of intelligence bored him. Shallow women, especially those caught up in image and materialism a little too much were not even worth a second date. Looks were certainly something, but it always got stifling after a while if there was nothing else going on. With Mary, however, everything was different. It occurred to him that his life before her was starting to fade into a dull – almost meaningless – background tapestry as he realised how she had kick-started something deep within him. She was a wake up call like he had never had before, and it wasn't just the strange circumstances of how she had come into his life. There was also the odd feeling he had in that he believed he was starting to understand himself a little better. And he was enchanted by her magnetism: he felt she had a certain light about her; an energy. He had already told her that she was someone who, depending on her mood, could brighten (or dim) any room she walked into. Her enquiring mind had won him easily, as did her down-to-earth ways. And her looks – they certainly could not be ignored: her face, distinguished and strong-looking, yet still very womanly; her dimpled cheeks; her blue eyes that seemed to look right into you – all framed by long, dark brown hair which tried to curl at every opportunity. Whether she was *the* one he wasn't sure yet, but no one else had ever come so close. Yet, he told himself time and time again that as she had appeared so strangely and so easily, she might just as easily and abruptly disappear from his life. Perhaps, he wondered, assuming her story was true, there was some mechanism in the universe that would 'put things right': that she could be swooped up and carried back to 1901 at any time. She could be an illusion about to disappear, as though she had never been there. He just could not know. It was all a huge risk. But one thing he did know was that they were on the same wavelength, finishing each other's sentences, knowing what the other meant before they had even got the words out, and just understanding each other. He had even had the impulse to say to her one evening, "I feel that I know you already – that I've known you for a very long time", to which she had smiled warmly, and replied, "I know how you feel. You seem curiously familiar to me too. Cut from the same cloth, I think." She had then looked away, seeming shy of the subject. But it was her arrival into his life – and, allegedly, his time – that concerned him more than anything else. He wondered whether any questions about her true identity had been raised through the incident at the lake. Did the UK's National Health Service now possess a permanent record of Mary Stepney being admitted to the hospital? Of course they would, and he knew that all it took was for someone to ask for her National Insurance number or even just her date of birth to realise something was not quite right. "Born in *eighteen* what? Sorry, I don't think I heard you right. Don't you mean *nineteen?* What was the date again?" She would have given her address as his house not that of her parents – he hoped. He would wait and keep his fingers crossed that nothing bad would happen.

THE HERO

The newspaper proclaimed, 'Woman heroically saves boys from certain death.' It was written large across the front page, accompanied by a photograph of the lake and the two boys standing smiling with their respective parents. There was no photograph of Mary, the article referring to this fact by saying, 'Unfortunately, we have been unable to obtain an interview with Mary Stepney, nor have we been able to get hold of a photograph. We are also not certain of her location at the moment, so have no way of knowing if she is still in the Dorking area. Perhaps the heroine is shy in coming forward, but we hope for a chance to speak with her soon.' Passages describing what happened used phrases such as 'immense courage' and 'true heroism'.

Another newspaper, one of the low-brow tabloid variety, had the headline, 'Winter wonderwoman!', supported by the most sensational language it could muster.

The phone calls and visits to the house scared James and Mary. They knew that journalists were adept at delving into people's pasts to enrich a story and fill more column inches: anything they could find would surely go in. James refused to open the door to them, and sent a message stating, 'Ms Stepney is greatly pleased that she was able to be of assistance to the boys and is absolutely delighted to hear that they are now in good health'. But the press wanted more.

* * *

"They're saying you're a hero!"

"Heroine, surely?"

"Whichever you prefer. Same thing."

"I saw on television the other night that the professional footballers are all heroes too. And so are the England cricket team."

Her tongue-in-cheek humour was not lost on James. "Well, we don't live in the days of the Greek heroes anymore. But you acted extremely bravely and heroically, risking your life to save theirs."

Mary eyed him thoughtfully. "James," she began, "it's a truly strange world now. It's very odd. I was merely doing the decent thing by rescuing those boys. Who wouldn't have tried? I could not have stood by and watched them drown. Who could? But I'm no superwoman. They were just very lucky lads. And I was very lucky. Why does this sort of thing make the papers want to make me into a celebrity? Is it just to sell more papers? I'll not be used for that purpose. Also, I don't want the attention. And what could I say to them anyway? I'm just an ordinary person. A schoolteacher turned writer!"

"Turned time traveller!" James added, winking. "You're not an ordinary person!"

"That's true, but they mustn't know that, of course. Why don't they look at the minds of these boys? How they even thought they could ride bicycles along a narrow structure suspended three feet off the ground I don't know. So foolish. And they'd had no manners when they knocked into me earlier." She told him about the way they had been riding prior to their arrival at the lake.

"But yet," she continued, deep in thought as she spoke, "I feel there's something that pushes us all together, makes us feel united, whether we like it or not, causing us to try to help one another and be kind. What is it?"

"Humanity?" suggested James.

"Yes. But it's more than that."

"Society?"

"Even less so. That word is just a word that describes us as a group, a collection of people, but there's so much more there, do you not agree?"

"Yes," James replied. "I do think so. Depends on what you believe too, I suppose. A politician named Margaret Thatcher once said there was no such thing as society."

"Well as long as she never attained any real power it didn't matter that she thought like that." She looked at James. "I hope she didn't."

James laughed heartedly.

They talked about politics, religion, spirituality, and about some quite unorthodox ideas that seemed to be spreading around the world about the essence of life itself. Concepts of indivisibility and connectedness swarmed through their minds, and the more her mental machinations danced and conspired with his own beliefs the more he wanted to kiss her.

* * *

Frustrated with not getting anything on Mary, two young male reporters from the tabloid newspaper, desperate for recognition and to further their careers, resorted to researching the strangely elusive hero. They could get a fair smattering of details without too much trouble – certain things were legally in the public domain – and all they had to do was gather it together. Something on her background, where she came from, how old she was, what she did for a living, her marital status and so forth. They also decided to spy on her home from a neighbouring house (someone who had been unable to resist the generous cash sum they offered as recompense for snooping from a bedroom window for hours on end). The journalists were determined and used to getting their way.

They watched, they waited, they took it in turns to sit at the window behind net curtains in the house which was perfectly situated directly across the road from James's house. It was a cheap shot, they knew, but they wanted to surprise and impress their boss as well as beat the competing broadsheet newspaper to a pictorial scoop on Mary (the broadsheet would never resort to such 'creative' means of obtaining photos, and the men knew it). They saw curtains open, curtains close, James going to work, James coming home from work, James putting wheelie bins out, James bringing wheelie bins in, James occasionally shutting the gate when the postman left it swinging open, and they saw the infrequent visitor to the house. They were getting nowhere, although had worked out that Mary must effectively be hiding in the house. Admittedly it was winter, but why, they wondered, would she be doing this?

They were, after a few days and to the detriment of their other work and their sanity, about to call it quits when something happened. One of them saw her. It was on a crisp sunny morning. James had left for work and Mary had decided it was all right to go out into the garden at the front and refill the bird feeders that hung from the rowan tree. She opened the side gate between the garage and the house and peeped around the corner. She slowly emerged, looking around furtively. Seeing no one, she opened the side gate, propping it open with a brick before disappearing. Shortly afterwards she reappeared, carrying a ladder. She placed it under the tree and, one by one, filled the birdfeeders with seeds and nuts. She scrubbed and refilled the birdbath which also hung in the tree, above the feeders. When she was finished she carried the ladder and the bags of feed with her back into the garage. Shutting the side gate she was gone again. That was all they got; that was all it took – they were ecstatic. Shooting rapid frame by rapid frame the journalist on duty at the window had missed no opportunity. His telescopic lens had been able to focus close-up on her face, capturing everything as she had gone about her business not aware that she was being filmed. It was a study of concentration, satisfaction and happiness. He rang his partner now off-duty and boasted that he'd finally 'got her'.

The headline shouted; it screamed out that a conquest had

been made. The innocent and oblivious subject was now secured and possessed for the world to see. Mary went on to be the main attraction of that week's paper, and the pictures were situated next to the write-up with all the 'facts' about her as obtained by the men. (They found a Mary Stepney born in Croydon thirty years earlier who they presumed to be her). The editor was thrilled and the journalists had scored career points as desired.

James spotted the offending publication as he stopped for petrol on his way home from work late one afternoon. Arriving home, he handed it to Mary. She took one look at the front page. There she was, plastered all across it with a photograph that very clearly showed her face. She threw the paper on the floor and flung herself onto the sofa, crying.

"It's no use," she howled, "they get me even when I just go out into the garden! I'm in prison, like a bird in a cage! An animal in a zoo!"

James moved closer and tried to console her. She pushed him away.

"I want to go home! I don't belong here! This is too much! This place is too much! It's horrible! You live in a horrible world! I'm being pushed too far now! I can't live here without being harassed! It's vulgar! This would never have happened in *my* time! Not like this! People had something called manners! Is this the same England? I ask you, is this the same England I used to know? I am doubting it more every day!"

"Hey, calm down! Ignore them! Don't worry…please."

"Have you read it?" she asked.

"No," he replied, "I've just glanced at it so far. I'll read it tonight after din—"

"They're going to come and take me away!" she interrupted. "Any day now your government, so concerned with control of the people, will come and take me somewhere. They'll think me a criminal! I've not been born even, according to your authorities. Oh, and I certainly haven't paid any income tax or, what is it,

National Insurance! Not ever! I'll be tortured!"

"Mary! Please! Nothing like that's going to happen. This is one of the most civilised countries in the world – believe it or not. People don't get treated like that here."

"What do you mean? Do they take them abroad to torture them?"

"No! Well, I don't know! But you don't need to worry."

"They'll want to treat me as though I'm an exhibit; a strange new breed of mammal. I'll be like Charles Darwin's specimens, although I'd like to see them find a jar big enough for me. They'll think I'm a liar. Or mad. Or both."

"Mary! You can't tell them the truth! They'll just think your parents broke the law not registering your birth in the civil records. And you *could* get around the rest – the no school records, no medical history, no tax, etc, by saying you lived abroad in some far-flung place. I dunno. Fiji? The Pitcairn Islands?"

"I'd rather the back blocks of Constantinople. Oh, what shall I do? I can't lie."

"Dry those tears first of all." He handed her a tissue.

"Where's my cotton handkerchief? You know I don't like wasting paper on my nose."

He sat down next to her.

"Mr Harvey," she began, reaching for his arm.

"Yes, Ms Stepney?"

"I'm a non-entity. A nobody. I don't exist. I'm not really here."

He looked upset. "But you *are* here! I don't like you saying that! *You are here!*"

"They'll take me away and torture me until I tell them who I really am."

"But you can't tell them anything different, can you? *Can you?*"

"NO!" She glared at him.

"Then they'll have to believe you."

"In the short time I've been here I've learned a little about how things operate. And I don't like what I've learned. They'll want to lock me up like some poor animal in a cage. They do terrible things to animals in the name of science! And that's what they'll do to me!"

"They won't lock you up," James comforted, rubbing her arm. He could see the fear in her eyes.

"James, please don't let them take me."

"I won't let them take you. But, I've just been thinking, they might wonder why they can't find any record of your parents' births or those of your siblings and so forth. It's been compulsory to register all births in this country since the 1870s."

"Ohhhhh," Mary wailed and held a cushion over her face.

For a moment James felt as though he had fallen into a scene from the *X-Files* or the old *Sapphire and Steel* he used to love when he was a child. Who was writing the script for this one?, he wondered absent-mindedly. And would it have a happy ending? Then a tiny, almost inaudible part of him whispered something about how it might be good if she is run through the system and found not there, at least then he would know for sure that she really might be from 1901. But he was ashamed of that voice now, that cold and almost callous voice of reason, and he chose to stifle it again, for the time being at least.

A few days later a letter arrived for Mary. It was from the police, they were nominating her for a bravery award. The letter praised her actions at the lake and drew attention to her 'uncommon heroism'. She had, they said, risked her own safety to save not only one but two others. They mentioned the difficult and challenging conditions of the rescue, and used the words 'courage' and 'bravery'. They also asked her whether she would mind attending an awards ceremony and allowing the press some time with her as well as reporters from their own organisations and other authorities associated with the police. Mary, although taken aback at receiving the letter, was determined not to let it upset her. The ceremony would not take place for some weeks, which gave her the comfort of having some time to make up her mind about what to do. But, time, allegedly, was also her nemesis and could not be trusted; it was the grand villain she accused of stealing her from her world and abandoning her in a strange new one – with added twists that hinted at it being nowhere near ready to relinquish its mighty grip on her.

* * *

Mary walked in slow, halting steps up to the front of the house. Sitting on a slight incline, the imposing Victorian red brick structure dwarfed the rectangular garden below. She studied the house carefully for any signs of life. Believing the occupants to be out, she crept up the front path, her eyes peering into the gloom through the windows. It was a quiet morning, and there seemed to be no one about anywhere in the neighbourhood. She began to relax a little. She looked around. She felt so much was still the same, and yet that so much was different. It was very strange, she thought, unable to not believe that the house was still her home; the house she had lived in from the age of seven – it felt almost an extension of her own body.

She froze. She had seen something that jarred her whole system. It was a low brick structure in the middle of the front garden. A small terrace set completely to flower garden had been constructed using a low wall made chiefly of brick, augmented with decorative grey stones of varying sizes and shapes. Stopping everything from sliding down the gentle slope, the structure acted both as a retaining wall and a beautifier. Without thinking, Mary fell to her knees beside it. It was not the structure so much as one detail it contained. Carved by hand on the side of the brickwork, in the creamy-brown mortar, were the initials *MS, TS, MS* and *JS*. Although covered over by lichen, the rough inscription remained just visible to the world. Mary felt her stomach heave and was powerless to prevent her torment rising. Totally consumed, her emotions surged, like a fountain of grief flowing upward and outward, from her old world to her new world, the feelings of a past time reincarnated. She slapped her hands onto the ground, pressing them angrily into the earth, as she stared into the handwritten initials. She saw her tears fall from her face, and watched as they soaked into the dirt. At least she was now, she felt, putting something of herself in there too, in where the others 'were'. As she howled, she reached down and plucked an interesting-looking stone from out of the ground near the base of the wall. It, she thought, had been part of the original garden wall, and had, she could tell, not been moved in all the time since. It was like reaching her hand back into her time. Instantly, to her it represented her old world in miniature, like a wonderful souvenir, and she held on to it tightly as if it was an embodiment of the whole of her past life and who she felt she was.

As she sat, she realised how delightfully peculiar the wall was – there would be no others quite like it. To her it was new, built only a year or so ago. She could remember the day well when her father, along with two of her brothers and her sister Matilda spent what seemed like most of the day out the front getting covered in filth and dirt and stuff that stuck like there was no tomorrow. It was a day of laughter and shenanigans; a good day, where the family had made something together. And they had done it without using skilled help, and had capped it off by proudly carving their initials as neatly and as deeply as they were able. She also remembered how her grandfather had been around that day, although not involved in the work – he was "beyond all that hard labour" he had said, laughing. She pictured his face, his deep brown eyes, brown like the earth, and his furrowed brow, decorated with unruly grey hair sitting above a long, cloud-like beard. He had watched the others working in the garden from his seat inside, by the window, while desperately wishing he had a camera. He had sat telling the family (not for the first time) about the time back in 1851, when he went to the Great Exhibition in London. He was, he stressed, *very* young at the time. It had been such a thrill, he said, to see one of the first ever photographs. It was a daguerreotype of the moon, by an American photographer, J.A. Whipple. There had been cameras on show and all the latest photographic inventions. If only, Mary thought, he could be here now with her to see the fantastic cameras and technology he would be absolutely astounded. She was. The staggering leap ahead in technology could not have been anticipated, nor even believed back in 1901. A few years after the Great Exhibition, Grandad had also been enthralled by the photographs in the newspaper from the Crimean War. It was almost like being there, he had said repeatedly, shaking his head in awe. Good old Grandad. Long gone now. Her mind wanted to stop crying but her emotions and her body felt caught up in the release of it all, and so she continued to wail, certain that no one was around to hear. She looked up at the front window of the living room and tried hard to imagine her grandfather's face looking out as it had for most of that day while the garden was having the work done. It had been sunny then, but now it was completely cloudy, and little could be seen in the room from outside. There were silhou-ettes, but they were new – new shapes from new objects that had not been there before. She stopped looking and returned her attention to the flower bed. She felt it strange how the flowers were completely different now too. How had the other ones fared? she wondered. Had they lasted months, years, decades? Who lived there now? Did they know the sweat and effort that had gone into digging the hole for the wall, getting it flat and deep enough? Did they know the money that had been saved for the modest number of bricks that had been bought straight from the man they knew at the brickworks up the road? Did they know the sum total of love and laughter that had gone into it? Of course not, she told herself. They probably didn't even look at the wall. Her crying continued, and she didn't realise that she was becoming louder. A firm tapping on her shoulder made her jump.

She turned and looked straight into the face of an irate-looking elderly man.

"What are you up to, eh?" the man demanded. "Would yer like me to call the police?"

She slowly gathered her wits. "Oh, no! I'm not doing anything! I'm only looking! I live here, errr...I mean, I used to live here!"

"You're not doing anything? Don't make me laugh. I watched yer walk up the path and crouch down 'ere. Yer casing the place!"

"I'm what?"

He tut-tutted. "Don't play innocent! I've got a good description of yer and I'm gonna ring the police now! Where's the blessed bobby when yer need 'im? Yer'll have to stick around while we wait fer'em to come!"

"WHAT?"

"But yer not coming near my house. You can stay 'ere, but come out on the street, off the property. I don't think the family who live 'ere will want you on their property any longer than yer've already been! Come on!" He gestured for Mary to walk to the pavement. "*Come on!*"

Seized by fear and embarrassment, she stood up and ran off along the street.

The man shouted angrily, "Don't think yer gonna get away with this! I'm ringing the police and I've got a good description of yer! Yer won't get away with doing this sort of thing!"

He had not deigned to tell her that he had recognised her from the newspapers as the 'local hero'. He had also not bothered to mention that her claim to having once lived there could not be possible since the family currently there had been in residence for more years than she had been on this earth.

Not stopping until she reached the corner of Turnpike Lane,

she had trouble believing what had just happened. She knew she had been a fool. Going up to the house and entering the property – she knew all along that that was the wrong thing to do, but she had just *had* to go there – she had felt compelled. But, she told herself, she hadn't harmed anyone or anything. Hadn't done anything except sit in someone's garden. She knew it was wrong in the eyes of the law and that the owners wouldn't like it, but she also believed that it wasn't 'really' wrong, under the circumstances. Nonetheless, she vowed never to do it again. After catching her breath, she walked back to James's house. Turning her left palm up she looked at the stone she had grabbed from the flower bed. She smiled an agonised smile. To her, a vestige of a life now gone, of a world swallowed up by time, the stone went on to become as precious to her as any material possession could ever be.

THE PHOTOGRAPHS

One evening, James and Mary were busily preparing dinner when the doorbell rang. A small, stooped elderly woman stood on the doorstep. She had a jute carrybag in one hand and was clutching a large framed picture in the other. Silently, and without taking her eyes off him, she held it out to James. Frowning, he took it and looked at it. It was a very old black and white photograph of a young woman wearing what looked like her Sunday best. The woman in the photograph looked to be aged in her late twenties and was standing confidently, her hair in a bun, wearing a long, dark-coloured dress adorned with white frilly cuffs and collar. In a heart-stopping instant, nerves flashed in his stomach.

Trembling, he handed the photograph back. "Uh, what is it that you want? I'm not sure I can help you…this is a *very* old photo. I'm not sure why you want me to see this. I'm sorry, but I don't know this person. Are you looking for somebody?"

She smiled faintly. "I don't think you understand, Mr Harvey. Take a closer look at the photo."

"Why? No! How do you know my name?"

With that, she plunged her hand into the bag she had with her and pulled out another photograph, a much smaller one. She showed it to James.

"Oh, please," he complained. "Not another! *Why? Why are you doing this?*"

"Take a look," the woman insisted.

He noticed it was the same young woman as in the other photograph, only this time she was standing next to an older man and woman – possibly her parents – in front of what looked to be the back door of a house. The man wore a suit and sported a large moustache. His arms were folded across his chest. The woman was wearing an apron over a long dress and holding a tray of baking. She had a stony expression. The young woman was standing slightly behind them, leaning against the house and was almost, but not quite, smiling.

"Read the inscription on the back."

He turned it over. In beautiful, flowing handwriting, someone had written, '*Mr. and Mrs. Maitland Stepney, with eldest daughter, Mary. Outside home, 5th August 1899.*'

He turned cold. The nerves in his stomach jangled more and he felt his legs go weak. This must be a dream, he thought. *This is not possible!*

Taking the photograph out of James's shaking hand, she placed it back in her bag and turned to walk away. James, dumbfounded, just stood there, unable to speak or respond in any way. The woman walked slowly down the path, opened the gate, closed it, and silently walked away, her movements laboured and stiff. James watched her until she was out of sight. He had to accept that there was only one possible explanation: *SHE KNEW!*

Walking uncertainly back into the house, he stumbled into the living room. He paused for a few seconds, gathering his thoughts. He knew he had to tell her. Holding this back from her would be too much – and would probably only cause more problems later.

Mary walked in from the kitchen. "Who was at the door? More press? Is something wrong?"

"Mary," he began hesitantly, "an old lady just came to the door."

"Mmm?"

"She had some photographs…two photographs."

"Photographs? Whatever were they of?"

"Uhhh…*you!*"

"I beg your pardon?"

"*They were of you!* But not more press photos; they were, er, they were old ones. Black and white. *Really* old. Mary—"

She fell against the kitchen door, grabbing the handle to steady herself. Staring down at the floor she mumbled, "How?"

"I don't know." He walked over and put his arm around her.

"How was I...what was I—?"

"In one it was you on your own, just standing there. Looked nice, actually. The other one you were with, I think, your parents. And you were standing with them outside your house. Your mother had been baking; she was holding a tray of food."

She gasped and slumped into his arms. "Oh, my goodness! Oh, my Lord! I remember them being taken. I remember them very well – it was only—" She stopped. "For the first one, Mother made us all go for pictures in our Sunday best. She wanted them for keepsakes. The one at the house was taken by a man who came to Dorking on a regular basis, photographing people in their daily work, even as they walked along the streets. My father befriended him and thought it would be rather fine if he came and photographed us with some of Mother's baking. How she did love to bake. The man thought it wouldn't hurt, and it was another customer for his business. Tell me—"

"What?"

"Tell me how she got them and who she was."

"I don't know! She didn't say who she was and I didn't think to ask. I thought she was a crackpot or up to no good."

"Well, I think somehow she must be very clever." She sat down on the sofa.

"We need to know how she worked out that you are the same Mary Stepney as the one in her old photos."

She nodded. "She must have them in her family – family heirlooms."

"I guess so, but she must know that the Mary Stepney in the photos should be well and truly dead by now. How she had the audacity – or madness even – to come to the house and do what she did."

"Yes, it's very strange. *Very strange*," she said, shaking her head.

"Mary?" James suddenly exclaimed.

"Yes?"

"This woman – she must be a relative of yours!" He started pacing around the room.

"What did she look like? Can you describe her?"

He thought for a moment. "Well, she just looked like an ordinary old woman. She was average height, a bit stooped. I can't really describe what she looked like. Pretty normal. Grey hair. You'd have to see her. But then you wouldn't recognise her anyway, would you, because she wouldn't have been born until well after 1901. Your lives couldn't possibly have overlapped!"

"You're right," she agreed glumly. "I keep forgetting things like that."

"So I wonder if maybe she was just someone not all there, you know what I mean? She might have recognised you from the newspapers and then spotted you in her family photos and thought you were one and the same, without having all her marbles present."

"Perhaps. James, anything seems possible these days!"

He laughed. "Not quite."

"Yes!" she countered forcefully. "Look at me! Am I not living proof that *anything* is possible?"

He frowned. She stood up and moved towards him.

"Please, James, you are the person always saying how people need to open their minds. And their hearts. You are always complaining about the closed minds, cold hearts and low aspirations."

"Yeah, all right! Point made."

"I think we ought to look out for this elderly lady. We must speak to her if we see her again. I need to ask her how she knows me and how she could possibly be in possession of pictures of me."

"She's mad! Cloud cuckoo land. Must be," James offered.

"Perhaps. Perhaps not."

"We'll see who's right."

* * *

"Ms Stepney?" the man called through the letter box. "Would you be interested in going on a reality TV show? It'll be filmed in the Bahamas and there'll be a tidy sum in it for you?"

James was at work and Mary was sitting on the stairs, waiting for the man to leave. He had seen her through the window, and had been ringing the door bell and knocking with the frenzy, Mary thought, of a man completely devoid of manners. It was no emergency, so why, she wondered, was he so insistent?

"Will you speak to me, *please? I'm* not wanting to upset you!"

"Please, just go away!" she pleaded.

"Ah! Ms Stepney!" he resumed, encouraged. "The figure could be in the vicinity of a hundred thousand pounds! Very negotiable!"

Mary scowled. She had not yet completely worked out the value of the British pound in the twenty-first century and thought this to be an absurdly high price to pay someone for what – she couldn't quite work out – seemed to have something to do with being filmed in your pyjamas. She knew what reality TV was, as James was always complaining about it. To her, though, TV was still a fascinating novelty, and she was able to sit through almost anything, reality or otherwise; the only exceptions being graphic violence and sexual explicitness, both of which shocked and upset her, causing her to refuse to watch.

She wondered whether James might like the money: a hundred thousand pounds – or anything in that vicinity – would certainly be one way to give him something back for all his kindness and generosity, as well as for her to have something to live on. She told the man to go away and send her a letter explaining what it was all about. She would then consider it in due course.

"Along with all my other offers!" she shouted, grinning slyly to herself.

The letter flap clunked shut and the man walked happily away. It was only then that Mary realised that she could never do any such thing: she was 'out there' enough now – too much, even. The continuous quizzing and querying was digging a deeper hole for her to fall further into as time went by. She tried hard to forget about the hundred thousand pounds.

HARD TIMES

It was a rare occasion for the family to be all together in one place. It always meant a crowded and noisy atmosphere, albeit usually a happy and good-humoured one. They sat on chairs arranged around the kitchen table; they sat on the floor and on stools placed wherever they could fit. They overlapped and their chairs butted into each other. Yet they thought nothing of this and of how they managed to all fit into a house of the size that, in the wealthier and more materialistic decades to come, would seem ludicrous and even shameful for housing this many people.

"As your father has lost his job," the mother began, "things will have to tighten up around here. I've arranged to take in washing and mending. I've placed a card in the newsagent's window and a few more around the area. I've told the neighbourhood, one-by-one, so word should get around pretty soon. But it won't do my hands any good."

"If Mary were still here we'd be all right," said Johnny. "She'd have helped somehow, she always did. She would've kept us happy no matter what. If only she hadn't been—"

"*Missing*," interrupted his mother. "She's *missing*."

The father's face tightened and his voice hinted at stifled emotion. "Our Mary's just missing. Nothing more. Our little black sheep has just wandered."

"She did like going up to London," said Andrew. "I reckon Jack the Ripper might have got her."

"DON'T YOU *EVER* TALK LIKE THAT!" the mother roared. "And don't *any* of you ever talk like that!" She drew a long breath. "That so-called Ripper hasn't killed in well over ten years. He's obviously not around anymore. Probably dead now. Besides, our Mary wasn't, er, the kind of lady he chose to butcher. We know that she had no plans to go up to London that day. She would've told us. She might have some peculiar ideas and opinions, but she isn't *that* much of a black sheep."

"Don't you mean dark horse?" questioned Elizabeth.

The mother ignored the comment. "She'd only planned to visit the grave of our Sarah, God bless her soul, you know that."

"I still wonder if she wasn't kidnapped and taken to the white slave trade or something equally hideous," said Rhoda. "She is so very pretty. That might have drawn them to her."

"White slave trade? Don't be so silly! Not around here!" the mother scolded.

"Stranger things have happened at sea, you know," said the father. "Still I have to say as I've said all along, I think she was out walking and she hurt herself and is still lying there, somewhere out of the way, perhaps in brambles or deep in the woods. She was such a lover of the woodland, you know. Always wanting to go out and look at things, fascinated by birds, bugs and beasts. Even climbed to the top of Leith Hill on her own in the dark once, remember? Had us worried sick for hours. She loved Leith Hill. She'd only wanted to be on her own to, what was it, think about the world or something, she said. There'd been a full moon and I reckon that had had something to do with it; can make people do daft things, it can. This time she probably broke her leg and wasn't able to move. No one came by. After a number of days out in the wild she…she succumbed. Winter and all, you know. Poor wench." He stamped his fist down gently on the table a few times. "That's what I think!"

Nobody spoke for a moment and the atmosphere was tense. A couple of chair legs scraped across the floorboards.

"Well, perhaps we'll never know!" he added. "Only the good Lord knows the answer!"

"Hmmff!" said Johnny. "That's if he really *is* good."

"Wash your mouth out, Jonathan Stepney!" the mother said fiercely.

"Well, if he's so good," added Lawrence, "why does he let things like this happen?"

Nobody spoke. Who could dare to challenge the very foundations of Christianity? Who wanted to look like a little devil amid the assuredly heaven-bound?

Eventually the mother spoke. "I'm afraid it's bread and dripping tonight. And if you're lucky there might be a few pieces of cheese left and a handful of potatoes and leeks from the garden."

Elizabeth's lip trembled and she burst into tears. "It's not fair! It's just not fair!" She stamped her feet on the floor.

"Hush, Lizzie," soothed her brother Thomas, seated next to her. "It'll be all right. You'll see." He turned to face his parents. "I might as well tell you all now. I'm going to see about a job on Monday."

"A job?" said Elizabeth, still sobbing. "But, Thomas, what about your schooling? It's terribly important that you get your education."

"It's also terribly important that this family eats and pays the rent."

"Yes!" agreed the father. "You can't eat arithmetic or English literature, as grand as they may be! Thomas knows that!"

Elizabeth visibly seethed, but she knew to say nothing.

The father continued. "If Mary were here she could've gone back to her teaching job at the school. The pay was reasonable, and it was a good steady job. And the ones in charge trusted her entirely. She could've risen in the job. Not like the ones I get. There aren't that many women around here with jobs as good as hers, jobs not affected by fashions or whims – teaching's a reliable profession to be in. Before she left it to…to sit and dream."

"Father!" the mother shouted. "Do not speak ill of—"

"The dead?"

"No! *Our daughter!*"

The mother got up from her chair, pushed it in carefully so as not to scratch the floor, then walked to the coal-fired range, busying herself with preparations for the evening meal, such as it was.

UMBILICAL CONNECTION

Mary's birthday was fast approaching and James wanted to give her something truly different, something unique that she would never forget. The thing he had in mind seemed to him to be far superior to anything he could buy in a shop. He had started secretly researching her family tree, compiling a folder of certificates, charts and various information. He had been downloading details from a variety of websites, as well as ordering birth, marriage and death certificates from the General Register Office. She had been a very easy person to research, and her siblings naturally even more so. The 1901 English Census was available on the Internet, and details of the occupants of her old home in Roseberry Lane appeared before his eyes. Seeing Mary's name, however, was an experience which shook him to his core. It was all very well to be friends with this woman and even have her living in the same house as him, but seeing her name turn up on a handwritten listing alongside the names of her parents and siblings – *in 1901* – was downright eerie. He had been able to get certificates for her parents: their births, their wedding and their deaths. It crossed his mind to look into this Mary Stepney and see if anything more than just her birth came to light. He felt duplicitous and somewhat ashamed of himself, but he felt powerfully compelled to do it all the same, and couldn't help remembering the conversation he had had with Bob at the pub, which was when the idea first entered his head. After obtaining her birth certificate he searched the records to see whether she had married, had had children – and, most crucially, whether she had died. To his relief and satisfaction, he could find no records of her doing any of those things, not in England or Wales anyway (and he wasn't going to start looking in Scottish or foreign records, or not yet, anyway).

Remembering the weathered headstone beside which he and

Mary had met, he found her sister Sarah's death – from pneumonia in March 1901, exactly as Mary had said. Searching on, he found details of the grandparents she so loved. He also found details of her grandparents' parents and was able to go back two further generations before the work became overly time-consuming and the trails more difficult to follow.

Mary's birthday rolled along and James presented her with the gift. As they sat down together in the evening to go through it her amazement was clear. She opened the folder with trembling hands. Seeing the names of her family members seemed almost too much for her. She had before her – sitting on her very lap – the lives, details and fates of her entire family; some more detailed than others. It took some time for her to read it all and to deal with the emotions that were brought forth. She smiled when she read details of births and marriages, but seeing the deaths was something she appeared not prepared for. She sat absorbed, reading slowly, uttering an occasional exclamation.

Her parents had both passed away in the 1930s. Mary gasped as she read that her parents were now dead – seeing it in print made it all the more shocking. Mother had had what appeared to be a heart attack. Father had gone downhill in every way possible it seemed after slipping over and breaking his leg. Mary said she was pleased that they had at least died of natural causes and had not had to endure the war a few years later.

Her little brother Johnny had not been so lucky. Brought to her mind so recently when she met James's young cousin Charlie, Johnny had fought in the First World War in the disastrous Gallipoli Campaign, and had been one of the many gunned down by the Turks. There was, apparently, a grave in Turkey containing what little they ever found of what they thought might be him.

Mary's sister Elizabeth had gone on to found a charity which built schools and hospitals in Africa. She married a British diplomat, had four children, and was awarded an OBE for her work in Africa. She had lived between Africa and Hampstead,

London. She died in 1969 on the day of the moon landing.

Mary's brother Thomas had fought in the First World War and was wounded in the trenches in France. He had been one of the thousands who had taken part in the infamous soldiers' Christmas truce of 1914, in particular the football games, England v Germany. Result: a draw. To them, the temporary truce and accompanying bonhomie had served to poignantly highlight the absurdity of the war. He was shot by a man who had been his friend the previous day. They had had no axes to grind, no hatred towards each other, no desire to kill, and had even stated out loud across the fields that they did not want to shoot each other. They had only wanted to win at football and share a Yuletide meal, along with a bit of singing. Thomas did not suffer badly from his wounds, but he returned to Surrey a broken man; a man who could seldom bring himself to talk about the war. He never married and lived alone with several animal companions, tending his beloved garden until his death in 1970.

Mary was shocked to see that her youngest sister, Rhoda, had been killed in the London Blitz while working for the Red Cross. She had been tending the sick and injured when a bomb struck the makeshift hospital. Mary commented that Rhoda was someone who could be called a true hero. The last time Mary had seen her she was still at school and had been severely reprimanded in front of her classmates for stealing a biscuit from the teacher's lunchbox.

Matilda, always sensible and even-tempered, had lived to a ripe age and eventually succumbed to age-related conditions in 1984. She had married a local farmer and raised three children on their farm in Surrey.

Andrew had joined up in the First World War and served as a cook in the camps in France. Returning uninjured to Britain at the end of the war, he opened a café in London. He married a woman he had employed as a cook and they had a family of four. Andrew died in 1964 from cancer.

Lawrence did not marry, but lived for many years in London with his close friend Theo until the time of his death from a heart attack in 1962. He was an enthusiastic collector of art and antiques.

Mary was stunned. James's work had been meticulous and the results were clear to see. She closed the folder and placed it on the coffee table. Looking down at the floor, avoiding his eye, she said nothing. He knew to wait for her to speak first. She eventually sat back in her seat and stared straight ahead, into space. He could tell she was absorbing a massive amount of information; it couldn't be done too quickly, nor could he, he knew, underestimate the emotional impact. And, he told himself, she naturally had no way of being ready for or expecting any of it. She showed no emotion and remained uncharacteristically quiet and inanimate. James went out to the kitchen to make some tea.

Then as if something had grabbed her and yanked her out of her seat, she leapt up and ran towards the front door. She opened it and flung herself outside as quickly as she could go. Slamming the door behind her she raced away.

James rushed to the front window and looked out. The gate was hanging open and there was no sign of her. He grabbed his keys and mobile phone, hastily put on a jacket and shoes and went outside. Left – no one, right – ditto. He tried to think of somewhere she might go but it seemed hopeless. He listened to the air. He thought he could hear the distant sound of running. He tried to catch up. He eventually caught sight of the hurrying figure. It was rounding the corner into Roseberry Lane. He stopped running and waited to see where she went. Sure enough she was outside her old home. He idled behind a lamppost, pretending to be making a call on his phone.

Give her some time, he thought. And some space. It must be pretty hard to be her right now…well, all the time actually now! What a hell of a burden she's got!

He waited some minutes. The figure in the distance sat down

on a wall that separated the property from the street. James relaxed and began walking away, to wait further out of sight. Just as he was leaving, he glanced back in time to see the silhouetted figure dash towards the house.

"Oh, no!" He ran.

When he got to her she was hunched over the letterbox, hanging tightly on to the knocker, pushing it repeatedly against the door. Fortunately, there seemed to be no one home. Her fingers were clasping the cold metal, determined not to let go. She swung her elbows and even her knees against the wood of the door, banging and crashing as loudly as she could.

"STOP IT!" James shouted. "You'll break something! Come away!"

She said nothing, but kept going at the door. He tried to prise her off.

A male voice boomed from behind them. "Is there something the matter? Can I help?" An elderly man stepped nearer. "I don't think they're home," he added.

"I'm sorry," said James, flustered, "it's just that she's, er, she's not well. She doesn't mean any harm to these people, whoever they are. She's not up to anything. Honestly. She was just...*leaving!*" He tried harder to extricate her fingers from the door.

She looked up at him. The sight that greeted him caused him to stop and draw breath sharply. It was not so much the flowing tears but something about her eyes; something about her tragic expression. In her he saw what he already knew in his mind, but this time it was visceral: the almost contagious energy about her of complete and utter despair. And grief: she had just lost her whole family.

After some time she relinquished her hold on the door and crumpled into a heap on the doorstep. She curled into a foetal position and rocked convulsively.

"Is she all right?" the man asked.

James didn't know what to say. He just stared at her face. Tears welled up in his own eyes, but he realised that he must be suffering the faintest modicum of what he thought she must be feeling.

At that moment torment was all she knew. Overwhelmed, she told herself in no uncertain terms that she was now reduced to a complete freak; a fleshy remnant of times gone by, times now dead in the ground. In her mind she was the *coup de théâtre* still on the earth when her show was well and truly over and the curtain had long since fallen. The feeling in her every bone, every organ, every cell was of wanting to escape her body. She wished for death and reunion with the ones she loved. But it was not to be, and she realised she had to accept defeat.

"God," she whispered under her breath, "why have you abandoned me here?"

"What did you say?" James leaned over her.

"Nothing. I'll go," she said quietly, attempting to stand. James helped her up. The old man bent down and peered into her face.

"WHAT ARE YOU DOING?" James snarled. "CAN'T YOU SEE SHE JUST WANTS TO BE LEFT ALONE?"

"I'm sorry," he replied, backing off, "only I think I've seen 'er before. She's been around 'ere trespassing recently. On this same property, yer know."

Mary flopped back on to the doorstep and moaned, wrapping her arms around her head, crying.

"What?" James queried. "What are you talking about?"

"Oh, nothing, nothing." The old man shrank back into the shadows and walked away. Over his shoulder he added, "I think there's a bit more to her than meets the eye now, isn't there?" He disappeared.

"Stupid old bastard," James muttered, as he helped the physically drained figure to her feet and slowly down the path to the street. She didn't speak and was still sobbing.

Suddenly, an energy surged within her and she roared, "I

HAVEN'T HAD TIME TO GRIEVE! I've lost them all! I can't take it all in! IT'S TOO MUCH! IT'S TOO MUCH!"

"I know. Let's just get you home now and we can talk about it."

"BUT I HAVEN'T HAD TIME TO GRIEVE!" she said, this time with even more ferocity.

"I know, I know."

"It's just too much! Can't cope!"

"Mary, I'm so sorry for upsetting you like this. Really. I didn't mean for it to be like this. I only wanted to give you something special…something that would mean a lot to you and that you could treasure. Better than something bought in a shop."

Sniffing hard and taking a long, audible breath, she said in a low voice, "James, you have given me so much more than I could ever have asked for. Your gift was something from the heart – from yours to mine."

He felt a pronounced twinge in his stomach.

She drew another loud breath through her tears. "You have helped me understand. And helped me accept where I am. I have never been given a present quite like this in all my life. It is wonderful. Thank you. Thank you, you dear sweet man."

He pulled her closer to him and hugged her. They had not hugged properly before. He felt her start crying again. Her fast and erratic breath seemed to go through him as well; her wet face seemed to be his wet face too, and he felt odd as he realised that the boundaries of their separate selves were being blurred together in this way. It was then that he realised he was crying too.

For a long time Mary said nothing about the unearthed family details, but as time passed she became more willing to discuss it. Although shocking with its godlike revelations, the dossier was of such importance to her that she kept it tucked away in her top drawer, out of harm's way, next to the stone.

* * *

One evening after dinner Mary and James went out for a walk around the neighbourhood. At the last minute they decided to include Roseberry Lane in their route, daring to go past what she now referred to as her 'old house'. It turned out to be non-eventful, however, with Mary benignly looking at the house as if it was encircled by a thick, invisible wall – some kind of force field – repelling her. James thought she had seemed sad but resigned. She had said little and just stood quietly. Later that evening back home, Mary picked up a magazine and spotted an article on people who are believed to have disappeared into thin air without trace. Police accounts of people who had gone to do something as unremarkable as getting out of their car and walking around to the back to scrape ice off the window when they suddenly vanished greatly interested Mary. She was surprised to read how many reliably witnessed and well-documented cases there were, and the mysterious subject pulled her own emotions to the surface.

"I feel," she began passionately, "like someone who is not in control! Yes! That's it! I'm just not in control!"

"What do you mean? Control of what?" James asked, slightly taken aback at her burst of intensity.

"I mean...ARRRGH! I feel as though I can't go back, even if I knew how to!" She sighed loudly and let out a mournful groan. "I've been here now for quite some time. I am strangely happy – except when I am being pursued by people." She paused, calming herself. "James, I have seen things, learned about things, done things, experienced things that no one in 1901 could ever have. I have walked through to the future and seen what it is like! The shocking reality of this world is now mine! James, it's hard to know how to put it, but...*I have a new life!*"

He just smiled.

"My dear Mr Harvey, I have outgrown my former life! I

acknowledge this is a terrible thing to say. It pains me to say it but I have outgrown 1901 and all that came with it. I feel ashamed to speak these words, but they are the truth. I feel like I am a person growing up and needing new clothes all the time, as I am constantly outgrowing them. New, bigger, different! All the time! And I don't feel that I've stopped growing, even now."

"But you must still have a strong attachment to 1901 – you can't pretend you haven't. It's your home."

"Yes, right you are. It is still my home." She walked around the room gesticulating with her arms as she spoke. Her whole persona, was impassioned. "I can move far away, I can walk, I can run, I can go by train or even plane, and I still can't get away from it. No matter where I go or what I do it's always with me, clasping on to me, *never* letting go! But it's not that I want it to let go. It's like an old friend, the sort that stays in your heart and mind forever with the deepest, sweetest affection. *It is love*, and being love it has no doubts or delusions. It's something big and strong and heavy that anchors me to one place. I suppose it stops me being tossed and tumbled, and yet I *feel* tossed and tumbled. But there's this thread, like an umbilical chord, which binds me and won't let me go. I am forever connected to 1901. It is not place. *It is time*. For people come and go, are born and die, like the yearly fall of leaves from the trees. People are transient here; only time stays. And now Old Father Time seems to have forgotten the rules. He is the drunken jester who has dropped his juggling balls while I am the one on whose head they have landed – the one who is paying the price of his carelessness."

THE INTERVIEW

The newspaper headline blared 'Is local hero a time traveller as well?' It was on the front page of the local broadsheet paper, a paper not particularly known for any sensationalist or tabloid tendencies. The article ran alongside a close-up of Mary, and centred around an allegation made by 'a local woman' that Mary had somehow 'slipped through' from over a hundred years ago to be walking the earth, according to the source, 'at a time that is not hers' and 'she should not be here!' The woman, referred to only as 'the source' (although the paper assured its readers that they did know her name and address), was reputedly in her eighties and claimed to have known Mary's family. Admitting that she did not know Mary personally, as she was born much later, the woman did claim to be a relative and said she had known most of Mary's siblings as well as her parents. She claimed to be in possession of photographs which 'proved' that Mary had been alive at the turn of the previous century. Naturally this story gave everyone a huge laugh and started no end of joking.

"Is it the first of April again?" a local radio station asked its listeners. "Why on earth has such a story even made it into the newspaper, let alone on to the front page?" they asked, bewildered. "What a waste of paper, waste of ink, waste of time! (No pun intended!)."

James and Mary went back into virtual hiding. They guessed the story must have something to do with their mysterious elderly caller with the photographs, and that she was most likely 'the source'.

It didn't take long before the competing tabloid paper got in on the act and sent a contingent of enthusiastic journalists back in pursuit of Mary, encouraged to use the most creative means of getting a story – anything they could remotely link in with the claim of time travel. They resumed their earlier campaign, and the letters and phone calls came rolling in (unanswered), and they even tried waiting on the doorstep for hours at a time, desperate to get more mileage out of the female 'Doctor Who of Dorking'. It was grossly irritating, and James and Mary were determined not to let it get to them. Not too much, anyway.

Mary eventually agreed to an interview with the local broadsheet. She thought this would get them – and hopefully the tabloid too – off their backs, and that once her interview was published the silly story of her being a time traveller would lose its appeal and vanish. She decided that if she went along with the story of time travel and just told the truth about everything it would seem to readers that she was just making fun of the situation and was wasting everyone's time. Or perhaps that she had well and truly lost her mind and was merely a pathetic idiot getting lots of attention, however brave and heroic her recent actions. Whichever way it turned out, she felt sure it would very quickly burn away to nothing and that then she could get on with leading as normal a life as possible.

JOURNALIST: "Is there any truth in the reported claim that you were born in 1871?"

MARY: "Yes. I was born in 1871."

JOURNALIST: "You don't mean *1971*?"

MARY: "No."

JOURNALIST: "Or 1981? Or close to?"

MARY: "No."

JOURNALIST: "Where were you born?"

MARY: "Near Dorking. Hazelwood."

JOURNALIST: "Not in a hospital?"

MARY: "No."

JOURNALIST: "What is your date of birth, if you don't mind?"

MARY: "The eighteenth of July."

JOURNALIST: "This should be able to be verified, you understand?"

MARY: "Yes, very well."

JOURNALIST: "If you really are over a hundred years old, why do you not look a day over thirty?"

MARY: (Visibly annoyed) "I moved from 1901 to this time in an instant. *So there is no reason why I should look over a hundred!*"

JOURNALIST: "What happened when you travelled from 1901? How did it happen?"

MARY: "I still do not understand what happened. One moment I was bent down paying my respects at my sister's grave and the next I was suddenly faced with a scene which looked similar...but was actually quite different. I didn't realise at first that I had travelled in time. Then I met a gentleman. It was he who helped me realise that I was no longer in my own time. He was, of course, just as surprised as I."

JOURNALIST: "So the whole experience was seamless?"

MARY: "Uhh?"

JOURNALIST: "Never mind. Were there any strange feelings or sights or sounds – anything? Any strange lights in the sky?"

MARY: "No. Nothing. I was looking at the lettering on my sister's gravestone when it happened. I do remember the lettering looked so fine and sharp at first – so new...and then it became less clear, harder to read. I didn't think much at the time, but it was peculiar. I think I must have moved into this time as I was focusing on the gravestone. I don't suppose that that could have caused it."

JOURNALIST: "Er, well, I guess we don't really know, do we?"

MARY: "No. I suppose not."

JOURNALIST: "Mary, are you happy here in this time?"

MARY: "I am, er...I am happy, yes. I like it in many ways, although not in others. There are many good things about this time. Like better transportation; mind you, much of it does frighten me still. I very much like the new cookers, the washing machines, electric irons, vacuum cleaners, central heating – oh, what a godsend!, refrigerators, freezers – oh, so many wonderful inventions! Oh, and I love the television and the radio and the music players. The advances in technology are just incredible! I rejoice every day at some of the things I am able to use and enjoy! So much labour is saved – you won't know how hard it was in my day. People had so little time to put their feet up. So many people became ill through their work, depending on what it was. A lot of people went to early graves. What a tragedy that is when it happens. There wasn't the National Health Service."

JOURNALIST: "Back onto the concept of free time, do you think we have a lot of leisure time now?"

MARY: "Yes! Except that so many people rush around like billio trying to fill it. It seems that family time and time to sit with folk has become less important, replaced by more…I suppose selfish and – what is that word I've learnt? – materialistic pursuits, like shopping. It's a sort of trap. I love the television, but it bombards you with messages to buy this, buy that, you're nobody without this, you're somebody with that. Sometimes I wonder if your powers that be just want you all to consume and nothing more; just add to the economy. Do you think that's possible?"

JOURNALIST: (Chuckles) "So, you see a lot that's wrong with the way our society is presently structured?"

MARY: "From what I've read and seen for myself I think that greed and power have continued to dominate. Greed for more and more money – I don't mean so much your ordinary person here, I mean the big companies. The power seems to be held by a small group of very wealthy people. And they will do almost anything to keep holding on to their power and control. Mr Harvey has told me that some of them have politicians sitting in their pockets, so to speak. That can't be right. I hope you don't mind me speaking frankly like this, but you did invite me here."

JOURNALIST: "No, that's fine. You do have some strong political opinions, especially for someone who says she has not been here very long."

MARY: "I just read a lot and am interested in the world. To not care about things like this would be, in my opinion, an act of negligence. It would make me complicit in the actions of these people and would just help them remain being so unfair and wrong in their ways. I care about things. I always have. I've also never had so much time for reading as I have now. I don't work, so I read a lot. And Jame— Mr Harvey has many good books and sources of information."

JOURNALIST: "May I ask if there's any particular reason why you don't work?"

MARY: "Well, Mr Harvey is very kind. He supports me and in return I do all the housework and chores. We prepare meals together though – he wants to do that, as he says I shouldn't do everything, but really I am his housekeeper now, I suppose."

JOURNALIST: "And why do you not look for a job?"

MARY: "I, er, don't think it would be a wise idea at the moment, with my unusual status. It would cause problems for me. Legally speaking, I don't exist, as my birth certificate is too old. I could not be part of the taxation system nor any other aspects that are looked at when one gets a job. But I used to work. I used to be a schoolteacher. I also used to write. I once had a story published in *The Times*."

JOURNALIST: "A story in *The Times*? Really? We'll look into that. Which school did you work at?"

MARY: "I'm sorry, I'd rather not say."

The journalist produces a photograph – the one of Mary standing with her parents, outside their house.

JOURNALIST: "Is this you?"

MARY: "From whom did you acquire that?"

JOURNALIST: "It was our source – the same source who told us that you are from 1901."

MARY: "Yes, that is me. I do not know who this source is – please tell me. Is it someone who thinks she knows me? A relative? Has she told you that I am saying I am from 1901?"

JOURNALIST: "I'm sorry, Mary, I'm not able to answer those questions; we have signed a confidentiality agreement with her. But I can tell you that she said she knew some of your brothers and sisters, and even your mum and dad."

MARY: "Oh."

JOURNALIST: "She says she *is* related to you, but I'm not able to tell you any more than that."

MARY: "Oh, no bother."

JOURNALIST: "What about your interests? We know you like reading and writing; what about other things, for example, do you have a favourite piece of music?"

MARY: "I have many. I very much enjoy the Adagio from the *Concierto de Aranjuez* by Rodrigo. It moves me like no other music. And Schubert's *Ave Maria* and *River of Tears* by Ararat. And Albert Ketèlbey – I find his music wonderfully varied, imaginative and delightfully theatrical. Also swing music, Al Bowlly, for example. And I like the work of George Gershwin and Noël Coward. And Petula Clark."

JOURNALIST: "Okay, quite eclectic. What about a favourite food and a favourite film?"

MARY: (Thoughtful for some time) "Oh, I'm happy with just a good, hearty vegetable stew. And I now like Indian food, so long as it's not too hot. I haven't eaten meat since 1891 – something which used to upset the applecart at home, but no matter now, huh. I confess to admiring the great George Bernard Shaw, and I feel he has influenced some of my thinking. As for a favourite film, I haven't one, although I do confess to liking *Singin' In The Rain* and *It's A Wonderful Life*. I like Buster Keaton and Charlie Chaplin. And the likes of Victoria Wood. I do like to laugh."

JOURNALIST: "So quite varied taste then. Some people might

think you would just like films set at the start of the twentieth century, or earlier."

MARY: "No, I'm not restricted like that at all. My mind isn't that narrow."

JOURNALIST: "Right. As I mentioned a minute ago, we know you like reading and writing. What about the performing arts? Have you ever gone to a play? Or even acted?"

MARY: (Looking irritated at the likely cloaked pointedness of this innocent-sounding question) "I was once told by an old aunt who loved the theatre that if you must do Shakespeare, always play royalty. I don't know who she thought I was, but, no, I never performed in anything, apart from a few amateur things when I was a pupil at school. I did see a couple of shows in London and one or two in Surrey. I liked the music halls best. I like the old art of singing, dancing and telling humorous stories. You always came away feeling good for all the singing and laughing. You don't have them anymore, not the same. You have all sorts of strange things now, some very good and some, er, not so clever or tasteful. I don't count tasteless things designed just to shock as the arts. To my thinking, the arts should be pure creativity and, preferably, beauty."

JOURNALIST: "I suppose it's the old question of what constitutes art. How does one define art? It's pretty difficult to be precise with any definition, don't you think?"

MARY: "Well I have been surprised to see it can now include a dead animal or an unmade bed."

JOURNALIST: "Mary, what do you think of our towns and cities now?"

MARY: "Well, I haven't been to terribly many yet, but from what I can see with my own eyes, and from television and from what Mr Harvey has told me, I can say that there seems to be a definite drive towards sameness. Networks of shops are taking over like lots of little empires and trying their best to oust out all the interesting and independent local shops. It must affect the level of specialised knowledge and expertise, and community relationships in general. But I don't want to say my opinion is better than anyone else's."

JOURNALIST: "I have to say you're certainly not alone with that opinion, it's been said many times by many people. Mary, what's your opinion on the role of women now?"

MARY: "Women seem to be a great deal freer and much more independent, in this country at least. Not all others though, I realise. I know in many countries it still isn't easy to be female. But for this country, I think it's a much better time now to be a woman than it was in my day. The vote has been a hard-won right – anyone who doesn't vote, male or female, has to be letting themselves and their country down. People died so that we could vote."

JOURNALIST: "What do you think about marriage and the different types of relationships now?"

MARY: "In my day, marriage was a sacred contract between a man and a woman. It came with obligations and expectations...and limitations, too. It made a union respectable and it meant you could live together and have children. Now things are so very different. It did shock me at first. But I've had time to think, and I've decided it's good that attitudes to marriage have changed, in that it's more fair now for the woman, but I still hold marriage as a very special thing. It shows a commitment to each other. I don't like all the legal aspects, but I understand there is much more scope now for tailoring it to how you want it, and dropping all that obey nonsense. I also think people must be accepting of those who want different types of relationships, apart from the traditional male-female. It's crucially important to be understanding and accepting of others. If we are all God's creatures then we must respect one another, for God would not have allowed there to be these differences if they were not meant to be. I believe the differences serve to help us, ultimately."

JOURNALIST: "Right, very interesting. So, Mary, are you anti-war?"

MARY: "Well, I am certainly not *for* war! I detest war. Only an idiot wouldn't."

JOURNALIST: "There are plenty of people who think war can be justified in certain circumstances. Would you agree?"

MARY: "I think the only time a war can be justified is when you are under very clear threat of imminent attack. I understand this was the case in the Second World War. I think Britain was justified in going to war then – there was absolutely no choice – I do not, however, regard the pursuit of power and national interests as sufficient justification to wage war."

JOURNALIST: "What do you think of the current perceived threat from terrorism?"

MARY: "I believe that no one should ever use violence to solve a problem. The terrorists are in the wrong. Violence is the last resort of the helpless and incompetent. But there is always a reason behind people's anger – it doesn't usually come about naturally for no reason."

JOURNALIST: "So you think terrorists have reasons behind their actions?"

MARY: "Of course. There is a reason behind everything. They have – very wrongly – chosen to use what is usually a smaller violence to fight what is normally a bigger, perhaps more insidious violence. Sometimes they are reacting to state terrorism, like taking of their land or whatever. But violence begets violence. It's a cycle of badness that breaks my heart and fills me with sorrow for the wrongs that are committed supposedly in the name of God or Allah or whoever."

JOURNALIST: "This brings us nicely on to religion. What is your view on religion? Are you a religious woman, Mary?"

MARY: "You may regret asking me this! I've rather a lot to say on religion these days! Before I came here, to this time, I was a good Christian woman. I more or less believed what I was told, but even then I did challenge a few parts of what we were supposed to believe. I tried to believe it when we were told things like we were the right religion and that all others were wrong: the Jews were wrong, the Moslems were wrong, the Buddhists were wrong, even the Catholics were wrong. Those we used to call savages were wrong – with their spirit gods and witchdoctors – barking up the wrong tree, as it were. We believed we should spread our wonderful Christianity to them, encourage them to convert and be saved; to stop their silly ways and ridiculous beliefs. Oh yes, and speak English too, enough of their native gibbering."

JOURNALIST: "That is what you thought?"

MARY: "That is what we were taught to think from an early age, just as our parents were and theirs before them. But as I said, I challenged some of it. It just didn't make complete sense to me, and I saw the contradictions and things that I thought, to put it plainly, were wrong."

JOURNALIST: "What do you think now?"

MARY: "Now I *know* that we were wrong. Yes, quite wrong. We were also barking up the wrong tree. Christianity is just another religion – another organised religion. We are no better than any of the others, only different. If you look more closely at the Bible and the views of some church leaders, you will see a fair number of contradictions and double standards. The Bible has been changed over the years and from what I can gather now only partially resembles the original texts. The views of men – and I mean men – have been added over the years; things to keep control over the people – and to stop women getting out of their place. Also justification for wars. What loving and tolerant god wants his people to go off and kill *other* god-worshipping people? How is that loving and tolerant? How is that looking after your flock? The words of more sacred texts than just the Bible have had their meanings altered and misinterpreted."

JOURNALIST: "So you think the Bible and other sacred books

have been hijacked?"

MARY: *"Hijacked? I'm sorry?"*

JOURNALIST: "Effectively stolen and used as a vehicle for another purpose."

MARY: "I suppose that's one way of putting it. If I may be so bold as to say, I think this world has a long tradition of using sacred books to peddle various messages. Wars committed in the name of God or whoever are a blasphemy. A blasphemy is saying that God made me do this, or God wants that family in that house over there to die, or God does not want those people in that country to have control over their own lives."

JOURNALIST: "So, if religion is this flawed, what do you suggest we have to replace it? Or are you an atheist now?"

MARY: "I am most certainly not an atheist. I believe in God, just not the orthodox view. I think we need to phase out orthodox religion and phase in a new kind of spirituality. Let me tell you something I don't tell many people."

JOURNALIST: "This interview will be read by a lot of people."

MARY: "No bother. I'm past being ashamed of my unusual opinions. I believe that the words 'love', 'life' and 'God' are interchangeable. I believe all three are one, and that this could even be called a new Holy Trinity."

JOURNALIST: "A new Holy Trinity? That's interesting."

MARY: "Yes. It helps one learn respect for life in all its forms. I wonder whether our children could benefit from being taught that they are part of this thing called life, and that they are one with God and with each other?"

JOURNALIST: "Interesting."

MARY: "God is love. And God is life. If God is life, then all life must be sacred. Yes? That means that all people, all animals and all living things are sacred."

JOURNALIST: "Those are some very deep and very serious statements – food for thought."

MARY: "I don't really want to say any more on this, not that there's not a lot more to be said. To stop destruction and wars and save this world it requires us to stop believing in the gods of yesterday...and instil respect for all life. That would mean changing our ideas to reflect reality and the love that I believe is permanently all around us. Get rid of the old violent, vengeful God of the past – who never even existed. God is not someone to fear. May I be so bold as to say religion doesn't seem to have worked? Its shortcomings are being revealed more and more. It's time for a change – big changes, and I think they're starting to happen. I hope so, anyway. But in the meantime it seems to be the case that we are rather spiritually poor, while being materially overdeveloped. It's all money and technology and things. Should we approve and admire every new science and technology, no matter what? Let's question how much faith we should put in these things before, not after, they are released into the world. And whether they are needed at all. I think we now know a lot but we understand very little, if that makes any sense. But going back to religious and spiritual matters – I wandered off the path a bit – my grandmother, bless her soul, used to tell me to count my blessings every day, and I think that would be helpful advice to anybody. I think there's some sort of law of attraction that then brings more for you to be grateful for, so it's an ever increasing thing. I'm still learning. I hope when I'm old I'll be as wise as she was. It's hard to explain all this in an interview. And I know it's sometimes easier to say these things than to do them, and no one can be perfectly angelic all the time, but the thing is to try to be true to who you really are. True to what is in your heart. So simple, but not always easy."

JOURNALIST: "Wow, some big ideas there. Worthy of further debate, to be sure. You seem to be someone who has thought a lot about a lot of things."

MARY: "I just wonder what your readers will think of my 'love', 'life', 'God' notion. As a concept, it actually gets bigger the more you think about it.

JOURNALIST: "Does it?"

MARY: "Yes. Readers could try it as a mental exercise, when they're alone and somewhere quiet, and see where it takes them."

JOURNALIST: "Perhaps I'll try that tonight, in the bath. Mary Stepney, wherever it is that you are from, you are a most fascinating and interesting person to talk to. I want to thank you for your time and for what I'm sure will both shock and stir many people."

MARY: "Thank you very much."

THE TIME TRAVELLER OUTED

The newspaper interview was picked up by other papers, the television, magazines and of course the Internet. Articles began appearing in national papers, particularly the tabloids, and Mary's supposedly ridiculous story seemed to be gaining, not losing, momentum. Her plan to stymie the talk of her being a time traveller had backfired. Reading the article in the local weekly paper, James commented that had she answered the questions in a less honest and more manipulative way she would not now be gaining notoriety. Had she made overtly outrageous comments things would be different, and she would be written off as a joker (or a nutter). He told her she should have said electricity was evil, or that people are all sinking into some sort of technologically-induced coma! Now she had not only excited the interest of the local area again, but was now attracting interest from all over the country. Where would it stop? She was fast becoming, James reckoned, an unwitting moth before the bright yet fickle light of media celebrity, the light that was so easily ignited, carried as it was on the still-smouldering embers of the local hero story. It was starting to get crazy. Letters began flooding in and the phone became busy with invitations for more interviews and 'chats', along with crank calls and calls from some who were simply *very* confused.

Mary didn't know what to do. She told James that she had truth-telling hard-wired in her brain and that she could not start lying or deliberately looking a fool for anybody. She was also starting to realise the financial value of doing deals before she did an interview. She knew there was big money around and being offered for little but her sitting down and chatting to someone for half an hour, or even just ten minutes. She could do that. She could sit, answer their questions and be pleasant, go home and show James the money she had earned. It was a great plan and would make them both more financially secure for little effort.

Mary embarked on a series of interviews. Some wanted to meet with her in her home area, while others wanted her to travel to them. She began catching the train on her own up to London where she would be met by bemused people who would whisk her off in black taxis to their offices or other locations. She seemed to have a canny knack for getting the negotiator to go up on, and sometimes even double, the original amount offered. She was treated well, although did get the distinct impression that she was nothing more than an intriguing novelty. And she knew that the prospects for being an intriguing novelty lay in the very definition of a novelty – that there would come a time when she was no longer new nor interesting. So she made haste. Yet she kept telling what she considered her truth and expressing her innermost opinions on a range of subjects, completely unaware that James was right: she was very much the delicate, winged innocent, fluttering gaily and obliviously in the face of dangerous, fast-moving headlights that were looming up – and were now almost upon her.

* * *

"D'you remember you asked me about Samuel Hodges being a relative?" George Hodges asked Mary, as the three of them sat in the living room one Sunday afternoon while the rain pelted down outside.

"Er, yes, I do," she replied, placing her cup of tea on the table. "I didn't mean to say it. I wasn't thinking straight."

"It's all right, love," he replied, wiping crumbs off his beard. "I understand now." He gave her a smile.

As if realising she had no choice, Mary succumbed, "He was your grandfather, wasn't he?"

"Yes. Do you know anything about him, love? Y'knew him,

didn't you?"

"George, your grandfather was a big man, like you. He had a beard too, and you actually look remarkably similar to him."

He smiled shyly and looked at the floor. "Good looking fellow then, eh?"

She laughed, continuing, "He would chat to me whenever we bumped into each other, which we did often. It was so different back then; you'd know your neighbours and share a great many things with them. Sometimes they were almost like family. Of course, it was possible to not have much in common with some of them, or even to not like them, just like today. But generally speaking there was a feeling of togetherness in each village. And reliance – you were reliant on other nearby people for so many things, and they would be reliant on you for something, even if it was just to help out when they were poorly. Someone in the village had to bake the bread, someone had to be able to mend roofs, fix a fence, shoe the horses. It was cooperation…and we all benefited. Samuel was a lovely, kind man. But he could be gruff at times. Sometimes you could look at him and just know that he was in one of those moods, so we used to hide from him then. You'd hear him whistling a lot. Whistling was much more common then, for some reason, not sure why. Oh, and he always had his pipe with him."

"Like me!" George said, tapping his jacket pocket.

"It was very normal then though, for a man to smoke a pipe. In winter you'd see these tiny puffs of smoke floating up into the air, like lots of miniature bonfires moving about."

"Sounds a lot like me, he does!" George chuckled. "I've got a few photos of him."

"You should get them put on disk," James said, "and get them redone. They can airbrush out the imperfections."

"What imperfections did he have?" George asked, surprised.

"Not *him! The pictures!*" James said, laughing.

"Oh."

"George, you are a little like someone from back then, in a way," Mary said. "I hope you don't mind me saying."

"Eh? No, I guess not. I know I'm an old-fashioned sort of fellow. Getting beyond some things – they're bringing out new stuff every day now, I can't keep up. And all the strange new words that ye keep hearin'."

"Do you want to keep up?" James asked.

"No, to tell you the truth. Why bother? I 'aven't the money to keep up, anyway. Mind you, there's a lot of people around here that seem to have a lot of money to throw around, much more so than in the old days. Might be wrong, but it's my impression."

"I think there's an awful lot of financially wealthy people in this area," James said.

Mary added, "It never used to be like that. In my day most of us were scratching around to make a living. If you worked hard you might be lucky and do well, but many people worked hard and still weren't lucky. There were many unpleasant jobs and no shortage of people queuing up to do them. Desperate, some people, poor souls. My family were more fortunate than unfortunate, although not at all wealthy. Money would rise and fall, like a choppy tide. I was lucky enough to be able to receive an education and to be able to buy the occasional book and go to see the occasional play or show. I think we were helped by the fact that Mother was good at making a little go a long way. If we had food no part was ever wasted. Nothing was allowed to go bad. We ate all the food we grew in our garden. That reminds me – do you know something else that surprises me about today?"

"What?" James asked.

"It's the wastage! And how few people grow any food in their gardens anymore. You go out to enormous shops and buy it there. I don't like supermarkets. They frazzle me. So much of the food doesn't look right – looks artificial – and there are just the same few varieties of apple, tomato and squash. Where are all the others? What's happened to them? And I've learnt something about the chemicals that are put in a lot of the food now. We had none of that – our food was all organic, of course, but we didn't have that name for it then. It was just food. Chemicals came later and, strange, isn't it, how it's turned out: food with chemicals is really the odd man out – the newcomer – not organic food. You know I've been reading a lot in the time I've been here. Oh, there's all these new books! They're new to me, anyway! Like E.M. Forster."

"And lately I've seen you reading Dorothy Parker and John Steinbeck." James added.

"Yes! *So many!* I would like to say to my two favourite gentlemen – that's the two of you, in case you wondered – that I could never leave this time period because of the books! And I was going to say I also read a few magazines – there are some very good ones. I especially like the ones about what life is like in other countries and—"

"It's interesting, George," James butted in, "for me to know a woman who hates women's magazines! She loathes them!"

"As I was saying before James so rudely interrupted me," she flashed him a mischievous grin, "I am *quite* amazed at how things are now. Many things just don't make sense and seem to be done for all the wrong reasons."

"Up with the revolution, eh?" George joked, grabbing a fistful of biscuits.

"Things have got to change," she added, "or…I don't know what will happen, but it's all gone very, very mad, as far as I can tell."

"Tell me, young lady, what was it like to ride in a carriage, behind horses? We really only see carriages in period dramas, don't we, lad? Apart from the monarch and people like the lord mayor, who use them on special occasions, and a lot of posh weddings. Not much other than that though, is there now?" He looked at James.

James nodded, adding, "I used to think horses and carriages

were something you would have just had to put up with back then – with no cars then it was a sort of a hardship. But I'm starting to think about them a bit differently now."

Mary, finishing off a biscuit, commented, "It was what we were used to. The Landau carriages, ahhh, they were handsome creations. Carriages weren't all the same; some were grand and others weren't. There were plenty of different types. Some were kept cleaner and in better condition than others. Some rattled so much you were sure they were going to break at any moment and land you head first in the mud. Wheels would go, of course, but there were wheelwrights in every village. Ooh, we did get stuck in the mud a lot. That was a jolly nuisance. You couldn't always be too precise about your arrival time. I liked it when I knew the horses were well looked after. One thing my whole family would get up in arms about was ill-treatment of horses. At least these days you have strong laws about these things – in this country anyway. Makes it harder and less acceptable for people to ill-treat animals – one good thing you moderns have done!"

"'Moderns', George, is Mary's latest word for us!" James said, laughing. "And I'm not sure that it's always used in a positive way either! I suppose it's the flipside of us saying oldies."

"You're just lookin' at us from a different angle, aren't you, lass?" George said to Mary, who smiled politely.

James added, "We're not used to having someone from the past looking at us…examining us and analysing us. It's such a reality check, I tell you. George, I find my conversations with Mary absolutely fascinating and they really make me think."

"Thank you, kind sir, although you do flatter me excessively. I'm sure you used to think before I arrived." She gave him a shy smile. "One more thing on riding in carriages," she continued, "was the slow pace. Oh, not good if you were in a hurry, if someone was having a baby or the like, but the rest of the time you could go at a nice pace, enjoy the scenery and be able to greet people you knew as you passed by. I remember riding home through the lanes in an open carriage one warm summers evening. It was only last summer in fact...well, the summer of 1901!" She took a deep breath and closed her eyes for a moment. "I can still remember the smell of the dry grass and the summer flowers: honeysuckle, night-scented stock, lavender. And fields of hay left out to dry. Mmmmm. Those are things that you have to miss when you fly along in cars. You don't even know they're there, it's just rush."

"I'd like to live on a farm and have horses," James remarked.

"Would you now?" George said. "Y'll need a bloody shed load of money to buy one, unless you move away somewhere cheaper than around here."

"Well, yeah, I know," James acknowledged. "Maybe one day, who knows. It'd be good to have more space. A bigger garden. Fruit trees. A cottage in the country, with views of woods and fields. I want trees around me. Must be getting mellow in my old age, huh? Would also quite like one of those long driveways to the house, with stones that crunch under tyres when someone drives up."

"And no mortgage, I suppose?" George asked.

James laughed. "Yeah, yeah, I know, in my dreams. No, I shouldn't say that. Maybe one day. Might make it my five-year plan!"

"It's my *hundred*-year plan!" joked Mary, as she poured them all another cup of tea.

LONDON UNDERGROUND (UN)LIMITED

The downward escalator was so steep and so long that with a bit of imagination the woman could imagine she was descending into another world. Instead of merely going from one London Underground line to another, deeper one, she was going to some infernal underworld with mischievous sprites and cackling demons with pitchforks in their hands. How clichéd, she thought, but it was symbolic nonetheless – going down to such depths. Whenever she thought about going into the older, deeper train lines in London – its Victorian labyrinth – she would shudder. A Tube fire was her greatest fear; a fear she was not even particularly conscious of having. It, too, lurked at the lowest of levels, deep and darkly subterranean.

With the three parallel escalators, two going down and one going up – and she being on the centre one – she could easily see the other two escalators, particularly the one going up past her on her right. It was on this Everest-scale upward escalator that she now rested her gaze.

She was musing about how she might one day write a children's book about some secret world existing beneath street level at Angel Station when she was abruptly jolted out of her imaginings. The passers by were flowing past in their usual, never-ending tidal flow. But her eyes could see something. The scene seemed to have started *blurring* before her eyes. She rubbed them. She blinked hard. Still the same. Rubbed them again, no change. Everything – people, the walls, the escalators and hand rails – now looked as though it were made of water: shimmering; fluid. Impossible. Shapes, colours and textures melded into each other – then, strangely, separated out again.

"What the hell!?" she said aloud, grabbing hard on to the rail with her right hand. "My eyes...must get my eyes checked! And soon! Woooaaaa!"

A man going up the other way caught her gaze. He appeared as if struck by some disturbing thought. But he was blurring too! His thick brown jacket changed tone and texture before her eyes; one moment wavy and rippling, the next an array of dark and light areas, merging in and out of each other. Yet she could tell it remained the same brown jacket. And his face. Staring as he was, his eyes seemed to move out nearer and nearer to her across the space. Nothing was staying still. It seemed as if one moving world was sitting directly on top of another moving world. And there was way too much movement going on for her liking. She was now gravely worried about her vision, trying to remember getting a bump on the head or something that could have caused this, but she couldn't think of anything.

She was now approaching the half-way point of the long descent. As she began to come level with the man she could see as much detail as the colour of his eyes and the blemishes on his skin. Her eyes explored his face watching his expression change to one of alarm – almost panic. As he passed by he swung his head round and looked back. His mouth was open and his eyes were wide. The woman was by now feeling absolutely certain that her eyes could not be trusted. And what the hell, she asked herself, almost screaming now inside her head, was he looking at her like that for?

But just at that same moment, several other people standing near the man also turned and looked in her direction.

"*Shit!*" she blurted. She craned her neck around to look at the man, just in time to see him reaching the top. As she watched, he stepped through what looked to her to be a watery-looking wall, but with nothing showing through from the other side. He vanished from her sight. All the people who had been around him on the escalator followed him, also vanishing through the watery portal, with none seeming at all perturbed about doing so.

It was now her turn to step off at the bottom. She looked back up. People flowed around her like a vast sea with the occasional cross-current, but she felt reassured that things looked normal again. No one else seemed bothered by anything strange. Wherever the man was he was now completely out of her range of vision. As she walked along the long corridor to the train platform she ran the scene over and over again in her mind. He was just an average Joe Public, she remembered; he was dressed for work in black trousers and a brown jacket. And carrying a top-opening brown leather bag, like the very practical ones she remembered her teachers at school having. Although, she reflected, she couldn't say he was dressed in the current fashions, he did look handsome, in a classic, manly way, with plenty of wool and corduroy. His hair was wavy and neatly combed back – even greased – in a 1950s James Dean sort of style. Very retro-looking, she thought. But it was the way he came into focus and went out of focus and came in and went out. Something had gone on that hadn't made a shred of sense. *I DIDN'T IMAGINE THIS!* she declared vehemently to herself. *IT WASN'T MY EYES! HE WAS FREAKED OUT ABOUT SEEING ME TOO!* Of all the uncanny experiences she had had in her life (and she could easily list a fair few) she had just had one that to her seemed inexplicable in every way, complying with none of the known laws of physics.

That night in bed her mind travelled to the middle of a solid object, where subatomic particles swarmed and swirled rapidly and endlessly, in a grand production choreographed by an invisible energy field. She dreamed she was right in there, in with the madly moving elements, caught up in the molecular frenzy that was energy made manifest. As she flowed with the currents she soon found herself face-to-face with the man in the brown jacket. He appeared all of a sudden, being projected out from one of the atoms. He was still looking at her. Only this time he was grinning inanely. The atom he was attached to kept flying in her face, teasingly, saying to her, *"Look, look! I am here! I am here!"* She panicked and woke with a start.

She had no idea that she had seen into the time we call 1955. She had no idea that the surprised man in 1955 was in a mild state of shock after seeing into what he could only imagine must be 'the future'. Neither told anybody.

THE MAN IN THE GREY SUIT

It was a gloomy, overcast day when the man came to the door. There was a ring of the doorbell followed a few seconds later by a sharp rapping. Mary, not expecting anyone, had been sitting, reading. Forgetting James's advice on opening the door to strangers while he was out, she flung it wide to find a tall man in a grey suit. He was clean-cut with short-cropped greying hair. He smiled, not warmly. He had brown eyes so unfathomable and dark – almost black – that they looked as though they could burn holes in anything they stared at long enough. He seemed to be a man with a purpose.

"Hello, are you Mary Stepney?" he asked.

"Yes," she replied, somewhat timidly, already wishing she hadn't opened the door.

"I'm from the Government – security service." He flashed an identity card which meant nothing to her. "I've been asked to interview you under the provisions of Section 5A of the new Security Act, as well as some possible immigration matters."

"What? Immigration? What is this about? What sort of interview do you want?" Her instinct was shouting *shut the door in his face! Keep him away!*

"Just routine, madam. But it will require you coming with me. Would you be able to come now for the interview?"

"Now? Truly? For how long? And, may I ask, to where would we be going?"

"Can't say how long. As long as it takes, I'm afraid. We're going to a Government office in Guildford. You know Guildford?"

"Can I leave a note for my…for James, er, Mr Harvey? I need to tell him where I'm going."

"I'm sorry, there's no time. My boss is waiting there now. I'd appreciate you getting your shoes on straight away. Grab a coat.

Handbag. That's all you'll need. You'll be home later."

Mary began hastily writing a note to James, but upon seeing the man's severely scowling face at the door she stopped. She collected her shoes, coat and handbag as instructed and went with him. As she pulled the front door to, it dawned on her that she had no way of knowing if what this man was saying was even true.

* * *

James arrived home from work later that day to an empty house. He found Mary's unfinished note on the kitchen table.

"What! What's happened? What's going on?" He then mumbled, "Where's my long, detailed note I always get? Where's my War and Peace? My...lovely big informative note? She *always* writes those! Never goes out without leaving a note!" He huffed, looking around in almost a panic. "MARY? MARY? *Where are you?*"

He spent the evening at home waiting for her return or the phone to ring. Nothing happened. As the time passed his imagination began to kick in. He went as far as imagining she had been sucked back through the wormhole or whatever it was she believed had brought her to the present date. He imagined she had been spirited away and dumped back in 1901. Would she remember any of this? Would she reappear a mere flicker of a second after she had vanished from 1901? In other words, would there even be any time to account for at the other end? She had had the presence of mind to start a note to him, but why had she not completed it? He could picture her, pen in hand, realising she was 'going'. Cell by cell, she was dematerialising and then rematerialising, her consciousness in tow. But, no! He stopped himself. She must still be here, somewhere. He checked and saw that she had taken her coat and handbag. And one of her pairs of shoes was missing. So she had gone out of the house. He checked that her stone was still there, in the drawer where she kept it. It was; likewise the family tree dossier. He then had peace of mind enough to know that she had not deliberately packed up for good. After walking around the neighbourhood, looking in all her regular haunts, he went home and went to bed, sleeping fitfully.

* * *

Meanwhile in Guildford, Mary had been bundled into a large room painted a pale blue, in which was arranged a single bed, a sofa, an armchair, and a table with a glass and a jug of water. A mirror and an old watercolour of Guildford cathedral adorned the wall. The room felt grimy and cold. A door opened to a small en suite bathroom. After being left waiting for fifteen minutes she was collected for the 'interview' and taken to another room.

The man glanced up at a camera mounted on the ceiling before placing a voice recorder on the desk between them. He began in a police-like manner, with the date, location and their names.

"Is your name really Mary Stepney?" he asked for the second time. He got a notepad out of his pocket and wrote in it.

"Yes, you know it is. What was yours again?"

"What is your date of birth?"

Mary gave him a dirty look.

"What is your age?"

"I'm as old as my tongue and a little older than my teeth."

"Very funny. What is your date of birth?"

She sighed heavily. "The eighteenth of July, 1871."

The man repeated that into the recorder. "That's the eighteenth of July, 1871. She is saying she is over one hundred years old, yet she appears to be aged approximately twenty-eight to thirty-four."

"How dare you! So rude! I'm thirty!" She turned away.

"Please face the desk, Ms Stepney."

Incensed, she knew there and then that she had to get out. And fast.

The questioning of her personal details continued. The man was thorough and relentless. He spoke loudly and clearly into the air above the voice recorder.

"And you are certain that you lived in the Dorking area in 1901 and that you were teleported to the present day?"

"Yes. If you mean transported."

"Yes. How did this happen?"

"I don't know. You tell me and then we'll both know."

"I repeat, how did this happen?"

"It just happened."

"No strange vision or scene?"

"No."

"No sudden haziness or fog?"

"No."

"No strange sounds?"

"No."

"Strange lights?"

"No."

"Smells?"

"No."

"What about other people. Were there any other people around you prior to your alleged disappearance from 1901?"

"No."

"Had you been drinking alcohol?"

"No!"

"What about the night before?"

"No!"

"Had you taken in any way any other substance which could induce hallucinations or distortions of the senses?"

"Definitely not!"

"Have you ever been diagnosed as suffering from schizo-phrenia?"

"From what? No!"

"Have you ever been diagnosed as suffering from any mental condition or illness?"

"No!"

"Ms Stepney, have you ever been in prison?"

"No!"

"Any other institution?"

"Only school."

"You know what I'm getting at, I don't mean school." He paused thoughtfully. "Mary, we would like you to undergo some tests."

Who is this 'we'? she wondered.

"Will you consent to the administering of a series of tests on you? Tests which will require you being hooked up to what we call a polygraph machine, which will not hurt you but could help us in our investigations? It is non-intrusive and harmless. Do I have your consent?"

Puzzled, she answered, "Yes, I suppose so."

"Good. And later we will most likely ask your consent for other tests, but I won't go into that just yet."

He walked over to a desk, opened a drawer and retrieved a small machine. He placed the machine on the desk, connected it to a laptop computer, and set about attaching several wires and monitoring devices to Mary's skin. She watched in horror but said nothing.

"Ms Stepney, are you in good health?"

"Yes."

"Are you taking any medication?"

"No."

"Have you taken any pain killers today?"

"No."

"Any aches or pains?"

"No."

"Headaches?"

"No, not recently."

"Good. Could you be pregnant?"

She gasped. "No."

"Good. Any physical ailments or conditions at the moment?"

"No. Apart from a severe case of being brassed off – ever heard of that one?"

He switched on the machine and fiddled with it as he spoke.

"Please just ignore the wires, they won't hurt you. Now please stay calm."

Mary looked at the wires and the points where they were attached to her. *Stay calm? Oh why didn't I just keep my blessed mouth shut?* she thought. *Why did I have to open the door and go with this man? I've got to get out of here!* Calm was one thing she did not feel.

"Ms Stepney, I want to ask you again. What is your true date of birth?"

"As I told you – the eighteenth of July 1871."

He watched the computer screen and made a note on his pad.

"And you are absolutely sure of that fact?"

"Of course."

"You would swear to it in a court of law?"

"Yes!"

"Would you say you're generally an honest person?"

"Yes."

More looking at the machine and writing notes.

"All the time?"

"Yes, I think so. I try to be. No one's perfect though."

"Have you ever taken drugs?"

"If you mean illegal drugs, then no, I have not."

"What about legal ones? Do you enjoy a tipple – alcohol?"

"Um, a little. An occasional glass of wine is nice and I like cocktails, but I don't get rotten drunk, if that's what you mean. I was brought up much better than that. I was not raised in this present time of liberalness."

"Ms Stepney, tell me the schools you attended and the years as best you can remember."

She relayed the details to him. He wrote more notes and kept looking at the computer screen.

"Please tell me the full names of your parents and the first names of your siblings."

She told him. She included Sarah, adding the comment that she was dead.

"Yes, Ms Stepney, and so are all the others!" he added brusquely.

"*Bastard!*" she hissed under her breath.

"I'm sorry, I didn't quite catch that."

"Nothing."

"Good. Now, tell me where you've worked and the years, as best you can remember."

The only paid employment she had had was at the school, and she knew the dates. She told him the address and a few details about her employer.

"So the head teacher, he must have been upset when you resigned…which was to do what? To become a writer?"

He studied the screen intently.

"Well, yes, he was. He wanted me to stay. He said I was a valuable member of staff, reliable and a very good teacher. But, yes, I wanted to write. I suggested I work just two or three days a week but he wouldn't have it. He said that my replacement wanted to work every day and every hour God sent. There was nothing left for me. I understood."

"And this writing…have you had anything published yet, or is that not the aim?"

"I've had a story published in *The Times*. I've told this at every jolly interview I've done! I'm sure you must know this already!"

"Just procedure, madam."

Then, like a thunderbolt out of the sky, he asked, "Ms Stepney, are you in love with this James Harvey?"

She gulped. "No!"

He watched the screen and the slightest of smiles passed over his lips. He wrote something down.

"Never mind, we'll move on to the next question. Ms Stepney, are you making the whole thing up, this story about being from 1901?"

She felt her blood rise again. "NO!"

"You don't seek attention? All this publicity?"

"NO! I DETEST IT!"

"Did you get a taste for being in the spotlight after you rescued those two boys from the lake?"

"No! I hate this attention! It's horrid! I want to go home!"

"Home to where? To 1901? Or to James Harvey's house?"

She groaned. "To Mr Harvey's house! But yes, sometimes I do want to go back to 1901! Of course I do! People like *you* make me want to go as far away as possible!"

The man looked at her and didn't say anything for a few moments. She feared he was going to give her an electric shock but it never came. After a few more questions and writing more notes he stood up and removed the wires from her skin and put the machine away in the drawer.

Mary was not allowed to go home. She was taken back to 'her' room and told she would be there until further notice. She did not fight. She did not resist. She showed a sudden passiveness that surprised the man. He was irritated that he could not read her anymore. After the interview her manner had changed, and she seemed less the sincere, matter-of-fact woman she had been previously. Her honesty and straightforwardness seemed to have mutated into a state of calm withdrawal. He did not know why, and to him it didn't seem to fit: she should be even more angry now; even more wanting to go home – wherever home was.

She now considered herself a homeless woman in an unknown prison of a building: she felt she had already lost her time and now her place was gone too.

* * *

"I will not be upset. I will not be sad. I am not upset. I am fine. I was fine before I met her and I'm *still fine!* So she's gone...oh well, Ms Victoriana, it was interesting while it lasted! Gone back...somewhere, eh?" Taking a deep breath, he mumbled, "I suppose at least I had the pleasure of meeting her."

He stood staring at the floor. He felt a well of sadness trying desperately to erupt at the surface, but he refused to let it.

"Had the pleasure...pleasure! Ha! How can you flit in and flit out, just like that? Gone. How can you do that? Hmmff. Goin' to the pub tonight anyway, catch up with Bob and...whoever. It's been a while. No, I was fine before and I'm fine now! Don't need her!" Realising he shouldn't be talking out loud like this, he stopped and made the desperate monologue go back inside, where it belonged. He tapped the side of his treasured Georgian wall barometer, feigning interest in its readings, then stomped off. Walking from room to room, he sensed her recent presence in each one of them, from the carefully folded washing to the immaculately made beds. The house was perfectly clean and tidy. There were cut flowers in a vase in the dining room, and the whole house just seemed wonderfully cared for. She had brought a bright energy and a freshness to the air itself, and a sensitive dignity which was difficult not to notice.

With her precious stone the biggest sticking point for James's calculation that she must simply have had to go out in a hurry, he alternated between believing she had been taken somewhere and believing she had gone on her own accord. The stone was something that she so cherished, he thought; it was like the only photo you have of someone very dear – it was something you must never, ever lose. It was the only tangible reminder of a life gone by; a life already lived and now finished. Unless, he postulated suspiciously, it really was all a hugely elaborate hoax after all, and she really couldn't care less about the stone. He chided himself for being so gullible. He poured himself an ale and decided to sit back and watch some football.

* * *

The man opened the door to Mary's room and found her sitting cross-legged on the bed, looking up at the light coming in through the window. He led her out of the room and along the corridor back to the room she had been in for the initial 'interview'. This time the room had been set up differently, with various equipment arranged around a chair and a large screen. There were cameras mounted on the ceiling and apparatuses which Mary could not identify. She was asked a couple of questions about her general health again before being seated in the chair and connected to ambiguous-looking items of equipment. She did not resist, and she only spoke when she was asked a question. When all the necessary connections had been made and the systems were ready, the session began. The man explained how she was to be shown a series of photographs and video clips on the large screen in front of her; each picture or video would be shown for exactly thirty seconds. She was instructed to look at them and not say anything.

The first picture came up. It was a photograph of a scene in Mary's home village taken in the late nineteenth century, showing residents clustering with their buckets around a village well. Mary smiled slightly and leaned forward to have a closer look. The next picture was a photo taken in more modern times of the exact same place, from a similar angle. This time Mary did not smile, although she did look interested. Following that was a short video clip of Margaret Thatcher stepping down from her premiership in 1990. Parts of the clip were replayed several times during its thirty second slot. Mary appeared impassive. The next item comprised pictures of Princess Diana's funeral procession in 1997. Again, Mary looked unmoved. That one was succeeded by a photograph of Queen Victoria. Mary instantly smiled. Her smile quickly vanished, however, when she saw the next image, which was a close-up of the front page of a British newspaper announcing the death of the elderly monarch. Mary leaned forward in her seat again, this time apparently to read as much of the article as her eyesight (and time) would allow. The next exhibit was a popular television advertisement from the 1980s – one aimed at teenagers and broadcast frequently at the time. It played for the whole thirty seconds, and throughout this time Mary's face betrayed no flicker of recognition or nostalgic fondness. Next up was a video of Madagascan lemurs happily leaping and dancing in their native habitat. Mary looked happy. After that came some iconographic video footage of the dismantling of the Berlin Wall. Mary looked intrigued but showed no emotion. The crunch came at the end, with the final image being an almost pornographic picture of a woman; the picture obviously chosen for its potential to shock any decent-minded Victorian lady. Mary frowned, pursed her lips and looked away, appearing embarrassed.

With the session over, she was thanked and led back to her room which, in the time she had been away, had been fitted with a small television. A desk and chair had also been brought in, and a pile of books delivered, along with writing equipment and a copy of the current *Radio Times*. It would appear that she was intended to remain there for some time.

* * *

James began looking for Mary in earnest. He rang the hospitals and the police, but to no avail. He asked neighbours if they had seen her leaving on the day she went missing, but no one had seen anything. Ironically, he felt he could have done with the pesky journalists hanging around, but they seemed to have moved off. He paced around the garden, looking for clues and anything different. Nothing. He checked his credit card account and found no new transactions, which he thought revealing, as he had given her a joint card (on an account specially set up) to allow her to go shopping without him occasionally and to always be able to get home. (He had known that getting her a card to access an albeit limited portion of his money might seem foolish and overly trusting, but he considered it to be a means of testing her true character – the litmus test of her honesty. So far, she had passed). Knowing now that she was likely to have been 'escorted' out of the house and away somewhere did not make for pleasant thoughts. He could think of only two possibilities: the first, a crazed member of the public who had seen her in the papers and on TV; and the second possibility, that someone from the Government had got hold of her. He felt that the latter was more likely. He turned to the Internet and began looking to see who might be most interested in Mary's case. In doing so he found what he believed to be the tip of the otherwise concealed, covertly operating iceberg that was the Secret Service. Something inside him – he could just feel it – told him that they (or GCHQ or some other limb of the amorphous, multi-headed national security beast) were the ones responsible for Mary's disappearance.

* * *

Mary was given further tests. One was a DNA test, in which her genetic material was obtained and analysed. They also ran blood tests, looking for certain antibodies, minerals, metals and other substances in her bloodstream. They checked for particular chemicals stored in fat deposits, bone and organs; and even investigated to see how much residue from pesticides she had in her body, comparing her with a typical (modern-day) Surrey woman of her age. They gave her IQ tests, emotional intelligence tests, personality tests, and grilled her face-to-face. They showed her more pictures and videos, and monitored her physiological and behavioural changes while she viewed them: blood pressure, heart rate, brain activity, facial expressions, body language. Few people had ever been as rigorously tested in this way, and the truth about Mary was something they were not going to let get the better of them. They had no plans to inflict pain, nor to deprive her in any way. They would move 'ever so slightly' towards that 'darker' end of the spectrum only if they 'had' to. But they found they did not have to, for the answer about Mary came to them surprisingly swiftly, albeit piece-by-piece. The disturbing truth about her began to emerge; a truth they were neither prepared nor easily able to accept, even though it was now becoming increasingly evident and indisputable.

* * *

James reached hesitantly for the phone. Dialling, he cleared his throat and waited. A recorded voice instructed him to press another button to get through to an operator. He waited. The operator put him through to a government department where he was told he was not able to speak to anyone but that he could leave a message. He left one, waited days, but did not get a reply.

He reported Mary to the Missing Persons Bureau and then decided to write to his local Member of Parliament. The MP, who James regarded as often appearing rather smug, with dubious ability to be particularly proactive or progressive (but very adept at keeping the support of his cronies and ensuring his own long tenure) replied that he was "terribly sorry" to hear that Mary had departed, but that perhaps she had gone back to 1901 and all would be well again. He added, "What a jolly adventure we've all had with her fantastic story", "hasn't it been entertaining?" and comments of the sort. He did end the letter with some common-sense advice on how the system works regarding missing persons – but nothing James did not already know. Privately, the

MP was of the mind that James had just been taken for a ride by a tremendously lying and deceitful woman who had inadvertently (although admittedly very heroically) happened to rescue two boys.

James sent a flurry of emails to the Government, targeting every department and agency he thought could be of any help. One email came back stating – without actually saying that they were talking about Mary – that persons may be held for questioning for up to three months with no automatic recourse to a solicitor if they are suspected under the new anti-terrorism laws. Incensed, James thundered back in reply, "BUT SHE IS NOT A TERRORIST!"

He despaired. Without the support of his MP it looked practically impossible to tap even a tiny chink from the shell that contained (and protected) the Government: the largely impenetrable fortress with its shadowy side of legislative excuses and secrecy. It seemed immune and disinterested in his impassioned appeal, but he could not give up – it was now his quest to find her.

Knowing that the first thing to do was to garner more support, James travelled down to Eastbourne to visit his parents. He knew it would be tough; he could imagine his mother lecturing him on getting involved with Mary, strange as she (allegedly) was, and he expected her to add that he should forget about her and just get on with his life. And that she wanted to see him happy, but also had visions of him marrying someone different from what she had judged Mary to be, from their one not so successful meeting; someone with a better background, who went to a good (expensive) school, had high aspirations, spoke eloquently about their travels in Brazil and Botswana; someone with poise, elegance, perhaps even taller and more assertive. His father, on the other hand, although prone to making the occasional highly embarrassing gaffe was more placid and down to earth, disliking unpleasantness and confrontations. And he liked most people. A retired civil servant, he had worked in central government at Whitehall for decades, slowly climbing the ladder until he reached, as he put it, "a high enough post – any higher than this and I feel some blighter'll come along and push me off." He still played golf with some of the chaps from the office, most of whom had also retired, or were not far off. The move from Dorking to Eastbourne at retirement had been partly practical (more house for your money) and partly so as to deter him from jumping on a train to London and returning to the office as a consultant or on some other basis, which was so often the way. Eastbourne was a lot further from London, and it offered, as well as invigorating sea air and seaside atmosphere, a laid-back life of what they hoped would be splendid isolation from the hectic goings on in the world.

Telling them about the situation and how Mary had evidently departed in unexplained haste, James decided to let them know a bit more about his true feelings for her, this woman who shared his wavelength and his opinions on life. His mother, at first haughty and dismissive, gradually came around to agreeing to help. It was his father, Frank, who was cooperative straight away, adamant that looking for Mary was the right thing to do. James told them how she had no family alive and no one in the world apart from him. It was this that swung James's mother around, touching on her sympathies. Frank wanted to speak to James's MP, keen to give him a swift nudge in the right direction, but James said not to, and that it might be better to just bypass the man and head straight for the jugular of power – or at least a major artery.

Frank began ringing and arranging to meet some of his former colleagues, particularly those still employed in government. They held a range of jobs, from positions of some power to positions with a modicum of power, through to people who knew someone with power to those who knew someone who knew someone with power, or – the commonest of all – those with no real power or links to power whatsoever. Carefully, and as diplomatically as possible, Frank Harvey began picking his way through his old workmates, talking, listening, appealing for a favour wherever possible and sucking up like never before. He went to London and met them in restaurants, pubs and clubs. He reminisced, he charmed, and he tried to get any information at all that might help. In the back of his mind he wondered whether they really did have her. What if, he postulated, she wasn't with them at all, but something else had happened? He would feel a right fool then if it came out that she had simply gone back to her New Age hang-out at Glastonbury, or wherever it was she originally hailed from. But trusting his son implicitly and desperately keen to help, he embarked on a mission, accumulating a file of information.

There was one contact who began to shine out as having a direct connection to people who could be of real help in the hunt for Mary. The man had had dealings with the nucleus of MI5, and had also gone to school with one or two of them, as well as with Frank. True Old Boys, he said, don't forget each other in a hurry. Frank nurtured his relationship with the man, who still worked at Whitehall and still had his finger on the proverbial pulse. As the pile of information on people currently in detention grew, Frank came to the conclusion that, if what he had been told was true, he had been given enough information to have a pretty good chance of finding Mary. It transpired that she had been removed from her home to go for questioning (a bit more than that, really, just nothing too drastic, the man had said) at a secret location in Surrey. Frank then asked him for a list of places used in Surrey for clandestine activities of this sort. Without actually betraying his employer and telling Frank where Mary was, the man passed him a list of locations in Surrey, their addresses and notes on each. It was left to Frank to work it out. The man would say no more, reminding him that he had already disclosed many more details than he was supposed to, and that he hoped he wouldn't be found out for having given him as much information as he had, even with the provisions of the Freedom of Information Act. Frank offered his profuse thanks and treated the man to an expensive lunch in one of the West End's top restaurants. It was a very small price to pay, he thought.

Frank sent the list of addresses to James, who studied it thoughtfully. It was hard to eliminate any or favour some above others, but James and his father agreed that they should start with the one nearest Dorking. It was a gamble, but if it didn't prove right they would just move to the next one, and so forth. James's parents suggested involving the press and having a high-profile demonstration at the location, rather than trying some covert action which, although less risky in the potential humiliation stakes, was bound to backfire in their faces and get them in huge trouble with the law.

* * *

Mary's disappearance was now making it into newspapers and websites, perpetuating her 'fame'. For many, she was a standing joke, nothing more, with newspaper headlines such as, 'Time travelling local hero goes missing' and 'What are religion's missing messages? Missing time traveller has the answers!'

The morning was still and sunny as James travelled to Guildford. Meeting his parents at a pre-arranged location, they joined with a handful of others, mostly friends and neighbours of James's parents rallied specially for the cause. James had made a selection of placards, all designed with media attention in mind. After handing them out, he began walking slowly towards the discreet reddish-brown brick building. Around it stood a few large trees and there was a small gravel carpark where a handful of cars were parked. A wrought iron gate was the only opening in the high brick wall that encircled the property. The gate was shut, with an automatic card-reader/intercom for cars that pulled up. A

closed-circuit television system protected the premises and little
could be seen through the windows. There was no sign saying
what the building was about, although James spotted a small
gold plaque beside the front door. The writing was too small for
him to see.

The picket began. James, his parents and the supporters alternated between standing and sitting on the ground in front of the
gates. When, at one stage a car drove up, they swarmed around
it and leered at the occupant. It was an unsmiling man in a grey
suit. He waved a card over a reader, the gates opened and he
drove in. James's mother rushed off in an attempt to follow the
car into the premises.

"*Edwina!*" Frank shouted. He and James grabbed her and
yanked her back.

"That's not the plan!" James said gruffly. "Not yet anyway!"

But, unaware to him, her main motivation was that she had
simply not wanted to have to come back a second day.

James's attempts to find his missing love were small-scale and
couldn't have been more straightforward, while the edifice
challenging him was of massive complexity and resources, and
made of the toughest steel. Mary's story of travelling from 1901
to the present was not an undemanding one; it spoke of possibilities not as yet common knowledge (if indeed they ever would
be); it seemed bewildering, yet was probably quite simple if the
facts could ever be laid bare. How her physical molecules,
energies and elaborate consciousness had travelled through time
(but not space) was an accidental achievement of the most
incredible kind. She was special. James was aware of the
daunting situation, but could not and would not give up: she
needed him now – she had no one else on earth, quite literally.
None of his anxiety about whether her story of her appearance
was true entered his head anymore; he just wanted her back.

As the day of action wore on, a representative eventually
emerged from the building. A middle-aged woman in a smart

suit crunched across the gravel car park and stood at the gate, wrapping her hands around the iron bars. She examined the small crowd. Around her neck was a staff pass with her name, title and a photo. Frank craned his neck to read the words but could not quite make them out. Before he could get any closer a gust of wind came and flipped the pass over.

In a loud, authoritarian voice the woman announced, "Excuse me! We don't know what you think coming here will achieve, but we think you should leave. There is no reason for you to be here. We have nothing to do with the woman you are looking for." She pointed at a nearby placard that read 'Free Mary Stepney – detained by UK spooks'.

"Yes, you do!" Frank retorted. "We know she's being kept here against her will!"

"Yes! Let her go!" roared Edwina.

"She is not here," the woman pleaded, trying to keep as calm as possible.

"Yes, she is and you know it! You must do," James said. "Who's in charge here?"

The woman looked crossly at him. "I am not at liberty to give out information. We are not negotiating with you. Please leave…and take your banners and any rubbish with you!"

"Any rubbish? Listen, we don't have to go," Frank said to the group. "We're legally entitled to make this protestation."

"Too right!" said Edwina.

The woman shook her head, turned and stomped off back into the building. Nothing more happened.

"We can't just do this every day and get ignored by them," said James.

"Where's the press?" Edwina asked. "James, I thought you'd rung them up."

"I did," he replied, "but it's not my fault if they've chosen not to turn up. I am a bit surprised."

Edwina threw her placard on to the ground and stood staring

down at it for several moments. "Frank – all the people you know in the civil service...and now *this!*"

"What?" asked an elderly woman seated close by on a fold-up chair. "Did someone say silver service? Surely not *here!*" She and a few others around her erupted into laughter.

Edwina scowled at the woman.

"Edwina, there's no point in losing your temper," Frank scolded. "That's not going to help things!"

"I HAVEN'T LOST MY TEMPER!" his wife bellowed back. "It's just that this seems so pointless! We're humiliating ourselves!"

"Mum," James began, "once we get the press on side we'll have a lot more power. Once they turn up we'll be in the papers, radio, TV and Internet. There's even some guy in the area who helps run an activist website which is viewed by people all over the world who are interested in this type of action. He could place some photos and stuff on the website, that would help. We'll get people on side. Just wait. Things'll happen."

She huffed. "All right! All right! Well, I'd like to know where these journalists are right now and why they aren't here. Standards these days in the papers! I mean they don't even bother to check their stories with two or three different sources anymore before they print them, did you know?"

"I'm sure they haven't done that for years!" added one of Frank and Edwina's neighbours.

"Yeah, the world seems to have dumbed down," remarked James, "crap, isn't it? Or perhaps I should say *innit?*"

Meanwhile, Frank was lost in thought, staring in at the building, watching for any signs of movement or anyone looking out at them. He wanted to know how rattled the occupants were by the protest. He tried to get a feel for the level of anxiety inside the building, but with no activity visible found it impossible to gauge.

More time elapsed, and eventually the group agreed to go

home. The press still had not arrived and the action seemed to have been successful in merely intriguing and bemusing the passing motorists and pedestrians. They agreed to meet the next day, and managed to get an assurance, more or less, from two local newspapers that they would be there at some stage.

The next day's protest at the same location began quietly, with James, his parents, the same neighbours as the previous day, plus a few extras roped in. There was no sign of the press until around 11am, when a large van pulled up and parked half on the pavement and half on the road, its hazard lights flashing. Out of it stepped two young people, a man and woman, one carrying recording equipment and the other armed with a clipboard. They moved quickly across to where the picketers had formed a huddle outside the closed black iron gates. After identifying themselves they went around speaking with members of the party, beginning with James, whom they recognised. It was his turn now to be wanting them around, a fact he privately suspected was the reason for their non-appearance the day before.

"James," the female reporter asked, after a series of questions and comments had been made, "do you feel certain that Mary is being held inside this building?"

"Yes, we're reasonably sure," he replied.

"Only reasonably? Why are you not completely sure?"

"Because, firstly, there are a number of places they may have taken her, but this is our prime suspect, if you like. Secondly, there is also the possibility, remote as I think it is, that after yesterday's protest they may have moved her somewhere else. We just can't be sure at this stage. But we are sure they have got her somewhere."

"So, if she isn't here, it will mean that, if nothing more, your action is symbolic and will tell the Government that you are on their case, as it were."

"Yes. A little bit like David and Goliath though, isn't it?"

The reporter smiled sympathetically. "Yes, I can see how you would see it like that."

"But don't forget something," his mother called out, "don't forget who won *that* particular battle!"

* * *

The involvement of the press heralded an abrupt turning of the tide. James began receiving calls from well-wishing strangers, and his parents' home in Eastbourne became a drop-in centre for people wanting to join the protest or give backing in some way. There seemed to be a great deal of support all round. The story about Mary, from the public's point of view, had turned from one of mirthful curiosity to one of genuine empathy. It was now a missing person case, and of someone who had, after all, heroically rescued two young boys from drowning. So what if she had said she was from the past? People seemed to have forgiven her for her craziness, and her name began to rise at last above the jokes and petty scandal to an altogether loftier status. Except for Edwina. She still did not like the thought of her son – her only son – being involved (although he still denied there was anything 'like that' going on) with someone who seemed to continually attract controversy. The freezing water of the lake at Hazelwood did little to cool Edwina's private scorn for her normally very sensible son.

On the third day on the picket lines the now much bigger crowd – comprising mostly retired Eastbournites, plus a few of James's neighbours (including George Hodges who, much to the disgust of most of the gathering, brought his pipe with him) – was beginning to organise itself into smaller factions, sharing food and bringing fold-up chairs to make the whole thing more comfortable. More placards were made, and Frank brought a radio along to ease the monotony, under the guise of listening out for any news broadcasts mentioning them. The only quibble then was which station to have it on.

They were not disappointed. The one o'clock news bulletin on BBC Radio 4 had an item on them. After that they started to become known, and instead of quizzical looks from passers by, they received honks and cheers. The occasional passing pedestrians would now smile and make eye contact – or even stop and chat – rather than just scurry past as they had been doing.

But still the iron gates did not open. Still there was no news and no sign of Mary.

THE LETTER, THE WITCH AND
THE WAYWARD

A mysterious letter arrived for James. It was posted in London's central SW1 postcode, and the envelope bore an unmistakable 'On Her Majesty's Service' emblazoned in red across the front. The letter was addressed to him personally, but was not the usual format: there was no letterhead and no name at the bottom – a most unofficial-looking letter springing from a most official-looking envelope. It stated that his current 'picketing of Government premises on the pretext of finding a missing person must cease immediately' and that any continuation of this activism 'could result in formal action being taken' against him and those 'accompanying' him. The author of the letter seemed aware that James held 'a list of information regarding covert Government addresses' and ordered that 'this list must not be shared with anyone, nor must it be copied in part or in full or reproduced in any way'. Furthermore, the list 'should be destroyed immediately'. And 'any further attempts to track down the missing woman could be regrettable'.

James felt a cold chill go through him. He rang his parents and told them to stop the action and tell everybody to forget the pickets. It just wasn't going to work. This David was not going to get the better of that Goliath after all. He read the letter to them and, predictably, they were horrified. They invited him to come and stay with them for a while until everything 'blew over', as they put it. James informed them that he could not come and stay as he had already taken too many days off work and it was too far to commute, and also that he didn't think it would 'blow over'. Regardless of all this he couldn't forget Mary, he told them. Her sudden entry into his life would not just 'blow over'. At least, he told them, he now knew for sure that the Government had her; he surmised that the OHMS envelope had been deliberately used to let him know in no uncertain terms that he had no chance of winning.

Frank was deeply concerned about the letter. He grappled with the notion of speaking to some of his old colleagues again. This situation simply would not do. He had worked for the Government for so many years; he had been a loyal, well-functioning wheel among the other loyal, well-functioning wheels and cogs and he felt profoundly betrayed. Edwina, on the other hand, although finding the letter shocking, was secretly pleased, thinking that this would put an end to the Mary saga. Life could now go on as normal, as it had before the woman's arrival into her son's life. He could get involved more in the local community in his area and get himself another girlfriend. Quite frankly, he should stop wasting time with girls *like her* anyway.

* * *

An elderly woman, bent and arthritic, walked slowly up to the wrought iron gates that shielded the building from the outside world. She stopped and held on to one of the bars, catching her breath. From her stooped position she lifted her head to look up at the building. For a few minutes she just stood there looking, before reaching into her bag. She brought something out and held it in her hands, her swollen joints and thick fingers dwarfing the small object. She seemed to speak out loud to herself for a few minutes, before shuffling off. She slowly rounded the corner and disappeared.

* * *

Two days later James was horrified to see another item on TV about his protest at the Government building, only this time it wasn't him and his entourage but a completely different group assembled. With eyes wide and disbelieving he watched the footage of around twenty elderly people sitting outside the black gates. With just three placards, the group was seated on deck chairs with cushions and the like, and – horror of horrors – chanting in a ritualistic manner. Candles and joss sticks burned, and soft, ethereal music played. Some were clutching photographs and other small items he couldn't quite identify.

The TV reporter said, "It is a special event for the local psychics, seers, shamans and even witches – white witches, I have been told. It is a coming together of people purporting to possess special powers and is something Guildford is not particularly accustomed to seeing, especially not out on the street like this."

It was, the journalist said, "An interesting assemblage. But will it help bring answers to those wanting to know the whereabouts of controversial missing Surrey heroine, Mary Stepney?"

And then James saw her – the old lady who had come to the door with the photographs. She was sitting on a striped deckchair chanting and holding up a photograph. The reporter went to her, asking her a few questions. She was named only as Agnes – *a relative of Mary Stepney.*

James decided to go to the next day's protest, ignoring the warning. He did, however, make something of an attempt to disguise himself, donning sunglasses and a cap. He felt ridiculous. He parked his car in a shoppers' car park in Dorking and walked to the railway station, choosing a twisting, turning route, moving at speed then stopping and waiting and watching for anyone following him. He meandered through the leafy council grounds and past the library, before crossing the busy A24 and heading along the street to reach the station. He boarded a train for Guildford, all the while watching for signs of anyone watching him. He knew it was paranoia, but since receiving the letter he thought anything was possible. Keeping himself concealed, he got off the train at Guildford and immediately boarded a bus to go the short distance to the protest.

Arriving, he was surprised to see the congregation had swelled since the previous day. There were now even more of them, not all of the same ilk, but mostly. Hesitantly, and with a lump in his throat, he approached the woman he now knew as Agnes. She looked up at him with a startled expression which quickly turned to one of happiness when she realised who he was. With an impulse of defiance, he tore off his sunglasses and hat, and sat down on the pavement below her, more or less hidden between other people. Looking into her eyes he sensed a whole world of things he could only guess at: a kindness and wisdom seemed to emanate from her, and a mischievous, youthful spirit shone through, contrasting with her body's apparent feebleness.

"I'm James Harvey," he said, wondering if she really had recognised him.

"I know," she replied huskily before clearing her throat.

"I just thought I'd come along and see how everyone was getting on here," he added.

"Why did you leave here – your demonstration, I mean?" she asked, before quickly adding, "Have you had people threaten you?"

He gasped. "Er, well…sort of…yes." He saw no reason for not telling her about the letter. As he told her what it contained she shook her head and looked up at the sky.

"That is to be expected from these people. They will bully you. But if you stand up to them *publicly* you should be all right. And I mean publicly. Let the people out there know your every move and you will have more protection."

"How?"

She smiled. "If everyone out there knows who you are and what you're doing, the authorities will be, in my opinion, less likely to hurt you or do anything nasty to you. You should tell the papers about the letter too, and any websites, or whatever that you are a member of. Don't cover up what the Government have done – their actions deserve to be spoken about."

"Yeah," he replied, "I think you're probably right. And safety in numbers, huh?"

"Yes."

"Please tell me, Agnes, how you know the truth about Mary."

She smiled and looked around as if searching for the right words. "James, I am a bit of a witch, I suppose."

"How can someone be a *bit of a witch?*"

"Well I guess I am a witch, yes. I don't go in for labels much, you see, but, yes, I am a witch – a white witch. Not the other kind."

He looked astonished.

"I thought you knew, smart boy like you!"

"How would I have known that? And I don't know why you think I'm smart!"

"Hmmff."

"Where did you get the photos of Mary from?" he asked.

"They were passed down to me from my grandmother. She used to tell me all about the people in the photos. She knew them all, every single one of them. I wrote down the names and dates, or rough dates at least, sometimes locations as well, on the backs, if they weren't already there. When I saw Mary's picture in the newspapers and then on television I thought how she reminded me so much of the pretty young lady in some of the old family photos. I talked to my dear friend Donald, who's here today," she gestured towards an elderly man seated a few metres away. "He told me that he caught the Stepney girl, as he called her, poking around more than once at a house on Roseberry Lane. He lives there, you see. He recognised her from the newspaper. He told me that she said she used to live in the house. It was odd. Very odd. We chatted about it…about her. I went and got my old family photos and Donald and I compared them with the newspaper pictures, just for fun, I assure you."

"So you knew it was her just from comparing pictures? You couldn't!"

She chuckled. "No, of course not! That would be madness! There was her story about having lived in the house – that seemed impossible. Donald has known all its occupants since about 1970, would you believe. So there we are, I admit that I then did a bit of a spell."

"*A bit of a spell?* Not quite a *whole* spell then?" he teased.

A look of merriment danced in her eyes and her face lit up. "I asked the forces that be to tell me whether she was the same person. I started to get a funny feeling that she was. It was a very peculiar feeling. And with what Donald was saying too. It seemed very very odd, of course!"

"You're telling me!"

She continued, still animated. "I was told that it was the exact same person. I was right! I then knew that my relative from all those years ago was still alive and walking this earth! A fantastic truth! I knew that somehow she had cheated time and had stayed here. Don't ask me how."

"She didn't so much stay here, Agnes, as come back."

"Eh?"

"Mary disappeared in 1901 and reappeared here, last November. She missed virtually the whole twentieth century!"

"What! Oh! So, she hasn't been alive all this time?"

"No."

"So, she's not like Virginia Woolf's Orlando?"

"Er, no."

"Well, well! That makes more sense now."

"*It does?*" he asked, puzzled.

"Oh yes, my boy, very much so."

PROFESSOR JOHN BEALE: PART ONE

Professor John Beale stood at the front of the room addressing a group of media professionals interested in finding out more about what the esteemed physicist thought was happening in the world: the odd, unexplained events that were now being reported on not only a daily basis, but even minute-by-minute. There were other explanations being put forward that did not involve physics or science, but Professor Beale's one, according to journalist Lyndsey Smith and several of her contemporaries, despite being about as radical as a scientific theory can be, was definitely the one out front by a country mile. It wasn't just what he said. There was something about his manner of presentation that made her and others sit up and listen, and suspend their disbelief for as long as he was speaking: in short, he was engaging and unexpectedly charismatic. An American by birth, the professor had lived in the UK for some time, while still retaining a partial Eastern New England accent. Emanating a likeable confidence, he had, through hard work, earned prestigious places at Princeton University, and now Cambridge. His wholesome, handsome looks had wide appeal, and over the years had made him the subject of a good many students' private imaginings that had nothing at all to do with subatomic particles.

The meeting was informal, more a talk than a lecture, and the professor had not long started on the subject so dear to his heart.

"Professor Beale," one of the journalists asked eagerly, "can you please tell us about how the atmosphere – or whatever – could be disturbed enough that the reported space-time anomalies are able to happen?"

He took a deep breath and thought about how much he would tell them about his theory on this occasion.

"I will answer your question, as that is what I'm here for, but

I would like to take you there via a slightly long and windy road, but it will be, ah, extremely scenic, and will take you to your answer. And it will all make sense in the end...*I hope!*

"Physics, particularly its quantum mechanics arm, is a mysterious subject. It is baffling; it is mind-bending – even to me, still, after all these years!" He laughed. "As a quantum physicist, I have found looking at the intimate functioning of the universe to be a highly challenging yet utterly fascinating area of study, as it makes us question what we believe can be possible; it leads many of us to believe some things that fly in the face of our old scientific teachings. That can be hard. That can be a real stretch. I'll get on to those in due course.

"The subject has its frontier scientists who seem a little like those brave souls so many centuries ago who said the world wasn't flat after all. They said that the world was in fact round: a sphere, to be precise. Very few people believed them at first and they were really mocked and vilified. Weren't some scientific heretics even murdered for what they were saying? New truths don't always get accepted easily, especially when they're controversial...and not always easy to grasp. Anyway, it's a little like that today, except people aren't going to be burnt at the stake for their views! I hope not, anyway! But the trouble is that so many people out there are still to open their minds and their hearts to accepting what has been proven in labs across the world, in good, proper experiments where the effects of extraneous factors influencing results have been prevented...and where sheer chance alone cannot explain the results. But many people," he sighed loudly, "even other scientists – *especially other scientists* – are scoffing at these experiments and the conclusions. Perhaps the scoffers are today's flat-earthers? Yet the implications of many valid and repeatable experiments that challenge the old classical physics are now slowing ebbing out of academia and into the real world, making their way into our culture and our understanding of the world in which we live. And not just physics findings, but also discoveries in cosmology and biology, and in many cases, if not most cases, the three are interrelated. But it is still very much early days. There is a heck of a long way still to go."

"I am – and I know others here will be too – very interested in finding out more about the controversial findings," remarked Lyndsey, "and I know you will be presenting them soon, but it's not the easiest subject for the average layperson to get their head around. Some of my colleagues here are fairly up to speed on the rock-bottom basics of what you are talking about, but there's so much here, and in your theory – what you've told me about it already – that we really need the subject explained as simply as possible." She glanced at her contemporaries and was met by nods and grunts of agreement.

"Okay, Lyndsey, thank you, and of course you're right. It's hard to know where to begin, and I haven't prepared a document or anything. The very mention of physics or quantum mechanics usually sends the non-physics person running. It can intimidate and bore – their eyes glaze over. I've seen it many times. But in order to give you a taste of it, with an emphasis on why I believe physics provides the explanation of how the Unexplained Visual Experiences are occurring, through giving us – if we know where to look – a flashing neon signpost pointing to the rather unlikely culprit – the cause or source of these UVEs around the world – I'll try to give you a summary of some basic findings and interpretations. We are going to have other talks, so this is just a start, an introduction." He paused thoughtfully.

"I'd like to preface it with a statement. I'd like to add that some people – not me, specifically – are saying that *part of* the reason for the serious decline in bee numbers is due to the same thing that I am going to blame for the appearance of the Unexplained Visual Experiences. There is a theory that this same culprit is partly responsible for the bees' increased susceptibility to various toxins and diseases through their immune systems becoming weakened. Some people are saying that humans and other animals are being similarly affected, with weakened immune systems, although there are of course myriad possible causes of these problems, and I'm not· commenting on bees or immune system problems, only the UVEs. But it is food for thought and something we should keep in mind.

"I have some big questions for you. Could it be possible that there are things that exist that we cannot perceive using our five senses or the mechanical apparatuses we have created to supplement them? Could it be possible that the universe is more than just objects moving about according to the classical laws of cause and effect? Could it be possible that what we call space is not empty and passive after all? Could so-called thin air actually be a place of busy activity?" He paused, and looked around, waiting for a reaction but, seeing none other than curiosity, carried on.

"Think of the vacuum we call space. It seems empty, just nothing. But it has been found that this vacuum we call empty space is anything but empty. It is an established fact that the vacuum is actually a sea, composed of waves which spread out through the universe. These waves are like the ripples on a pond. Scientists refer to this field of wave energy in various terms, such as the Zero-Point Field, or just the Field. Whatever you want to call it, it is space...*and time*. In fact, it seems to be *everything*. It comprises supercharged energy, sometimes known as Zero-Point Energy or vacuum energy.[4] It is thought that everything taps into this supercharged field to get energy. This means that a proton, that most elemental part of an atom, refuels by tapping into the Zero-Point Field, this so-called empty space; therefore the Field accounts for the stability of atoms and, therefore, all matter."

Noticing the now pained expressions of concentration on the faces of many of his audience, he began to speak more slowly.

"So, Nature's fields of energy and information are in the air, so to speak. We could say that the inherent energies in the Field, along with all the fields and forces that exist in Nature together form a Unified Field. Or matrix. It seems that our so-called empty space is a cauldron of seething energies. It is hard to imagine that what on the surface appears to be just thin air can hold so much and do so much. I like to tell students to keep in mind that most of the universe is invisible. We see everything our eyes are able to see, but all the rest that's going on is invisible – *to us*.

"As the Field is self-generating, which I'll explain soon, it logically leads us on to the question to be asked – the big question we're talking about: can it be disturbed by us in such a way that could possibly result in the strange happenings that are now occurring everywhere around the world – such as the terrible plane crash in Mexico that Lyndsey reported on? That is a question we will return to once I've explained some more about the background to my theory, but keep it under your hats for now.

"Now, these particles – these protons, electrons, etc – are not solid objects. You've probably heard that before – that nothing is truly solid. At the subatomic level things are not solid but are vibrating, indeterminate packets of energy that cannot easily be quantified or measured.[5] At its core, everything consists of pure energy. *We* are all made up of energy that vibrates so fast we appear as solid matter.

"Now, one of the really odd things about subatomic energy is what scientists say is its way of becoming a wave or a particle seemingly at the drop of a hat. It 'decides' what it will be. And it can, just like that," he clicked his fingers, "become either. Uncertainty is the only thing we can be certain of here.

"I swear I am not making this up as I go!" He winked at a woman whose mouth was hanging open.

"You've perhaps already heard about this: the effect of an observer makes a difference to subatomic energy. That's what makes it take form. It has been found that when a wave of energy receives attention – such as by someone observing or measuring it – it forms a particle, or matter. In other words, it then 'freezes' into a particular state. After we have finished looking or measuring, the particle returns back into the ether-like background of all possibilities.[6] No entity exists in a permanent, stable form. The punch-line of the observer effect is that the thoughts or beliefs of the scientist doing the observing shape the outcome! It seems to go against what we think should happen, doesn't it?

"It's just as well you're all sitting down, because it gets even stranger! It was back in 1982 when things really started to rock and roll. A French physicist using particles proved that an event at one location can affect an event at another location without any apparent mechanism for communication between the two locations.[7] Communication was immediate, as if space and time did not exist. So, our old physics theory that nothing can travel faster than the speed of light wasn't quite right. It would seem that energy doesn't need to travel – it is already one with all other energy – interconnected. Now, that *has* to sound strange to anyone who hasn't heard this before, huh? Albert Einstein, decades earlier, knew about this and had called it 'spooky action at a distance'."

"That is unbelievable!" exclaimed a young woman in the audience. "I'm trying hard to keep up! My mind is freakin' out a bit, I have to say! It's mind-boggling! Is all this – what you're saying – now widely accepted?"

"Yes, it is, although there are a few different schools of thought regarding interpretation, meaning, and so forth. I agree with you that it is mind-boggling. But not all minds want to be boggled. Studies contributing to what seems to be a new, emerging worldview have shown that our old subject-object split is no longer the entire story. There now seems to be no objective reality. That, my esteemed audience, is pretty heavy stuff." His face then became uncharacteristically serious as he searched the faces for signs of genuine comprehension of his last point. "Okay, more on that later. Back to what I was saying a minute ago. Sometimes these packets of energy behave as particles, sometimes as waves. The key concept here is potentiality. Potential. I know, a little confusing. Very uncertain. I see your bewilderment; I see your puzzled faces. What this means is that there is a state of pure potentiality – of infinite possibility – in these subatomic entities at all times. Think about that. Think about the scope: nothing is certain, but everything is possible. And just as a bit of background I should add that subatomic particles have no standing on their own; you must look at their relationships: they are interdependent and indivisible. They are all related: everything depends on everything else. One big system.

"I said I'd explain how the Field is self-generating. What happens is fluctuations of the waves in the Zero-Point Field drive the motion of subatomic particles, and all movement of these particles in turn generates the Zero-Point Field. The flow of life-energy, one could say, continuously regenerates the universal energy. It is a self-perpetuating feedback loop across the universe. Incidentally, this must be the best possible source of energy anyone could ever tap into. Work is being done on this, I know, but it's still some way off till we can run our cars and our TVs on quantum energy, if ever it could be possible. *I would love to see the day!* And, while I'm digressing slightly, before you can ask, I have no intention of explaining the whys and hows of the fluctuations in the waves, which is probably a relief to you all!" He grinned at the journalists, who by this time were uncharacteristically quiet and motionless, as if frozen in their seats.

"When I use the word universal to describe the flow of energy I am not using that word loosely – we *are* talking the universe here. The waves in the Zero-Point Field extend from one end of the universe to another. This means that they effectively tie every part of the universe to every other part. It is all connected. *Everything* is connected, *literally*. People talk more about connectedness these days, and this is where it stems from. As humans, we exchange information with this field of quantum fluctuation. This, however, has the effect of blurring the boundaries between us and everything else."

He paused, looking at each face in turn. All were silent and nobody took their eyes off him. He could tell that the proverbial penny had not as yet completely dropped.

He spoke slowly, selecting his words with care. "What all this means is that it challenges our notions of self and separateness. What it means is that all matter and life in the universe is literally connected. And, what's more, we are connected to the farthest reaches of the universe through this fluctuating field of waves. Everything is one; you cannot chop it up into pieces or segments and think that by looking at just a little bit that you are understanding the whole. This topic needs to be explored in much more depth later."

A couple of people whispered and one giggled.

"Yes, it's very weird and highly controversial, I appreciate that. But don't worry, it's all good!

"I want to briefly touch now on climate. The atmosphere is giving us extremes of weather and sudden changes in climate, much more sudden than has been normal for the Earth. Climate destabilisation is a term we now hear more and more. The atmospheric changes are causing changes in the oceans as well, as glaciers and polar ice caps melt, releasing large quantities of fresh water into salty currents with potentially far-reaching implications for heavily populated continents like Europe. In addition to climate destabilisation, the atmosphere, or, more correctly, the biosphere – which is basically everything: land, living organisms and atmosphere – is now reacting in what seems to be an unwanted yet very natural way to human activities of a highly technological nature. Now, I'm not talking about the burning of fossil fuels here, but other things.

"We have been bombarding the air with all sorts of heavy

artillery for years; I don't mean bombs and weapons but new and more insidious forms of energy. Things we can't see. There is now a heck of a lot of radiation bouncing around: transmitters, mobile phone masts, all sorts of wireless technology, etc, etc, even our electricity meters emit wireless radiation. But while all this is constantly washing around in the air, soup-like – electrosmog or electropollution some people call it – it's small beer compared to some big emissions that are happening out there." He cleared his throat and paused, as if to gather his thoughts.

"A great deal of covert military experimentation has been taking place for decades. These trials occur without the knowledge of citizens, in fact great pains are taken to keep them secret. I am specifically talking about experiments with electromagnetic energy, experiments with sound waves – ones we can't hear, experiments with time, experiments with space and experiments in invisibility. Do any of you know about the famous Philadelphia Experiment?[8] This sort of unusual experimenting has not stopped, but has in fact continued and even increased. Invisibility with anti-radar cloaking is after all the perfect way to sneak into enemy territory and to avoid being a target. On a slightly different note, many of us have heard about the HAARP project[9], in which the US military have built the world's biggest radio-frequency-radiation transmitter and are blasting high-frequency microwave radiation up at the ionosphere, the uppermost protective layer around the planet. It's for scientific and military applications, like knocking out communications and so forth. And I'm certainly not saying it's so, but it is thought by some that there could be other more sinister objectives, such as using electromagnetic technology for the aim of, and I quote, 'manipulating and disturbing human mental processes through pulsed radio-frequency radiation…over large geographical areas'.[10] And weather manipulation, like setting off earthquakes and volcanoes. There are a lot of people back home in the States who are concerned that things like this could even be a possibility. And I do say *possibility*, because we don't as yet know; however, worries like that aside, looking at just the issues of energy and radiation, we are continually pulsing out substantial amounts of human-made electromagnetic energy into the naturally-present electromagnetic energy which already exists in our global environment without understanding what might constitute too much. A critical mass. An overload – sending the planet's force fields into disarray. That's what the crux of my argument is – that we *have* reached critical mass and that the planet is saying enough already. The Earth's protective electromagnetic fields appear to have been damaged. So have we created – and now opened – a Pandora's Box? I think we have.

"To spell it out, I believe Nature is reacting by not being able to prevent some time-space anomalies from happening – the Unexplained Visual Experiences, or UVEs.

"As we did not until relatively recently realise that there exists this complex sea of energy in the air already – the Zero-Point Field – we did not know that this vast structure of energy exchange exists not just in the air but in and around every object in the universe, binding everything together, all planets, all stars and all the spaces between them."

He paused for a moment, and looked contemplative.

"The Field of energy holds everything together, in place, and, as I mentioned, enables relationships and communication between distant objects and organisms. It is structural, and it is quite literally the glue of the universe. If we humans had different sorts of eyes perhaps we would be able to see it. The Field of quantum waves of energy could be crudely likened to a cobweb, one which has been tweaked and poked and stretched for a long time now but has seemed to cope okay and still been able to function properly. But, as it became more damaged, we started inadvertently affecting the navigational and radar capability of some animals – whales, dolphins, migratory geese, etc. Their remote sensing abilities were impaired and they would head off in completely the wrong direction, often with unfortunate consequences. But no other signs or symptoms of a disturbed natural world really came to our attention, and yet they must have been there for a long time, building up. And we seemed not to worry too much about the whales and birds and so forth that we affected – because their plight didn't directly affect *us humans*, you see. We knew it was sad, but it was just 'one of those things'. Our species is very self-, or should I say human-centred.

"It is only now with newer and more powerful technology that the fabric of our world has reached a state whereby it has trouble maintaining its normality at the most fundamental level. It still operates normally almost all the time, but the fabric seems to be so damaged in places – so thin and threadbare – that these strange occurrences, these Unexplained Visual Experiences as we are calling them, are now happening at an accelerating rate.

"In the sea of energy, the conditions have become just right it seems for seemingly random fragments of past times to pop into our time. The timelines are becoming a bit jumbled. Tangled. This is teaching us that we may now need to write a few new laws of physics, because we certainly have not yet got hold of all the rules. We're still very much learning, and we should feel no shame in admitting that.

"Now, let's go back and look once more at the Field in a bit more detail. The devil is in the detail, as you people well know. I hope you're still holding onto your hats – your journalistic mortar boards! What I'm about to say, although hopefully fascinating, might not seem terribly relevant to a discussion about UVEs but, believe me, it is, and just how it fits in will be revealed.

"The Field creates a medium enabling particles, atoms and molecules to 'speak' to each other more or less instantaneously. I'm not sure how many of you know about the experiments – and there have been many – where people have been able to use their thoughts to apparently affect external matter, such as water, human cells and machinery. So, expanding on the effect that an observer has, which I mentioned a little while ago, individuals have been found to be able to affect other things, living or otherwise, through attention. And, specifically, *intention*. I could direct you to a swathe of what are fairly conclusive experiments on this subject; experiments that have found that thoughts and intentions can have measurable effects on a target person, animal or object. Even so-called telepathic activities such as remote viewing have been able to be demonstrated in the lab.[11] Yes, that's *in the lab*. I won't go into remote viewing here, but plenty of information is now available.

"Scientists have been able to change the acid balance in containers of water through human intention,[12] and have been able to change the physical structure and inherent quality of water through directing specific emotional and environmental 'signals' to it.[13] This has been done repeatedly. And intentions have been able to be stored, if you like, in a simple electronic device – a machine. These machines, if you put them next to some water, can affect the water in measurable ways. There have been many other similarly fascinating incidents of this sort of phenomenon. This is frontier science – why is all this stuff not being publicised more?! All are examples of the mind working outside the body. It's what some people call the *non-local* mind.[14] Scientists at the cutting edge believe that when we are alive in our bodies our consciousness is present everywhere in the body at once, not just in the head, and that we naturally extend beyond our bodies with this non-local mind ability. I think this is much too complex a subject to discuss here, but if anyone wants to come and see me after the session I can refer them to several studies on a unified theory of mind and matter. They provide good physical evidence of a world completely interconnected at the most fundamental level.[15]

"Might it be possible, therefore, to say that we humans

possess a great deal more mind power than we thought? Obviously, it's up to the individual to be interested in this or not be interested, but, at an anecdotal level, I'm sure most of us have had times when we've suspected that a bad mood we've been in has affected our computer or our car or some other machinery. I know I have. Most of us have had a plethora of odd occurrences where our intuition has made us suspect that there is more to this existence than we have been led to believe; that we are not confined to our heads and bodies and, dare I say it, nor are we so separate from each other."

"And every*thing*?" questioned one of the journalists.

"Exactly! Now, there is one more thing about the Zero-Point Field that I'd like you to know. I could leave it out, but…I've decided just now to include it.

"The Field is, as you already know, a vast sea of energy. I've mentioned how it functions and how it is self-perpetuating, and how the energy within it behaves, but many of you seated here today may not be aware that it is not only energy but also a recording medium." He paused to allow his words to sink in.

"That's right. You heard right. To add to the general weirdness of the Field, it seems that it is busily imprinting events that have happened in the universe.[16] Amazingly, it is now believed that the Zero-Point Field carries information on everyone who has ever existed and on everything that has ever happened. All knowledge; all events; all history of the cosmos. It is stored there, in the fabric of the Field. Many of us have heard of the Akashic records. They're also known as the Universal Mind, the mind of God or Allah, and so forth; and in the Bible it's called the Book of Life. And for those of you who believe in karma, well, if it exists, then this is where it is all recorded and how it happens. Anyway, I realise it's not the easiest thing to comprehend – I, myself, have had to grapple with it – and a lot of people like to pooh-pooh this, but the waves do appear to be a complete archive, if you like, on all people, all places, all events, all animals, everything. All cats, all cows, all rainy Sundays, all apple pies have been imprinted in a permanent record. Imagine all the kind words you've ever said – or otherwise! All the times you've smiled at someone, or helped someone – made someone feel good. Every sparrow is known unto them. Every hair on your head. In Indian culture there is air, fire, water, earth and akasha – the universal womb, so to speak. So, the Field is said to be, among other things, the universal records, and virtually all religions have spoken of these records, and it is exciting to say that cutting-edge scientists are now busy working on understanding this, and a new, revolutionary picture of the universe is fast emerging.

"It seems all knowledge and information is there, as well, of course, as the vast amount of energy. It is a unified information- and memory-field. Proponents of this view state that there is nothing that is not there. *Nothing at all.* They say there is nowhere else.

"This is big stuff. I know I'm throwing a lot at you at once. It must seem a bit heavy to those who haven't heard any of this before. I can see by the looks on some of your faces that this talk is going to lead to some spin-off talks! And I'm in trouble with a few of you, aren't I? I'm going to carry on regardless!

"So, how do our minds really work then? It is now being said that we are all continually interacting with the information in the Field at a sub-conscious level. The studies I'm talking about here conclude that the brain is the middle man, so to speak, between us and the Field. What we have lurking, or in some cases rattling, in the space between our ears is now believed to be a retrieval mechanism tapping into the Field – and a frequency analyser, stopping us becoming overwhelmed by the limitless information contained in the Field."[17]

"What about consciousness?" asked one of the journalists.

"That's one of the big questions. Materialist scientists – the mainstream, in other words – maintain that awareness, or consciousness, is basically just a biochemical secretion; that we are basically just walking, talking chemistry sets. Now, who here feels that they are just a biochemical secretion? Anybody?"

No hands went up.

"No, neither do I. In fact, I find it insulting. There is so much overwhelming empirical evidence pointing *away* from that conclusion. And non-empirical evidence – although scientists don't pay any serious attention to that. But there is so much work still ahead of us: we need to incorporate consciousness into science. Some people already even say that in reality the field of science sits *inside* consciousness, not outside. They say that universal consciousness, not matter, is the foundation of all existence – of everything that is.[18] If this is true, then consciousness is the precursor to physicality. I hope this is all making sense. Or that *some* of it is making sense." He took a drink of water and cleared his throat.

"Professor Beale," Lyndsey began, "is what you are saying that there is now scientific proof that the likes of René Descartes were wrong and that Mother Nature is not mechanistic, random and without order, but is inherently intelligent and purposeful? That the universe is…well, this is going to rankle with some people, but does it now seem that the universe is conscious?"

"Again, I need to stress that it's up to the individual to decide what they take from all this, but, yes, it could well be argued that based on scientific findings the universe does seem to be conscious. Ergo, it is intelligent and purposeful." There was a ripple of reaction in the room. "Furthermore, to use your Descartes analogy, 'I think, therefore I am' now becomes 'I think, therefore I *affect*'. I affect energy, circumstances, matter, other living beings, etc.

"As I said a little while ago, some scientists now believe that consciousness, not matter, is the foundation of everything that is. There is a constant flow of information at the quantum level between everything, including organisms and their environment, consciousness and energy, and so forth. If we are in the right frame of mind – and that means being more active in your right brain hemisphere than your left, incidentally – things like creativity, inspiration and intuition come to us from the Field – we learn how to interact with it and reap the rewards. Getting in the 'zone' – this is where the zone is.

"It seems, therefore, that there are two levels of *physical* reality and not just one: there is the world we already know – the world we see around us, plus there's the world that we cannot see – the world of the very tiny, quantum processes going on all around us. This is where intention is effective; this is where it all happens. And what about after we die? One well-regarded scientist has said that when we die we experience a 'decoupling' of our frequency or life force from the matter of our cells.[19] He believes that we are then returned to the Field – the home of the spirit world; the home of everything.

"Now, if an observer, by the very act of observing, is able to settle an electron into a set state, in my mind it begs the question to what extent could he or she influence reality on a grand scale?"

The professor paused and looked keenly at his audience. "We now know that intention can influence outside entities, so…there is a lot to think about. We now know that people who are close to each other, such as a happily bonded couple, have an effect nearly six times as great as single operators in influencing the outcome of trials involving instruments called random event generators.[20] Random event generators are mathematical machines that work in their own mechanical way, oblivious to outside forces, until, that is, someone comes along and makes them behave oddly. These machines have even been taken to locations and events where there has been a powerful collective mood with an intense atmosphere. At the peak of the intensity these machines have reacted out of the ordinary, in a way that seems impossible. Yet this has been repeated time after time.[21] We think that the Field has been behaving differently at these times and we put this down to living beings imprinting upon the Field. This consciousness in action includes at times what could be called a collective consciousness. We've all heard this term before. The feeling in places like London at the end of the Second World War with the street parties and so forth; the Woodstock concert in 1969; the death of Princess Diana; the aftermath of the 2001 World Trade Centre attacks – these were examples of our collective consciousness in action. People talk about an atmosphere, something almost palpable. It's an intensity that is shared. And now it can also be measured.

"Evidence suggests that when we wish or intend for something to happen we are sending it 'out there': it gets imprinted in the Field and it is made real, so to speak. It seems that *thoughts are things*. Thoughts are things that affect other things. And that affect yourself. You can hurt yourself or someone else, or help someone. And not just some*one*, but many people. And not just people – animals, whole species, entire communities and regions. Once day we might even choose to go global with these abilities – these abilities to help."

"Here, here."

"I know it sounds very weird, like Alice's Adventures in Wonderland come to life—"

"Alice on heroin!" interjected a man near the back. Everybody laughed.

"But there really is nothing hocus-pocus about all the things I've just said. I know it's heavy stuff, and can be hard to grasp – I'm sorry if I've left your heads spinning. I know that a recording of this talk will be made available, so that might help, as I know there's a lot to take in here. But this is the truth that is emerging about the basic composition and functioning of our universe. Like it or loathe it, it isn't going to go away. This is being talked about more and more now, although I expect believers in the current paradigm – the current ideas – will take a long time to change. That's always the way. And there are so many – *so many*

– vested interests that will want to keep things the way they are, and that means keep the thinking the way it currently is. So, as you people all know, it partly depends on who owns the media: the TV channel, the website, the newspaper, the magazine, and so forth. Even who owns the bookstore. And it's hard to be different from everyone else. It's hard to be someone standing on the sidelines, telling a different story to what everyone else is saying. But we have to ask ourselves whether for the sake of us all that is what now must be done.

"I recommend that journalists such as yourselves – those of a more, shall we say, open-minded and critical-thinking bent – go and find out more. See what you can take from all this stuff. Does any of it work for you or resonate with you? If so, maybe you should consider going about spreading the word. You are journalists – you hold *so much power* in today's world. So much power to influence. I wonder what would happen if more people understood this stuff at the layman's level. I wonder what the world would be like if the average person knew that there is an underlying order to everything – a governing intelligence. What would happen if they started to think that existence isn't random and isolated and purely genetic; that we are not alone, and that we are all part of the most wonderful web of life and of exciting potentiality? *What would happen?* We can use this to heal ourselves, to heal others and to heal the planet. I personally think its time has come! It is desperately needed and we are ready for this! I would like you to go forth and help the world...NOW!"

UNCIVIL SERVICE

Frank Harvey leapt on to the back of the old schoolmate at Whitehall who had given him the list of government houses. Deciding he had nothing to lose, Frank tried for more information, going so far as demanding to have Mary released from wherever it was she was being held and to know who it was that had sent the threatening letter to James. But this time the man refused to help. Old school chums or not, the man would go no further. From his home by the sea Frank began firing another series of brickbats up to London, at the edifice he had once laughingly called his 'home away from home'. To him now, his years of loyal and dedicated civil service seemed to count for very little. As if forgetting that he had already managed to extract something important which he should not have been given, he began to postulate that central government was, and always had been, a one-way street: you were required to bend and buckle as far as you could for The Establishment, but if you dared question anything or ask for anything above the ordinary in return you were whistling in the wind.

Frank ignored his wife's pleas for him to give up on Mary. He would walk around the house humming quietly, his gaze miles away, lost in invented scenarios of confrontations with his former colleagues. He could picture himself with them, seated around a wooden table, coffee cups, pads and diaries at hand, warming their hands over old radiators, complaining about early morning meetings. And then the vision would mutate from comfortable routine to one of defensive words, hardened expressions and thinly concealed resentment. If he allowed the fantasy to continue after that it inevitably became a shouting match, with red faces, lost tempers and someone storming out of the room – which was what he felt like doing whenever Edwina's pestering got too much. He would stomp outside, don his forest-green wellington boots, and get stuck in to the pruning or weeding or general tidying up. There was always something to do in the garden. Edwina, more content to stay indoors unless the sun was streaming down, worried that he might be biting off more than he could chew; no one who wanted a nice quiet life – especially one at lovely, peaceful Eastbourne – chose to take on The Establishment. Sure, you could sign the occasional petition or write to your MP, but you did not go marching in, guns blazing, and insist that people divulge classified information. And certainly not twice! Once was enough! And, my word, he should be grateful for getting that! He can be so pig-headed! Normally so placid and easy-going, now, thanks to this Stepney woman, he's going much too far. Surely James's girlfriend or whatever she is isn't worth all this. This Government is not renowned for any particularly unscrupulous behaviour – they will let her go soon, if she really is no threat to the country. The UK, Edwina thought, is not one of those countries that does illegal and immoral things to its citizenry. They tend to treat their own pretty well. Although there were, she admitted in the back of her mind, a few question marks hanging over some incidents that had leaked out – but who was to say? Surely not Frank!

Frank whistled defiantly as he noticed Edwina looking out the kitchen window at him, mouthing something about another email coming through from someone or other in the Government. He should read it, she said, calling up at the open window which was not open quite enough to allow him to catch all her words.

"Eh?" he shot her a puzzled look. A clump of soil dropped off the spade he was holding.

"Another angry email!" she yelled up at the window, standing on her tip-toes.

"Oh," he replied, "another one. Hmmff. Something'll turn up."

"Yes! Probably the same people as those you say took Mary Stepney!"

"Don't be silly!" He went to walk away, looking for places to use his spade.

"Frank! Just give up! It's not going to work! They'll let her go when they're good and ready, not before. What makes you think you can shake the tree so much that it drops what you want? It's foolish! You'll be put on a list!"

"I'm sure I already *am* on a list!" At that moment he noticed that the young buddleia needed the secateurs. Grabbing them from where he had left them on the patio he headed down the garden to the small tree.

"Aargh!" Edwina growled, storming off upstairs.

Later Frank read through the emails, spotting the one that had so upset his wife. It was from a former work acquaintance, someone who had been the sort to say yes to absolutely everything you asked. A yes-and-I'll-do-that-for-you-right-now type of person. More precisely, he was a how-high-would-you-like-me-to-jump? sort of person. Good to have in any office, so long as they can actually think for themselves as well. This chap, according to Frank, was an excellent all-rounder, not one to really be in charge of anything, but he wasn't and never had been, so he fared well. Frank had asked him to chase up the old school chum for him. The Yes Man had initially told Frank that he would chase the man up, no problem, they were on good terms. But then something must have been said, Frank thought, for the Yes Man to be sending him an email telling him politely but firmly to back off and stop hassling the Old Boy; it wasn't going to get anywhere, the Yes Man said, as no one there could disclose classified information, no matter what, especially to someone who didn't even work in Whitehall anymore. Unaware of Frank's earlier success in getting secret information, the Yes Man at last demonstrated that he did in fact have the ability to say no, even if it was on behalf of someone else, while stressing to Frank that in the interests of security, strict rules and regulations had to be followed. Frank felt that it was almost patronising, and saw it as a declaration of exactly where the line lay. His sudden feeling of disconnection and isolation from the old network – the complex but comfortable mechanism he had been a part of – hit him hard.

THE WOMAN IN THE ROOM

Agnes stood at the door of the house waiting for someone to let her in. It had been a long trek by train, having to go through London on the way, and then finding not just the house but the road it was on had been like an expedition across Africa for the taxi driver. A remote former mansion in a remote part of north-eastern Essex had made for a scenic, yet tiring journey for one her age.

Looking up, she admired the Victorian architecture with its fancy adornments and styles. Aesthetics, she mused, were all important: this life is too precious to spend without surrounding yourself with beauty when at all possible. She noticed the way a leafy climber wound its way determinedly up a wooden pillar and hung freely at the top, looking to go even higher. She ran her fingers across its glossy leaves.

"The sky's the limit, my friend," she murmured.

There was a buzzing sound and the door opened. Standing in the doorway was a tall, skinny man dressed in a dark suit. He smiled politely, exposing oversized teeth.

"Mrs Woodham-Walter, do come in."

"Thank you." She wiped her shoes on the mat and stepped inside. The entry hall was lit by a series of lights suspended low from the ceiling. She noticed several unmarked doors to the sides. It all looked very nondescript, with a large room at the end of the hall, well-illuminated, with what looked like partitioned offices.

"I have to ask you for some ID, please. Passport? Driving licence?"

"Oh, yes," she fumbled and produced her driving licence from her handbag.

He dashed to a nearby photocopying machine and took a quick scan before handing the card back.

"Thank you. In here, please," he motioned her towards one of the side rooms. The door opened from the other side. A stern-looking man in a grey suit asked her to sit down with him at a desk.

"Mrs Woodham-Walter, you understand this is most unorthodox." He sat down, scraping his chair across the wooden floor as if to emphasise the seriousness of his words.

She wasn't sure if it was a statement or a question. "Yes, I know. I can but try, you see."

"Hmmm."

She tried to smile at him but knew it wouldn't wash.

"You have been very," he paused, "successful at determining her location."

Agnes said nothing.

"You know we had to move her from Surrey because of you, and now you have found her once again. It is most impressive. I don't know how you could have known; this has been a closely guarded operation. Perhaps we should have you in here as well?"

Still she said nothing.

Sighing, he added, "So you see we are allowing you this visit on the condition that you maintain *strict* confidentiality. We have decided that there is no point in moving her again, as you'd most likely be able to find her, even if we took her to the Isle of Skye or a cave in the Pennines."

She looked down at her hands.

"So, whilst you are not out of our sight, it has been agreed to let you have this visit. One visit only. Make the most of it."

He picked up a piece of paper and looked at it for a few moments.

"I need you to sign this. I'll wait for you to read it through first if you want." He handed it to her. "It's a statement saying that you will not disclose to anyone any details of anything you see, hear or witness here today. You are forbidden from telling anyone about the location of this house and what is contained here – not that you will see much, of course. This is important for security reasons, you understand?"

She knew it was a question that time. "Yes, I understand. I'll sign." She duly complied and returned the paper.

"Thank you." He took it, signed it, and stapled it to another piece of paper then placed it on the desk.

For a few tense moments they just looked at each other. She cleared her throat. He looked at his watch, and pushed a few keys on his laptop computer before getting up and leaving the room.

As he went he said, "Please wait in here. Someone will be in shortly to get you." The door shut and she heard some quiet discussion outside in the corridor.

She waited, too frightened to move in case they heard the chair creak and thought she was up to something. Snooping. She wouldn't want to get on the wrong side of these people, she could tell that much. But she could not stop her eyes moving around the room, taking in as much as they could. Not a lot to see, she thought. It looked like a normal enough office. Except that she thought it was not at all personalised; it was as though this man – if indeed it was his office – had not wanted to grace it with any family photos, certificates, cute or funny things – nothing. Not even a personal interest-type calendar to be seen. He must, she thought, not feel particularly at home here. Must have a strong cut-off between his private self and his working environment. At work just to work and nothing else. Or perhaps, she wondered, he thought he might get the chop at any time. There was, she thought, a feeling in the very air that it might be that sort of place. That would make me not want to bring much of my true self to work too, she thought. The door swung open. It was the man who had let her into the building. With a sweep of his thin arm he invited her to follow him out of the room and along the corridor. He ushered her into a small room and on to one of four chairs. The room also had a square table and a telephone mounted on the wall. There was little else. He left without saying anything.

Again, Agnes waited. She sat patiently, this time with not much to look at or think about, except what she was there for.

A few minutes later the door opened. Standing before her was a pale woman wearing ill-fitting jeans and a baggy sweatshirt. Her head was down and she seemed to not want to make eye contact. The door closed behind her and a woman's voice called out to Agnes, "Mrs Woodham-Walter, you have fifteen minutes. If you need anything please dial 1 on the phone in there. The door will be locked until the fifteen minutes is up."

Agnes's mouth hung open as she looked the woman up and down. "My dear child...what have they done to you?!"

* * *

James resumed his solitary existence, reading books again, going to the pub with friends and watching football on the TV. His interest in local history went on the backburner. He didn't want to be reminded of 'the past' in any way. He tried hard to think of things other than Mary, trying to engross himself in as many interests as he could. He travelled down to Eastbourne one Sunday for lunch with his parents; however, all that his father could talk about was how to try further to get Mary released. His mother went about trying to shut her husband up, but James guessed that this was due not to the pain of the subject, but to her unwillingness to pursue the matter any further.

"Your cousin Charlie's just had his fourth birthday," Edwina commented as she passed the dish of potatoes to James.

"Has he? He's such a lovely kid. Must've been a bit of a rave, eh?"

"It was lovely. Your father and I went."

"Why wasn't I invited?"

"We thought you'd be out picketing with those, er...those

people who have taken over the picket at Guildford."

"*Those people*, as you put it, have not taken over!" James argued. "They're just maintaining a visible protest. For God's sake, they're fantastic! What they're doing is really admirable!"

"Aren't they a bunch of retired witches and the like?" Frank asked.

"Don't be silly!" said Edwina. "Witches don't retire. They keep going."

"They are retired, yes," James said. "But witches? A few of them, maybe. But certainly not all. Anyway, does that matter? They are people who care – and who have the time and motivation to do something about it. Without them out there this pressure on the Government would have dissolved by now." He averted his eyes from his father as he spoke. "It's not as though anyone else is doing anything!"

With that, Frank reared up out of his seat. "I'll have you know that I have pushed every button and tried to twist every bloody arm I ever thought I could twist to get her out of there! It's not my fault if once you've left the civil service no one pays any attention to you!"

"Frank! Calm down!" Edwina tried to pull him back down into his seat.

After seething for a moment he sat down.

"Dad, I'm sorry," James said, "I really am. I know you've tried to move mountains. It's just that nothing's happening and she's still in there. It's so unfair. It's just not right that they can do this!"

"With the anti-terrorism laws now they can do virtually whatever they want," Edwina remarked. At least we're not as bad as some countries here."

"What are you saying?" James demanded. "That she's *probably* not being held in a black site, as a ghost detainee, or being tortured? And what? Because we're far too civilised for that sort of thing? Don't make me laugh!"

Edwina ignored the remark, continuing, "But I know our

country is by no means lily-white—perhaps often guilty through association. Perhaps the CIA are behind all this? Yes, I'm sure that will be the explanation!"

"Could also be immigration issues they're interested in," Frank offered. "I wonder."

"She's English! And she's done nothing wrong!" James insisted. "That rumour that she's from 1901 is why they've taken her, it's about—"

"Hang on," his father butted in, "she's been going around telling people in interviews that she *is* from 1901, so it's not exactly a rumour."

"Yeah, okay, but the whole 1901 thing is why they've taken her."

"Well they must be totally bonkers believing that!" said Edwina, with a mouthful of food. "How could anyone believe that?"

"Absolutely!" Frank agreed. "But I know they're very interested in these space-time anomalies that are happening. UVEs, or whatever they're called. They're employing more people to look into this sort of thing now, and I know GCHQ are well into it."

"Waste of taxpayers' money!" said Edwina. "They could spend that money on making sure our local councils are better funded, so that they can perform all their services properly!"

"Probably comes under the black budget," James mumbled.

Frank's fists hit the table on either side of his plate as he boomed, "The whole world is a bloody shambles!"

James, calmer now than both his parents, added, "So I don't know what we can do now except wait. They should release her soon, surely."

"I think you might be being a bit on the naïve side," said Frank.

"I think they'll *have* to release her soon," James continued. "It's not like she's a threat to the country. They'll just be doing tests and things."

"Ooh, horrible," said Edwina, screwing up her face.

"Yes," Frank began. "I suppose to them she's a bit like an alien discovered inside a spaceship that's crashed."

"When was this?" asked Edwina.

"No! I'm speaking hypothetically. They'll want to test her like she's a tree or a rock or something where you can measure the age – the level of molecular decay or something, isn't it? Carbon testing?"

"Frank, don't be silly. How can they carbon date a person?"

"I don't know. They'll find a way, I'm sure."

James smiled wryly, shaking his head. "Even if they could do that – which, come to think of it, I'm sure they can – the age of her body doesn't reflect the fact that she was born in 1871."

"WHAT!" erupted Edwina. "You don't seriously believe that she has travelled from the past to the present?"

"I wasn't saying that. What I mean is if they tested her they wouldn't have success in proving this story, anyway. They'd have to let her go."

"Still being naïve, I say," said Frank, reaching for the salt.

"We'll see," said James, hurrying through his meal so that he could leave.

* * *

"Mary, I…" Agnes didn't know what to say or where to begin.

There was no response.

"Mary, I've come to talk to you, to see how you are."

"Ma'am," came the reply, still not looking.

"Sit down…please sit down," Agnes dragged a chair closer. "What have they done to you? Please talk to me, Mary."

Slowly, the figure sat down, looked without interest around the room and glanced at Agnes.

Mary spoke quietly, "You're not from here. You're not one of them."

"No, dear," Agnes replied. "I'm not one of these people. Heaven forbid. Listen, we only have fifteen minutes, so I need to speak fairly quickly."

"Very well."

"Mary, I have been tracking you down. I know they moved you up here from Surrey recently. Are you being treated all right?"

Mary shrugged her shoulders and mumbled, "Mmmm. Not badly."

"Hmmff. Well you don't look that great if you'll forgive me for saying."

Mary said nothing.

Agnes moved closer to Mary and deliberately and noisily scraped the soles of her shoes across the wooden floor as she whispered in her ear.

"Listen, I want to get you out of here. I'll bet they've bugged the room and there's probably a camera somewhere, so I'll try and say some things so they can't hear."

Mary nodded.

Agnes continued whispering, "I might be able to get you out. I will devote myself to doing this, and doing this as soon as I can. You poor girl, you don't deserve to be held prisoner like this. You must be freed. Leave it to me. I can work wonders. I found you here and got myself in here, didn't I?"

Mary turned and looked at her with a new interest. Her eyes scanned Agnes's face, around and around, and down to take in the entire extent of the bent old woman seated beside her.

Agnes stopped scraping her shoes and moved back to her previous position.

"So, Mary," she resumed her normal pitch, "I hope you're eating all right. Are you?"

"Who-who are you?" Mary enquired.

Agnes smiled. She placed her hand on top of Mary's. "I'm terribly sorry. Mary, my dear, my name is Agnes Woodham-

Walter. I need to confess that I'm the person who went to the newspaper with the old photos of you. And I told them that you're from 1901. Mary...*I am so sorry.* I am *really sorry.* I didn't realise what I was doing. I did it for the sake of truth. I believe strongly in truth. And I guess I thought that somehow it would be good for people to know this – good for them, somehow. But I now know that what I've done has caused you no end of problems. *And now this!"* She gestured around the room. "Locked up! It's all my fault and I'm so sorry! And I'll make it up to you...by what I said a minute ago. And there's something else I should tell you. I'm a relative of yours. That's how I had the photographs of you."

Mary's eyes widened and she stared dumbstruck at Agnes. Then a flash of joy swept across her face.

"A relative? Truly?"

"Yes! My parents were Alfred and Matilda Perkins. Matilda – my mother – was your sister Matilda! Mary, you're my aunt!"

Mary gasped and her hands flew up to her face. Her eyes watered.

Agnes was radiant. "It's true! Isn't it all so incredible! I'm so excited that you're here! Not *here* in this building, of course, but at this period in time, I mean. But it must be so unfathomably hard for you. I can only begin to imagine."

"Yes, I have to admit it isn't easy. Are you really who you say you are?"

"Yes! I grew up in the same area as you, only much later. I inherited a lot of photos from my mum when she died. Oops..."

"It's all right," Mary said calmly, "I know they're all dead now. Of course they would be. I know about the dates and who did what – James, Mr Harvey – has put together a most thorough and wonderful family history book for me. It was his gift to me for my last birthday." She suddenly looked sad.

"Oh, how lovely! He's a very nice man, isn't he?" Agnes said.

"Yes," Mary said at a near whisper. "Mrs Woodham-Walter,

do you know how he is getting along? They haven't taken him as well, have they?"

"Oh, please call me Agnes. No, they haven't taken him. He's fine. He misses you terribly though, and is trying to find you. And he's been taking leave from his job to picket outside a Government building in Guildford – the one you were being held in before I, er...before I contacted them."

"Oh, please tell him he must not do that! He must go back to work! He must not lose his job over me! Tell him I'm not there now anyway."

Agnes thought for a moment before replying, "Mary, I can't tell anyone that you've been moved here to Essex. I signed an agreement."

"I'm in Essex?" Mary said, startled. "I had no idea. They don't tell me anything. I knew we travelled some distance. I had only a small window. I knew we passed through a long tunnel."

"Yes, I suppose that would've been when you drove under the Thames at the Dartford crossing. You're now located about twenty minutes out of Colchester. Very pretty countryside, not that that's any comfort to you."

"Oh." Mary thought for a moment. "I'm afraid geography played second fiddle to my English literature studies."

Agnes smiled warmly. "Are they treating you well?" she asked.

"I'm all right. They feed me well, I must say, but as they have removed my freedom...I must say that no, I am not being treated well. I have committed no crime except being different. I am no threat to anyone, yet they talk about security concerns. They say they are allowed to do this because of some laws they have. It's ridiculous and makes no sense to me, but what is there for me to do? What sort of country has this become? Or is it just the changed times we are part of? I wonder. And what will they get from holding me here?"

"Information, I suppose. How they'll be able to work out how you got here is anybody's guess though. I don't see how they'll be able to. Listen, are they hurting you at all? I can get you a solicitor. Heaven knows, you should have one!"

"No, it doesn't matter. Not yet anyway. If I'm here much longer though I might want one, only I don't know how I'd pay for one."

"I don't think you need to worry about things like that."

"Yes, but they cost more money than I have...don't they?"

"I don't think you'd have to pay for a solicitor, dear, I think you have access by right."

Mary nodded gratefully. "Oh. And no, they're not hurting me. They are, however, subjecting me to a barrage of tests. Some are just medical and nothing much. Some are so silly. Some are baffling. And some are plain vulgar and distasteful."

Agnes looked uneasy. "Nothing they shouldn't be doing, I hope?"

"No, I suppose not. I just think them showing me photographs of all sorts of things can get a little tedious and some of the photographs are not particularly suitable for ladies or polite society, if you know what I mean."

"Oh, I see, well anyway, as I said before, you'll be fine, just hold on...you know." She winked at Mary.

"Oh, yes...I, er, hope so." Mary replied uncertainly.

"Mary, I'm family, remember that. And I remember what my sweet old uncle Thomas used to say."

Mary gasped.

"Yes, your brother Thomas, he'd say 'Chin up old hen, the fox hasn't got you yet!'"

Mary leaned forward with excitement. "*Yes! Thomas!* Dear Thomas! He *did* say that! I remember! You really *are* family! You remember his silly old saying! Bless you, Agnes! And thank you, *thank you* for coming to see me! You have restored my faith and hope."

Agnes beamed. "Good! Those are things you must *never* lose, no matter what! I can only imagine how hard all this must be for you. Now I think our fifteen minutes must be near a close. Best not be whipped away in mid-sentence, eh?"

* * *

As Agnes's train snaked its way across the flat Essex countryside she had time to think. She was still formulating her plan when the tranquil greenery increasingly gave way to old terrace housing, row upon row, heralding the arrival into central London. At Liverpool Street Station the train terminated and she had to get off and make her way across town to Victoria Station, from where she caught her train home. She was just coming to a decision about what to do when the train finally rolled in to Dorking. Exhausted, Agnes spent the remainder of the day going over and over her plan in her mind: it must work; it *had* to work – Mary's freedom and wellbeing depended on it. But it had to be done in such a way that none of the authorities holding Mary would know it was happening. How to outsmart those who consider themselves the pinnacle of smartness; those supposedly able to extract information from anyone, anywhere, about anything. That evening she rang Donald and put her scheme before him.

"WHAT!" he shouted, causing her to move the phone away from her ear. "Yer must be mad, woman! How can that work?"

"Donald! It can work, you'll see! I have thought this through, you know. I've thought about possible pitfalls at every stage, or at least I think I have. I'm pretty sure I've got a plan which has a very good chance of succeeding. It feels like the thing to do. Oh, have faith in me!"

"Oh, yer crazy woman! I hope it does work. If it doesn't yer may find yerself in more than just a spot of bother."

"I know."

"And yer'll have police and secret wotsits following yer

around and listening in on yer phone calls."

"What?"

"Yer might already 'ave that now!"

"No! Donald, don't be so paranoid. They haven't got enough reason yet to do that to me!"

"Hmmff. You know what they can be like."

"Yes," she conceded. "Although they'd have to believe me to be an actual threat to do that, wouldn't they?"

"Well, I suppose so."

"Well, how could they consider *me* to be a threat? An old woman. A feisty, it could be said eccentric woman...just a relative of Mary's. How is that a threat?"

"Yes, they shouldn't think that you are. Not at this stage anyway. Mind you, 'ow did they respond to you knowing where Mary is? That must be drawing attention to yerself, considerable attention."

"Yes, actually Donald, I've just realised that they could be thinking I'm a very big risk. Come to think of it, they probably are listening in to this phone call now!"

"I haven't heard that funny clicking sound though that they say you get," Donald said, "so maybe they haven't got round to it yet."

"Oh, this just sends shivers up my spine! I've got to go away and rethink. Donald I'll let you know what I decide."

PROFESSOR JOHN BEALE: PART TWO

Professor John Beale was at his desk, wading through recently received emails. Some he could ignore, some he needed to read then file, while others needed some sort of response. Seeing one he had received from someone who called himself an under-graduate psychology student, his blood boiled as he read his request for comment. The lengthy diatribe proposed that the weird space-time events happening around the world were likely to be due to nothing more than the effect of drink or drugs, people wanting to be in the limelight, and even mass halluci-nation. Professor Beale swore as he scrolled down the screen until he came to:

> '...it is a well-known premise of psychology that mass hallucination can and does occur. It has been reported in many parts of the world. The 'witnesses' are usually all together in one place when it happens. It's a kind of self-hypnosis. The term mass hallucination would certainly explain these peculiar events in which people report seeing into the past or the future or some other anomaly. I would welcome your comments.'

He didn't know where to begin. He had an impulse to just ignore the email, but couldn't resist sending a short rebuttal.

'Rather than just attempt to debunk your notions of mass hallucination, alcohol, drugs, etc as the explanation', he wrote, determined to be brief and not waste much time on this shrink-in-the-making or wannabe Freud, 'I would simply say that there appears to be a large number of sightings where the witness or witnesses were responsible and trusted members of society, such as court judges, academics, air force officers and senior police. It certainly seems that there are too many of these happenings for them all to be dismissed outright as false or otherwise halluci- natory. I suggest you delve deeper into some of these cases and try to put your personal opinions on hold. Remember, good and proper science is where the investigator is open to whatever outcome, and is not conducting research as a *fait accompli*. (You seem to already 'know' the answer). I would add that anecdotal information suggests that only a proportion of the sightings are being officially reported – most go unreported for fear of ridicule. I don't blame them. So, for the sake of gathering good, sound data and arriving at sensible conclusions, please refrain from calling them hallucinators, drunks, drug-takers, liars, idiots, attention-seekers and whatever else you threw at them in your email. Regards, John Beale.'

He clicked on 'send' and a feeling of satisfaction went through him. There you go, you smug little bastard, take that! He decided that if the student emailed again he would ignore him.

John Beale's preferred explanation for the strange goings on was one he had told very few people – until now. Not many, he had felt, in his wider professional circle would accept his version of how and why things were going awry in the biosphere. Yet to him it was an accepted fact that science had now demonstrated (and explained) at least the mechanical side of how some very bizarre and even supposedly supernatural phenomena was able to occur. He was impressed by the work done by scientists at hallowed universities such as Princeton, Stanford and Vienna, particularly their ability to show, through what was deemed to be scientifically robust experimentation, the extraordinary features of the very fabric of the universe at its smallest, most mystifying levels, and how it is receptive to the actions of living beings. Through what seemed to be intelligent, natural law, he saw how potentiality and innate connectedness formed the basis for all life, all matter and all the spaces in between things. Tying this together came the conclusion, abhorred by run-of-the-mill scientists, that the universe seemed to possess so much more than rocks, gases, DNA and predictability.

* * *

"Professor Beale," Lyndsey Smith began, at the start of another of the professor's talks to interested journalists, "would you mind talking about the Unexplained Visual Experiences, the UVEs, in a little more detail for us, please? I mean, maybe a bit more on how they happen and what they are. Your last talk was mostly about quantum physics, the universe and all the incredible findings – it was quite heady stuff – so I think it would be good to maybe zoom in a bit more to the UVEs this time. Is that all right?"

"Okay, Lyndsey, sure. Well, I'll start at the beginning of how the theory on UVEs coalesced in my mind. It came about when I started thinking about the atmosphere and these UVEs happening 'in the air', as it were. This is an oversimplification of my thought processes, but I remembered what the 'air' is actually made up of, and all of a sudden I had one of those eureka moments – you know what I mean? – when all the dots suddenly joined up in a flash. All of a sudden it seemed clear. I thought more about the reality of what so-called 'thin air' actually comprises, and how it has far-reaching implications for us all. And I tell you, I became very excited.

"My theory is that our impact – human impact – has upset the planet's energy fields via our colossal discharges of radiation, which I talked about last time, and that this overload of the wrong kind of energy is sending through apparently spurious scenes backward and forward through time – notice the events are not space or place anomalies: most of the reported events seem to be of *that same place but just a different time*. That is significant. It is the time variable which is going awry. I haven't witnessed one of these events, incidentally. Has anyone here?"

People looked at each other and shook their heads.

"Okay. When two different time periods collide, as it were,

with each other, they are each slipping into the other time. A vision of the past means you have slipped into the past temporarily. It also means that the person in the past seeing you has slipped into their future temporarily. You both appear real to each other. For a few moments you are in each other's time. I don't think they are ghostly re-enactments or mirages of reality – I think they *are* reality. I am starting to call them timeslips, for it seems time really does slip and fall down – it rips open and the fabric is rent until by some law of the universe it is repaired very quickly. It is unsustainable and it repairs itself. We cannot, of course, have more than one time existing simultaneously at the same place. The much publicised air crash in Mexico last year – Lyndsey, I know you were there reporting on it after it happened – where the mountains were said to melt away – into what, we never did find out – was, I think, an example of time slipping back a heck of a long way. I don't know if they saw dinosaurs or what, it wasn't clear from the flight recording, but it may well have gone back to before there were even mountains there. It could even have been before the continents all drifted to their present positions."

"What! So you think the pilots could have been looking at Pangaea or Gondwanaland?" Lyndsey enquired, amazed.

"Possibly, yes," the professor replied. "Or at any stage before the mountain range was formed through the geological processes that made them what they are today. It might not have had forest cover. It might have had very different vegetation – the last ice age ended only around ten thousand years ago, after all, and that meant most places had different land cover to what they have today."

"But, Professor Beale, the crash happened in *this* time though," Lyndsey added. "The wreckage was strewn across the forest in *our* time. I went there and saw it. I reported on it. Surely, if they had come down in another time the wreckage would have been invisible to us as the plane would have been lost to the other time."

"Correct," said Professor Beale, "so the apparition must have ended by the time they hit the ground. Most of these apparitions only last maybe a minute at most. There are some, but not many, documented cases lasting longer than that. Also, the present time was co-existing with the other time, so it's not clear how that would have affected it."

"That was so tragic," remarked one of the other journalists. "So many people died. If the universe is more or less conscious and intelligent, as you said in your last talk, why would it let people die like that? Where's the intelligence in that?"

The professor had encountered that question recently, while discussing the subject with his wife. He felt he was on solid ground.

"I believe that the universe only lets someone die – or be born – if it is meant to be. Meant to be according to the laws of the universe. You can shoot me down for saying that and call me callous or a heretic, but I believe that with a complex interplay between free will and destiny it results in there being a time for everything, and that nothing is random or without meaning.

The woman seated next to Lyndsey spoke up, "You still haven't explained *how* your theory about radiation works. *How on earth* do you think we could possibly be able to upset the energy field of something so vast and powerful as the mechanism that regulates the whole time-space thing? And, even if you can explain the mechanics of it, what do you see as the way forward?"

This is it, he told himself – a time to be careful. Looking at her directly, he answered, "I'm going to speak about that soon – I'm still fine-tuning my theory, really – but I can state emphatically that we have changed this planet almost beyond recognition since we exploded in population and became the industrial and technological giants that we are today."

"Perhaps in a later talk you'll be able to tell us how it all happens, as well as your conclusions and what the implications are?" offered Lyndsey, smiling knowingly at the professor.

"Perhaps," he conceded, smiling back.

* * *

Arriving home utterly exhausted, the professor bid his wife a hasty goodnight and went to bed. She carried him up a cup of hot chocolate mixed with his favourite tipple. He drank it and was asleep within minutes.

An old song he liked started playing. *'Time, flowing like a river, to the sea, you and me, you and me...till we meet again...'* What his wife was doing playing it when she knew he was trying to sleep he didn't know, although he was enjoying it in a hazy sort of way.

As it played he thought the house was starting to smell most unusual – of bracing sea air, of all things. *Ah, lovely*, he thought. The sea! What a wonderful smell! *'I must go down to the seas again, to the lonely sea and the sky. And all I ask is a tall ship and a star to steer her by'!* [22] Ahhh! Flung spray! Blown spume! *SPUME!* Good word! Seagulls crying! The pop music was drowned out by the sound of crashing waves; they roared in his ears and blew sheets of cold, salty spray across his face. He had forgotten how alive the sea made him feel. He inhaled deeply and sighed. After some minutes of sheer enjoyment, despite the salt stinging his eyes, he turned away. He was met with an alarming spectacle. It was his old school friend, Howard. He was bent over, polishing his motorbike – the one he had had when they were at school together in Massachusetts all those years ago.

"Howard!" John yelped.

Howard turned and smiled broadly, beckoning John to go over and have a look at his bike.

"But Howard," he began, "I don't understand! How did you get here?"

Howard, still smiling, replied cheerfully, "John, what a thing to ask! Just how far away did you think I was? Distance is nothin'! Get your head round it, man!"

John was even more confused. "But you got rid of that bike when you moved to Boston. I don't understand."

"Yeah, but isn't it great?"

"I – I don't know."

Howard's face seemed to be frozen in its smile. Slowly, the shiny motorbike dimmed and in its place stood a huge almond tree. Spinning around to ask Howard what the hell was going on, John noticed there was no trace of his friend anymore. He seemed to have gone as abruptly as he had arrived. Then John found himself chewing on one of the almonds. Surprise gave way to enjoyment – it was delicious. He closed his eyes and enjoyed its unique taste. There was nothing quite like almonds, he thought. Subtle flavour. And oh so healthy. Reaching out to the tree to grab another one, although he couldn't for the life of him remember getting the first one, he became aware of there now being an enormously high wire fence in the spot where Howard had just been. It reminded him of the fences around tennis courts, to stop the balls going out, only this one was even higher – much higher. He went over to it. As he stood there, pressed up against the fence, the wires began to blur together before his eyes, becoming what resembled – to his thinking – a cinema screen. On it appeared a scene of thousands of ocean gulls flying towards him. It was then that he realised they really *were* flying towards him: becoming three-dimensional, they seemed to dart – all a flap and screeching – out of the picture, as if they would go through him. He dropped down and sat on the ground to watch. The birds flew noisily overhead. Feeling something land on his lap, he looked down expecting to see something wet and unpleasant, only to see a length of sugar cane. One of the birds must've dropped it, he thought. It didn't put him off trying it. As he chewed the end of the stick a glorious sweetness filled his mouth.

"Mmmmm. Not too sweet, just right." He had another suck.

He recalled the time he and his wife had stopped to watch sugarcane workers loading up one of the sugar trains in rural Egypt. It had been one of those wonderful vignette moments that had stuck in his mind.

Just then it started snowing – and snowing hard. Soft, fluffy snow soon surrounded him in drifts. Sitting in its midst, he ran his hands through it. It was like soft cotton wool and felt immensely comforting. His warm hands melted the crystals almost on touch. Squeezing a handful together, it quickly became a small block of ice and he rubbed it across his forehead. Scooping up handfuls he threw it into the air. Powdery white spray contrasted against the blue sky – which was now devoid of gulls, he noticed. With increasing joy, he threw handfuls up, down, sideways, wherever he could. He wrote his initials in it. He thought it was funny how his hands weren't suffering from the cold of the snow.

Thinking he should get up and take a look around, he stood up, brushing the snow off his clothes. At that moment his nose was accosted by the smell of what seemed to be a wet dog.

"Euch!" he said out loud, fanning the air with his hand.

A wet Irish wolfhound galloped past him, flicking snow as he went.

"Hey!" John looked for an accompanying person but saw no one.

He walked on for some distance in the direction that the dog had taken. He was in the middle of a vast plain with a few trees and not much else. The dog became a speck in the distance then disappeared. As John walked past one grove of trees there appeared, as if looming out of nowhere, a rather rotund elderly woman reciting something John vaguely recognised. She was standing in a theatrical pose with her arms moving expressively and her voice loud and captivating.

"If music be the food of love, play on;
Give me excess of it, that, surfeiting,

The appetite may sicken, and so die.
That strain again! it had a dying fall:
O! it came o'er my ear like the sweet sound
That breathes upon a bank of violets,
Stealing and giving odour. Enough! no more:
'Tis not sweet now as it was before.[23] *Huh?... who are you?*"

"Who am *I*? Who are *you?*" he countered. "A bit of a strange place to be quoting Shakespeare! Are you rehearsing for something?"

With an angry expression, she turned and pointed towards what was an audience of at least a hundred people seated in a dimly-lit theatre.

Delete 'he heard a wind start blowing' through to the note reference (including it) & join up sentences so that it reads: 'As he reached backstage the dark wood of the theatre...'

"WHAT THE—!" He jumped. He scooted to the side to leave the stage. As he reached backstage the dark wood of the theatre dissolved before his unbelieving eyes, becoming an orchard of orange trees.

"How did that happen?" he said, walking up to the first tree of what looked to be hundreds. The leaves were so green; intensely so, he thought. And as for the fruit... He plucked a large, ripe orange from the tree. He sniffed it, made an appreciative noise, then embarked on peeling it with his fingers. He remembered how hard it was to peel an orange this way. Determinedly grabbing out a chunk of the fruit he leaned forward as he took a bite. Instantly the juice burst into his mouth, causing him to eat it furiously, driven by its smell and taste and the exquisite sensation of the juice running down his throat. Its acid seemed alive in his body, like a healing balm, determined to eradicate anything non-wholesome.

"That was simply one of the best oranges I've tasted in a *long* time," he said. He wiped his mouth with the back of his hand. "Dee-licious!"

A dark-skinned girl wearing Arab clothing rode past on a camel. She nodded to him and kept going.

"Hello!" he called cheerfully, but she was gone.

As he stood in the orange grove he wished he had his wife with him to share in these wacky adventures. She should be here, he thought, *she'd love this!*

Then what felt like a powerful gust of wind blew up beneath him, sending him into the air, tumbling this way and that. Panicking, aware that it had all of a sudden become like the memorable tornado scene from the 1939 film *The Wizard of Oz*, in which houses, cows and witches on bicycles are tossed through the Kansas sky, he tried to grab one of the trees, but they seemed to be getting smaller – or were they just getting further away? His helpless body was hurled around in the air like a leaf in an autumn storm. After a while he managed to stabilise himself to the extent that he stopped tumbling uncontrollably. Then waves of something that felt like water rocked him, reminding him of when he used to go out with Howard when they were little, in Howard's tiny yacht. The waves came rhythmically – not consistently spaced, but spaced enough for him to begin to manage the way his body moved in response. He was just getting used to the movements and actually rather enjoying himself, when what looked to be shapeless glowing packets – of what he wasn't quite sure – came travelling towards him, riding the waves. The packets would flash into solids then miniature waves, then back to solids then back to miniature waves.

This is insane! he thought. And am I on the ground again, or what? *What are these things?* He watched them for a while. They were everywhere, on every wave and between every wave. Then he decided to let his mind have some fun. He tried an experiment. He selected one of the packets as it approached and thought of something it could become.

"Okay, first one," he said. "You become a frog."

It duly complied. A green frog with large orange feet

appeared on the wave and hopped to one side, disappearing into the undulating distance.

"Now, a red sports car. *Wow!*" A car washed up almost at his feet. The engine was revving and the door opened for him to get in.

"Uh, no, I don't think so. This is crazy enough already!" It drove away on its own.

Possibilities raced through his mind. What else could he wish for and make real? He saw a twin-cam Harley Davidson roll up, dangerously zig-zagging as it stormed by. He saw a woman who looked a lot like Marlene Dietrich effortlessly surfing the waves, while smoking – complete with cigarette holder – and wearing a see-through bikini. *Mmmm,* he thought. Tearing himself away, he saw himself stepping up to a stage and being awarded a Nobel Prize in Physics. After the very solid appearance of an English country cottage draped in wisteria he tired of it all, saying out loud, "Okay, okay! I think I get the picture! *Now, a way out of here! Please!*"

The phrase 'sometimes a wave, sometimes a particle' echoed through his mind repeatedly, like a mantra.

"John! JOHN! *JOHN!*" It was his wife's voice. She was patting him on the cheeks. Groggily, he opened his eyes and looked at her.

"Sometimes a wave, sometimes a particle."

"What?"

"Sometimes a wa—. Holy shit! Sweetheart, you wouldn't believe the dream I've just had!"

"Try me," she replied, caressing him tenderly. "You have been making a *lot* of noise for the past half-hour!"

"Phew!" He looked for more drink in his mug by the bed but was disappointed to find it empty.

"Want another?" she asked.

"Yeah. No. I don't know. Whatever you put in it…you could sell it and make a fortune!"

She frowned. "It was just the usual. Oh…yeah, that's right, I confess I accidentally tipped a little more spirit into your cup than I was intending. I didn't have my glasses on! I'm sorry if I've overdosed you, but I'm sure it was pretty much just the usual!"

"Oh, no! Well that dream I just had certainly wasn't just the usual! Do you have any idea how brilliantly alive I feel?"

She smiled, perplexed.

"I feel like I've been, I dunno, digitally enhanced!"

"Huh? Meaning what, exactly?"

"I've just seen and tasted and smelt and heard and felt the most amazing things! I've just kinda tripped, actually, I think. Not sure why. It was such a mixture of good and not so good! I know lack of sleep combined with alcohol always does make my mind flip out. Those oranges were—"

"Oranges?"

"Yeah. Growing on trees."

"That's where they usually grow."

"Ha ha. The taste was better than real. More vivid. More depth."

"Glad to hear you've had a nice time."

"Except for the Shakespeare play I walked into the middle of. Whew, that was highly embarrassing."

She laughed. "You dreamt about Shakespeare! Serves you right!"

"Hey, I don't mind Shakespeare. I'm not a complete philistine, you know."

She laughed. "So what do you think it all means? Anything or nothing?"

"I could sum it up in one word: potentiality. You know what I mean. Or I could say that I think it means I need a holiday – that's probably more to the point."

John Beale's vivid dream, although confusing him more than any other dream he had ever had, left him with an enduring thought of what seemed to be limitless possibilities of the Zero-

Point Field. He wondered how true it was that wishes and intentions openly expressed can actually cause something to happen and, if so, what the time lag was for manifesting something. The glowing packets of energy in the dream enthralled him: absolute potentiality was the most exciting concept he could think of. In the space he had been in, seeing the instantaneous materialisation of the things he had wished for had been a surreal experience. He knew that the wide-awake world in which he was now safely back doesn't quite work like that; the heavy world of matter, where earthly vibrations are slow and cumbersome. Things spin more slowly, and restrictions, real and imagined, press in on every possible scenario. The thing would be, he resolved, to try to remove as many of those restrictions as possible. But how? He was determined to know the whole truth about how to live life to its fullest, its most glorious – tapping into its awesome potential – and how to feel, right down to his very cells, the underlying quantum world that he now wanted to rush out and tell everyone about.

THE WOMAN IN THE BED

The door opened and Agnes was led inside, past the room in which she had previously met with Mary, and to what looked like a large bedroom. The room was furnished with a single bed and an assortment of furniture, including a desk and two chairs, a TV and an ensuite bathroom. There was a bay window with a curved seat running along its entirety. Mary was sitting at the window, reading. She looked up. A wide smile instantly spread across her face.

"Mrs Woodham-Walter!"

"Hello, Mary!"

"I didn't know you were coming! Nobody told me! Please sit down!" She quickly tossed her book aside and made room beside her.

The door was closed and locked from the other side. A stern voice called out, "You have half an hour for this visit, no more. If you need anything you'll have to knock loudly on the door, as there's no phone in the room."

"Please call me Agnes, for heaven's sake, dear!"

"Thank you, and I shall call you niece one day too, if I may!" she said with a mischievous wink.

Agnes laughed. "You seem in better spirits this time. Much better than last time. Is there any reason, or have I just caught you at a good time?"

Mary grabbed hold of Agnes's hand as she replied, "I'm much happier now and it's because of *you!* Because you have come all this way to see me and are trying to get me out. And because you are part of my family – I thought there was no one left that I could call family, but you have changed all that. You are like an angel appearing to me!"

"Oh, really," said Agnes, embarrassed, "I'm no angel, I assure you! I'm sure your captors don't think I'm one either, annoying them the way I am!"

"Yes, I'd thought you were not allowed another visit. How have you managed this? And half an hour this time. Such luxury."

Agnes looked knowingly at Mary and said in a hushed voice, "I have been very fortunate in my, shall we call them negotiations, with the authorities. It seems they are easily intimidated by what they don't understand – me, in this case. As well as you, of course. So I had a kind of bargaining power. I think I might have almost exhausted my credit now though." She chuckled.

"So this might be your last visit," Mary asked sadly, still clutching Agnes's hand.

"Don't worry dear, I'll get you out."

"They might lock you up too, if you're not careful. They just came for me, completely unannounced. A man in a grey suit knocked on the door and just took me. It was all too too much. No consideration whatsoever. No time to tell James. Or to pack. Be warned."

"I will be careful," Agnes assured.

"How is James?"

"He is well. Still desperately wanting to get you out of here. He told me that his father's been busy trying to get you released. He has connections in government, you see. Only he's retired now and doesn't seem to be getting anywhere. He's not part of the system now, so he shouldn't expect miracles."

"Oh, that's very kind of him. I hardly know the man. We didn't particularly hit it off when we met. His wife was worse though." She slapped her hands over her mouth. "Oh, I shouldn't have said that! Please don't tell James I said that!"

"Of course not. Listen, Mary, I have a plan which I think may well work. I want to try it now, before our half hour is up. Let me tell you what it is."

Still mindful of the room possibly being bugged, she whispered in Mary's ear and explained the scheme she had cooked up in the time since their last meeting. Mary was astounded. It seemed to her like something straight out of a novel, not real life. Yet here was her stooped and elderly niece – who seemed of course like she should have been the one who was the old aunt – persuading her to undertake a highly risky-sounding act.

A screen stood in one corner of the room. Mary and Agnes repositioned it, went behind and took off their outer layers of clothing. Agnes struggled to put on Mary's jeans, finding the waist impossible to do up, so she made sure she had a belt on and pulled the jumper down far enough to cover things. Mary donned Agnes's dress, overcoat and shoes.

Still whispering, Agnes said, "I had the hood of the coat on over my head when I walked into the building. It's a big, roomy hood, so you can use that, and you'd need to, anyway, to hide your face. Remember, I have a bit of a stoop, so don't run out the door with your perfect posture, will you?"

"All right," Mary whispered back, "I won't utter a word either, if I can help it, not a dicky bird. But what about you?"

"I'll feign a tummy upset or something and will go to bed in my clothes and partly wrap myself up in the bedclothes, and I'll be turned away from the door when they look in. They'll see the clothes and assume it's you in bed. Should be all right for a little while – long enough to give you a head start and get you to Donald and his wife Lynne who are waiting in their car for you right now, to drive you away. They're not going to drive you home, as the authorities would look there straight away, so they're kindly taking you to their small cottage by the sea up in Norfolk, at a place called Cromer. I don't know if you know it."

Mary shook her head.

Agnes continued, "It's miles away from Surrey, so hopefully you can stay hidden for a while."

"But, Agnes, what about you? You'll be in so much trouble here when they realise what we've done. Talk about upsetting the applecart! I don't want you to be left here!"

"Don't worry about me dear. I can look after myself. I just want you out of here and to go away with Donald and Lynne. Please take my word that you can trust them; they've been friends of mine for many years. They'll look after you and will get you home before long, somehow. We haven't worked that bit out yet, it depends on how things go."

"You'll be in so much trouble."

"I know, I know. But listen, it's you they're interested in and want to lock up, not me. I want you to go to the press as soon as you can and tell them the whole story. More than one paper if you can. TV too. Radio. Definitely the BBC. Everything. This must be made public. They can't be allowed to get away with things like this. We voted this government in to be fair, not to treat people like this."

"Oh, Agnes, your mother was a good woman, wasn't she?"

"Yes, she was. Why do you ask?"

"Because you are such a good woman and I know that goodness can flow from one good person to another."

"My mother would have kittens if she could see me doing this!" Agnes added, half-joking.

"Matilda lived to be quite old, didn't she?"

"Yes. Certainly reached her three-score and ten, as we used to say."

"And then some," Mary added, laughing nervously. Her face became anxious once more.

Agnes grabbed her hands. "The minutes are ticking by and you need to get going. The time has come; we must now put the plan into action. Now, it's a plan as daft as a brush, I'll admit, but we'll give it a go, eh?"

They discussed the strategy for Mary leaving the room, saying goodbye to the officer on duty and departing the building. She would not bother to sign herself out in the visitors' book. She was told what the car and its occupants looked like, and exactly where they were parked. It was agreed that she needed to leave as quickly as possible, and with as few words as necessary. Once out of the building Mary was to hobble slowly away (in case someone was watching from inside) and round the corner to a side road, where the 'get-away car' was waiting.

The moment arrived. When the half hour was up the two had said their goodbyes and were ready. A young woman came and unlocked the door, calling out for Agnes to leave. With Agnes lying in the bed, facing the other way, Mary shuffled, head down, out of the room and headed for the front door without a word. Fearful of the rapidly approaching footsteps, she let herself out and walked slowly out of the property. The door did not re-open, much to her relief, and with her heart pounding in her chest she walked along the road following Agnes's instructions. She spotted the car parked up the side road. The elderly man and woman bundled her into the back seat and took off. The journey took them on to the back roads of Essex and up to the flat expanses of Suffolk and then Norfolk. They slowed down once they passed Ipswich, but were reluctant to stop for any reason until they reached the house on the Norfolk coast.

Meanwhile, Agnes was ready for the trouble that she knew would come very soon; she was only too aware that once she had their attention there was no way she could successfully masquerade as Mary for more than minutes, or even seconds. Desperate to buy her as much time as possible, she lay low, quietly on the bed, careful not to turn over or show her face to anyone who might look in at her. She said a silent prayer and gradually dozed off.

While asleep, Agnes missed seeing the member of staff come into the room, bringing with her a plate of dinner and some drinks. The young woman placed the tray down on a small table in the room and called to Mary to come and get her dinner. Hearing nothing, she glanced at the occupant of the bed. Something suddenly rang alarm bells. Not only had Mary crawled into bed at a funny time of the day (which wasn't like her) but she seemed to have aged prematurely since the visit from her relative! A surprising number of wrinkles and even tufts of grey hair seemed to have developed in that very short time.

* * *

"Oh, here's a phone," Lynne said excitedly to Mary, passing it to her. "I've switched it on and – please don't think I'm being patronising, but do you know how to use one like this?"

"Yes, well, enough to make a phone call. That's something I have learned." She tapped in a number and waited.

"Hello?" came the voice.

"James?"

"Mary? Is that you?"

"Yes! I've escaped! They've been holding me in Essex. They moved me from Surrey. Agnes – you know her, don't you – she came to see me today and we exchanged identities!"

"WHAT!"

"And I'm now in a car with two very kind friends of hers, and we're heading for the Norfolk coast, to their holiday cottage at Cromer!"

"What! I don't believe it! Cromer? Isn't that up in East Anglia somewhere?"

"Yes, Norfolk. On the coast."

"I don't believe it! Who are the people you're with?"

"Mr and Mrs Lambie."

"Donald and Lynne!" Lynne called from the front.

"I heard. Mary, I didn't know about this! Nothing! Why didn't she tell me she was doing this? I could've done something; I could've helped."

"It's all right," she said, "it's just nice to hear your voice again. It's been so long. I've missed you so much. I've really missed you."

"Really? I've, uh...I've missed you too. I really wish you were here with me." There was a pause. "When are you coming home?"

Mary smiled. "I don't know when I'll be able to. I'll do my best to get back soon. But those people will be looking for me at any moment, if not already. It won't take them long to realise what's happened. I only wish Agnes hadn't put herself in such danger for me. She's so wonderful. And you'll never guess what? *She's my niece!*"

"WHAT?"

"My niece! She told me that she's my sister Matilda's daughter."

"Oh. And are you sure that she is?"

"Oh, yes! I believe her."

"What's her name then? Agnes who?"

"Woodham-Walter."

"Oh, right." He remembered the name from the dossier he had put together for her. "Anyway, where exactly are you now?"

"Mr Lambie, where are we now?"

"We've just come into Bury St. Edmonds," Donald replied.

Mary and James chatted on for a few more minutes before Mary handed the phone back, giving profuse thanks. They drove on through the heart of East Anglia, happy in the thought that, although Agnes was indeed in grave trouble, Mary had back the most precious thing she had ever possessed and could ever possess – her freedom.

* * *

Agnes was harshly evicted from her bed. At the young woman's behest, a troop of three men and one other woman stormed into the room and stood staring in disbelief at the elderly figure seated crestfallen on the bed. Shouting erupted and tempers flared. The young woman who had been monitoring Agnes's visit now stood cowering in the corner, dodging verbal salvos.

"It's not my bleedin' fault!" she protested. "I was never told to watch them! It was only an old lady visiting her! How was I supposed to know they'd cooked all this up?"

The grey-suited man who seemed to be in charge then directed his rage to a man who was standing next to him.

"Brian, I said we should've been properly monitoring the visits, but, no, I'm told we haven't enough money for the equipment! Bloody budgets! Not necessary to have a camera in her room! That's what you told me!"

"Yes, I know, I know! There isn't the money to watch the ones who aren't seen as high security risks or risks to themselves. This could not have been foreseen. We can't have CCTV in every room. And we have to have someone not only watching but listening as well. Do you know how much a trained surveillance expert costs per hour? It's not just someone watching screens, you know."

"I don't care what they cost! Couldn't we have had someone actually just stand in the room with them for the visit like they do in prisons? I suppose that would be against some law of civil liberties or something? Or was it just that we don't have enough people? Someone had to be making the tea, I suppose. And answering those always-urgent emails from HQ. Without descending any further into sarcasm I suppose I can only say I think we've learnt a lesson here." He turned back to Agnes. "Before we arrest you on the grounds of impersonating another individual, and aiding and abetting the escape of a person in custody, I want you to tell me where Mary Stepney is."

The young woman hurriedly left the room. Agnes looked straight ahead of her, ignoring the faces. She replied quietly, "I will not."

A hint of a snarl curled the man's lips. He placed his face in front of Agnes's. "Tell me where she is."

She turned away. "I will not."

The two apparently most senior men exchanged glances.

"Listen, we will let you go and won't press charges if you tell us where she is."

She sighed. "I will not let you apprehend her again. She has done nothing wrong. You have held her for far too long already, not that you should have held her at all. She is who she says she is, nothing more, nothing less. Forget studying her and just accept that her story is true."

"Mrs Woodham-Walter, you talk too much!" he snapped. "And yes we *do* know what her story is. We know her *true* story."

"Well, good then, what more can you hope to get from her? Blood? Oh, that's right, you've already taken that."

"That's our business, not yours!"

"This isn't a democracy when people like you are allowed to do things like this to decent and innocent people!" she said bitterly. "People who have committed no crime! In fact, she's quite the opposite. She is a pillar of society. What sort of thugs are you? You should have more respect for people! You disgust me! You act like legitimised criminals!"

"*SHUT UP!* The abuse stops there!"

She refused to recognise the rumblings of fear. She ran through in her mind the old adage she had known for many years: *Fear knocked at the door. Faith answered. There was no one there.* She repeated it silently a few times. It seemed to help. Sitting proudly, she looked straight ahead defiantly; she would not break.

* * *

Mary kept herself hidden inside the modest house that looked out across green heathland to the beach and open sea. She would watch people amble past the house to go to the beach, and could see part of the sandy expanses from an upstairs window. It was from this window that she would sit, able to see a scattering of small screens arranged in the sand to block out the wind and afford some privacy (that rare gem, she thought, in this time of so many people). Donald and Lynne stayed with her, providing food and supplies they had brought with them up from Surrey. Their cottage, which they occasionally hired out on a weekly basis, was already well stocked with books, magazines and games, so Mary was able to busy herself. She settled in as best she could, feeling awkwardly yet overwhelmingly grateful towards her elderly benefactors. She mused over how strange it was that she only knew Donald previously through him catching her at the house on Roseberry Lane – twice – doing things she knew she ought not to have been doing. Funny how life can turn, she told herself. She grew quickly to like them, and they treated her well, with no end of caring and fussing. She was advised against phoning James anymore as his phone was, they said, very likely to be 'being listened to' by now. They thought she seemed genuinely quite aghast at what the modern-day powers were able to do, yet they couldn't help wondering what she must have thought of how similar matters used to be conducted 'in her time' (much worse, they were sure). She told them how she felt her long-held beliefs and the rosy image she had of her glorious England were becoming ever more tarnished as reality hit hard – although she did go to pains to stress to Donald and Lynne that she was still, and always would be, patriotic; and that she still loved her country just as much as ever. She explained how she had already learnt, reluctantly, from discussions with James that the British Empire had not been entirely a good thing, and that now she was fast learning about the lack of wisdom inherent, it seemed, in so many of the people running the country, and indeed countries the world over. With their liking of secret dealings and their inability to always disclose their true motives for making some decisions, they could facilitate vested interests and be a law unto themselves. She wondered who they really represented and how they slept at night, yet it was she who was the one having trouble doing so.

Three days later they came. It was in the still of the early morning. A van quietly pulled up in front of the cottage. Its occupants got out and crept up to the house, surrounding it as quietly and stealthily as a pack of lions circling a solitary deer. Decisively, they pounced. They plucked Mary from her bed as she lay sleeping and took her away with them. They left the other two standing on the front doorstep, gasping in disbelief. Donald and Lynne could do nothing except feel that they had failed her in a monumental way. The van drove away and no further communication was made.

FAIR IS FOUL AND FOUL IS FAIR

"This is another fine mess you've got yourself into, Agnes. Okay, now get yourself out of it."

Unable to sleep, she got out of bed. She had been thinking long and hard to remember some spells, but was hazy on which ones to use. She could dredge up a few, but found it only easy to remember ones she had had cause to use more than once. She had never been held against her will before. She had never been in this much trouble before. She decided to cobble a spell together and hope for the best. Not being in possession of her books and usual assortment of plants and various required objects she was forced to make do with what she had, which was not much. She had not been allowed to remain in Mary's room and had been moved to makeshift quarters further up the corridor, and as such had precious little at her disposal. Two days earlier, she had asked the people holding her if they would be so kind as to get her some sage bushes, lavender oil and a few crystals for her spells. They saw no harm in indulging a foolish old woman. Impressed by the ease with which they had given her these things, she later asked for – and duly received – a packet of candles, some thread and some twine, a hearth brush, a bell, a few bowls, a compass, some salt, some incense and an incense burner, and a box of matches. She did laugh to herself at their willingness to give her the matches: she could be planning, for all they knew, to burn the place down in order to make her escape. The matches were sought supposedly so that she could, as she put it, 'have a little smoke occasionally to relieve the monotony' (they also got her some cigarettes), with them unaware that she had never smoked in her life and had no intention of doing so. She also needed something of the earth. Spotting a potted plant resting on the windowsill she now had all she needed. With her own 'special' knife, white-handled with a curved blade (confiscated by the authorities on her arrival at the house but later given back, after her plaintive request – and their realisation of how blunt and non-menacing it was), she slowly and gently cut a side branch off the plant, praying as she did it. She filled a bowl with water from the tap over the handbasin. She sat down at the small table, which was to be her improvised altar, and, after consecrating the space and the items within it, she arranged everything in front of her; her focus on the now-lighted candle.

Relaxing, she worked herself into a suitable state of mind and began invoking energy. She chanted softly, "Eko, eko, azarak, eko, eko, zomelak, eko, eko, cernunnos, eko, eko, aradia," becoming louder as she went, reaching a crescendo.

She then moved on to specific spells, her head swaying gently from side to side as she was swept along with the mood of the moment. The flame flickered and grew into a slender spire of luminous orange. The bowl of water took on a subtle apricot hue and the plant looked on with living, breathing steadfastness. Agnes suddenly realised she needed a stone. She removed the Celtic pendant from around her neck and placed it next to the other items. She now had everything she thought she needed, a ramshackle assortment as it was. Creating carefully crafted images in her mind, she visualised freedom and happiness for both herself and Mary. She took care that the images endured in her conscious mind throughout the duration of the spells. She felt the magic of the air increase, and at that point she began to feel that something good was definitely going to result from what she was doing. She now just had to wait, and repeat the spells and visualisations as often as she could.

After she had finished, she said aloud, "Never, ever, give up! Out of this situation only good will come…only good will come. I am safe."

Satisfied, she crawled back into the bed and was able to sleep at last. Little did she know that at the very same time Mary was also communicating with the powers that be, asking for exactly the same things, just in a different way.

Agnes heard a van drive up to the building and knew instantly that it was bringing Mary back. She chided herself on enacting a plan that had been so foolish that it had resulted in them both being locked up. She wished she had spent more time coming up with a better scheme, one less doomed to failure, instead of giving in to her impatience. Mary was returned to the same room she had been in before. The people in charge made them swap their clothing back but forbade them from meeting.

It had not been as difficult as Agnes had expected for the authorities to find Mary. Hidden, supposedly safe in the cottage on the Norfolk coast, Mary and her rescuers had spent a cosy, yet naïve, three days. However, as low as they had kept their heads they were unable to stop the authorities' relentless searching through phone records, emails and whatever else they could lay their hands on. There were enough records legally available to them that showed a strong friendship between Agnes and the Lambies. Plus there was the easily accessible information about properties. The house in Norfolk, being owned by the Lambies, was an obvious choice needing to be checked. The final thing that had clinched it was how, according to their neighbours, the Lambies had gone away on holiday on what was the very same day that Mary had made her escape.

Donald and Lynne returned home to Surrey feeling low. Wishing they had taken her to a friend's house instead of one that they themselves owned, they saw how inept they had been. They speculated that doing something like sending her under another name to a bed and breakfast in the wilds of Scotland might have proved safer. As Mary, virtually possessionless as well as (allegedly) stateless, had no passport or official papers she could not have been sent abroad; but, they realised, there were still so many remote hiding places they could have taken her to, even in such an overcrowded isle. Hindsight, as always, was a perfect tool for providing the answers.

Donald had embarked on a programme of intense prayer and meditation, pursuing his plan of 'second-to-last resort'. Once a conventionally religious man, he had gone on to abandon orthodoxy for the Spiritualist Church, which had surprised a lot of people. Finding comfort and peace from knowing the 'other side', he turned his back on what he had been raised to believe and, bit-by-bit, assembled his own picture of what he believed life to be about. When he and Lynne met Agnes another, even stranger door had opened, albeit one he did not particularly want to step through. Although they did join in on the occasional witches' (or seers', or shamans', as some of them preferred) evenings with Agnes and her friends (more for social reasons than anything), Donald was reluctant to dabble in something that, although used to do good (or so they always insisted), still spooked him a little. As time passed he grew increasingly anxious, and decided it was time for his plan of 'last resort': as an adjunct to his praying and meditating he would now consult the one and only book he and Lynne had on the 'other' subject: a kind of user's guide for entry level white witchcraft.

* * *

Feeling acutely alone in his struggle, James was determined to speak face-to-face with the one person he saw as providing the only chance of help he now had. In possession of Donald's mobile phone number, he rang him to see how Mary was. Upon being told the terrible news he had the realisation that Agnes must now also be imprisoned. He turned up on Donald's doorstep a few minutes later. They sat down over tea to talk about what to do. The plan became to get a lawyer on side and to send out more letters, this time including one to the prime minister. Rattle more cages, they decided. Engage the media again. Make it an issue. And they would contact their member of

Parliament again – he must, they reckoned, be nagged some more; even the 'uncooperative old bastard', as they called him, must have a social conscience hidden somewhere deep within him, they thought. They resolved to pick and dig and get completely under his skin.

Meanwhile, the two men were not – although they thought they were – the only ones still thinking about how to secure Mary and Agnes's freedom. James's father resumed his efforts with a vengeance, fuelled by the fact that there were now two innocent, non-threatening women being held against their wills for no good reason. Still ignored, and now building up an increasingly sour reputation among those he once worked with, he kept going, poking sticks at the government.

Agnes got into a habit of doing spells in her cell. With little else to do – few of the books she had been supplied with appealed to her, and she didn't care much for TV – she had time to think hard and remember spells, as well as concoct new ones. Trying to recollect the underlying premises, she was forced to decide what sorts of incantations might be best used under the circumstances. She appealed to the forces of light and the energies of the universe. She appealed to the spirit of goodness and the spirit of all life. Her spells sounded a lot like prayers; some were silent, some were not; and she found herself saying them at all times of the day, no matter what she was doing.

Agnes was largely left alone by the authorities. Believing she had some power over them, she had confidence that something would happen and that she would be sent home soon. Occasionally one of the people working in the house would come by and ask her a few questions. Privately, she thought that they wanted to use her abilities. She knew she could be an asset to them and she knew that they knew that. Whether she was to help them solve crimes or sniff out other countries' state secrets, she knew she was worth more on side than off. And unprosecuted rather than prosecuted.

GLOBAL REACTION

The matter of how and why the world was experiencing a sudden spate of what appeared to be supernatural visions became the subject of increased international discussion. Emerging out of easy joke material into the arena of serious debate, the topic was picked up by more and more people around the globe. Everyone from politicians, local authorities and police through to shop workers, taxi drivers and bartenders talked about it and slipped it into conversation at any chance, and the media found it exceptionally fertile ground. Minds were challenged, and many found it all very exciting. Speculation abounded as to the cause of the happenings, and there were still those who chose to disbelieve all reports, no matter who or where they were from, refusing point blank to entertain the idea that such things were even happening. A degree of polarity ensued, with divisions of believers and non-believers forming; although the vast majority were of the opinion that something very strange *was* indeed happening.

Some of the world's religious fundamentalists decided that the events were real but were only explicable as acts of a very angry, spiteful god who was choosing to punish His children for their sins. Theirs was a god who was said to be loving and tolerant and understanding on the one hand, yet simultaneously intolerant, vengeful and destructive on the other. This God of Fear and Mixed Messages reigned supreme for many, allowing the flock to hold up filters to incoming information, separating out what they wanted to believe from what they did not want to believe, yet with most still considering themselves fair, open and tolerant at all times.

There was another sector of the population that saw the alleged timeslips as nothing more than a conspiracy plot: the ruling élite desperate to instil yet more fear into the population at large. Fear, it had long been said, was a vote-winner and a known motivator for people to favour certain political parties. The conspiracy theorists suggested that there had been no more of the funny happenings than was normal – there was always a steady stream of such reports, they argued – this was just scare-mongering. The governments would, they proclaimed in one of their more colourful theories, announce any day now that a particular country dubbed by some as 'evil' and plotting to bomb certain other countries 'off the map' was responsible for the strange occurrences, and that therefore we cannot rule out the possibility of 'having' to go to war against them. They would say 'we must defend ourselves against this very real threat that is, according to our intelligence services, using sophisticated technological methods to induce hallucination in our people.' Or, perhaps, the theorists speculated, the authorities wanted to force-medicate or imprison (or even worse) some of their own citizens, and this was one way of singling them out, by putting some drug in their water supply or gas through their letter box.

Another group scattered across the world thought the strange happenings were the first outward sign of humanity's transition to the next stage of human evolution. They maintained that evolution, by its very definition, was an ongoing process and therefore never stopped. Driven by natural laws and guided by the human animal's inherent spirituality we are all, they said, on our own paths to greater love, peace, wisdom and enlightenment. The individuals who have had the strange experiences must be highly evolved souls, they said, and must have increased their earthly molecular vibrations to such a high rate that they are able, from time to time, to see past our time and into another, with the other dimensions beginning to unfold to them. It was stated as signifying an important and exciting phase of humanity's progression on to better ways of being.

And there was yet another group, a very significant chunk of the world's billions, who had the notion that the occurrences were some sort of distortion in time, as unbelievable as it may seem. These people could not, however, come up with reasons for it happening, nor could they explain the huge number of strange sightings, other than to suggest that there might be sunspots or solar storms or some such natural phenomena somehow causing reports to rise above the 'normal' background rate for perceived inexplicable goings-on. They tended to expect the reported happenings to drop off at any time and return to the usual (extremely infrequent) level.

Globally, there was no shortage of explanations and no end to people's imaginings of the overall cause. At last people began to be more willing to come forward publicly and talk about their experiences. The BBC, with its public service ear to the ground, wasted no time in discussing the 'new' phenomenon of Unexplained Visual Experiences.

BBC RADIO CONTINUITY ANNOUNCER: "And now on Radio 4 it's time for Melvyn Bingley in our Manchester studio to present this week's *In The News*."

MELVYN BINGLEY: "Hello. Good morning and welcome to a discussion about the so-called Unexplained Visual Experiences – the UVEs – also referred to by some as timeslips. Whatever they are and whatever we call them they seem to be happening around the world on a daily basis now, with many incidents being reported every day. Here in the studio in Manchester I have two guests with me. Hello to Lyndsey Smith, international correspondent for TV's Channel 4 News, and hello to David Montgomery from Greater Manchester Police, who has recently witnessed one of the bizarre experiences. First of all, can we come to you, David Montgomery. David, can you please tell us what happened to you?"

DAVID MONTGOMERY: "Hello Melvyn. I was out walking the dog one morning. Our home is in Manchester, so we often take the dog out in the car to the countryside. We were out in an area just to the east of Manchester, well outside the city, just off the A628, and we were heading along a footpath which runs across a field and up a hill when it happened. I'm used to the walk; I've done it on and off for the last I don't know how many years, so the place is very familiar to me. I was walking along, the dog was running ahead of me."

MELVYN BINGLEY: "What kind of day was it?"

DAVID MONTGOMERY: "It was a bit misty but the sun was breaking through. Not a heavy mist; you could still see very well. The dog came back to me yapping. I looked at her then looked back up the hill and noticed a house that, well, frankly shouldn't have been there."

MELVYN BINGLEY: "When you say it shouldn't have been there, do you mean it was completely out of place – and that it had not been there before?"

DAVID MONTGOMERY: "Yes. I've walked up that hill for years, it's a place I really like so I go back a lot, and there's always been an open space, with a scattering of trees, not much else. Some woodland to the sides. And now there was this house. Well, of course I was completely taken aback. I froze in my tracks. The dog, as I said, was back with me, barking. Kind of a low growl. She wrapped herself tightly around my legs which she only does when she's scared, and that only added to my feeling that I could trust my senses and that something was very wrong."

MELVYN BINGLEY: "So you think she saw it too?"

DAVID MONTGOMERY: "Yes, I think she did."

MELVYN BINGLEY: "What sort of house was it?"

DAVID MONTGOMERY: "It looked like a nice enough old country cottage. Not very big, and not in the best state, I must say, but definitely occupied. There was washing on a line tied between two trees. There was a vegetable garden. And I remember plants growing up the outside of the house. Ivy, I think, and what looked like wisteria. Smoke was coming from the chimney and there was a low light inside."

MELVYN BINGLEY: "Did you see any people or any activity going on anywhere?"

DAVID MONTGOMERY: "There was a man outside the house doing something. It looked like he was repairing some part of the house – wood work, I think. I managed to walk a bit closer and I think I must have stared at the man, because he looked at me with a puzzled expression, although he didn't look half as puzzled as I felt."

MELVYN BINGLEY: "What sort of clothing was he wearing? Was there anything about him that stood out in your mind?"

DAVID MONTGOMERY: "I remember thinking he looked quite poor. He was wearing what looked to be an old suit; dressed up in what would once have been smart clothing but wasn't anymore. Not much else about him really. He had a beard."

MELVYN BINGLEY: "Did you see any cars parked anywhere?"

DAVID MONTGOMERY: "No. I did, however, see two horses in a field close by the house. There was a barn too, oh and a shed with what looked like a heck of a pile of coal inside – the door was open."

MELVYN BINGLEY: "So what happened next?"

DAVID MONTGOMERY: "The man started to walk towards me. I stayed where I was. The dog was still with me; she was still scared. The man got closer and as he approached he looked increasingly fascinated by me. But as he was getting very close it all went...it disappeared. That was when what must have been a mirage vanished and it was back to what it normally looked like on the hill – with no house."

MELVYN BINGLEY: "So it all vanished. What did you do then?"

DAVID MONTGOMERY: "Well, I can assure you that the dog and I wasted no time in getting back to the car. We took off and went home quick smart. I told my wife and a few other people.

Brave or foolish, I don't know, but I couldn't help it. A thing like that affects you so much. You can't concentrate on anything else for a long while either, as it sort of takes over your mind for a bit. You constantly try to work out what happened, and replay it over and over again."

MELVYN BINGLEY: "Do you have any personal opinions on what happened?"

DAVID MONTGOMERY: "I call it a mirage. It was some sort of temporary illusion. Whether it was a straight out scene from the past I don't know. Part of me thinks that it may well have been, but of course I can't be sure. It has been suggested to me that I look in our local archives to see if there ever was such a house standing on the hill. I know I didn't imagine it. Let me just say that whilst I do drink in moderation I can assure you and the listeners that I had not had one that *morning*, nor even the night before. And I'm not taking any pills or, well, anything at all."

MELVYN BINGLEY: "You have in fact been called one of the more reliable and credible witnesses of these phenomena. I think it's something about your employment – we haven't as yet told the listeners, but we'll tell them now, that your job within the Greater Manchester Police is as detective inspector, so a pretty responsible position."

DAVID MONTGOMERY: "Yes, well, hopefully I can help some of those who have had their sightings scoffed at. These unexplained phenomena are happening to all sorts of people from all walks. At least I consider myself well trained to take any flak I might get!"

MELVYN BINGLEY: "I'm sure you are. Thank you, David Montgomery. Now if we can move on to Lyndsey Smith. Lyndsey you've been reporting on several high-profile UVE cases around the world. What's your take – your personal opinion – on what might be going on?"

LYNDSEY SMITH: "Melvyn, I've been absolutely astounded by these cases. As you know, I reported on the plane crash in

Mexico, which was the first high-profile occurrence of this sort. It marked the start really of the subject being in the media. It wasn't like other plane crashes, if you know what I mean, where causes are found usually quite soon after the incident. The crash in Mexico was very different. The autopsies on the pilot and co-pilot showed no traces of anything abnormal: no drugs, no alcohol, no suspicious substances. The men flying the plane were of excellent reputation among Mexico's pilots, and there were no contributory factors identified. Investigators have as yet found no faults with the plane after examining the wreckage, although I know investigations are still ongoing. According to the flight recorder the pilots said they saw the landscape change before their eyes. They were flying over what is a very uniform region – uniformly mountainous, that is – so there would not have been a change in land use or any topographical changes to the extent that would make them have that sort of reaction. And they knew the area. The plane was flying correctly on course and it was going normally until, well, we've all heard the unusual conversation that was recorded on the plane's flight recorder."

MELVYN BINGLEY: "So, do you have any ideas about what could be happening?"

LYNDSEY SMITH: "I'm finding it very hard to decide what is going on with any degree of certainty except to say that glimpses into other times does *seem* to be what is happening in at least some of the cases. It feels strange me saying that publically, I can tell you! It's my personal opinion. I don't know about all of them; the one in Mexico is less clear – the plane crash, I mean. It could have been a time anomaly, but there is nothing to substantiate that. If it were the case, then it's possible that the pilots saw back in time to a different era, when the landscape was different – that would mean a very long time ago. It's also possible that by the time they crashlanded the UVE had finished, which would explain why the wreckage was found in our time. But some of the well-publicised occurrences seem to be something different.

Some of them consist of animals behaving unusually, like disappearing. Huge flocks of birds, for example, congregating en masse and then just disappearing up into the sky – flying up into the upper reaches of the atmosphere. We have no idea what that is about. Perhaps they are seeing something we can't see."

MELVYN BINGLEY: "Yes, right. Those ones are extremely puzzling. So it appears the one in Mexico – the plane crash – could, to use your words, have been a time anomaly. If it was, what would you say might be causing such an occurrence? Or, in other words, whatever these things are, why should they be happening all of a sudden?"

LYNDSEY SMITH: "Generally speaking, I don't think these unexplained anomalies are caused by hallucination. I don't think the people are all intoxicated or all under the influence of anything. I don't think they're all making it up. There will probably be some fraudulent cases, but I think they will prove to be the exception. We know there have always been unexplained phenomena and incidences of things such as this sort of thing happening. Our history is littered with stories of people seeing into what appeared to be another place or another time, so this sort of thing is not completely unheard of. But with the upsurge in these phenomena it is clear that something new is happening.

MELVYN BINGLEY: "It has been said that because most sightings are going unreported – many people just don't want to cause a fuss or attract attention – there is little opportunity as yet for a full and proper analysis, which would, I presume, include knowing whether there is any special distribution of events or patterns of occurrence?"

LYNDSEY SMITH: "That's right – to a point. But as there are still *plenty* of reported cases coming in, we are able to look at things like geographic patterns and so forth from that data, which is substantial. I believe the databases are already huge, and growing by the day. The events are on the increase and will most likely continue to increase until some particular remedial action takes place. I've been following what's being said by several groups and some professions, and it's got me thinking that orthodox investigations probably won't come up with the whole explanation on their own."

MELVYN BINGLEY: "Really?"

LYNDSEY SMITH: "Yes. Our government and the scientists and other experts that they've commissioned to look into the matter might find it hard to identify the root cause of the UVEs. My hunch is that it will take an unorthodox approach to find the answers. I've been talking to a scientist who in the start was giving almost underground talks to small groups. His views could very aptly be described as unorthodox. Professor John Beale of Cambridge University thinks the UVEs are a natural response to certain human activities on the planet. He speaks about quantum physics, technology and the biosphere. Although he is a conventionally-trained physicist he takes a very broad, you could say holistic approach, and is quite radical. It gets complicated, I can tell you! He talks of waves and particles, uncertainty and probability. He is big on interconnectedness, which is the cornerstone of his theory. It's all, he says, under-pinned by the potentiality contained in the very air and space around us, and the unpredictability inherent in the subatomic world."

MELVYN BINGLEY: "So, he is advocating the cause as being human activities, via the microscopically small quantum world that exists all around us?"

LYNDSEY SMITH: "Yes. The Zero-Point Field – the so-called 'thin air' all around us and extending into space – has been affected, he says, by the world's colossal discharges of man-made radiation into the biosphere. He speaks of a critical mass – a tipping point – as the reason for the UVEs happening. He is quite convincing, I have to say. The only way to find out is to immedi-ately reduce or even halt all our discharges of this kind of radiation and to see if the UVEs stop. I think we'd soon know."

MELVYN BINGLEY: "That's one thing currently being discussed at international level. I understand the theory has much top-level support, as well as many fierce opponents."

LYNDSEY SMITH: "That's right. We're waiting on what will come from that. There is currently a bill before the United Nations. But one thing we do know for sure is that we seem to have developed the most incredible rips or tears, if you like, in the space-time fabric of our world. Sounds very sci-fi, doesn't it?"

MELVYN BINGLEY: "Very Doctor Who."

LYNDSEY SMITH: "Yes! But is Professor Beale right? That knowledge will be vital in not only understanding but perhaps also in fixing the situation – if we are able. We must have a stable universe. If things are to go increasingly awry where will it end? I wouldn't want to live in a world of chaos, where the laws of physics or whatever had become so warped that you or someone you love could disappear at any moment!"

MELVYN BINGLEY: "Heaven forbid!"

LYNDSEY SMITH: "That's why we *must* find out what is going on – we must find the truth as quickly as possible. We don't as yet know for certain what the critical factors are, but things are going very awry. We have many questions to answer. Can we fix it? How can we as a species possibly affect space and time? Is it really because of the huge amounts of radiation being blasted around the place on an ever-increasing magnitude? Is our planet really becoming more unstable? Is it really true that people are not only disappearing but also appearing? And from other times?"

MELVYN BINGLEY: "Is that last question a reference by any chance to cases such as Mary Stepney?"

LYNDSEY SMITH: "Yes. She has supposedly, and I stress supposedly, materialised from 1901."

MELVYN BINGLEY: "And she has now either disappeared again – back to 1901, or some other time or place even – or is, as some people allege, being held in secret detention by the UK

Government or the CIA."

LYNDSEY SMITH: "That's right. That's another mystery. But whether she is a genuine by-product of these timeslips is something we don't as yet know for certain. There have long been stories of people appearing and disappearing, mainly disappearing."

MELVYN BINGLEY: "You mean just suddenly into the ether?"

LYNDSEY SMITH: "Yes."

MELVYN BINGLEY: "It seems that whether we call them timeslips or Unexplained Visual Experiences or just strange goings-on, they constitute a very weighty and nebulous subject."

LYNDSEY SMITH: "Yes, and I have a hunch that the eventual conclusion – with the implications for how we live in this world – will be one that crosses boundaries, disciplines, theologies, ideologies, sciences – everything. Borders, ethnicities, the lot. Strangely enough it could be quite unifying. The world is facing this situation together. It's something very serious, and possibly cataclysmic. It may mean that humanity has an awful lot to learn and that our world will have to swallow one big bitter pill."

MELVYN BINGLEY: "So, although you say it's a problem, and use the word cataclysmic, you also said you thought it could be quite unifying. Does that mean then that you think it will ultimately turn out to be something good or something bad?"

LYNDSEY SMITH: "I think it has the potential to be either good or bad. I think this is a two-headed beast."

MELVYN BINGLEY: "A rather cryptic answer. So you are backing the radiation hypothesis as your number one theory?"

LYNDSEY SMITH: "Yes, at this stage."

MELVYN BINGLEY: "Although is it not, for some people, a bit too fringe? From what I know about this theory I can speculate that if this bill is passed with urgency by the United Nations, as most commentators suspect it will be, it would spell immense changes to life the world over. We would have to turn our backs on a great deal of technology and return to living simpler lives – a little like the life that Mary Stepney says she has come from."

LYNDSEY SMITH: "That would be a strange irony, wouldn't it?"

MELVYN BINGLEY: "Yes. But could all this be a little too radical? It is still only a theory, after all."

LYNDSEY SMITH: "Yes, but as you know, Melvyn, many of humanity's grandest and brightest ideas and innovations started out as radical and unorthodox. Even heretical. And who's to say what will happen if we don't at least try to alleviate the current situation? If it's broken, we need to fix it."

MELVYN BINGLEY: "Too true. So there we have it. No absolutely clear direction yet on what is causing these phenomena, but we await the decision from the United Nations regarding the urgent bill currently before them, which would enforce what has been called the biggest experiment ever under-taken. People are working hard trying to find an explanation for the UVEs – and trying to work out what we need to do to stop these things from happening. So we wait with bated breath. Thank you very much to Lyndsey Smith and Detective Inspector David Montgomery."

FATES

Agnes, although possessing a strength and resilience that belied her feeble appearance, sorely missed the comforts of her home. Her home-made arthritis salve and her own bed were the two things she missed most. She had always been able to endure uncomfortable beds, bad food and things not going her way, but now that her bones had twisted and weakened she was suffering more than ever. She prayed for relief but it didn't always come. She tried to use her powers of remote viewing to 'go' into Mary's room and see how she was, but as soon as her abilities in that direction began to allow her some movement out of her body, a sharp ache in her bones would distract her and jolt her back, terminating the journey prematurely.

One morning the man in the grey suit came in to her room. He asked her to go with him to a room where he said they were waiting to do some tests. She grudgingly obliged and he led her to a room full of unusual-looking equipment and a large desk. He got her to sit on a chair in the middle of the room. The thought that flashed across her mind was that she was going to be punished for not telling them where Mary was when she was missing. She also thought they wanted to investigate her 'abilities'. At that moment she determined to shut them off as if they did not exist within her. She would share nothing with these people: no secrets, no techniques, no knowledge, no ancient wisdom, no nothing. If she did otherwise, it would be, she mused, like trying to sow seeds in hard, infertile ground: these people were of a different mindset, not ready or able to appreciate, let alone respect, things like this that they could have no control over.

She was made to undergo a series of tests over a few weeks. She was more or less forced to give her consent to these tests, some of which were simple question and answer sessions while others were more serious, involving hypnosis and even, on one occasion, brainwave monitoring. As best as she was able, she blocked their endeavours, erecting brick walls in her mind whenever she thought they were on to something. They gave her classic psychic tests of guess-the-shapes-on-the-cards, and she deliberately got them wrong, resulting in a score of even less than one would expect from chance alone. She began to sense their growing frustration with her.

* * *

One day Agnes handed one of the staff an envelope.

"I want you to give this letter to Mary Stepney. Please make sure she gets it. No funny business. It's just family stuff, so of no interest to you people. Don't keep it from her. You know that I'll know if you do; I've put a spell on it in so far as I'll know the moment she reads it."

"You and your spells! Gives me the willies! A long letter, is it?" the young woman enquired.

"No, not particularly. But it's not short, either. It took me a long time to tell her everything I want her to know. It's hard for me to write. I wish I'd had my computer to do it on, but you people are making sure that I'm here and not at home."

"Don't worry, Agnes, I'm sure you'll be out of here before too long."

Agnes stared at the woman. "How can you say that? You keep saying that. Tell me, do you know something?"

"Not exactly, but I'm just hopeful for you. I know it's hard for you here. I don't think you should be here, but what I think doesn't matter."

The woman patted Agnes on the arm, smiled and walked away with the letter.

"My dear Mary,

There is the very real possibility that we may never see each other again, so I am writing this to you in the hope that you get it and that it finds you fit and well, despite your being in this rotten place. Of course I hope you get out soon. I know my weary old body is getting the better of me. The nice young woman who usually looks after me has let slip more than once that I might be being released soon. I hope she is right. I'm not sure how much more of this I can stand.

I would like you to know some more about the family. I hope you don't mind. I think you will be interested.

My late husband, Stanley, couldn't have children, so we never had any (although I did offer to see if the good-looking postman we had then would be able to do me any favours, but Stanley refused to let me! A naughty little joke, if you don't mind. I said he could deliver every day, except Sundays! I think Stanley was worried I might be serious!). Anyway, we thought of adopting, but with all the red tape and the time it takes we never bothered to apply. We always, it seemed, had nieces and nephews around, and cousins, so there were plenty of children in our lives and, let me assure you, enough presents to buy! I do miss Stan. He passed away from leukaemia twenty years ago.

My mother – your sister Matilda – was a very kind woman. She lived a simple life on the farm. We never had terribly much money but we made do. Better off than many folk, I must say. We grew most of our own food and would swap things with neighbouring families and everyone we knew. My father, Alfred, worked hard on the farm. I had two older siblings, Michael and Andrew. They are both dead now."

She went on to give details of names, dates, occupations and assorted information about all the family members she could think of. She ended the letter with, *"Meeting you has changed my life. You have enriched it beyond your imagining. You are a rare sort of gift to this world, if I may use that word, for I feel you are a gift. You are special, and you have an innocence about you that is beautiful. And you are wise beyond your years – I would say an old soul. I hope you stay with James. I think you would be good together. Please know that he thinks an awful lot of you – I know that for sure from spending time with him recently (and I think he loves you! – another naughty comment!).*

When you get out of here don't be angry for what they've done to you. Don't be bitter. Accept that this was your path and move on. Nothing happens without a reason. Just make your life as happy as you can, and design your life to be exactly what you want it to be from this point on. Have faith and be confident. My mother used to say don't worry until worry meets you. Don't forget the angels are always there with you and they cannot do enough for you, so don't hesitate to ask them for help whenever you need it, even for small things. Be happy, and always take good care of yourself.

Bye just now – until we meet again.

God bless and lots of love,

Agnes

xx"

Mary was given the letter, but not before it had been steamed open and its contents read. It shocked Mary, who was still coming to terms with having a living relative, let alone hearing about dozens of people, still living, to whom she was now suddenly connected. Her hitherto tenuous bonds with the modern world were being forged and strengthened, link by link, like molten metal being shaped into something more solid. The picture before her was growing bigger, as the hordes, it seemed, of new relatives made her feel an uneasy excitement.

* * *

"Oh, I can't bear this place anymore!" Agnes shouted at the young woman who came into her room carrying a tray of lunch. "Why am I being treated in this manner? I have told you I need my medication – please allow me the dignity of going home and getting it, at least!"

"I'm sorry, Agnes," the woman said quietly, "I can't do

anything, it's not up to me. I've told them how you feel. It's up to them."

"The pumped-up lout in the grey suit, you mean?"

The woman smiled. "I'm not sure who you mean."

"Yes you are!"

"Yes, all right. You'll have to speak to him. He's not so bad when you get to know him…or so I'm told."

Agnes smiled. "You don't like him either. You're a good judge of character. What are you doing here? You should go and work somewhere else. You're very good at your job. Go into a caring environment, somewhere where ethics are important."

"I was always under the impression that working for the government *was* a respectable job!"

"Well, yes, most of it is, but I'm not so sure about here. I can't really recommend their sort of hospitality."

"You're trying to get rid of me, aren't you! It won't work, I'm afraid. I'm paid too well here, can't afford to leave, much as I'd like to. Real hard people, some of the people here – the ones in charge, I mean. Real hard nuts."

"Hmmff." Agnes took her plate and began eating. "Do you know something?"

"What?"

"You stay here, earning lots of money, but you're miserable."

"Yeah."

"Is that what you want your life to be? You can make it different. Think, my dear, about what your ideal life would *feel* like, and how happy it would make you. Try *feeling* that happiness, if you know what I mean. And then put the steps in motion to make it real. I'm sure it will happen for you if you keep that focus."

"We'll see."

"And do you know something else?"

"What?"

"I'm sure this is hospital food, and a bad hospital at that. Or is it leftover from a bad airline meal? What I wouldn't give for some decent cooking. *Like my own! Cooked in my own kitchen! Get the hint!*"

The woman smiled and left the room.

From that day on, Agnes saw only dark clouds. Her spirit, characteristically buoyant and expressive, was as though in a box being squashed and squeezed and stamped on. She gradually became quieter and more introverted. Her spells were done more to break the monotony now than anything else, and she preferred the company of the books she was given to that of any of the people there, even the young woman. She longed to make a desperate break and see Mary, but knew the door was always locked and that security had been tightened after what they had done. Living more and more inside herself she was beginning to reach a lonely but peaceful place where no one could hurt her or make her do things she didn't want to do. And where no one could find her. She began to go there more often, particularly at night, as she lay in bed. The room would all but disappear and she would slip into this better place, somewhere kinder and gentler, where she was not a prisoner and where she could feel an all encompassing love. She could make herself move and travel beyond the four walls: she at last saw Mary again; she saw her home and her garden. She saw freedom and she did not want to go back. It was during one of these times late at night that she was to deliberately venture further – beyond the point of return.

It was early the next morning when Agnes's body was discovered. The young woman who had gone in carrying breakfast screamed as she realised the smiling woman in the bed was not breathing. At that moment a shock wave was generated, rippling outward through the people involved in her detainment and to their superiors, jolting them hard. A pre-existing clash of opinions within the covert government agency was revealed, and the question of officialdom's right to act in secrecy and with near impunity was dragged out into the public arena for discussion by an insider who was sick of it all – someone who wanted a new occupation and a new employer, even if her pay would be much less.

* * *

Agnes's death was revealed to her closest relatives, who notified Donald. The news hit him with such force that he walked around in a daze for some time, wandering over to her garden and just sitting there, staring at her flowers. Angry with the circumstances of her passing he contacted several people, including James. Donald wrote to the member of Parliament, the newspapers and even the prime minister. He sent the news as quickly and as widely as possible, and was pleasantly surprised when someone from the news media contacted him back and wanted to take the story to national prominence.

James's father emailed his former government colleagues, complaining to them about the 'suspicious' death in custody. He tried his hardest to prick consciences – even just one. They should not have been holding her in the first place, he told them; her death in these circumstances was scandalous and warranted an independent inquiry. In one of the messages he received back he was told that this would now mean that Mary Stepney would be taken even further below the radar; that she would probably be moved again and kept even further from public scrutiny and from any chance of anyone finding out anything about her. The ones involved would likely close rank, the source said, and there would be little chance of anyone seeing Mary Stepney again for a long time. In response, Frank managed to mobilise a few supporters to go up to London and stage a picket as close as they were allowed to get to outside Number Ten, Downing Street. After spending a few hours trying to explain to police and passers by what they were doing, they returned home somewhat deflated, feeling that they had wasted their time.

* * *

Weeks later, it was a Saturday just like any other Saturday for James. He had slept in, had breakfast, done some cleaning and tidying and was getting ready to catch up with friends to go and see a game of football. He liked the atmosphere and camaraderie. The heightened expectation and intensity of emotion at the matches was cathartic, and it was always an enjoyable day out. They would meet at whatever railway station was nearest the game, then afterwards, whether their team had won or not, they would go to a pub for a couple of hours before heading off to a nearby curry house. Like him, his friends were not typical hardcore football fans either, and most of them found it was subsumed amid a variety of other interests and activities in their busy lives, such as going out with the wife or doing a spot of DIY. They talked about refurbishing Victorian flats and which new Audi they wanted to buy (usually a pipe dream); and the ones with children worried about Internet perverts and how to restrict the kids' use of the computer without them noticing.

It was on this particular Saturday that just as James was preparing to go out a car pulled up outside. The doorbell rang. Opening it, he was greeted by two serious-looking men. They stood tall, effectively propping up a nervous and bashful-looking woman who looked meek and diminutive beside them. It was Mary.

PROFESSOR JOHN BEALE: PART THREE

As more and more strange accounts streamed in from all corners of the globe it was becoming almost a joke, but one without a punchline. It was all about people, places and objects. Appearances and disappearances. Believing the eyes or not believing the eyes. Although there was considerable debate raging like a firestorm around the world, in scientific circles one man's bold theories had risen to the top and were now attracting the attention of the world's serious media and those outside his normal sphere of influence.

As a well-attended press conference in London came to a close, Professor John Beale changed gear and gave an impassioned, off-the-cuff speech that was to go down in history. A flaming shot across the bow for those on board SS Earth, he spoke his mind with complete candour, unconcerned about who he might offend or what hackles he might raise.

As he looked around at the large, animated audience he thought to himself 'desperate times call for desperate measures; desperate measures need desperate words to make them happen.'

"Well, ladies and gentlemen, that's really it, the why and how of my theory. So, in a nutshell, we have reached a critical mass of accumulated electromagnetic radiation – caused by us adding to what is already there naturally – and this unnaturally ionised atmosphere causes a radiation overload, which causes unforeseeable magnetic storms of such concentrated magnitude that UVEs are formed in the air. Temporarily. Like silent mini-tornadoes, the magnetic storms travel at lightning speed, but randomly, hitting places even miles away from the source of the radiation. So that is as much as I can say on the UVEs to a general audience, but I would like to elaborate here, as I have been given such a great opportunity to talk to the world – and my allocated time is not yet up." He took a couple of deep breaths, adjusted his tie, and cast a sweeping eye across his audience.

"I think what I am about to say is of critical importance, although there will be many people who will not welcome my desperate words; those whose existing ideas and beliefs will be greatly challenged through what I have to say. Please believe me when I say that I truly respect our differences of opinion; however, as a man of science I believe the truth must out, no matter what it is, and that it is now time for us as a global society to move forward – and to admit that we've got some things wrong and that we need to look with some urgency at what serves our highest needs – and what doesn't.

"Science is a story, told to us in instalments: bit-by-bit, knowledge comes to us, and this knowledge needs to be constantly revised and corrected. These scientific stories create our perception of the universe and how it operates. Importantly, from these stories we have shaped our societal structures, like our relationships with our environment, relationships with other people, how we do business, how we teach our children, how we organise our countries, and even how we define many things. Now, imagine for a minute if you will, that some of these stories are *wrong*. Imagine that some of the most fundamental ones are wildly off-track, and that we are now working out the *real* scientific stories. Please take a leap of faith with me here.

"Now, the scientific stories that underpin our societies on this planet are based on the concept of separateness: the separation of mind from matter, the separation of the material world from the spiritual world. Also, the separation of science from spirituality, and I could give you many other examples, even things like the separation of art from daily life. What this means is that we think our reality comprises separate, finite, measurable parts. It's what we were brought up to believe. We see ourselves as separate from one another, with an underlying philosophy of predictability, scientific certainty, fixed boundaries and so forth. After the

Enlightenment we shifted away from seeing ourselves within Nature to us standing apart from it. Now we see ourselves as superior to everything else on the planet, with the Earth being a place 'outside' us, with resources for us to do what we like with – consequently, we became detached 'managers' and exploiters of 'resources'. We have had to have this human-centred belief in separateness for us to continue to believe in evil, in perfection, in good versus evil, and that for every winner there must be a loser. Eat or be eaten; I win, you lose. This aggressively independent way of thinking – which is currently our prevailing Western belief or paradigm – states that nothing non-local can exist. This means that under the existing separateness model there can be no such things as fields of connected energy at the quantum level, no such thing as the wave-particle uncertainty phenomenon, no such thing as the observer effect on a wave or particle, and certainly no such thing as psychic energy or any of that spooky stuff. A belief in separateness does not allow for an all-encompassing spirituality or the collective consciousness. Separateness, therefore, would infer that what frontier scientists have been proving in labs across the world for decades now involving various non-separate things cannot possibly happen. *But it has.* These things *have* happened. Fact. Empirical evidence. Hard science. Proper scientists doing proper experiments. So, what do we do? Where to from here?

"The Buddha said, 'This life of separateness may be compared to a dream, a phantasm, a bubble, a shadow, a drop of dew, a flash of lightning'. Separateness is illusionary: me and you; us and them. The concept of 'other' looms large, and something or someone deemed 'other' often doesn't seem to matter to us. That can be harmful. And dangerous. From when we are very young we are spoon-fed these notions, as our parents were and their parents before them. We're not bad, we're just misled. But the end result is that we have gone on to build our world based on an erroneous and constricted viewpoint.

"But now, as some of you here today have heard me say in previous talks, cutting-edge scientists are rewriting the books, at last getting at the real truth. A physicist pal of mine put it that they are at the frontier of the frontier. Let's hope this frontier becomes less edge and more mainstream very soon.

"There has been the revelation that our quantum field of energy existing all around us holds us all together in an invisible web. It is a vast web of connection, with an information transfer constantly taking place between living things and their environment. The brain and DNA receive and transmit information from the Zero-Point Field. Scientists have evidence which suggests that consciousness is a substance external to our bodies. Consciousness is, of course, instrumental in shaping our world, and top scientists have demonstrated that thought forms are an aspect of transmitted energy. Thoughts are capable of profoundly affecting all aspects of our lives; with every thought we think and every judgement we hold we are affecting our world.

"Now, all this could be – and is being said by many – to prove the existence of God, or Allah, or whatever name you like to use, by showing that a higher consciousness is out there. And yes, it has also been said that God does not need science to prove anything, and that spiritual truths are not dependent on science. I totally accept that. But science affects the mindset and therefore the activities and lives of so many people in these times that it is worth making these connections and drawing these implications for the greater good. Spirituality does not need science's approval, but it now has it anyway!

"Science and religion need no longer stand opposing each other, tearing strips off each other at every chance: there can now be one unified vision of existence. This is big stuff! We are all part of a larger whole. You can happily wave goodbye to the idea that we are alone and isolated, living out desperate lives on a lonely planet in an indifferent universe. But the where to from here question is not an easy one: we now need to rethink our definitions of ourselves and all life. And this message, should it be fully absorbed and internalised, will allow us to break away from the fear and hate that currently dominate so much of our world and cause so much hardship, violence and misery. Greed. Poverty. Inequality. Etcetera. The list is long.

"But we're up against an old science, a big and strong scientific establishment, whose main quest nowadays is for grants. We have now entered a time of transition, with people unsure and disoriented, searching for the truth about the human experience and looking for ways to heal the world. This is a time where cooperation is needed, and where an acceptance of uncertainty will prove most helpful. The materialist storybook, based on separateness, that we have adopted for the past few hundred years is the colossus that can at last be brought to its knees, as we begin to integrate all fields of knowledge together into a single unified paradigm. This would result in a new, holistic worldview. And this new worldview would avoid or at least mitigate a world-systems catastrophe, which seems to be where we're heading right now. This new worldview generously provides us with a better understanding of who we are and where we are going.

He cleared his throat and continued. "Changing tack for a minute – back to the UVEs, which are, of course, the reason we came together to have this conference. The military of some countries are wanting to exploit these time-space anomalies. They would like to be able to control them and use them for their own purposes, each country with its own separate agenda and separate national interests. I personally do not think this is a good idea. I think this is *so* much bigger than all of us that it cannot be looked at simply in terms of what we humans can get out of it. Is it right to be expressing the – incidentally very separatist – notion of trying to dominate and control so much of Mother Nature, or God, or whatever you want to call it? Is it right for us to have a new mindset – one that is healthy for us and the entire planet? Could it be a good idea to look at how we can better live in harmony with our world again? Is there any truth in the accusation that the current business-as-usual scenario involves tyranny against the natural world? Perhaps some of us forget that we are animals too. Do we, as human animals, have any more right to be here than any other species?"

There was a rumble of noisy unease in some parts of the conference hall.

"Someone just yelled out something about the Bible. I know what you are referring to. That's something to be worked through, but not in this forum. Are there any contradictions in the Bible already? I'm asking this rhetorically; I don't need to hear any answers. I have a sneaking suspicion that there are. But I also know that the Bible and other holy books do say to love, respect and care for all around you as you would wish for yourself; and all around you can be your next-door neighbour, a stray dog, the soil, a river, a tribe in the Amazon.

"And while I've got us all together, under the microscope...I would like to shove into the light one of our big contradictions that we share as a society. Let's release it to the light. Let's stop hiding it in the shadows. Some of our contradictions are very big and like a room with an elephant in it that everyone's pretending isn't there. What elephant? A lot of you might not like what I'm about to say, but perhaps it's time this was said, and I just touched on this a minute ago.

"I wonder, do we *really* have any more right to be here than any other species? Are we really superior to animals? Or to rainforests? Do we have the right to kill for fun? To take a life and call it sport? Or to take a life and call it fine food? What are veal crates really all about? Do we have the right to torture animals in laboratories? Or for so-called traditional medicine? Or breed cats and dogs for fur – and food? And what's it with extracting bear bile from live bears? Or the slow death of harpooned whales? I'll ask again: do animals also have the right to life?

"Most of us say we love animals – we might have some companion animals at home. And yet we are happy for someone else to kill and cut up *other* animals so that we can buy their bodily remains in neat little packages in the shop. Or buy products made from their bodies. Do I say, oh, it's all right as it's one I don't know? What sort of life do animals have the right to? Hmmm. Is there a definite whiff of hypocrisy here, or is it just my imagination?"

There was a noticeable increase in agitation, with some attendees arguing with others, and one or two shouting angrily.

"Ahem! When you've calmed down! These comments I have just made were, I confess, a sneaky little experiment, if you like...and most of you just gave me a *very clear result!* Not all of you though. But, boy! Have I really hit a nerve! This, dear audience, is highly controversial stuff, attacking you right at the core of your belief system. *See how very, very deeply ingrained the belief in separateness is?* See how much reaction I've just got! My word! Did you feel how your blood pressure went up when I just said all those things about what we do to animals? This really does show how things are with us humans, doesn't it! What I was saying about separateness – you have just illustrated it for yourselves by the type of reaction you had."

He paused, watching the animated audience and wondered what his previous smaller audiences of journalists would have been like, were it merely that group in front of him. They slowly quietened as he continued.

"Perhaps we have simply forgotten that animals are our friends and, in some cases, our close cousins. It was Albert Einstein who once commented that 'our task must be to free ourselves from this prison by widening our circles of compassion to embrace all living creatures and the whole of Nature in its beauty'. The prison he was referring to was the delusion of a separate consciousness. He believed that 'reality is merely an illusion, albeit a very persistent one'. The phrase 'keeping it real' suddenly takes on a whole new meaning, huh?

"Many of us live in places and situations we might not have chosen had we felt we had more of a choice. Many live surrounded by walls, cars, noise and rush. Or in abusive relationships. Many live doing jobs that aren't what we would choose in our hearts. Or by not being true to ourselves in some way. Denying ourselves. Suppressing ourselves. Harming ourselves. Perhaps many of us have forgotten who we are and what we are. Perhaps we have forgotten how to live in our world, and that we are part of the *natural world*, not the world of concrete and steel and toxins and isolation. How many of you here know the smell of the mountains? Or the feel of the salty spray of the sea on your face?" The memory of his recent vivid dream flashed through his mind, and he had to suppress a smile. He looked around and noticed a jumble of reactions and emotions.

"Okay, well, perhaps some of us have forgotten what it feels like to be properly *alive?* As awful as that sounds, and I'm certainly not putting myself above anyone here, in *anything* that I am saying – I am just a messenger – but perhaps, just perhaps, Nature Deficit Disorder is a really real condition of modern times? Perhaps we are too removed – too urbanised, too sanitised, too disinfected? Too disengaged?

"I'm not sure what you're all thinking right now, you've gone very quiet! It's good for us to hear different opinions, isn't it? It's good for us to think outside our normal lives and about other possibilities. It's good for us. But, have we really forgotten so much about who we really are? Some social scientists say that to compensate with life in the modern world we load our lives with *things,* seeing material success as the best way forward. And, to a point it is, but they say that things can only satisfy at a shallow level and only temporarily at that. Deeper satisfaction cannot be purchased. But we already know that, don't we? The materially wealthy buy a new car and computer every few years. We discard things so easily now and buy new stuff so easily. We are lured and seduced from all sides. Products are designed to not last. We throw things out and demand that new ones be made from the earth's *finite* resources. Finite – that means there is a limit to them. And this failure to ever be completely satisfied leads to other problems. We drink and take drugs and we connect ourselves up to the latest gadget so that we aren't alone with ourselves and our thoughts – and whatever is beyond that. Then we don't have to think. Sometimes it can hurt to think; some thoughts are painful.

"We robotically repeat the mantra of *must have more money,* no matter how much we already have; must have economic growth. Short-term financial gain. Must keep producing more and more. Must keep getting more and more. But hey, true wealth is abundance that does not cause scarcity or any other problems further afield or further down the track. So, do we have true wealth? Shouldn't we have it by now if our materialistic world was *the way?* This was wasn't mean to be permanent, you know, once people had all the material things they needed the original plan was to level off production, not accelerate it. That little part of history's been forgotten. Hmmm, so how come with all these things we're never satisfied? What is the meaning of life? How come we are trapped in a system *which does not work?* All this can make us less happy than we could be. Can make us lonely. Isolated. Some people become heavily reliant on different things – to work; to making money; to substances – alcohol, drugs; to things like shopping, sex, religion and bad habits. Our true essence and what we deep down know is the right way is pushed still further aside and we may even become ill. A lot of health researchers are now certain that many illnesses are made worse – or even caused – by our thoughts. And, if we feel troubled, taking things like anti-depressants is not the answer. It's a big bad mix of stuff we *are* able to extricate ourselves from. But I'm not saying it's easy. I'm not saying that at all."

Pausing, he studied the audience reactions, which were still wildly diverse. He carried on.

"We need to think about this and the things I touched on earlier, and not just do what our parents did and their parents before them. It's not caveman days anymore. Or the Wild West. Let's move on. We're not pioneers on the Oregon Trail. All that is behind us. Again, I say it – *let's move on!* Let's think for ourselves about how we want this world to be. Let's reinvent ourselves and our society in our grandest vision of who we really are! Let's start redesigning. To quote from Gandhi, 'you must *be* the change you wish to see in the world'.

"Let's look at what we've created. Let's really look. Not just fob it off. The world we have created and are continuously creating is the legacy we leave to our children's children. What sort of world and human society are we designing for them? Is it a good one, getting better all the time? If it's not, then do you think that maybe one or two things I'm saying here just *might* be right? Maybe just worth exploring even *a little?* We all have a choice, and we all are powerful co-creators of the world. Imagine what we could do if we all empowered ourselves! If we acted together in unison – as a strong collective – we could get anything done!

"The ground is fertile and ready, and we are now being handed the seeds. And the light is always right there ready to make it all happen. We see chinks of light from time to time, but most of us are too afraid to go towards this light."

"Because we're not dead yet!" heckled a young male journalist in the front row.

Smiling at him, Professor Beale resumed. "That's true, my friend! And isn't it great? We're not just too afraid to see things for what they really are, we're also too busy. Too busy with working and watching TV. We have forgotten much wisdom we used to know – like where there is a will there is a way.

"It is a fact now scientifically proven that if you are optimistic you are likely to live significantly longer than if you are not.[24]

And that if you believe unfalteringly that things will turn out well in a certain situation they usually do; there's a lot of truth in self-fulfilling prophecies. The power of intention is formidable – all sorts of amazing things can be achieved by us willing them to happen.[25] [26] The power of love is not just a pop song but describes the strongest, most enduring thing that exists. Yes, it sounds hippie, but, frankly, too bad. Compared to love, things like steel and carbon nanotubes bend like marshmallow.

"Experiments in 'conscious evolution' are taking place right now, as I speak. These are people who are reconnecting with our innate personal powers: our mind power. And our heart power. Add to these the laws of attraction. And the power of prayer – prayer can move mountains. The laws of attraction mean that we attract similar things to what we are projecting and being, such as gratitude: if you actively express gratitude, you will attract more and more reasons to feel grateful. That sort of thing.

"To summarise, we humans need to change the way we live in this world. And we need to do it, like, yesterday. There is an urgent need for a return to a position of custodian, with an abandonment of the current assumption of entitlement. To move away from being preoccupied with trade to being preoccupied with morals would be a good thing. By stepping out of the current paradigm and waking up we can create a fantastic quality of life. And with having more quality of life we are more content, we consume less of the earth's resources, we care more, and we look after each other and our beautiful world more. And that would mean that we live in harmony with it, seeing ourselves as *part of it,* not separate from it. Yes, we are *part* of Nature, not separate from it – any separation is an illusion, as I outlined earlier. That is such an important point. Our survival utterly depends on an extraordinary living web of planetary life. Someone once said, and I quote, 'In discovering we live within a living universe, we open to the heartening knowledge that we are one of her precious offspring, seeking communion with her depths'.[27]

"And I am saying all this stuff not because I'm a mouthy so-and-so, but because if we evolve a little bit more – spiritually, I mean – we would then stop our interfering with our planet's functioning and these damned Unexplained Visual Experiences would cease."

He wondered why his microphone had not been switched off. *Surely,* he thought, *to so many this talk must feel like a hell of a hiding.* Most people were looking stunned. A few looked deliriously happy. There weren't many left looking angry, as those ones had all walked out much earlier.

"See, I did have a point with all this, and that was it! Please think about what I have said! I know I've said a lot here, and as this last part has not been a planned speech it has been somewhat unstructured. I hope I've made sense all the same. And, critically, as far as this now admittedly very hijacked speech goes – I make no apologies for that – I want to end by reiterating the main point that I am trying to make, which is that by making some big changes to how we think and how we live and how we view the universe – based on this new frontier science – not only would we help ourselves transform our lives, but we would also enable the planet to survive…and we would *bring an end to the space-time anomalies* – our current symptom of the increasing chaos of an unhappy Earth!"

DECISIONS

Ushering them into the living room, James was unsure whether to make cups of tea or prepare vials of arsenic. Righteous indignation threatened to spill off his tongue at any moment but he held back. Equally incensed and aggrieved, he felt it would be justified to let them have it – for Mary, for Agnes and for Agnes's death – but a part of him wondered if perhaps it might be better to keep the lid firmly on the venom and just accept Mary's return with gratitude and joy.

"Mr Harvey," one of the men began, "as you can see we are returning Mary to her home. She has undergone a variety of tests and has been treated with the utmost care, I can assure you."

James said nothing but took a deep breath. His face was hard.

The man continued, "We know there's been a media circus, but we would like you to understand that it is over now, and that she is able to stay here with you. But we are required to look at possible counselling needs she may have as a result of her, er, treatment."

"Nothing much," assured the other man, "just routine for people who have been in detention for as long as she has. Not quite the Guantanamo Bay sort of thing but, you know, just wanting to make sure that she can settle back into society with no problems."

There was a tense silence in the room.

The first man spoke again, "Well, we must be off. We were just tasked with dropping her home. We hope that in time you'll accept why we acted in the way we did and that we were only trying to understand the truth about her."

"And there were some immigration questions hanging over her, too," the other man chipped in.

"She's not a bloody object! She has got a name!" James blared.

The first man continued undeterred, "I'm not at liberty to

divulge, but I can say that she has given a lot of people something to think about. Her truth is shocking. How she got here, we are still trying to figure out. We do not consider her a security risk, nor are there outstanding immigration matters."

"Anymore," the second man added.

"We have gathered data on her and will hold it in a databank. We have decided, with support from the prime minister's office, to issue her with enough identification papers so as to allow her to work here and live a normal life—"

"What!" James interrupted. "You'll give her papers so that she can work! And pay tax! So bloody good of you!"

"A courier will arrive in the next few days with a passport, birth certificate and other papers for her. This will stop the media fawning all over her once they get the idea that she isn't what they thought." He stood and headed towards the door. The other man leapt up and followed, pausing along the way to admire James's antique wall barometer. He ran his fingers along the thermometer part.

"TAKE YOUR HANDS OFF IT!" James barked.

The man jumped back.

The first man carried on, "Oh, and Mrs Woodham-Walter's death was, I can assure you, tragic as it was, due to natural causes and was in no way related to her detention. She died peacefully in her sleep and was found in the morning...actually looked happy. She was smiling and—"

"YOU SICK BASTARDS! GET OUT OF MY HOUSE – NOW!" James lunged at the men and as they were stepping out he slammed the door on their heels.

He looked back at Mary. She got off the sofa and went to him. For a long minute they looked at each other, saying nothing. Then they clasped each other tightly and stayed there until their bodies began to ache from the position.

* * *

As they became reacquainted with each other nothing else mattered; time seemed to stand still. Mary's state was delicate. She had lost weight, looked pale and miserable and kept bursting into tears. After they had talked for some time, James gently sat her down and excused himself while he made a few quick phone calls, letting his parents and Donald know of her safe return. He then returned to her and they continued talking.

"Mary, I've nearly been arrested, and my father has made himself practically an official enemy of the state. We've been contacting everyone we could think of. No one would tell us where you were after you were moved to Essex. Did you know it was Agnes who knew for sure that you were in the house in Guildford? She reckoned she could do this thing – distant viewing or remote viewing, I think it's called. My father thought you might be there too, but Agnes was the only one that got to them, you know, she became a massive pain in the neck for them. That's why they moved you from Guildford to Essex – to get away from her prying and her all-seeing eye."

Mary smiled weakly.

"I didn't know that she was going to rescue you that day. She just did it, in cahoots with Donald and Lynne. I'm just so fucked off it didn't work."

She elbowed him. "Don't swear."

"Sorry. Been on my own too long."

"But," Mary began, "it wasn't right for Agnes to be there. It was just horrible the way it turned out for her. She shouldn't have had to go through it. She shouldn't have had to die there – in a soulless place like that." She wept.

* * *

The passport and papers arrived, and gradually Mary settled back into her life with James, telling him about her experience, and through that talking, understanding and working through her feelings. She had had a lot of time to think, and through the anguish and uncertainty a clarity of mind and heart was emerging.

"I thought I was going to be made to wear the broad arrow, but fortunately I wasn't".

"What's the broad arrow?" James asked.

"The arrow markings on convicts' uniforms," she replied. "Some people call them the Devil's claws."

He smiled. "I don't think it would have been a good look for you."

"No. Instead they gave me a few very ordinary clothes to wear, none of which fitted me properly. When I had to wear Agnes's clothes, God bless her soul, I was too tall and not the right shape. I felt like a right mad thing when I walked up that road to the car when I escaped! I must have looked completely mad!"

"I'm just pleased they didn't hurt you – and that they've let you go at last."

"James, they *did* hurt me."

He looked at her inquisitively.

"Oh, you men! They may not have flogged me or tortured my body, but they kept me in a glass jar, like some poor specimen of Darwin's, and they would examine me and test me. And watch me. And prod me. And make me endure the most hellish boredom. It was so monotonous…and made me very, very low. It was routine. And there was seldom anyone to talk to. Only one window to look out usually: only one side of the world existed; I knew the sun had risen but could never see it happening. They may not have hurt my flesh, but they deprived me of the open air, the sunlight, the sights of the world, the smells of the world, the sounds, the freedom to come and go as I wish, and the freedom to be who I am. They hurt me in ways that bruises and beatings could not have. I've realised so acutely that one's freedom is the most valuable thing, far more valuable than any pearls or diamonds or glittery riches. Without freedom, any person is a pauper. I read in a book while I was in there that 'life without liberty is like a body without spirit'.[28] I have decided that there is a very fine line we all tread, and that the object is not to cross the line. Although in my case, the line was ill-defined and arbitrarily drawn up, with me not fitting properly on either side – which is why they took me."

"But now you've got papers, an identity. So you've been given a place on one side of the line, the side that lets you have freedom and as normal a life as possible under the circumstances."

"James, freedom also depends on who is defining it. That is something to consider. I know that through the years there has been a lot of misuse and twisting of the concept of freedom. You know I've read George Orwell's *1984*. I know how language can be craftily used by people pursuing a particular agenda."

"Okay, well, you'll have as good a freedom as almost anybody has."

"James, I shall *never* be able to have a normal life here! I shall never be able to consider myself completely free. If I am lucky I may never be imprisoned again, but I will always be just a visitor here, someone from somewhere else – that can never change. But," she sighed, "no matter."

"I know," he said quietly.

"I have papers now which say I was born *after you were*. They are useful, but they are lies. My life is to be lived around lies or else I will get in more trouble. Ironic, isn't it? I used to always get in trouble *for* telling lies! Now I am torn between telling the truth and telling lies. History – my year of birth – has been rewritten for the sake of convenience. It doesn't seem right. Yet without the lies I could not get by in your world, and would, had I not met you and you been the wonderful person you are, very likely have ended up in some ghastly institution or homeless on the streets. The truth would have been unpalatable and unacceptable, and I would have had to live my life here as a freak that no one believed and that no one wanted to know." She started to cry. "A freak cared for by no one and loved by no one."

He hugged her. "But that hasn't happened, and you're not alone, you're here with me. It's all right."

"It just makes me so aware of that line I was talking about – that knife edge. It hovers close, even with you in my life, looking after me. I can almost feel its cold metal blade…"

"Come on, a little less dramatic, it's all right," he soothed.

"And what about the other people?" she asked. "The others like me?"

"Huh? What others?"

"Surely there are others like me, others who have been swept up by this unexplained time…thing and dumped here. Or perhaps dumped into other times. I pity them. At least I am fortunate. I have had Providence on my side…and now *you*." She caressed James's face. He smiled without saying anything. He could feel his stomach nerves on fire and heat rising to his face.

"James, I know I am truly blessed! And I am indescribably *overjoyed* to be back here with you! I am counting my blessings…and I have *so many!*"

* * *

Mary sat down to read her mail. She was still receiving a steady stream of letters from people either just wanting to say hello and tell her how much they were behind her, or from people with commercial interests – wanting to have her on a TV show or get her to endorse a product, or write lengthy biographical articles on her. She turned them all down, telling them she simply wanted a normal, private life, away from the stare of the public eye. Some mail was nasty, and suggesting that she was nothing but a fraud, but those letters were quickly put to one side and binned. She came to one letter which had a local solicitor's stamp on the front. Uneasily, she opened it and read its contents.

"With the death of Mrs Agnes Woodham-Walter and the subsequent sale of her property" Mary was "to receive the sum of one hundred thousand pounds".

The overall total had apparently been apportioned between herself and several other relatives, and the hundred thousand pounds was required to be banked into her bank account at her nearest convenience. Once the firm received the bank details Mary's money would be duly deposited.

She dropped the letter on to James's lap.

"Read this."

He read it from start to finish without speaking then looked at her. "This is incredible! Mary, this niece of yours just keeps surprising us! This is *fantastic* news for you!"

"I know. God bless her soul. She's like a guardian angel. When will she stop helping me? Even now that she's dead she's still helping me! I've never known anybody quite like her."

"Me neither. She was one in a million. I wish I'd known her sooner."

"She was the salt of the earth, just like her mother before her."

"Mary, this is fantastic!"

"James, it's a lot of money. I've never heard of anyone having anywhere remotely near this much money."

"It sure is a lot!" He looked at her seriously for a moment before continuing, "Mary, I've been thinking."

"Yes?"

"I've been thinking that we should sell this house and move away."

"What?" She looked at him.

"Sell and go somewhere. Travel first, see the world together, then settle somewhere different. Abroad, perhaps."

"Oh."

"Well, what do you think?"

"It's certainly an interesting proposition, but I need some time to think. Would it be respectable for me to be with you, doing all that?"

"Mary! Times have changed! No one would think anything less of you!"

"Well, what did you have in mind?"

"We could do a world trip first, then move to somewhere like, I'm not sure, but I was thinking of maybe Italy or France. Or even Australia or New Zealand."

"Goodness! Do you remember what I told you about New Zealand that day we met?"

"Sort of. Something negative," he said.

"I'm sorry, but that was my impression."

"It's changed a lot since 1901!"

"I know! Everywhere has! I've had to revise my opinions on a lot of things!"

"So what do you think now? Not just New Zealand – that might be a bit too far away, but what about Australia? You know, it's a darn sight warmer out there!"

"Yes, all very well if you don't mind big horrid bugs and snakes and crocodiles and sports fanatics everywhere! And those strange accents!"

He laughed. "That's the one! You crack me up. I'll tell you what. How about we travel to these places, as well as many others, and see what we think first-hand before we make up our minds? That would make a lot of sense, wouldn't it?"

"Yes, that would be..." she paused, looking at him. "That would be absolutely marvellous! That's so exciting, I can hardly wait!" She leaned over and kissed him on the cheek. He grabbed her and kissed her on the lips. She made the decision there and then that she could quite happily spend the rest of her life with this man.

* * *

Arrangements were made for the house to be put on the market. The money bequeathed from Agnes was banked into a joint account they opened specially, and was to be added to from the sale of James's house. Even with what he still owed on his mortgage they would walk away with a tidy sum. With the two amounts put together they felt sure they would be able to travel well and then make a good start wherever in the world they wanted to settle.

* * *

It was on the same day that contracts were exchanged on the property that James came home early from work, surprising Mary, who was busily tidying the garden at the front of the house.

"Hello!" she offered, startled. "It's only half-past three! They haven't fired you, have they?"

Grinning, he put her gardening tools out of sight around the corner, then swept her up in his arms. He carried her out to the car, depositing her gently inside.

"Mr Harvey, you've gone mad!"

He shut the door, got in and drove them away.

"What are you doing? Where are we going? My handbag is in the house. And look at how I'm dressed."

He said nothing.

"My hands are dirty and I'm dressed in scruffy clothes with dirt on them! And I'm sure my hair has bits of the garden in it! I can't go out like this!"

He still said nothing.

"Tell me! You *have* gone mad! It had to happen, didn't it? *I've* driven you mad, haven't I?" She laughed.

He drove them to the foot of Leith Hill, the highest point in south-east England. Reaching the car park James stopped the car and got out. He raced around to her door and took her by the hand. He then led her up a long and steep track up the hill. Despite her inevitable questions and protestations he carried on without a word. Eventually reaching the top, they looked around at the view over Surrey. It was a clear day and without the haze that so often clung to the landscape. Smiling, and with a glint of something she had not seen in his eyes before, he led her to a spot on the grass, not far from the eighteenth-century tower that marked the top of the hill. He reached into his jacket pocket then fell to one knee before her.

"Mary, I have brought you here for a reason. I hope it's a good reason. I was wondering, and have been wondering for a while now, um…Mary, would you make me a happy man and agree to be my wife?"

She gasped. Their eyes locked together for a long moment.

"James, oh James! You have swept me off my feet, but I'm afraid you'll have to ask my father's permission!"

The look of utter horror that flashed across James's face made Mary eventually burst out laughing.

"Yes! Yes! I will marry you! I can think of nothing I would rather do!"

He looked relieved. "Phew! Great! Fantastic!" He placed a ring on her finger.

She fell to her knees and kissed him passionately.

* * *

The feeling was as though a new layer, something soft and comforting, had been wrapped around the two of them. From this cotton wool-like encapsulation Mary seemed happy, but shadows still lurked behind the smiles and excited talk. Privately, she was apprehensive, wondering what her parents would think of her marrying and settling in this world of the future – and of her possibly even leaving the country.

She told herself that her mother would say, "Try to come home! Try everything you can think of to come home! Go back to the churchyard, to Sarah's grave, and sit there, looking at the headstone as you were doing when you were so cruelly and freakishly taken from us. Pray to God and think about your family, grieving and bereft in their poor house with only just enough food to warm their bellies. Pray to our gracious and generous Lord for a swift return to 1901! To things and people as they were and as they are supposed to be! Return to those you love and who love you! COME HOME! COME HOME! COME HOME!"

Mary searched her whole being for a shred of a clue about what she should do. She had told James she would marry him, but that, she knew, was spoken out of impulse and emotion, not after careful thought. She was taken by surprise, and was flattered and excited by the proposition.

She could hear her father saying, "Don't rush in to anything, my girl. Step carefully, for the road is always full of hazards." He would want her home too, to earn money for the household and to be there for them when they were old and needed care. "No need to marry," he might say, "unless you are really sure, and unless you believe you could not live without this person. And if you do marry, stay close. Don't tarry too long out and about – we will need your assistance when we're old."

The guilt and angst struck her sharply, and like a large thorn it pricked through to her core, reaching her heart and almost drawing blood.

Mary told James that she did not want to try to go back home anymore. She said she felt sure that whatever peculiarity of Nature had existed in the churchyard that day no longer existed there and had closed up or moved elsewhere. She had been back to visit Sarah's grave on several occasions since moving in with James, and on not one of those occasions had she felt or thought that the opportunity existed for her to return, Alice-like, through any invisible rabbit hole. But how could she detect the oppor-tunity, she pondered, unless she was actually transported? Could the space-time 'hole' be felt or touched? Did it have a surface or a texture? Did it have a sound? Or a smell? Or a vibration or resonance in the air? Would it make the ground tremble like a small earthquake? Would it make you feel a certain feeling – queasy? Or something extra-sensory? And the biggest question of all: would it be visible to the human eye, with its ability to see only a small part of what was really there? She knew none of the answers and could remember nothing of her journey on that fateful day: it had been over before she had known it had even happened. But nonetheless she helped James and his parents plan the wedding, even with her heart aching for her family and the beloved land she would soon be leaving behind, possibly forever.

MARY'S DREAM

Preparations were made for leaving and the house was packed up. James's parents were going to take most of their things, but the large items of furniture had to go into storage until the date to be shipped out. Boxes were stacked high in the living room, giving the appearance of a small warehouse, and they lived amid chaos for a few days.

On one of those chaotic days while James was out taking care of some last minute arrangements Mary was at home, sitting on one of the boxes enjoying a cup of tea. Exhausted, she lay back and slumped into a position that allowed her to drift into a light sleep. Wafting in and out of consciousness, she eventually abandoned herself to the heavy fatigue that gripped her.

As the sleep deepened, she was sure that she was also sitting up again, holding her cup of tea. As she sipped, a movement caught her eye. Next to one of the piles of boxes she spotted a hazy shadow. Puzzled, she blinked her eyes a few times. From the fuzziness she began to see the image of a person. She fumbled with her cup of tea and almost dropped it on to the floor. A few drops flew out and the cup fell, clanking loudly on to the saucer.

"You'd better be careful, my dear. You don't want to have to come back to clean that up!"

Mary's jaw fell open. She was unable to speak.

"I see the cat's got your tongue, eh! Never used to happen much before, did it!" The figure laughed. "You were always one for a great deal of conversation – good conversation, I might add."

"Er," Mary began hesitantly, "is that really *you*?"

"Well, yes. It is I, the woman who gave birth to you well over a hundred years ago! What a thought! Such a long time! It's lovely, very lovely to see you, my dear. We did miss you so."

Mary gasped. "I...I missed you too! Still do!"

Silence.

"Have you not got anything to talk about?"

Mary fidgeted. "Um, are you all right? I mean, what's it like...wherever you are?"

"Oh, my child. I am fine, and this place is the most wonderful place. But we don't need to discuss that. We want to say how happy we are for you to be marrying."

Mary's eyes moistened.

"I am delighted for you, and you must stop worrying about what we think about what you are doing. You are doing the right thing marrying Mr Harvey. Be happy. Enjoy the freedom which this world can give you. And be yourself."

Mary cleared her throat. "Thank you. That means very much to me."

"And speaking of freedom, that is one thing we have here too."

"Freedom to do this? To talk to me?" Mary asked.

"Yes. Sometimes. Rarely though. It is only allowed if the person being visited will benefit from the visit. It has to fit in with things destined for the person. Often we come to you when you are asleep at night."

"Oh." She was still at a loss for words.

"Are you going to ask anything else before I go?"

"You're going? Already?"

"I can stay a little longer."

"Mother, are you one of these Unexplained Visual Experiences that are happening everywhere just now?"

Her mother smiled. "Like you, you mean?"

Mary nodded.

"No. This is different."

"Oh."

"And I know you've been wondering – everyone in the family knows about what you've been doing and we approve of what you are doing, not that you need our approval. Getting married and moving out of England are two very big things. We think it is good and we are very pleased for you. Please stop entertaining the thought that you are somehow turning your back on us by leaving England. You are not. You are no closer to us here than anywhere else in the world. We can see that things could be quite difficult for you here in England if you were to stay. So, go, my dear, and see the world. It is something your father and I were not able to do. There was no way for us to up sticks, but you can. Your mind is big and wide and needs the whole world as its home, not just one little corner. You are a woman of the world in the best sense, and you are gifted with great intelligence and the ability to write well – which is something you must try to do again. Perhaps when you are settled."

Mary looked stunned. Her mother had never supported her writing before and it seemed strange for her to be saying these things now.

"Thank you, mother. *Thank you very much!*"

"And something else I know you're wondering about...your family's fine and happy and everyone sends their love. Your father is here with me now."

A tall figure stepped forward from the shadows.

"Father!"

"Hello, Mary, my girl. It's strange how it's all turned out, isn't it? For all those years you were missing I thought you were dead. I was certain – for over thirty odd years!"

"I was *here!*"

"I know. It's all right now. Everything's all right now."

"It wasn't my fault! I'm so sorry for putting you through that! It must have been dreadful. I can't begin to imagine. First you lost Sarah, then me. And both in the same year."

"It's all right now, love." He moved to stand beside her and placed a hand on her shoulder. She jumped at his touch.

"You thought I couldn't touch you," he said softly.

Mary nodded, sobbing and wiping her eyes.

"The good Lord gives us many abilities in your world; you would be surprised."

"Mary," her mother began, "I know you remember us often. We are all fine now. And Sarah is with us again. We are with all your brothers and sisters."

Mary buried her face in her hands for a moment. "Ohhhh, this is all too much to take in at once! My head's swimming! I can't believe it!"

There was silence.

"Mary," her mother eventually said, "I have someone else here who would like to say hello."

Out of the gloom next to her mother the figure of a woman slowly materialised. Mary had to blink the tears from her eyes. She drew a sharp intake of breath as the features took form.

"Agnes? *Agnes! Oh, Agnes, I'm so sorry! I'm so sorry that you—*"

"Died?" Agnes suggested.

"Yes! I'm so sorry! And I want to thank you for everything you did. You truly went above and beyond…" She burst into tears again, managing to add, "Thank you, Agnes. Thank you."

Agnes looked moved. "Please don't be upset. It was my time to go. It had been written in the stars at the moment of my birth."

Mary shook her head. "I have so much to learn, haven't I?"

The other three smiled.

"Agnes, I got your letter, it was wonderful. I've still got it; I'm keeping it always. And thank you *so very much* for what you left me. You didn't have to—"

"Shush! I had enough money tied up in that old house to go around. It made me so happy seeing you that day you found out about it. You are now able to make a good new start somewhere else, away from all the past which still clings to you like mud while you remain here. It is healthy for you not to forget but to experience somewhere else. Get out there! It's a big, exciting world!"

"Before we go," her mother began, "we just want to say that we are always but a hair's breadth away from you. If you call us we will come. If you need help, just ask. There are many, not just us, who are here to help, especially if you ask for it. Keep trusting your instincts and your heart. Your head may lie to you and play games, but your heart will always be true to you. Your life is with Mr Harvey now and he is a good man. He will take care of you and will keep you safe in a world which is not really yours. He is someone who loves you deeply and he can be trusted. Enjoy your life in this world and always be true to yourself. I love you, my daughter. We all do." Her mother then stepped back, visibly upset, before melting away into the air of the room.

Her father followed on with, "My love goes with you, my girl. You make us proud, you do. Goodbye just now…and make sure you do that writing." He touched her again on the shoulder before departing.

"Goodbye, dear," said Agnes. "Enjoy your life, but never forget who you are and where you came from. Gather the wisdom of the ages and help carry it back to the people, to the generations who are now so very much in need of it. Be a messenger. Spread wisdom through your writing. And through how you live your life – try to be an example. God bless you." She stepped back and slowly dissolved away. Mary had noticed that Agnes was no longer stooped but had been standing erectly with good posture, and looking considerably younger too.

Thinking that the visit was over, Mary began to cry. As she did, she was startled to see, for a few seconds only, her sister Matilda. She was standing in the middle of the room, grinning and waving madly. The vision broke away back into the ether, leaving nothing but boxes and what Mary had always thought to be thin air.

THE TREATY OF SHANGHAI

With halting steps and much to-ing and fro-ing the Treaty of Shanghai lurched into being. Words like 'desperate', 'cut-throat' and 'highly pressured' were bandied about by commentators, and it was true that the diverse nations involved had had to get through months of investigating, discussing, lobbying, arguing and general haggling. The treaty took all the skills and extraordinary patience that its politicians and negotiators could muster, and it was hailed universally as a mammoth achievement. The agreement eventually forged was revolutionary: its international commitment was to put the world to right, at least in some ways. It was formally agreed by all nations that the unexplained time anomalies were not a good thing, and that they were a danger to society the world over, particularly with aviation and other forms of transport incurring many deaths due to these bizarre occurrences. Many people took a lot of persuading, first, that there was actually a problem and, second, that the problem was caused by human activity. This initial period of flapping and floundering went on for some time, with vested interests – of which there were *many* – stepping up to the plate to authoritatively and categorically deny any link between their technology and the UVEs. They claimed that no one had been able to prove scientifically any link between their products and the UVEs. They maintained that the arguments being put forth by experts such as Professor John Beale were at best spurious, and, at worst, conspiratorial: that because he held such strong desires for the world to change he was using his position of scientific influence as a tool for leveraging the world back into some neo-hippie New Age, low-technology place; a place without the wonderful array of machines that serve us so well today. Did he never go shopping?, they asked. Did he not own a mobile phone? Anyway, they argued, these sorts of things – unexplained mysteries of the paranormal variety – had happened for as long as humanity had been on the planet, and were just freaks of Nature.

Opponents of the vested interests countered that, yes, paranormal activity involving what were termed timeslips had been happening for as long as people had lived on the planet, that was true. But, while some degree of 'that sort of thing' did seem natural, the very big and frightening number happening now had crossed out of 'natural' phenomena and into unnatural phenomena. They added that there had also been the suggestion that the disappearing bee populations over the past several years had been partly caused by radiation. The hypothesis was that bees' absorption of certain pulses of radiation weakened their immune systems and increased their susceptibility to various diseases. Coupled with this was the theory in some quarters that the health of human and non-human animals was damaged by doses of too much radiation, including the type that pulsed at a frequency that could disturb, or even interrupt, the functioning of the heart.

With these additional horrific possibilities weighing heavily on their shoulders something had to be done, whether one believed all the theories or not; and speculation as to what else could unravel was anybody's guess: the fear of yet more UVE-type things happening was enough to galvanise world leaders into agreeing to suspend the use and manufacturing of all radiation-emitting gadgets and gizmos with immediate effect. In a legal thunderbolt, the world was changed. The list of banned technologies and activities was long, and included passages on emerging technology and clandestine official 'black budget stuff', as some media called it. Forests of mobile phone masts, as well as hardware pertaining to Wi-Fi were reduced to leftover relics of what was now seen as flawed technology. Coming down like a hammer on areas most people had not thought of, such as aeronautics, the navy and defence in general, it was a contentious treaty and remained riven by doubters and naysayers, who, as well as vilifying a certain physics professor, repeatedly insisted that the whole thing was a plot by the Left to pacify all nations and return them to darker days, sparking visions of everyone having to wear hair-shirts, grow their own food and plough fields with oxen once more. But despite the angry protests the treaty was signed, and once implemented it heralded the return of calmer, safer times. Or at least calm *time*. And safe *time*.

THE CITY OF LIGHT

A string quartet consisting of two violinists, a viola player and a cello player, all wearing top hats and tails, welcomed people as they stepped on board the boat. Frank and Edwina stood near them, greeting the guests, who arrived more or less all at once. After a head count and check through of the guest list the festivities got underway. Minutes later, the vessel slipped its moorings and was off, gliding through the calm water with ease and certainty. The guests found seats on the deck or inside and settled into a cosy ride. One of the world's grandest cities was to be theirs for the day.

"Ahhh, la ligne de vie de Paris!" exclaimed Edwina, admiring the view.

"Yes," Frank agreed, "perhaps more so in the past than now, but it's still an important river, even if it is just used mainly for the likes of us tourists."

"Tourists...travellers...Johnny foreigners!" James quipped.

"Some of us more than others," Mary quietly replied.

Edwina became serious as she began, "Mary, we must get to know each other better. A lot has happened since we first met, that day at James's house, when I suppose I put my foot in it about your family...of course I didn't know. How was I to know? But as you're about to become my daughter-in-law in approximately ten minutes' time..." She looked into the distance, lost in thought.

"Mary," Frank said, saving the situation, "how's your geography?"

"Oh, nothing to write home about, that's for sure. Not as good as it ought to be. Why do you ask?"

"I'm sure you must have a reasonable idea of what Paris is like."

"Mmmm, I suppose so, but only in general terms and not the

things that have happened since 1901."

"There are some interesting things in our view at the moment, it's almost out of sight but you can just see...look over there." He pointed. "There's the tip of the glass pyramid that marks the entrance to the Louvre."

"Oh...yes, I see. What a sight. Not quite like the ones in Egypt though!" Mary said, laughing.

"No," Frank replied seriously. "And up that way, on the other side, is the Musée d'Orsay. Brilliant art in there, my word. Although nowhere beats the Louvre."

"Except perhaps the National Gallery in London," said Edwina. "*That* is something. We've got *so many* great works there."

"Yes, I know," Frank placated. "Look," he said, turning back to Mary, "you can see so much when you sail down this river. Do you see it? For a city, Paris has got so much. Fantastic designs, best in the world, if you ask me. You just have to look around. There's such an emphasis on beauty and good design. Such flair. Even the street lights are stylish. Why can't we make ours like that?"

"I wouldn't go too far with flattering the French," Edwina said.

"Why ever not, dear?" Frank asked, winking at James and Mary.

She laughed nervously, replying, "Oh, for goodness sake! Well, for a start, *they're French!*"

Mary smiled. "You're like my parents and grandparents! They didn't care much for the French, either. I suppose it must've been because of Trafalgar and all the other battles in the past."

"There you go, love," joked Frank, "you're a bit of a dinosaur! Sharing views with people born in the nineteenth century! I thought you liked to be more up-to-date than that!"

She glared at him and said nothing.

"Mum, how can you hate people you don't even know?"

James asked.

"It's a collective thing. Not individual. And I don't *hate* them, that's too strong."

"Yes," Frank interjected, "you've had to accept Mary's story, which is extremely hard to believe really, so why can't you make the leap with your mind to getting rid of these silly prejudices? We're all capable of changing the way we think and act and making everything much better."

She pursed her lips and looked the other way.

"Edwina, love, we're not picking on you, honestly."

She huffed. "Frank, please don't spoil this special day. We're supposed to be focusing on our son and his lovely wife-to-be."

"That's true; our lovely daughter-in-law-to-be. The one with the unbelievable story. Which we now believe. We've made our minds break out of their old ways of thinking and accept new things. As hard as it's been, we've *had* to. I think it's bloody exciting!"

James spoke up, "Okay…I think we've driven into a conversational cul-de-sac! Mary, let's mingle." He took her arm and attempted to whisk her away, but she stopped him.

"Yes, that's right," Mary said to Frank and Edwina. "Your daughter-in-law-to-be – the one with the French ancestry!"

"What? *Really?*" James looked surprised.

"Yes. Going back on my father's mother's side there was a French woman who moved to England because she fell in love with an Englishman."

"I didn't know that."

"It's true. It gave my family a dilemma at times about whether to like or loath the French."

"So, I believe they chose loathing," Edwina said slyly.

Mary sighed. "Yes, but it was only mild, to be honest. They weren't as bad as, um…as some. But they'd never met their French ancestor – she died in the eighteenth century, well before my grandparents were born. My parents and grandparents never met any French people in their whole lives."

"They didn't travel, did they?" James asked.

"No. It wasn't like today."

Frank chuckled. "So, Edwina, are you going to go home and tip out all our French wine, sell your French car, change your Internet provider, never eat French fries again and...what else can I think of?"

"No!" She turned her back on her husband.

"Dad, you're going a bit far. You're giving her a hard time, it's not really fair. I think you should lay off."

Frank thought for a moment then placed his hand on her arm. "I'm sorry, love. Went a bit far."

She said nothing.

"Did I tell you that we're booked into the Paris Ritz for dinner tomorrow night?"

She spun around and her face lit up. "Are we really?"

"Yes. Should be nice, shouldn't it?"

"Ooh, lovely! Although we'll probably still be full from all the lovely food we'll be having today!"

"Not *us!*" Frank said, laughing, playfully nudging his wife in the ribs.

"Look at this!" Mary called, pointing. "Do you all see the water – the way it's so glassy just over there? What a picture!"

The hung their heads over the side.

"It is remarkable," said Edwina. "So calm. Not a single ripple down there."

"If you look really hard," Mary continued, "you can see your own reflection, even from this height. I can see mine." She waved to herself.

James saw his, then commented, "I see you too. A nice bright hat – very modern...*this time!* Ultra white dress! Dazzling! Look at that! And the face – radiant! In fact, a fine fettle of a woman! Good enough to marry, methinks!" He gave her a quick kiss.

"I can see myself, I think," said Frank. "Uh, yes! That's me.

Very respectable looking chap! Hello! Heh! You know it's actually quite impressive to be able to do that from up here."

Edwina squinted and moved her head from side to side. "I must be looking in the wrong place. I can't see my reflection. No, I can't see myself. How come you can see yourselves?"

"Just keep looking, dear, keep looking."

"We have to go," James said, tugging Mary away. They walked up the stairs to the front of the boat in time to see the minister shuffling about, making last minute preparations. Seeing them approaching in their finery he smiled, guiding them to their positions. He reminded them where they would have to stand, and confirmed a few of the formalities. The minister, along with everyone else present, had been transported over en masse from London via the Eurostar train, and had arrived at Paris's Gare du Nord station the previous afternoon. It was a happy entourage, with assorted friends and relatives of James, including his sister and her family, who made the long journey from New Zealand. Mary did not have anyone she could invite, apart from Donald and Lynne, who were thrilled to receive an invitation.

Mary dashed off to find Donald, who was to escort her along the centre of the deck, between the two blocks of seating. The musicians played a lively rendition of Handel's *Arrival of the Queen of Sheba* while the crowd settled into the seats on deck. Gradually, they quietened. The ceremony began just as the boat was rounding the northern side of Paris's centrepiece, the Ile de la Cité. The gothic towers of Notre Dame came into view as the music stopped and the minister began to speak. The couple had chosen to write their own words and employ a style completely of their own. The minister read his rites and the couple made their vows.

"...This marriage provides not obligations but opportunities. Opportunities for growth, for full self-expression, for lifting your lives to their highest potential, for healing every false thought or small idea you ever had about yourself, and for ultimate reunion with God through the communion of your two souls.

"This is a Holy Communion, a journey through life with one you love as an equal partner, sharing equally both the authority and the responsibilities inherent in any partnership, bearing equally what burdens there may be, basking equally in the glories. Is that the vision you wish to enter into now?"

"It is," they both said. Further vows were made.

James finished off his part of the ceremony with, "I, James, ask you, Mary, to be my partner, my lover, my friend and my wife. I announce and declare my intention to give you my deepest friendship and love, not only when your moments are high, but when they are low. Not only when you are acting with love, but when you are not. I further announce before God and those here present that I will seek always to see the light of divinity within you and seek always to share the light of divinity within me, and especially in whatever moments of darkness may come.

"It is my intention to be with you forever in a holy partnership of the soul that we may do together God's work sharing all that is good within us with all those whose lives we touch."

The minister concluded, "We observe joyfully that you have declared yourselves to be husband and wife. Let us join now in prayer. Spirit of love and life, out of this whole world two souls have found each other. Their destinies shall now be woven into one design, and their perils and their joys shall not be known apart.

"James and Mary, may your home be a place of happiness for all who enter it; a place where the old and the young are renewed in each other's company, a place for growing and a place for sharing, a place for music and a place for laughter, a place for prayer and a place for love.

"May those who are nearest to you be constantly enriched by the beauty and the bounty of your love for one another, may your work be a joy of your life that serves the world, and may your days be good and long upon the Earth." [29]

"Amen."

The quartet struck up with Beethoven's *Ode to Joy* as the couple strode slowly to the back of the boat. A warm breeze sent ripples in the fabric of Mary's dress as she walked, reminding James of the moment when he had first set eyes on her, with her old overcoat flapping in the chilly wind that had howled through the graveyard on that November day, which now seemed so long ago. He smiled to himself at the memory of the unusual scene that had unfolded outside the church. She lifted her head and inhaled the river air deeply, drinking in the moment. She squeezed his hand and smiled. They kissed and held each other.

Edwina blew her nose several times as she walked along to congratulate the pair, who were by then becoming busily ensconced with photographers.

"Brilliant ceremony!" Frank said, walking beside her. "Loved the words. They've done a fantastic job of putting pen to paper. Surprised me. Didn't know the boy had it in him! Much better than the usual pap you get at weddings."

"Frank, shush!"

After the photographs, the newlyweds, with Edwina and Frank, walked down to below deck, where a sumptuous banquet was laid out on several long tables positioned end to end. The music played and champagne flowed. Everybody was seated and the speeches began. Some were witty and deliberately amusing, while others were amusing in ways that had perhaps not been intended.

James stood and, guided by some handwritten notes, ad-libbed freely. After thanking everyone for coming, and thanking the best man, bridesmaids, minister and several others, he continued, "It's really great to have you all here with us today, here in this brilliant city, and on this wonderful river. I'm not one for formal speeches, so I'm pretty much making it up as I go. So, please, bear with me. Now, as you all know, Mary and I met under extremely odd circumstances. It was as though we were in a play and my role was as an average English chap, into football, going to the pub, usual stuff. There was no special person in my life. Then in walks a woman who comes from such a different place – to put it mildly – that for a while our two worlds collided as we endeavoured to get to know each other and understand each other. As you can appreciate, it took a while for me to trust Mary and believe what she told me about herself. We didn't want to be together at first. We were reluctant housemates. I wanted Mary to go home and she wanted to go home. But for whatever reason she couldn't. And in the time since then we have really got to know each other. We have each had to understand each other. And our two different worlds have at last come together as one.

"I feel that Mary is the warmest, sweetest, most truthful and sincere, most caring, funniest and easily one of the smartest people I've ever met. And she's as wise as an old owl. Because of necessity really I have got her thinking about things that she would never have thought about, and she has got me looking at things in a way that I probably never would've otherwise. She has taught me that some old ways are worth keeping, and are just sensible. And I've shown her that some of our modern ways *are* an improvement on things and are frankly a lot more fun, like TV…and central heating. She won't argue with those! And I've been enlightened about things like growing food and living more sanely with the rest of Mother Nature. And much more. It's mix and match – and why not? She has taught me to appreciate things in life that I previously took for granted. I was rushing here and there without really seeing anything; I was missing sights, smells, feelings, experiences. I was being a bloke! Mary's shown me so much, and I'm pleased to say it's because of her that not only am I putting on weight like never before, but I am planning on growing fruit and vegetables as soon as we get settled into our new home. That should be fun. I am now more aware of the specialness – is that a word? – of life in general, every living being and living thing with which we share this wonderful world. Mary has inspired me to reach higher," his voice broke as he spoke. "She has inspired me to open myself to what life can offer. I'll stop before I get too carried away!"

"Elle est une femme très inspirante!" boomed Edwina, who had already drunk two glasses of champagne.

James grinned at his mother. "Oui, et très belle, aussi – very beautiful, also! That goes without saying, although I want to say it; I want her to hear me saying it. What first drew my attention to her was her amazing eyes and her dimples—"

"Y'd better stop there!" interrupted George Hodges cheerfully. "It's good to keep some things private, isn't it, lad? We really don't need to know where the dimples are!" He winked at James.

"The dimples are *on her cheeks!*"

There was a ripple of laughter. Mary held her head in her hands.

"Please! *On her face!* You can see them!"

More hoots of laughter.

"Moving swiftly on," he said, "I would like to say how proud and utterly overjoyed I am to be marrying Mary Stepney." Turning to face her he said, "Mary, I love you and want to thank you for marrying me."

They kissed.

Visibly moved, Mary followed with, "James, thank you so much! That's all I can say – thank you! You are too too kind! I haven't prepared a speech—?"

"I wouldn't worry!" James leapt in. "I didn't end up reading what I'd written down!"

"—as I was told I wouldn't need to make one if I didn't want to, but I would just like to say a few words all the same. I know you're all waiting to get into the food! I can see some people looking eagerly at the chocolate gateau!" She winked at Edwina, who hastily looked away.

"I would just like to say that it is thrilling to be here – not only here in Paris, a city I always dreamed of coming to but never actually thought I would – but also to be here in this time. Yes, I know the subject makes a lot of people feel uncomfortable, and I can see a few people shuffling already. But I believe in the truth at all times, and I cannot pretend to be someone I am not. I am someone who somehow, by some freak of Nature I suppose, fell through a disturbed area of the air – for want of a better explanation – and ended up here, at a different time. I had done nothing to cause it and it did take some time for me to believe that I really was here. It all seemed like a fevered dream for the first few weeks. But out of all this mystery something good, no, something *great*, has come. I have met the most wonderful man, someone so considerate and kind and gentle, someone warm, someone capable, someone with a great mind and who cares deeply about a lot of things. And who cares about me. He could have told me to go away as soon as we met – I know it was very hard for him to accept me. He could have booked me into the nearest lunatic asylum or whatever you call them these days, but thank heavens he didn't! I no longer wish to return to my home time. The suffering I left behind is now over – I'm referring to my dear family. I now wish to stay here and make my life here, with James, together seeing and experiencing this occasionally terrifying, but exciting and wonderful world. This is the happiest time of my life and I want to thank James for that – and also thank all you dear people here with us in Paris for coming over to be with us to share this day. You are all very dear to me, every one of you, please remember that. Thank you! Thank you! God bless!"

A toast was made and there was a roar of applause. After a speech by the best man, James's friend Bob, the dining began and an upbeat atmosphere prevailed.

The day wore on and the boat drifted lazily along. They had first gone in an easterly direction until reaching the Ile de la Cité, where they had turned and headed west, travelling many kilometres at a slow and at times almost stationary pace. The sun was setting as they turned again to return to the starting point: the jetty below the Pont Neuf. With the disappearing sun, the City of Light let her fabled magic rain down: a bold Parisian Blue sky transformed itself into a blue-black blanket covering the city. An orange blush coloured the bottom half of the sky, painting black silhouettes of buildings and bridges and casting a warm glow on the faces of the partygoers. Slowly, the orange became murky as it receded into the blue-black, but not before it had cast a spell on everyone there.

The couple were now married; wedded together indefinitely, and Mary was firmly enmeshed in the present-day world. With every advancing moment she was inextricably woven more and more into the fabric of the present, while the past was fast decaying and disappearing behind her, like the layers of the fallen – digested, literally, into the earth, unseen, below the surface of future generations.

* * *

James and Mary travelled the world for six months before deciding to make the big move abroad, to Australia. Mary resolved to begin writing again, while James planned to seek work as a history tutor, with a view to becoming a lecturer. Meanwhile, they joined up with an international study looking at the UVEs: the weird events which were to go down in history as spurring the planet's inhabitants on to looking at the world – and even existence itself – very differently. A new global mindset was fast growing out of the old one; the one which through its ignorance had caused a dramatic malfunctioning of the nuts and bolts which hold the world together. Although Mary was never to completely understand the hows and whys of her appearance in the modern world, she knew one thing for sure: that there was only one time – the eternal moment of the present; and that this world and the onion layers of the worlds within and beyond are as marvellous and as full of surprises as any that could be concocted through fiction.

NOTES

1 From poem 'The Triumph of Life' by Percy Bysshe Shelley (1822).

2 Poem 'In Flanders Fields' by John McCrae (1915).

3 Poem 'I'm nobody! Who are you?' by Emily Dickinson (1861).

4 First proposed by Albert Einstein and Otto Stern, 1913.

5 Werner Heisenberg - 'Uncertainty Principle', 1927.

6 The 'Copenhagen Interpretation' (Niels Bohr, Werner Heisenberg and others), 1924-27.

7 Alain Aspect, at the École Normale Supérieure de Cachan, France, 1982.

8 An alleged American military experiment conducted in 1943, in which US Navy destroyer the *USS Eldridge* was to be rendered invisible to human observers for a brief period of time.

9 'HAARP' is the High Frequency Active Auroral Research Program, jointly funded by the US Air Force, the US Navy, the University of Alaska and the Defense Advanced Research Projects Agency (DARPA).

10 Dr. Nick Begich and Jeane Manning 'Angels Don't Play This Haarp: Advances in Tesla Technology' (Earthpulse Press, 1997).

11 Long-running studies of remote perception at Stanford Research Institute (SRI) (Stanford University) and Princeton Engineering Anomalies Research (PEAR) (Princeton University).

12 William Tiller.

13 Masaru Emoto.

14 Scientists who have undertaken notable work in this area include (but by no means limited to): Dick Bierman, William Braud, Brenda Dunne, Amit Goswami, Robert Jahn, Roger

Nelson, Harold Puthoff, Dean Radin, Marilyn Schlitz, Helmut Schmidt, Gary Schwartz, Rupert Sheldrake, Russell Targ and William Tiller.

15 Scientists who have worked on a unified theory of mind and matter have included (but by no means limited to): David Bohm, Ervin László, Fritz-Albert Popp, Karl Pribram and Walter Schempp.

16 Lynne McTaggart, 'The Field' (Element, 2001).

17 Karl Pribram; Ervin László and others.

18 Amit Goswami and others.

19 Fritz-Albert Popp.

20 Robert Jahn and Brenda Dunne.

21 Scientists who have studied the ability of living beings to imprint upon the Field via random event generators and similar have included (but by no means limited to): Dick Bierman, Roger Nelson, Dean Radin and Dieter Vaitl.

22 From poem 'Sea Fever' by John Masefield (1902).

23 The opening scene from 'Twelfth Night' by William Shakespeare (c1601).

24 A 30-year patient study conducted by Dr. Toshihiko Marutaat et al at the Mayo Clinic, USA, 2000.

25 The Intention Experiment currently being conducted by a group of American, British, German and Russian scientists (www.theintentionexperiment.com).

26 Dr. Rene Peoc'h in collaboration with the Fondation Marcel et Monique Odier de Psycho-Physique, Cologny, Switzerland (www.evasion.ch/radiesthesie/odier/welcome .htm).

27 Author, media commentator and social scientist Duane Elgin, in *Resurgence* magazine, Issue 256, 2009.

28 Khalil Gibran, Lebanese-born writer, poet, artist and philosopher (1883-1931).

29 Extracted from example wedding vows in 'Conversations with God Book 3', Neale Donald Walsch, Hodder and Stoughton, London 1999.

Roundfire Books put simply, publish great stories. Whether it's literary or popular, a gentle tale or a pulsating thriller, the connecting theme in all Roundfire fiction titles is that once you pick them up you won't want to put them down.